Highway 61

Resurfaced

Highway 61 Resurfaced

BILL FITZHUGH

WILLIAM MORROW
An Imprint of HarperCollins*Publishers*

This book is a work of fiction. The characters, incidents, and dialogue are drawn from the author's imagination and are not to be construed as real. Any resemblance to actual events or persons, living or dead, is entirely coincidental.

HarperCollins books may be purchased for educational, business, or sales promotional use. For information please write: Special Markets Department, HarperCollins Publishers Inc., 10 East 53rd Street, New York, NY 10022.

FIRST EDITION

Designed by Nicola Ferguson

Printed on acid-free paper

Library of Congress Cataloging-in-Publication Data

Fitzhugh, Bill.
Highway 61 resurfaced / by Bill Fitzhugh.—1st ed.
    p. cm.
ISBN 0-06-059761-5 (acid-free paper)
1. Private investigators—Mississippi—Fiction. 2. United States Highway 61—Fiction. 3. Radio broadcasters—Fiction. 4. Disc jockeys—Fiction. 5. Mississippi—Fiction. I. Title.

PS3556.I8552H54 2005
813'.54—dc22   2004061081

05   06   07   08   09   JTC/RRD   10   9   8   7   6   5   4   3   2   1

To Kendall, my reason
for not singing the blues

Acknowledgments

Most of the research for this book fell into one of three, some-times overlapping areas: music, history, and medicine. My grati-tude to the following for help in these areas:

J. Fred Knobloch, Alan Stoker, and Tim Whitsett for informa-tion on subjects ranging from the twelve-bar form to obsolete recording technologies. I also referred to *All Music Guide* (*The Blues*) for biographical information on the Delta blues artists mentioned in these pages.

Billy Johnson, proprietor of the Highway 61 Blues Museum in Leland, Mississippi, for permission to use information from his article "Skin Balls, Good Times, and the Blues" (published in *The Leland Progress,* 7/12/01). Thanks to Jamie Tate for introducing me to Billy and for showing me around Leland. I also found invaluable information on playing "skin" in Zora Neale Hurston's "Mules and Men," as well as in the University of Virginia "E-project" created by Laura Grand-Jean (http://xroads.virginia .edu/~MA01/Grand-Jean/Hurston/Chapters/glossary.html).

The beautiful, brilliant, and funny Frances Powers, who shared her memories of growing up in Vicksburg, including the fact that she learned to smoke cigarettes down in Marcus Bottoms, and who, later, introduced me to Jamie Tate.

On issues of law enforcement and incarceration in the Magnolia State, thanks to Martin Hegwood, fellow novelist and attorney with the Mississippi secretary of state's office, and Bill Greenleaf at the Mississippi State Penitentiary at Parchman.

Dr. Cris Glick answered all my medical questions, no matter how ridiculous. Judge Tom Givens shared his knowledge of Prohibition-era Mississippi. Carol Puckett Dailey showed me around Greenwood and the rest of Leflore County and hooked me up with Duff Dorrough, who helped out from Ruleville to Parchman and back. Fish Michie pointed me toward Po Monkeys.

Thanks to Dan Baum and Margaret L. Knox, for permission to draw on their article "Jake Leg" (published in *The New Yorker*, 9/15/03), which was in turn based on research by Dr. John Morgan, professor at the City University of New York.

Mike Corley and Jerry Rushing at WQBC and George Mayer at "The Vicksburg" for giving Rick Shannon a place to work and live.

In matters of language, dialect, and dialogue I referred to *You All Spoken Here* by Roy Wilder Jr. (University of Georgia Press); *Juba to Jive—A Dictionary of African-American Slang* by Clarence Major (Penguin); and *A Blues Life* by Henry Townsend as told to Bill Greensmith (University of Illinois Press).

In writing about aspects of the radio industry in the south, I relied on C. Joseph Pusateri's article "Radio Industry" published in the *Encyclopedia of Southern Culture* (University of North Carolina Press).

In addition to time spent roaming around the Mississippi Delta, I referred to the following for images of the region: *Juke Joint,* photographs by Birney Imes (University Press of

Mississippi); *Delta Time—Mississippi Photographs* by Ken Light **ix** (Smithsonian Institute Press); and "Junior's Juke Joint," a Web site created by John L. Doughty Jr. (www.deltablues.net)

Thanks as always to D. Victor Hawkins, Janine Smith, Kendall Fitzhugh, and Tom Dupree for their notes. And to Maureen O'Brien, who, putting it mildly, had a rough summer and still managed to shepherd the project to the end. Also a big thanks to her assistant, Stephanie Fraser, and everyone at HarperCollins who makes these books happen, most especially Michael Morrison. And to Jimmy Vines for everything.

Highway 61 ⬛ Resurfaced

DURDEN TATE WAS a wealthy man. His company had a lock on 80 percent of the specialty-fats-and-oils market for fast-food restaurants in Mississippi, Louisiana, and Arkansas. Durden Tate's company had achieved this extraordinary market share by creating a superior product, a frying fat based on a flavorful blend of deodorized palm oil and refined pork lard. Tru-Fry 2000, as it was known, boasted elevated oxidation resistance, a high smoke point, and true frying longevity. As a result, every time a donut, a catfish, or a basket of fries was lowered into a bubbling vat in this part of the country, the odds were good that it was Durden Tate's fat.

As part of his commitment to quality, Durden spent four days a week visiting restaurants that used his product. After ten years of sampling crispy-fried hash browns at breakfast, corn dogs and fried pies at lunch, and hush puppies with dinner, the once trim and athletic Mr. Tate was pushing 320 pounds.

His wife, Wanda Lee Henshaw Tate, put up with his obesity and his frequent absence not only because she'd meant it when she'd said "for better or for worse" but also because Durden had come through on the "for richer or for poorer" part of the deal. But when she began to suspect Durden was cheating, she decided to get out. And she wasn't about to leave empty-handed. She'd put fifteen of the best years of her life into the marriage and felt she was owed something.

But Wanda Lee needed proof. She needed some photos, something that would make the divorce easy and the alimony as fat as Durden's lard ass. So she pulled out the phone book and looked under "Investigators."

--- --- --- --- --- --- --- ---

RICK WAITED UNTIL dusk before sneaking into the weedy field just off Highway 61, on the outskirts of Port Gibson, Mississippi. On the far end of the field was the back of the Pine Grove Motor Inn, where Durden Tate had checked in an hour earlier, and not for the first time since Rick had been following him. Rick had a camera bag slung over his shoulder and high hopes that Durden hadn't drawn the curtains all the way.

It was a typical Mississippi summer night, warm and sticky as a sweet pastry. Rick was sweating before he'd gone fifty feet. Halfway across the field, with burrs scratching through his socks and ticks scaling his legs, Rick stepped into a mud hole, sinking past his ankle. He pulled back, losing his shoe. Sewer gas filled his nose and he struggled against the gag reflex. In the waning summer light, he looked down to see the mud oozing into his size 10.

Rick stood there like a flamingo, thinking about the pair of boots in his truck. Sure the loafers were more comfortable, but, well, too late now. It turned out he was standing above an underground wastewater treatment pipe that had been leaking for a week. The rest of the field between Rick and the motel was a

rotten-egg swamp. The mosquitoes arrived just as the sun set. He tried to remember if the West Nile virus had been reported in Claiborne County yet.

Having no better option, he stuck his foot back into the ghastly muck, retrieved his shoe, and continued toward the Pine Grove Motor Inn. By the time he reached the motel, both of Rick's feet were soaked through with sewage, his arms and neck were riddled with insect bites, and he reeked of shit. But he still had a job to do, so he crept along underneath the rear windows of the motel, peeking in each one until he found Durden Tate's room. The good news was that the curtain was halfway open and Rick could see Tate sitting on the end of the bed. The bad news was that he was naked, all 320 pounds of him. The TV cast a bluish tint onto his blubbery folds. He had a beer in one hand and the remote in the other. Behind him on the bed were two paper sacks and his Dopp kit.

Durden began to talk, but because of the angle Rick couldn't see who he was talking to. Though Tate's voice was muffled, Rick could tell he was sweet-talking somebody. It appeared that the recipient of the honeyed words was lying on the floor. Durden reached behind him and grabbed one of the sacks. It was filled with onion rings from the burger joint across the highway. He continued his sweet-talking as he ate the fried onions. He tossed one to the floor, presumably for his companion. Why was she down there? Was Durden in a domination-submission relationship? Rick hadn't figured him for the type but, as he knew, people will surprise you. Rick popped off the lens cap and waited for the leather hood to come out. Durden ate the onions slowly, eyes closed, lips glistening with grease. By the time he finished, there was still no sign of the submissive lover. Maybe she's tied up, Rick thought.

A moment later, Durden reached into the other paper sack and pulled out a jar of peanut butter. He unzipped his Dopp kit and removed a tongue depressor. He scooped a wad of peanut butter onto the wooden stick, then crossed his legs and began smearing the goo between his toes. It looked to be smooth, not crunchy. Rick exposed a few frames of film.

When Durden finished with the left foot, he lowered it to the floor, then shouted, "No!" at his lover. He crossed his legs the other way and took his time smearing the peanut butter between the toes of his right foot. He licked the tongue depressor and chased it with some beer, then he leaned back on the bed and said something like, "Okay, c'mon, baby."

She was stout. Her hair was black, and she had a tongue the likes of which Rick had never seen on a woman. This was due largely to the fact that she was a Labrador retriever. She gave every indication that she was enjoying herself and, as she licked the peanut butter from between his toes, Durden Tate moaned and flogged himself as though he might win a prize for it. "Good girl," he seemed to be saying over and over. "Good girrrrl."

Figuring with no small amount of dread that this was merely foreplay, Rick snapped off a dozen pics, leaving another twenty exposures before he'd have to change rolls. Fortunately, Durden liked doing this with the lights on, so there was no need for a flash. When the poor dog finished with his toes, Durden sat up and reached for the peanut butter again. Rick got a queasy feeling about what was coming and figured right then and there that he'd make two sets of prints, one for Wanda Lee, one for the ASPCA.

Rick was reaching into his camera bag for a zoom when he heard a man say, "Hold it right there, pervert." All things considered, Rick hardly thought that was a fair characterization. He turned and saw the man from the Port Gibson Police Department, gun in one hand, flashlight in the other. "Now you just back away from that window and ease on over here, boy."

"This isn't what it looks like," Rick said.

"Yeah? What's it look like?"

"Like I'm a pervert," Rick said.

"That's right, what we call felonious trespass. That's a fancy term for a peeping Tom, so let's go."

Rick slapped at a mosquito buzzing his ear. "Actually, I'm a private investigator."

"Uh-huh." The cop gestured with his gun. "Well, just bring your Rockford files on over here."

Rick pointed at the window. "There's a man in there about to have sex with a dog."

"And what? You wanna watch?"

Rick couldn't believe this guy. "Did you hear me? I said sex with a dog."

"And who're you to be passin' judgment?" the cop asked. "You sayin' you ain't never laid no pipe with uh ugly girl?" He stuck his nose in Rick's direction and sniffed. " 'At's bullshit. Now, c'mon, you're under arrest."

THE GUARD, CASTING a friendly smile, leaned against the cell bars. "You sure you don't want to stay?"

"Much is I love you," Clarence said, "I think I stayed long enough."

"Well, all right then. You 'bout ready?"

"All packed, boss." Clarence stepped out of the shadow of his cell, his tight gray coils like snow on cured tobacco. His face was seventy-two years of troubles, yet it shined with the dignity of a man undefeated.

"Well, all right then." The guard gestured toward the freedom Clarence never should have lost and said, "C'mon."

Clarence walked out of his cell for the last time. Never looked back, not once. No good memories in there. Eyes always forward. He said his good-byes on the move too. He wasn't going to stop until somebody made him. He'd been waiting too long to get going.

He walked into the administration office wearing the itchy black-and-white-striped pants, the ring-arounds, as they called them, and a coarse prisoner's smock with MDOC CONVICT on the back. There was paperwork to do, and they checked his fingerprints to make sure they were releasing the right man, but they didn't look too close. They all knew who he was. He was an institution within the institution.

A woman behind the counter reached over and pressed something into his hand. Clarence looked in his broad rough palm and saw a small gold cross on a chain. The woman smiled at him and said, "Now is the day of your salvation. You take care of yourself."

"Thank you," he said. "You know I will."

They gave him a hundred dollars gate money and what they called adequate free-world shirt and pants. He was glad to wear anything besides the convict uniform he'd worn most of his life. The striped outfit was a cell unto itself, a further humiliation, bars within bars. Clarence had been a fine dresser back in his day, a real dandy. He looked in the mirror after changing and thought "adequate" was about the best you could say for the clothes they'd given him this time. But that was a small thing, easy to fix once he got to town. He couldn't let that bother him. He had bigger fish to fry.

The warden gestured toward the door. "Somebody meetin' you out there, Clarence?"

"No, suh, ain't nobody out there for me, but I'll be all right.

They's a man down in Jackson I'm 'onna see, gonna help me out. I'll send y'all a postcard from the zoo." They all smiled at that and then it was time to go. They let Clarence out the gate right there on Highway 49, where he'd come in fifty years ago, and told him where to go to catch the bus.

He stood there for an hour, watching the traffic, measuring his emotions, not sure if he felt the way he was supposed to feel getting out after all this time. He figured he mostly felt the same, probably take a while for it to sink in. When the bus finally got there, he saw how the people looked at him as he came up the stairs in his thrift-store outfit. He didn't guess he could blame them, the bus stopping so close to Parchman and all. But nobody bothered him, probably figured a man his age wasn't going to cause them any trouble. And he wasn't. Clarence was saving the trouble for someone else.

— — — — — — — —

RICK MADE BAIL with three other overnight guests of the Port Gibson Police Department. Fred, a lanky mechanic who had been drunk and disorderly. A roofer named Charlie who was busted for breaking and entering. And Paul, a small-business owner who'd spent the night on a domestic-battery charge.

The four men signed for their stuff and headed for the door. Rick, the only one not suffering from a hangover, was the first outside. He shaded his eyes against a blinding sun, then watched in dismay as the other three men shuffled out of the jail and into the arms of significant others. They all hugged and swore they were sorry, vowed it would never happen again. Rick couldn't believe it. A drunk, a thief, and a wife beater were doing better than he was, and he wondered what it must be like to have a woman like that. One who not only puts up with your stupidity, but who's willing to pay to get you back for more.

It made him think of Traci, the love whom circumstance had forced him to leave behind when he came to Vicksburg. Traci would've bailed him out and picked him up if he'd stayed with her. But he hadn't. Rick missed her, but he understood why she couldn't come. She liked her home and didn't want to uproot her daughter just to chase a disc jockey, let alone one who got shot at, like he had. Rick ran up his phone bill trying to talk her into moving, but when she started making noise about reconciling with her ex, Rick figured it was time to move on. Still, he couldn't help but think how nice it would've been to walk out of jail and into Traci's arms.

As Rick headed for the impound lot, he tried not to dwell on the fact that he had no one to blame but himself. He'd spent most of his life dodging commitment and the ties that bind in exchange for the alternative. Early in his radio career, there had been some logic to this, but the older he got, the better he could see the advantage of having a solid relationship with someone other than a bail bondsman.

Shrugging off his regrets, Rick got his truck and headed back to Vicksburg. He'd been there a few months and, so far, it was working out all right. Weeknights he did a shift at WVBR-FM, a classic rock station where he had the freedom to play what he wanted. During the day he ran his private-investigation business, which he called Rockin' Vestigations.

Rick was a radio veteran but relatively new at the PI game. He'd been in the former all his life and had stumbled into the latter after solving a multiple-murder case while working at WAOR-FM, in McRae, Mississippi, where he'd met Traci. In the course of solving that crime, he'd suffered a serious gunshot wound and had his picture splashed on the front page of every paper in the state. With no small amount of encouragement from Rick, the press portrayed him as a dashing, hard-boiled, rock 'n' roll, flirting-with-danger kinda guy. And without much effort, Rick had parlayed his sudden celebrity into the new line of work.

When he opened Rockin' Vestigations, he'd had a few things to learn. First, most of his work would be done at a computer. But not always. PIs still had to follow people now and then. And most of the people he was hired to follow did their running around at night, when Rick was on the air. So he found a couple of younger operatives whose primary qualifications were that they owned camera equipment and a car. They were freelancers, on call. They did the grunt work, except on occasions when Rick wanted to make sure he got the goods for particularly wealthy clients like Wanda Lee Henshaw Tate.

After the thing in McRae, during which Rick had found himself without a weapon at precisely the moment he needed one, he decided to get strapped. He bought a .38 and took a concealed-weapons class. He was a good shot, a natural. But given the statistics on firearm deaths, he rarely carried the gun. Still, he kept it, just in case.

His radio job provided a modest, if steady paycheck. He planned to build his PI résumé and client base to the point that he could get out of radio before Clean Signal Radio Corporation owned every last rock station in the country and played nothing but Zeppelin's "Whole Lotta Love" between fifteen-minute commercial breaks.

So, despite the fact that the cops had taken his film, that he was out on bail, and that he smelled like the inside of an outhouse, Rick felt like his train was on the tracks. It was true that he wasn't in danger of getting rich as a private investigator, but after so many years of watching the body of FM rock radio rotting in front of his eyes, he felt good that he was at least doing

Highway 61 Resurfaced

something to improve his future. The way he figured it, rock radio wouldn't live forever, but he could always count on people to lie, cheat, and steal.

So far Rick had caught a busload of cheating spouses, had tracked down a dozen check kiters, and had gathered evidence on a group running a disability-insurance scam. It wasn't the cure for cancer, but it beat the hell out of playing "Free Bird."

Rick eased his pickup onto the Clay Street exit. He had time to get a shower and a nap before starting his eight o'clock shift. He passed the faded green-and-white sign for the Southern Pride Apartments. The building itself was gone but its foundation still sat proudly on the lot, as if waiting for that part of the south to rise again. The road sloped toward historic downtown. Rick's apartment was ahead on the right, a twelve-story redbrick build-ing with "The Vicksburg" painted down the side in large, bold letters just like it was when it opened in 1928, the year before the great Delta flood. Before being converted to apartments, the Vicksburg had been a classic river-city hotel like the Peabody in Memphis, though somewhat less grand. And without the ducks.

Rick parked in the lot behind the building but couldn't bring himself to get out. It was ninety-five outside and humid enough to wither a man. He sat there soaking up the AC. But then he saw Veronica pull in to her parking spot. She was a cocktail waitress at the Isle of Capri, with a one-bedroom on the fifth floor. They'd met the day Rick moved in. He'd flirted, but she was either play-ing hard to get or dropping hints that she wasn't interested. Rick had a hard time distinguishing between the two. He wasn't sure if he was really attracted to Veronica or if she simply reminded him of Traci. He figured it was the excessive eye makeup they both wore, but it didn't hurt that Veronica's waitress outfit was on the skimpy side and that she had the legs for it.

Rick got out of the truck. The humidity hit him like a pan of used motor oil. He shook it off and slung his camera bag over his shoulder. He knew he looked pretty rough but figured he'd make up a rollicking story about how he'd just returned from a wild night in New Orleans partying with the Neville Brothers. He headed for the back door, getting there just in time to hold it open for her. "Hey, Veronica," he said. "How you doin'?"

Her face wrinkled as she passed. "Fine," she said. "But you seem to be attracting flies."

2

AS THEY CROSSED the lobby, Rick fumbled through a convoluted story about a wild night at Tipitina's involving Dr. John and a backed-up toilet, but Veronica wasn't buying it. "Do me a *big* favor?" she said as she boarded the elevator.

"Name it."

She pushed the close button and said, "Take the stairs."

"Uh." Rick pointed to the ceiling and said, "I'm up on seven."

As the door began to close, Veronica cast a damning glance at Rick's waistline. "The exercise'll do you good."

As Rick huffed up to the seventh floor, he came to terms with the fact that Veronica wasn't playing hard to get so much as she was saying he smelled like crap and was fat to boot.

He was sweating and out of breath when he reached his apartment, a one-bedroom with a thumbnail kitchen. But it had a view over part of the city and the confluence of the Yazoo and Mississippi Rivers. At four-fifty a month, not a bad place for a single guy with no romantic prospects.

He turned the shower on and stepped in fully dressed.

He'd probably have to throw the shoes out, but he thought it best to rinse everything off before making any decisions. As he dried off, he checked the answering machine at his office. Only one call. He picked up the phone and punched her number. "Wanda Lee? It's Rick." He listened for a moment before he said, "Yeah, I'm back. But things didn't go exactly as planned. I know, I'm sorry, but I—" She cut him off with another question. He said, "I'll tell you all about it tomorrow. I got a couple of things to do this afternoon and I'm on the air tonight, so just meet me at my office, say, tomorrow at two?"

Thanks to Charlie, Fred, and Paul, with their erratic tales of innocence and police brutality, Rick hadn't gotten much sleep in the Port Gibson jail. He hoped to get a couple of hours before going to work. But just as he lay on the sofa and draped his arm over his eyes, he had an idea. One that might make up for the misadventure at the Pine Grove Motor Inn. "Damn." He sat up, grabbed the phone book, and looked up a number. When a young woman answered, Rick said, "Yeah, you got anything that looks like a black Lab?"

— — — — — — — — —

THE ANIMAL SHELTER was down on Washington, south of town, in a converted cotton warehouse on the river. Rick parked in the gravel lot, grabbed his camera bag, and headed for the building. He noticed a Piggly Wiggly sack next to the front door. It struck him as odd since as far as he knew Vicksburg didn't have a Piggly Wiggly. He also thought it was odd because the sack was, in fact, wiggling. A moment later it fell over and out tumbled a kitten. It was the mangiest critter Rick had ever seen: dirty gray, sick, and scrawny. The kitten shook his head and got to his feet looking around, dazed. His eyes seemed to be set too far apart and his ears were too big for his head. The kitten pranced into Rick's path as if using his last bit of strength to make a good impression on someone who might help.

Now Rick was a pretty soft touch, but being unsure what flea-borne diseases might be transmittable these days, he was reluctant to touch the thing with his hands. Instead, he used his foot to herd the kitten gently back into the sack before taking it inside. There was a riot of dog, cat, and exotic bird noises coming from the depths of the warehouse, but the front office was empty. Rick put the sack on the counter and rang the bell for assistance. A moment later, a harried young woman with a one-eyed cockatoo on her shoulder stepped into the room. "Can I hep you?" It was the bird speaking, in a southern accent no less.

Rick looked at the bird's empty eye socket, then at the woman, and said, "Yeah, I'm the guy who called about the black Lab."

The woman nodded, then looked at the wiggling sack. "What's that?"

"Oh, I found that outside," Rick said. "It's a kitten. I guess somebody left it."

"Uh-huh." The woman looked in the sack, then shook her head. "Damn." She pushed it toward Rick and said, "You'll have to keep it."

"It's not mine."

"Uh-huh."

"Really."

"I don't care," she said. "If you give it to me, I'll just have to put it down. You want to be responsible for that? You want me to kill this little guy?"

"Well, no, of course not but . . . look, like I said on the phone, I just need to take a couple of photos and I'll be out of your hair."

"Uh-huh."

"Can I hep you?" The cockatoo let out a piercing screech, "Aaaaccck!" It began to bob and weave on the woman's shoulder, then it screamed, "Youth in Asia!"

"Listen," the woman said, wagging her finger at the bag, "I don't have the time, money, or staff to take that sick little cat. Aside from whatever medical attention it needs, and it looks like it needs plenty, somebody's either going to have to nurse that thing for weeks or we're gonna have to put it down. Now, you say you don't want that to happen, but you don't want the responsibility either, which means you expect me to take it. So, if you want something from me, it's only fair I get something from you."

Rick held up a hand and said, "I understand." He pulled out his wallet. "How much?"

She shook her head. "Take the kitten."

"I can't," Rick said, trying to sound sympathetic. "I live in an apartment. They don't allow pets." It was a lie but had a legitimate ring to it. Several residents at the Vicksburg had cats and a few had small, yappy dogs.

The woman folded her arms. "No kitten, no photos."

The cockatoo leaned toward Rick and screamed again, "Can I hep you?" Its empty eye socket looked like a piece of dried fruit. "Aaaaccck!"

"Look, I appreciate what—"

"No, you look! We have to put down three and a half million cats and dogs each year."

Rick looked around in disbelief. "What, here?"

"No, nationally, you idiot!"

"Hey, there's no call for personal attacks."

"Aaaaccck!" The cockatoo raised up and flashed his sulphur yellow crest.

The woman closed her eyes and took a deep breath. She

looked at Rick and said, "You're right. I'm sorry. I tell you what, you don't want the kitten, it's okay."

"It's not that I don't want it," Rick said. "It's just, the building has rules."

"No pets allowed."

"Exactly. My hands are tied."

She relaxed a bit. Her expression softened and she said, "I hope you understand, I have to try to find them homes. We just can't save of all of them."

"I appreciate that," Rick said. "I wish I could help you out. And I'll be glad to make a donation. In fact, I don't know if I mentioned this, but I work at a local radio station. Maybe we could do some sort of fund-raiser for the shelter, a pet-adoption-day sort of thing, you know, raise awareness, whatever."

"That would be great." She waved for Rick to follow her. "C'mon in the back and bring that kitty. I'll show you the dog I was thinking of for the pictures."

Rick picked up the bag and followed the woman down a hallway. She led him to a small room and locked the door behind them, which made Rick wonder. "Just put the bag on the table," she said as she went to a cabinet and opened a drawer.

As he stood there, Rick wondered if Veronica liked cats. She didn't seem like a cat person, but even so, everybody loves kittens, right? Maybe he should take this one, might be just what he needed to break the ice with Veronica. Rick could see her face as the elevator door opened and he was standing there with that poor little kitten, all precious and pathetic. She'd say, "Awwww. He's so cute." Then again, what if she was a dog person? What would she think then? Single guy with a cat might look a little gay, he thought. Of course, women do seem to like gay men. Maybe he could parlay all that into a scenario where, late one night, over drinks, he would confess his sexual confusion to her and express his desire to find the right woman to help prove he was . . . No, Rick thought, bad plan. Leave the cat.

"Okay, here you go." The woman turned around and offered Rick a syringe loaded with a clear liquid. She nodded toward the sack. "Just stick it in anywhere."

"What?" Rick took a step back. "Are you crazy? I'm not going to do that."

The woman reached into the sack with her free hand and pulled the kitten out. "Look, you said you can't keep him. I told you we'd just have to put him to sleep, right? So that's what we're going to do. Now, you want to hold him while I do it, or you want me to hold him while you do it?"

The cockatoo said, "Youth in Asia!"

Rick hesitated, not sure what to do. Then he reached out. "Give him to me." He took the kitten and said, "Can you recommend a good vet?"

--- --- --- --- --- --- ---

"**FOR STARTERS, HE'S** dehydrated and malnourished," the young man at the pet store said. "You should take him to a vet."

"I did," Rick said. "They were closed. I'll go back tomorrow." He bought a bottle of electrolyte solution, some kitten formula, and an eyedropper. There was a film-processing kiosk in the parking lot, so he dropped off the roll of film he'd shot at the shelter, then went to the station. He wrapped the kitten in a towel and set him on one of the turntables while he worked. The poor little guy had barely moved since. Rick didn't know if he was sleeping or dying or some of both. Between songs, Rick tried to feed him with the eyedropper, but he wasn't sure how much was actually getting in.

At the top of the hour, Rick put on his headphones and cleared his throat. He opened his mike and said, "You're listening to Vicksburg's classic rock monster, WVBR-FM." In the background, the kitten made a wet, snoring sound. "I'm Rick Shannon and this is the Allman Brothers Band with Blind Willie McTell's 'Statesboro Blues.' "

Rick killed his mike and pulled off his headphones. He leaned over and looked at the kitten. His eyes were weepy and his nostrils were mostly covered with a brownish crust. Rick got a tissue and picked the kitten's nose so he could breathe easier. "All right, you need a name," he said, looking into the widely spaced eyes. "How 'bout Wheezy?" The kitten didn't respond. "Wait, that was one of Snow White's little friends, wasn't it? The asthmatic dwarf? Disney would probably sue us." He stroked the kitten's head. "We'll come up with something."

The request line was blinking, but Rick needed to figure out his next two songs before answering. He pulled ZZ Top's second album and cued "Just Got Paid." But then what? Rick glanced at the big map on the wall that showed the coverage area of the station's fifty-thousand-watt transmitter. The shadowy blue circle was cut like a pie on the east/west axis by Interstate 20 and north and south by Highway 61. Rick smiled and spoke to the kitten. "Can't believe I hadn't thought of this before." He pulled Dylan's *Highway 61 Revisited*. As he reviewed the song list, Rick hit the speakerphone and said, "VBR."

"Yes hello thank you," a young woman said. "Hi wait a second I need to do something." She spoke as though unaware of the concept of punctuation.

Rick waited a moment before he said, "Did you have a request?"

"Wait yes okay you're still coming in," the woman said. "Is anyone else listening that's the sort of thing that's good to know is anyone else listening?"

"You mean to the station?" Rick sensed that one of this woman's tubes had burned out.

"No no no on the line," she said. "Sometimes they listen on the line it's one of the ways they keep track of us but here's the thing," she said. "I'm getting your signal through my teeth and it hurts when you play certain songs and I wanted to see if we could make a deal somehow because I could have been rich."

"No kidding?"

"Yeah, I'm related to the guy who first bottled Coca-Cola right here in Vicksburg in 1894 but wait I lost your signal again I'll have to call you back." And she hung up.

"Well thanks for calling," Rick said, thinking of the Atlanta Rhythm Section song "Crazy." It was the sort of call deejays came to expect, especially on the late shifts. He started ZZ Top, then hit the request line again. "VBR."

"Hey, dude, you're rockin' with the Allmans and the Top, but I got two words for you."

"Shoot."

"More Lynyrd Skynyrd."

Rick didn't want to get into a math argument, so he agreed to play "I Know a Little" and let it go at that. It was a typical night. A bored cashier at a convenience store wanted to hear David Bowie. A bunch of welders down at LeTourneau's Marine Construction facility needed some Jeff Beck. A car full of gamblers driving down to the casinos from Yazoo City had to hear their lucky Bad Company song. He cued the Dylan, then hit the speakerphone. "VBR."

"Yes, hello." It was another woman. "Is this the request line?"

"Yeah, what can I—"

"Is this the guy on the air?"

"Yep."

"Are you the deejay who's also a private detective?"

Rick grabbed the handset. "That's me," he said. "Rick Shannon, president of Rockin' Vestigations with offices in New York, Paris, and Vicksburg. What can I do for you?"

"I need help finding someone," the woman said in an accent soft as old cotton money.

"That's one of my specialties," Rick said. "Who are we trying to find?"

"My grandfather."

"I see. Has he wandered off?"

"No, nothing like that," the woman said. "In fact, I thought he was dead. That's what I'd been told when I was young, but I have a feeling he's still alive and I'd like to meet him before it's too late."

"What makes you think he's alive all of a sudden?"

The woman hesitated before saying, "I got a strange phone call the other day. A man asking for him, like they thought he might be staying with me."

"Did he say who he was?"

"No, he hung up when I asked," she said. "I know it's not much to work with, but can you help me?"

"Sure," Rick said. "No problem. What's your name?"

"Lollie Woolfolk."

"Miss Woolfolk, do you have reason to believe your grandfather is still in Mississippi?"

"If he's still alive, that would be my guess," she said. "But I can't say for sure. That side of the family's spread all over the Delta. He could be anywhere, I s'pose."

"Doesn't matter," Rick said. "If he's still around, I can find him. Can you come to my office so we can meet? I'll need to get some more information."

"Of course. Where are you located?"

Rick gave her the address and said, "When would you like to come in?"

"Would tomorrow be all right?"

"Let me check my calendar." Rick picked up the program log and riffled it near the phone. "Boy, tomorrow morning's booked solid." He wanted to sound like his services were in great demand, plus he liked to sleep late. "I've got a two o'clock that should be pretty quick. How's two-thirty?" She made the appointment and hung up.

The ZZ Top was running out. Rick grabbed his headphones, opened the mike, and said, "I think it's time to revisit Highway 61. Here's Bob Dylan with 'Tombstone Blues.'"

3

THINGS HAD CHANGED since the last time Clarence had been on a bus, so he sat up front by a window all the way to Jackson. The Greyhound station was in the shadow of a bluff crowned with the dome of the Old Capitol building. Clarence had planned to walk from there to his meeting, but when he saw the line of taxis he decided to treat himself. Let someone else carry him, save his tired old ankles.

The dark-skinned driver looked in the mirror and asked "Where to?" in a funny way. Clarence leaned forward and said, "Goin' to the Mayflower. But we got time, drive around first." He wanted to see how things had changed.

"Yes, sir. Very good."

Clarence sat back thinking about the changes he was already seeing. This strange man—Indian, he assumed—calling him "sir" and driving him around downtown Jackson. It was like the dream he'd been having for fifty years, where he had an entourage and a driver and a tailor making his suits. But Clarence already had a driver in mind and it wasn't this man.

As they climbed the hill toward State Street, Clarence

asked the driver where he was from. It was a place called Madras, in India, but he'd lived here for twelve years. When Clarence asked how he'd ended up in Jackson, the man explained that his uncle owned several motels in the Delta. "I came to work for him, but it was too boring," he said with disdain. "Checking in, checking out." He shook his head. "I could not stand it. I prefer to move around, to see things, to meet people." As he turned onto Pearl Street, the driver glanced in his mirror and said, "This is where you are from?"

"Naw." Clarence shook his head. "I'm from up near Dockery Farms," he said. "Small town called Drew. But I used to get down here now and then, long time ago."

"How long?"

"I was twenny-two," Clarence said. "I'm seventy-two now."

The driver let go with a low whistle. "You are visiting family?"

Clarence shook his head. "Takin' care of some business."

The driver suddenly honked his horn and leaned out his window to shout at a passing cabdriver, "Keep it between the lines!" The other driver, a younger white guy, laughed and shouted something back, but Clarence couldn't tell what.

"You like it here?"

"Oh, very much," the driver said.

"People treat you all right?"

The driver glanced at Clarence in the mirror. "You mean because I am so dark?"

Clarence nodded.

He gave a rueful smile and said, "Where I am from, we have what is called a caste system. I am used to the way some people act superior." He shook his head. "It is amusing to me how people here act as if the southern white man invented prejudice." He glanced in the mirror and said, "You will find it everywhere, I promise."

Clarence figured he was right, but it crossed his mind that even if prejudice wasn't invented in the deep south, it may have been perfected here. As they cruised around the city, Clarence maintained a steady stream of commentary about the way things had been the last time he was here. A few blocks onto Farish Street, something caught his eye. He pointed at a storefront and said, "Now right there, I remember, was old furniture store run by the McMurray family. Mrs. McMurray, Lillian was her name, she and her husband made a little studio in the back and they made some records."

"What kind?"

"Good ones," Clarence said with a regal nod. "Called it Diamond Recording Studios. That's still clear. They label was called Trumpet Records. They was big-time, now. Had plenny hits. Elmore James did 'Dust My Broom' back up in there. Sonny Boy Williamson cut 'Eyesight to the Blind' for 'em, and by that I'm talkin' about Rice Miller, not John Lee Williamson, the other one."

Clarence had to explain to his confused driver that there had been two men, both harp players, who called themselves Sonny Boy Williamson. There was John Lee Williamson up in Chicago, probably the most influential harp player of the prewar blues. Then there was Rice Miller, who was blowing harp down in Mississippi and Arkansas and eventually ended up as the star of the *King Biscuit Time* radio show on KFFA, in Helena, Arkansas. The show's sponsor figured they could sell more goods if they got Rice Miller to pass himself off as the more famous Chicago harp player, despite the fact that the two men sounded nothing alike. It worked. And a few years later, when John Lee was murdered during a robbery, Rice Miller began calling himself the Original Sonny Boy Williamson.

Clarence got a sad look in his eye when he said, "I was s'posed to go cut a few sides there myself." His voice trailed off as they drove on, past a row of shotgun houses. "But I never got back down here till now."

"Did you know this is an historic district? Built by former slaves," the driver said. "I read in the newspaper how this was once a thriving community for the blacks."

"Mmm-hmm," Clarence said. "Sho was. And I spent some time here when that was the case. Knew a nice gal stayed over on Amite Street. I got right enthused about her, but I can't think of her name right now." He shook his head thinking about how that girl had made his heart jump. "It's just a faded thing now, though," he said. "I can't even see her face. But I recall she had a funny high-pitch voice. And she laughed a lot. Sho did." Back on Pearl Street, Clarence craned his head to look as they passed the dilapidated Summers Hotel. "The only place a black man could get a room back then, he said. "That or stay at a private home."

"The Subway Lounge there is famous," the driver said. "I go sometimes on the weekends, for the music."

"I was gone by the time they started doing music there," Clarence said. He had the driver turn around and go up Capitol Street past the Illinois Central Depot, which was getting a face-lift, and the King Edward Hotel, which was all boarded up.

It was all different, Clarence thought. He couldn't even tell where the Heidelberg Hotel used to be. As they drove up Capitol Street past the McCoy Federal Building and the big banks, Clarence stared in wonder at what looked to him like a seamlessly integrated society. Black professionals—men and women—coming out of office buildings with white coworkers, talking and laughing and carrying on. He knew things had changed, of course, but seeing it with his own eyes, and not just on television, packed an unexpected punch, a good one. "Ain't nothin' like it used to be," he said.

"Yes," the driver said. "Everything changes."

Clarence noticed the clock on the side of the Lamar Life Building. It was just about time. He had the driver turn back and take him to his appointment.

The Mayflower was Jackson's oldest surviving restaurant. Clarence stood outside, looking at the fancy neon sign and the glass bricks, thinking about how he couldn't even walk in there last time he was here. And even though he could now, he felt funny going through the front door. He had a feeling like someone was going to grab him by the scruff of his shirt and show his black ass to the street, but no one even looked up from their tables. This was going to take some getting used to.

A white lady approached him and said, "One for lunch?" Clarence looked at her for a few seconds without speaking. She smiled gently, thinking he was hard of hearing, like her own grandfather. She spoke a little louder. "Sir? Just one?"

Clarence shook himself back to this strange new world. "No, ma'am, I'm looking for a Mr. Jeremy Lynch. Said to meet him here."

"Yes, sir," she said. "If you'd follow me, he's sitting in the back."

She showed him to the table where Mr. Lynch was waiting. Clarence sat down, said hello. It was the first time he'd seen the man without a thick pane of glass between them. They'd met only the one time, when Mr. Lynch had come to see him at Parchman. His head was bigger than Clarence remembered, and it looked like he spent more time on his hair than a man should.

Mr. Lynch said, "You okay?"

Clarence went mute, staring at the man, and overcome by a wave of misgiving and suspicion like nothing he'd ever known. Back inside, he knew the rules and who he could trust, and he wasn't troubled with doubt. But he was now, and he didn't like it.

He wasn't sure if he could live out here in an uncertain world, and he wasn't sure about this deal he'd made. Maybe he was being set up. Or maybe this was a dream, maybe none of this was real. Maybe he was going to wake up back in unit 17 where things were more predictable.

Mr. Lynch reached over and touched his arm. "Clarence, you all right?"

The touch brought him back. He managed to nod and say, "Uh-huh." He took a drink of water. They told him he'd have moments like this, that his mind would have to get accustomed to things and that it wouldn't be easy. When they said that, Clarence thought they were crazy. Easy? You think doing fifty years is easy? Fifty years he should've been somewhere else, like with that gal with the high-pitched voice, playing his music, raising children, having their children sit on his lap and listen to him play the guitar. How hard could freedom be? But he could tell they were right. It was going to take some effort. He had to get a grip. A grip on his thoughts and fears and doubts. He had to trust Mr. Lynch. Nobody else was offering to help. He had to keep his end of the bargain. Clarence looked at his lawyer and said, "You still got them tapes?"

Lynch smiled reassuringly. "Of course I do. Locked in the safe in my office. Would you like to go and see?"

Clarence shook his head. "No, sir. I'm just askin'."

Lynch waved off the concern. "I understand. You want to be sure. I don't blame you." He took a pack of crackers from the red plastic basket on the table. He opened it and said, "So, how's it feel to be a free man?"

"Different," Clarence said as he looked around the restaurant. "Feels different than I thought."

"I bet." Lynch sprinkled some Tabasco on his cracker and nibbled it. "Well, look, I'm sure it's gonna take some time to adjust.

Maybe you want to see a psychologist or some kind of counselor, help you deal with the transition."

Clarence shook his head and stared a hole in Mr. Lynch's head. He didn't have any use for that kind of nonsense.

"Or not." Lynch stopped a passing waitress. "Hon, bring me some of that Come Back Sauce, would'ja?" He leaned down to open his briefcase and pulled out a manila envelope that he put on Clarence's side of the table. "That ought to hold you for a little while," he said. "You know where you're staying? I need to know where I can find you."

"Saw hotel up the street. Figured it'd do."

Lynch leaned forward onto the table and glanced slyly at the envelope. "What's the first thing you gonna do with that, get you some pussy?" Clarence's face hardened in a way Jeremy Lynch had never seen. A prison-yard stare. "None of my damn business," Lynch said, holding his hands up. "You're right. Just curious. Forget I asked."

Clarence glanced down at his clothes and said, "I'm gone get a new suit."

— — — — — — — — —

"**AWWW, HE'S SO** cute," she said when she saw the kitten. "What's his name?"

"Crusty," Rick said. "Crusty Boogers."

The woman at the vet's office gave Rick a disapproving look. "That's terrible."

Rick acted as offended as she did. "He doesn't seem to mind."

The woman made a disagreeable noise and continued the paperwork. "And how are you going to pay for it?" Her tone suggesting that Rick didn't look like the kind of guy who could afford their services.

"I was thinking about using money," Rick said. "I didn't know I had options. You guys do stuff on trade or barter?"

She remained unamused. "We'll need a credit card for a deposit."

"Deposit? You're not doing a heart transplant. How much is this going to cost?"

"That's a sick cat. It can get expensive."

"Naaahhh." Rick looked at Crusty. "Probably just a bath, some food, and whatever shots he needs for a license."

"That's what everybody thinks, but they're wrong. How much are you willing to spend?"

"I tell you what," Rick said, handing over his credit card. "Do an exam and call me with your estimate." He gave her his business card. "I'll be at that number the rest of the day."

— — — — — — — — —

RICK PICKED UP the film he'd dropped off the day before, then headed for the offices of Rockin' Vestigations.

It was a block from his apartment, on the second floor of a re-stored building that dated to the 1890s. Named after the merchant who'd run a dry-goods business there, the Adolph Rose Building had a sign in front that promised antiques, art, a café, and a theater. The latter was a reference to the old Strand Theater next door. Long boarded up, the Strand had originally featured first-run motion pictures, then B-movie classics like *Queen of Sheba*. At the end it was showing a Civil War documentary appropriately called *The Vanishing Glory*.

The first floor housed Adolph Rose Antiques. Their show-room was filled with antebellum armoires, canopy beds, and dressers. There were also displays and glass cases filled with Civil War battlefield relics ranging from swords and socket bayonets to Confederate belt buckles and Union artillery projectiles. The

Highway 61 Resurfaced

proprietor was an affable man who answered to the name of Pee Wee Milkwood.

During the day, Rick's clients came through the antiques showroom to a wide staircase leading up to a hallway that fed the rented offices on the second floor. There was a back entrance up an exterior metal staircase for use after regular business hours. Rick had "Rockin' Vestigations" painted on the frosted glass of the door, like something from a Sam Spade movie. Inside there was a small reception area with a door leading to Rick's office, which was furnished with a desk, three filing cabinets, two chairs for clients, and a small table. There were large arched windows that looked out over Clay Street. The effect was a sort of southern noir.

Just after two, Rick was sitting behind his desk, saying, "Don't worry about it, Wanda Lee. I was only in jail the one night."

"Well, I'm still sorry," she said, sitting on the other side of the desk, rooting through her purse. "But did you at least get the pictures?"

"No, I'm afraid the Port Gibson police decided to keep those, since they weren't convinced I was who and what I claimed to be. But it's okay, I don't think you need them."

Wanda Lee pulled a pack of gum from her purse. "You want some?"

"No, thanks."

She unwrapped two sticks and popped them into her mouth. "But you said the pictures would be the key."

Rick smiled. "And they will be, Wanda Lee. I promise." He opened his desk drawer and pulled out a large manila envelope containing the set of eight-by-ten black and whites he'd picked up earlier. "Now, before I show these to you, let me tell you exactly what I saw."

Wanda Lee sat up straight and listened intently but didn't

seem the least bit shocked by what she heard. In fact, by the time Rick finished, she looked downright disappointed. She sat back in her chair and thought about it for a moment before she said, "Well, I mean, does that count as cheatin'? You know what I'm talkin' about? I mean, you think a judge'll call that adultery?"

"I doubt it'll go that far, Wanda Lee." He handed her the photos.

She flipped through them quickly, then paused at one. "Those ain't Durden's feet," she said, pointing. "He's got more hair on his toe knuckles."

"Yes," Rick said. "I know."

"But that sure is a pretty dog."

Rick took the photos and put them back in the envelope. "Wanda Lee, here's what I suggest, and I've already talked to your attorney about this. Make a lunch date with Durden, somewhere he won't want to raise a fuss, like a place that buys his Tru-Fry 2000. You'll show up with your attorney. Your lawyer will inform your husband that you want a divorce and that you expect it quick and easy. When Durden starts to squawk, your attorney will flash a couple of these pictures and then mention the public nature of a divorce trial and the likely damage to his reputation should he become too closely associated with the word 'bestiality.' "

Wanda Lee thought on that for a moment before she said, "You think that'll be enough? Ole Durden ain't got much shame."

Rick nodded and said, "I think he's got that much." He stood and walked her to the door. "Everything's going to work out just fine, you'll see." He held up the pictures. "I'll get these over to your lawyer this afternoon." Wanda Lee thanked him and went on her way.

Rick sat at the receptionist's desk to address the envelope.

He'd was licking the flap when Lollie Woolfolk came in like a cool breeze in a pink gingham sundress. She was shorter than she sounded on the phone, Rick thought. Early thirties, beauty-parlor blond, with a ripe-peach complexion and intriguing cheekbones. Rick just stared at her, his tongue on the flap.

"Rick Shannon?"

He nodded as though guilty of something quick and shallow.

She smiled and casually gestured at his tongue pressed to the gummy flap. "Stuck?"

"Huh? Oh." Flustered, Rick sealed the envelope and tossed it on the desk. "Sorry, I was . . . you surprised me."

She stepped into the room and said, "You should be careful doing that. I got a paper cut on my tongue once. It hurt like the devil." She stuck her tongue out, touched the tip with her finger, made a pained face.

Rick wanted to examine her for scars, but instead he stood and held out his hand. "You must be Miss Woolfolk."

"You can call me Lollie." She looked as soft as a magnolia petal.

Rick showed her into his office and offered her coffee. She took it with sugar. He asked her to fill out a client-information sheet. Pointing to the bottom of the form, he said, "Down there, if you'll give me whatever information you can on your grandfather. Date and place of birth, where he worked, anything that'll help me get started."

Lollie was halfway through the form when the phone rang. Rick excused himself and took the call out at the reception desk. "Rockin' Vestigations, Rick Shannon speaking." It was the woman from the veterinary clinic. She had the results of the doctor's exam. "How is he?" Rick asked.

"Sick," the woman said. "I need your authorization to go ahead with more blood tests and treatments."

"It'd be quicker to say what's not," she said. "Poor little guy's malnourished and dehydrated. He has flea anemia, amoebic parasites, worms, ear mites, his temperature's low, he has some sort of upper-respiratory problem, and he only weighs about two ounces. He has slight polychromasia, moderate anisocytosis, and the doctor thinks he has a viral infection in his sinuses."

Rick wasn't sure what it all meant, but he could hear the cash register ringing in the background. He said, "Is there any good news?"

"X ray indicates he doesn't have fluid around the heart or any pulmonary lesions, but his stomach is full of air. We have him in an oxygen tent right now and we've got him on vitamins, Terramycin, Clavamox, Albon, ViSorbin . . ."

Ka-ching, ka-ching, ka-ching. "What do I owe so far?"

"About four hundred dollars." Rick was quiet for a moment before the woman said, "So, do you want us to continue or should we terminate?" While Rick tried, in silence, to figure out where the money would come from, the woman took the opportunity to say, "Seems like a waste to stop now, don't you think?"

Rick thought about the kitten looking up at him from the bottom of the Piggly Wiggly sack, then he looked into his office at his new client. Well dressed, well heeled. He'd get a few hundred bucks for finding her grandpa. "What the hell," he said finally. "In for a penny, in for a pound. When can I pick him up?"

"End of the day if you wanna do everything yourself. Or you can leave him with us and we'll do it."

"How much to leave him overnight?" Rick paused to listen, then said, "I'll be there before you close." He hung up and returned to his office.

Lollie handed the form to Rick and said, "Do you work

alone, Mr. Shannon? The reason I ask is, I was hoping you'd be able to dedicate full-time to finding my grandfather."

"Don't worry," he said. "I have operatives. But I'll handle this personally." He glanced at the form to see how much he had to work with. "All right, let's see. Mr. Tucker Woolfolk, approximately seventy-three, born in Issaquena County, et cetera, et cetera." He read to the part about occupations, then stopped and looked at Lollie. "Theater manager and faith healer?"

She looked down in what Rick took as embarrassed amusement. "Yeah, from what I gather, he was sort of a showman, though snake-oil salesman may be a better term. It's all kind of vague because I heard all these stories as a kid, but I think he may have traveled around the state with a kind of, I don't know what you'd call it, a kind of minstrel or medicine show, you know, musicians, dancers, stuff like that. This was back in the forties or fifties."

"Sounds like quite a character."

"That's what I gather."

"Do you have any photographs?"

"No, I've never even seen one. I have no idea what he looks like."

"How about your parents? Are they still—"

She shook her head. "They're both dead," she said. "Car accident."

"Sorry to hear that."

She accepted Rick's sympathy with a sad smile. "Thanks." She sipped her coffee. "Oh, I didn't write this down," she said, tipping her cup toward the form. "I think he worked in radio for a time. You know how they used to do live music broadcasts from stations? My mom said he'd been the host on one of those, sort of like the *King Biscuit Time* they do up in Helena, Arkansas, that kind of thing."

"Where was this?"

"I'm not sure," she said. "It could have been in Greenwood or Memphis for all I know. Like I said, this is stuff my mom used to tell me when I was young." She finished her coffee and set the cup on Rick's desk. "That's all I can think of."

"Tell me about this phone call you got. You didn't recognize the voice?"

Lollie shrugged. "No, just some man. Black, I think." She got out of the chair and went to the wall where Rick had several framed newspaper articles about the case he had solved in McRae. "Only thing I'm sure of is, it wasn't anyone I know."

"And he asked for your grandfather?"

"Yeah, said he was trying to find Tucker Woolfolk. When I asked who was calling, the man hung up."

"Can you think of anything else? Did he have brothers or sisters?"

"Not that I know of," she said, moving from one article to the next.

"How about his wife?"

She looked over her shoulder at Rick. "My grandmother? That's who I was named after. But I don't know anything about her, not even her maiden name. I think she died pretty young." Lollie pointed to a photo of Rick in one of the articles. In it, he had peeled back the gauze to show the twelve-gauge wound on his neck. "What's it like to get shot?"

Rick struck a nonchalant pose, his hand casually touching the scar. "Let's just say it hurts more than a paper cut on the tongue."

She laughed at that and said, "I bet it does."

There was an awkward silence before Rick said, "Now, the only thing left to discuss is the matter of my retainer."

"Of course." Lollie crossed to Rick's desk and opened her purse. She was about to reach in, then paused. She looked at him and said, "Did you know your grandparents, Mr. Shannon?"

He figured she was angling for a sentimentality discount. "I knew two of the four."

"I didn't know any of mine," Lollie said. "But I'd like to. I don't have any other family left." She pulled a white envelope from her purse and handed it to Rick. "I hope this will be enough to get started."

Rick casually looked inside. It was five hundred dollars.

RICK SHOWED UP at the vet's office with the most expensive cat carrier they'd ever seen. It had a fleece-lined, battery-powered heating pad on the bottom.

The vet gave Rick a sack full of eardrops, eyedrops, pills, ointments, and nutritional supplements. Then she handed him a pack of tissues and said, "He has sneezing fits."

"Fits?" Rick looked at the small ball of orange fur. "How much snot could he produce?"

"You'll be surprised."

Rick put Crusty in the carrier and took him out to his truck. He set him on the front seat while he looked through the boxes of pet stuff in the back. There was a top-of-the-line kitty condo, two scratching posts, an automated kitty-litter box, and assorted furry toys. He found the seat-belt adaptor for the carrier, secured it in the passenger seat, then headed for the station.

He turned on the radio. "That's the Sippie Wallace classic 'Mighty Tight Woman,' from Bonnie Raitt's first album. I'm Mike Rushing, and you're listening to WVBR-FM, classic rock from the banks of the big river." Rushing was Rick's boss as well as the station owner. He was an aging hippie who'd inherited some money in the late sixties and opened a record store in Jackson. Parlayed that into half a dozen stores around the state, then sold before file swapping killed the retail record business; walked away with a bundle. He moved to Vicksburg, bought the radio station, and did the three-to-eight shift.

WVBR held one of the oldest radio licenses in the state, still broadcasting from the original building out on Porters Chapel Road. It was a small, quasi-Mission-style building, an irregular cube, almost windowless, sitting on the edge of a field near some woods on the outskirts of town. The entire building was a cozy eight hundred square feet, but what it lacked in size it made up for in character. The studio had a lived-in, communal funkiness. The walls were papered with backstage passes, classic album artwork, and old head-shop posters of Dylan, Hendrix, Easy Rider, and R. Crumb's doo-dah man truckin' down the road. The transmitter tower was in the field next to the station.

Rick parked in front of the studio. "We're here," he said to Crusty. "You ready to rock and roll?" The kitty raised his head slightly and opened his mouth, but he didn't say anything. "Oh, that's right," Rick said. "It's time for food or medicine or something." He looked at the instructions. "Well, soon. Just hang in there." Rick got out of the truck and stretched. The nearby woods were pulsing with cicadas. He looked up at the stars and saw the flashing red lights at the top of the station's antennae and thought about what he might play first on tonight's show. Cat Stevens? Cat Mother and the All Night News Boys?

He opened the passenger door and undid the seat belt. Crusty made a feeble mewling noise when Rick picked up the carrier. He looked inside. Crusty was curled up on the pad, barely moving. As he headed for the building, Rick worried that the little guy might not make it.

He walked into the studio just as Mike said, "That's Joplin and the Full Tilt Boogie Band with 'Half Moon' on WVBR. Rick Shannon's next, redefining classic rock, so stay tuned." He went into a commercial break and pulled off his headphones. He pointed at the cat carrier and said, "What's that?"

"My new life partner," Rick said. "Crusty Boogers." He spoke to the cat. "Crusty, this is my boss."

Mike looked inside the carrier. "She seems a little young to be in a relationship."

"It's a he."

He looked at Rick, eyebrows arched. "Sorry, I didn't know you went that way."

"Hey, I saw a man having sex with a dog the other day. I've got pictures if you want to see."

"Maybe another time," Mike said as he put his headphones on and waited for the spot break to end. "That does it for me," he said. "I'll be back tomorrow, but for now, I'm leaving you with 'Questions 67 and 68.' Here's CTA on VBR." He pulled off his headphones and said, "Just a thought, but if you open with 'Rainy Day Women # 12 and 35,' you can go into a whole numbers set."

Rick mulled it over for a moment, then said, "Paul Simon. 'Fifty Ways to Lose Your Lover.' "

" 'Hey Nineteen.' Steely Dan."

Rick snapped his finger. "Oh! I was going to say 'Rikki Don't Lose That Number.' "

"Ewww, clever boy. How about '19th Nervous Breakdown'?"

" 'Rude Awakening #2.' "

"Don't know it."

"Creedence."

"Oh. Then back to Chicago for '25 or 6 to 4.' "

Rick held up his hands to surrender. "I'm opening with something for Crusty."

"Lemme guess." Mike gathered his things and cleared out from behind the board. " 'Cat Scratch Fever?' "

"Cats hate Ted Nugent. Everybody knows that." Rick sat down behind the console and pulled the computer keyboard close. The studio equipment was mostly digital. Mike had stored a vast library of classic rock on the hard drives and if you knew what you were doing, you could almost program your entire show in forty-five minutes. Rick tapped out Elton John's name and scrolled down the song list, then made a selection.

Coming up on the top of the hour, Rick cleared his throat, opened his mike, and said, "This is WVBR-FM, Vicksburg. Classic rock for kitties." He went into "Honky Cat" by Elton John.

"Very nice," Mike said. "Have a good show. See you tomorrow."

As Elton sang about quitting those days and his redneck ways, Rick pulled out the instructions for Crusty. Ointment in the eyes, drops in the ears, a handful of pills down the hatch chased with a syringe of sticky kitty formula. When he finished, Crusty was lying in Rick's lap, feeble and pathetic. Rick cued up an Otis Redding song, then went to a commercial.

After the spot set, Rick opened his mike and said, "Well, friends, I've got some news to share with y'all. And it's good news, I think, and it's this: I have adopted. That's right, there's a new member in the Shannon family and I've got him here with me in the studio. Now I know what a lot of you must be thinking. That Rick Shannon's not exactly what you'd call prime parent material. And if that's what you are thinking, you'll be relieved to know that I've adopted a child of the feline persuasion. Weighing in at two pounds and one ounce, with a nice head of striped orange hair, I'd like you-all to meet Crusty Boogers." Rick gently lifted Crusty to the mike, hoping he might meow. Instead he

started sneezing like a machine gun. "Whoa!" Strands of stringy **41**
opaque mucus shot out of the tiny nostrils in every direction.
"Eww! Not on the mixing board! No, no, no!" Rick had never
seen anything like it. "My shirt!" Crusty must have sneezed
twenty times in five seconds before running out of gas, dazed and
exhausted. Rick laid him back on the heated pad in the carrier.
There was a moment of dead air before he said, "Boy oh boy."

"Well," Rick said. "There's a waxy cat goober dangling from
the microphone like a hanged man." He paused. "I'm not sure I
can describe it any better than that, and why would you want me
to?" He wiped it off with a tissue. "Suffice it to say, Crusty's
boogers aren't always crusty. The vet says it's a viral problem in the
sinuses that triggers a bacteriological problem that triggers all the,
uh, what'll we call it? All the discharge. Well, anyway, I better start
cleaning this up. Meantime, let's dedicate this next one to the
sickest little kitty in show business. Here's 'Mr. Pitiful' on
WVBR-FM."

GOING INTO THE last hour of his shift, the phones got
quiet and Crusty fell asleep without any further sneezing attacks. Rick had requests for a couple of lengthy tracks, so he
cued them up, starting with Boz Scaggs's version of "Loan Me
a Dime." He figured it was a good opportunity to start looking
for Tucker Woolfolk.

In his brief time as a PI, Rick had learned that most of his
work, at least in the preliminary stages, would be done sitting
down. The databases that are at the core of every conspiracy nut's
nightmares are gold mines for private investigators. If you exist in
real life, you exist in a database somewhere. If you're looking for
someone as old as Tucker Woolfolk, the best place to start might

Highway 61 Resurfaced

be the Social Security Death Master File. If he found Mr. Wool-folk there, he'd save himself a lot of time and increase his average per-hour pay. Unfortunately, the death master file database isn't perfect, being largely incomplete for the years prior to 1980. Another pitfall was having to know the exact name under which the subject was listed in the system. Was it Tucker A. Woolfolk, or maybe H. Tucker Woolfolk? Lollie hadn't listed any initials one way or another. Rick tried several variations but didn't get any hits. It was tempting to think this meant the man was alive and well and living somewhere, but it was just as likely that he'd died before 1980 or that he had a middle name Rick didn't know about.

Just for grins, Rick did a multiple-engine search on the last name. This was usually a waste of time unless the name was extremely uncommon. Sure enough, "Woolfolk" generated nearly 53,000 results. Rick glanced at the first fifty but the answer wasn't there.

The request line started to blink, so he picked it up. "VBR."

" 'TVC 15,' 'Eight Days a Week,' 'Five to One,' and '905.' "

Rick laughed and said, "Oh, hey, Mike. You're still working on that number set?"

"Yeah, once I get started on these things . . ."

"Let's see, 'TVC 15' is Bowie, 'Eight Days a Week' is Beatles. What were the other two?"

"Doors and the Who."

"Hey, listen," Rick said, "I hope you don't mind, but I did a sort of impromptu pitch tonight to raise money for the local animal shelter."

"No, I heard that. It was good. I'll contact them tomorrow and set up something formal." He paused a moment before he said, " 'Horse With No Name.' "

"Okay, uh, 'Wild Dogs,' Tommy Bolin."

" 'Diamond Dogs,' Bowie."

"Pink Floyd's *Animals*. That's 'Pigs on the Wing' and 'Sheep.' "

" 'Birds,' Neil Young."

"Stones, 'Monkey Man.' "

"Get back to work."

"Right. See ya."

As he hung up, Rick thought of another song for the number set, a classic. His favorite version was by Commander Cody and His Lost Planet Airmen. "Riot in Cell Block #9." This, in turn, reminded Rick that the next place to look for Tucker Woolfolk was prison. Based on Lollie's description of her grandfather as a con man, it didn't seem like too big a stretch. Rick logged on to the U.S. Bureau of Prisons Web site and did a series of searches but came up empty again. It was possible, if Woolfolk was incarcerated, that he was in a state or county lockup. Rick took a few minutes to run the name through a few of the Mississippi correctional institutions, but he came up empty.

As midnight approached, Rick figured he'd operate under the assumption that Tucker Woolfolk was out there somewhere. And with that in mind, Rick selected his last song for the night, Edgar Winter's White Trash doing "Still Alive and Well."

THIS WAS A first for Rick. Every time he'd looked for someone, he'd found them in one or more of the traditional databases. But not Tucker Woolfolk. Rick's best guess was that he was missing part of the man's name. He'd call Lollie tomorrow and see if she had any ideas on that.

As he drove home with Crusty asleep in his carrier, Rick started thinking about what Lollie had said about her grandfather being a snake-oil salesman traveling with shows in the south. It seemed a safe assumption that much had been written on the subject and now Rick was going to have to dig through all that. He didn't know if there were any statistics to back him up but, based on his experience, he figured Mississippi had a higher ratio of historians per capita than most states. You couldn't swing a dead catfish in Warren County without hitting somebody who claimed to be an expert on the Civil War, or civil rights, the blues, the boll weevil, or anything else having to do with the Magnolia State. Some were apologists for terrible things that had happened, while others seemed bent on demonizing aspects of the culture that were largely benign. But one thing was certain, there was no shortage of people interested in the state's past, ranging from cockeyed hobbyists to the Center for the Study of Southern Culture at Ole Miss.

Rick suspected someone out there was an expert on the traveling shows that used to crisscross the south. And if Tucker Woolfolk had been associated with them, maybe there was some mention of him in somebody's thesis.

He got back to the Vicksburg around twelve-thirty. He gave Crusty his last feeding and tried putting him to bed in his new kitty condo, but Crusty wouldn't have anything to do with it, preferring instead the carrier's heated pad. Rick grabbed a beer and his cigar box. He loaded his pipe, took a hit, then got online and started poking around. As expected, the history of minstrel and medicine shows was well documented. Both had roots in European traditions dating back hundreds of years. In the U.S. they were traced from as early as 1820 to as late as the 1950s.

If Tucker Woolfolk was in his early seventies, he'd have been old enough to see the last of the minstrel shows that had lingered in the south long after they'd died off in the rest of the country. And if he'd been a theater manager of some sort, as Lollie said, he might even have promoted shows such as the Silas Green Minstrels out of New Orleans, the Cavalcade from Mobile, Alabama, or the Vernon Brothers from Macon, Georgia, as they passed through Mississippi. These troupes of string bands, singers, acrobats, and dancers were, in some instances, whites performing in black face. But there were also all-black troupes owned by black entrepreneurs and, in time, there were even some integrated shows.

It occurred to Rick that in their own way, these traveling companies foreshadowed radio and television, each troupe a different channel to divert you from your troubles. This was especially true of the medicine shows that, like the modern infomercial, used entertainment and celebrities to gather a crowd before selling magic elixirs. Click, Sammy Green's Minstrel Show, click, the Darktown Scandals Revue, click, the Jay C. Lintler Mighty Minstrel Show, and dozens more.

Rick came across one particular production that caught his eye. He noticed it for two reasons. First because it was based out of Port Gibson, Mississippi, in whose jail Rick had enjoyed a night of hospitality, and second because the name sounded familiar. F. S. Wolcott's Rabbit Foot Minstrels was a traveling show that, at one time or another, featured many of the great entertainers of the century. Legendary performers such as W. C. Handy, Ma Rainey, Jelly Roll Morton, and Dizzy Gillespie performed with F. S. Wolcott's show, as did Rufus Thomas, the R&B great out of Memphis who was a comedian with the Rabbit Foot Minstrels in the mid-1930s. Rick knew Rufus Thomas not from the minstrel stage, but from radio in the 1960s and '70s, when he had big hits with "Walking the Dog" and "Do the Funky Chicken."

Rick pushed back from his computer and walked over to the window. He looked out toward the river, trying to figure out why F. S. Wolcott's name seemed so familiar. He saw the lights of a tugboat as it chugged and churned up muddy water it was too dark to see. He took another toke on his pipe and a moment later it hit him. He went to his record collection and pulled The Band's 1970 album, *Stage Fright,* and there it was: side two, track two, "The W. S. Walcott Medicine Show." The last name was "Walcott" instead of "Wolcott," and it was a "medicine show" instead of "minstrels" and it was "W.S." instead of "F.S.," but even with those differences it was too close to be a coincidence.

Rick slipped the record out of the sleeve and onto the turntable. He dropped the needle into the groove, and a moment later, loping, earthy music carried him inside a faith healer's tent where the real deal was going on and Garth Hudson was blowing his sax among the losers and winners and saints and sinners.

The Band was one of Rick's favorites. As much as anybody, they defined the music of the sixties and early seventies, which made it that much harder to understand why classic rock stations by and large didn't play them anymore. For a group comprised of four Canadians and one guy from Marvell, Arkansas, The Band was oddly steeped in Americana and exhibited a fondness for romantic images of the American south in songs like "The Night They Drove Old Dixie Down" and "King Harvest" with its portrayal of Depression-era sharecroppers.

Rick went back to the computer to look for the connection. He found it quickly. The story went like this: The Band's drummer, Levon Helm, had seen F. S. Wolcott's Rabbit Foot Minstrels as a kid in Arkansas and had been particularly struck by a singer billed as the lady with the million-dollar smile. She was known as Diamond Teeth Mary, though in the song she's referred to (for reasons that went unexplained) as Miss Brer Foxhole, "She's got diamonds in her teeth." But the weird thing was that Levon Helm didn't write "The W. S. Walcott Medicine Show." That credit belonged to Robbie Robertson, his bandmate from Toronto. Rick figured that since Helm was never much of a songwriter, he told the story about Diamond Teeth Mary to Robertson, who put it to music and didn't bother to share the publishing rights.

Rick chuckled when it dawned on him that he'd wandered a bit off subject, a not uncommon thing when he got stoned. So where was he? Oh yeah, Tucker Woolfolk. While it was possible the man had connections to the minstrel productions of the day, it seemed more likely that he'd been involved in the medicine shows that followed minstrelsy and which borrowed the traditional entertainment forms to lure audiences for pitchmen selling alcohol-based "medicine products" as a way to skirt Prohibition.

Surfing Web sites, he read about the Kickapoo Indian Medicine Company of New Haven, Connecticut; The Clifton Remedy Company; and Hamlin's Wizard Oil Company. Finally he came across an oral history by an obscure Delta harp player known as Itta Bena Slim. He recounted a story about a medicine show he'd been with in the 1940s that ran into some legal troubles outside Tchula, Mississippi. Itta Bena Slim said the promoter had shorted the local constabulary on his cut of the profits, contrary to the established custom. He said the man who had cheated the sheriff got out of Holmes County by the skin of his teeth. When asked if he remembered the man's name, Itta Bena Slim said, "Oh, yeah, he was Mr. Robert T. Woolfolk."

THE NAME PUT Rick in business. He plugged it into the Social Security Death Master File to check again. As far as he could tell, Mr. Woolfolk was still alive. He plugged the name into another multiengine search and got a few more hits, each yielding some good information.

Rick searched for a phone number in Mississippi. Once you've got a phone number, you're home free. If you're trying to find someone who doesn't want to be found, you simply look the number up in a reverse directory or, in many cases, you can type the number into a search engine and get the name and address you're looking for. Of course, all that depends on how much the subject is moving around. Rick figured that at Tucker Woolfolk's age, he was tending toward stationary, so that probably wouldn't apply. If he got a number that led to an address, he'd call and say he was with the cable company or somebody and needed to confirm his information for their records. Then he'd need to confirm that this was, in fact, the Tucker Woolfolk his client was looking for. He couldn't just call and be honest about it either; Lollie had asked Rick not to tell her grandfather she wanted to meet him. She wanted it to be a surprise, and Rick didn't want to ruin that. He could just imagine the old man's face when this woman showed up and introduced herself: "Grandpa!"

Rick suddenly had a dark notion though he wasn't sure what had prompted it. He didn't think of himself as unnecessarily cynical but he also wasn't naive. Rick told people he was in the information business. It had a nice, sanitary ring to it, but there was no way around the fact that his livelihood relied on the sordid nature of the human being. He was in the squalid business of providing proof that people were scum. Rick's career depended on distrust—wives suspicious of their husbands, insurance companies suspicious of claimants, employers suspicious of their employees. Rick had been hired for all these reasons and each time found that the client's distrust was fully warranted.

But he knew his clients weren't the only ones who had reason to be suspicious. Distrust was a two-way street. Just as his clients had reason to be suspicious, Rick had to be wary of his clients. As far as he knew, all his previous clients had been truthful about why they'd wanted the information they did. And though he had no reason to think Lollie had lied, he'd still had this strange thought. What if she hadn't been honest about why she wanted to find her grandfather? It wasn't uncommon for people to hire a PI under false pretenses. Was it possible she was interested in something other than a friendly family reunion?

Only one thing came to mind, and it struck Rick as wildly southern Gothic and clichéd: some sort of multigenerational tragedy steeped in deviance, alcoholism, and repressed memories. What if, he thought, Lollie wanted to take Tucker Woolfolk to court for having sexually abused her as a child or something along those lines?

Rick shook his head and wondered where that Tennessee

Williams moment had come from. Maybe a subconscious reaction to the town's abundance of Victorian architecture and the constant assault of antebellum imagery on everything from restaurant menus to the Mississippi River flood wall. On the other hand, the idea wasn't so far-fetched as to be dismissed out of hand. But, in any event, it didn't matter to Rick. His loyalty was with his client. He'd just take the whole thing at face value and move ahead.

There was one listing in Mississippi for an R. T. Woolfolk at an address in Belzoni, a small Delta town in Humphreys County about ninety minutes north of Vicksburg. Rick plugged the address into an online map site and found it was just north of the town, near Fisk Bayou and Cemetery Road.

— — — — — — — —

RICK CALLED THE number the next morning and confirmed that the old man who answered was the Robert Tucker Woolfolk who had once been run out of Tchula, Mississippi. "I told him I was a writer doing an article on the old minstrel and medicine shows in the south," Rick said into the phone. "He was a little skeptical at first, but once I got him talking, I didn't think he'd stop." He gave Lollie the address and phone number he'd found.

"This is fantastic," she said. "I am so thrilled, I can't thank you enough. You've got to tell me everything he said. I want to know whatever you found out."

"Sure, you want to meet at my office this afternoon?"

"No," she said quickly. "This calls for a celebration. I'm taking you out for a fancy dinner, tonight. You can tell me then. How about André's at the Cedar Grove Inn?"

"Much as I'd love to, I have to work tonight."

"Oh, that's right. How about tomorrow? You don't work Saturdays, do you?"

Rick could hear the excitement in her voice. "No, I don't do weekends," he said. "What time?"

"I'll make reservations for seven-thirty."

After hanging up, Rick did a little more research. He felt that he needed to give Lollie something other than an address and phone number to justify the five hundred she'd given him. Within an hour he had put together an interesting, if superficial, biography of Robert Tucker Woolfolk. Sometimes the work was so easy, Rick felt guilty. But he was learning to get over that.

Rick closed the file and went to check on Crusty. He was still lethargic and his tiny nostrils were clogged. Rick had learned that a flat wooden toothpick was the best way to pick Crusty's nose. The vet said it would be a while before the antibiotics would subdue the bacteria problem. But since that was just a symptom of the underlying viral problem, for which they had no cure, the snot would return after the course of antibiotics. In other words, the vet had said, "You're going to be picking this cat's nose for the rest of his life."

--- --- --- --- --- --- ---

SATURDAY MORNING AFTER starting coffee, Rick went downstairs and grabbed a copy of the *Vicksburg Post*. When he got back, Crusty was walking around for the first time since he'd been there. He wandered into a patch of sunlight and stopped as if he'd hit a force field. He rolled around on the warm carpet for a moment then began grooming himself, which seemed like a good sign. Rick sat at the table near the window overlooking the business district and the river beyond. Skies were clear and it seemed like you could see halfway across Louisiana.

He was looking forward to his evening. Deliver some good news to a customer, get the word of mouth going, have a nice meal at the client's expense. He'd heard good things about the restaurant at the Cedar Grove, one of the town's antebellum bed and breakfasts, famous among other things for having a cannonball lodged in the parlor wall.

He poured a second cup of coffee and picked up the paper, snapping the crease. He glanced down at Crusty. "Says here the river fell from twenty-three feet to eighteen-point-three on the Vicksburg gauge. Forecasters say it'll be fourteen feet today. What else? The county election commission approved Jerry Dale Lyons to run in the district one supervisor's race. Seems there was a question of where Mr. Lyons really lived that placed his candidacy as an independent in question." Rick turned the page. "Hey, the new Super Gorilla class of drill rigs built by LeTourneau was completed at the Sabine Pass facility over in Texas." Rick read the preseason analysis for the local high school football teams before turning to the obituaries.

"Well, let's see who's gone gently into the good night." Rick worked his way down the list, pausing to dwell on causes of death and the hobbies of the deceased. But it was a name that really got his attention. "Jesus!" Rick spewed hot coffee all over the place. He'd never seen Crusty move so fast. Rick grabbed a paper towel to wipe the window before reading the particulars: "Local businessman Durden Tate suffered a massive heart attack at the Biscuit Company Café yesterday afternoon. Mr. Tate was having lunch with his wife, Wanda Lee Henshaw Tate, and another man. Paramedics were unable to revive him and he was declared dead at the scene." Rick lowered the paper and looked around the apartment. Crusty was peeking out from under the sofa. "Sorry," Rick said.

- - - - - - - - -

BLIND BUDDY COTTON could see a lot better than his name or his dark glasses would lead a stranger to believe. But the way he figured it, if a guy from Tennessee could call himself Mississippi Fred McDowell, Buddy Cotton could call himself blind. At eighty-three, he looked and played the part, always letting someone lead him on and off the stage at blues festivals and clubs. Even kept a cane near his chair on the porch where he spent most of his days, just in case somebody showed up and wanted what they considered authenticity more than the truth.

Buddy knew that most of the original bluesmen with that nickname had earned it. Blind Lemon Jefferson, Blind Willie McTell, and Blind Blake were all born sightless. Blind Boy Fuller's eyes dried up on him before he was twenty. Blind John Davis stepped on a nail when he was nine. The infection took his sight. And Blind Willie Johnson lost his when his stepmama threw some lye at his daddy but missed and blinded Willie instead. There's a reason to sing the blues.

And while it was true he needed glasses for his "stigmatism," Buddy Cotton called himself blind mostly for marketing purposes.

He was sitting on the porch of his little house a few miles out of Ruleville, Mississippi. The exterior was rough cypress board with corrugated tin for the roof and the skirting around the bottom, like a prosperous sharecropper's shack. The inside wasn't quite as bluesy, what with the big-screen TV and the hot tub and a few other items catering to Buddy's fondness for creature comforts. He owned it all free and clear plus the land it sat on, surrounded by good cotton that somebody else was farming. He'd done all right for himself playing the blues, and he'd taken care of his money. Bottom rail on top now, and he'd earned every bit of it the hard way.

Highway 61 Resurfaced

It was ninety-six degrees in Sunflower County and Buddy was wearing the same gray porkpie hat he always did. Under the shade of the rusted tin roof, he seemed immune to the swelter. His face betrayed no emotion, like black wax poured into an indifferent mask long ago. He had a 1946 Gibson L-7 in his lap, a guitar he'd owned since it was new. He held a kitchen knife in his left hand. He was dragging it up and down the strings, torturing a cry from the instrument, like it was a safety valve for his own soul.

It was around noon when Buddy noticed a car turn off Highway 8 and start up the dirt road toward his place. He aimed his sunglasses toward the cloud of dust. His eyes were good enough to see it was Big Walter Johnson's car, that old Chevy Impala with the busted headlight and bad suspension. Buddy started tapping his heel to a medium tempo that matched the way the car bounced up the rutted road. He plucked a note and slid the knife down the strings and sang, "I gots dust on my mem'ries, can't seem to 'member a thing."

The Impala kept rolling and bouncing toward the house, a brown cumulus in its wake.

"I gots dust on my mem'ries, can't seem to 'member a thing."

The car pulled up. Big Walter's round, shiny face behind the dirty windshield.

"She said we had a honeymoon and now she wants a weddin' ring."

Big Walter waited for the dust to settle before he got out of the car. Buddy hunched over the guitar and attacked the strings, his heel keeping time during the ride. Big Walter got out and took a few steps toward the porch. He pulled a handkerchief from his pocket and wiped at the roll of fat on his neck. "Hey, Buddy, ain't you hot with that hat on?"

Buddy just slithered the knife up the neck of the guitar in reply.

Big Walter listened for a moment before he said, "That somethin' new? Sound a little like 'Steady Rollin' Man.' "

Buddy scowled and demonstrated the difference between the songs.

"Oh yeah," Big Walter said, pointing at the guitar. "I see what you mean." He stepped closer and put a foot on the first step. "Listen, I just hert some news," Big Walter said. "Thought you'd wanna know."

Buddy bent a note, then growled, "Yo' phone busted?"

When Big Walter smiled, the sun reflected off a gold-rimmed tooth. "I was passin' by," he said, dabbing his forehead with the handkerchief.

Buddy pushed his chin toward the old Impala and said, "Why you still in that raggedy-assed ride?"

Big Walter looked at the car, then back at Buddy. "Runs okay."

"Huh, I 'spect that's all you need." Buddy stopped playing and leaned forward on the guitar. "What's cookin' brings you out here?"

Big Walter waved his hanky toward the Sunflower River, a few miles to the west. "I's talkin' to old Cooter and them earlier, over to Cleveland. Hert Clarence's done got out."

Buddy nearly dropped the knife. He shook his head and said, "Can't be. He still gots some long years to pull, dudn't he?" He had a different grip on the knife now, not so much for playing.

Big Walter shrugged. "I'm just sayin' what I hert, Buddy. Old Cooter swears it's true. Figure he's comin' home." The gold-rimmed tooth peeked out again. "Thought you'd wanna know, thas all."

Buddy never changed expression. He just watched Big Walter go back to his car and get in. He turned the Impala around, then rolled down his window and looked out at Buddy. "He gets back? Maybe y'all do another show together." Big Walter waved and laughed as he drove down the dirt road, back toward Highway 8.

Buddy looked out over the hot-skillet landscape and thought about what might happen if old Cooter was right. If Clarence came home, it was more likely there'd be trouble than a show. He figured the others knew by now or would soon. Lord. They were all too damn old for trouble, Buddy thought, but that wouldn't keep it from their doors, just not how things worked out here.

Buddy felt the thing in his chest and he started to cough. After a struggle, he brought something up. He leaned and spit it to the dirt, then sat back in his chair to catch his breath. The end wasn't far off now. He could see it from where he was. He could taste it every time he coughed. Buddy had always hoped Jesus would call him in his sleep, but now he feared he'd be awake for it. He looked down at his left hand, the pads of his fingers broad from seventy years of playing. He pressed the strings to the wood and began to pick the notes to "Hellhound on My Trail."

THE VISITATION FOR Durden Tate was from five to eight. Rick arrived at a quarter to seven, figuring he could pay his respects before going to dinner with Lollie.

He opened the heavy doors of the funeral home and stepped inside. Two visitations were under way. In the state room to his right, Rick could see a few elderly women slumped in their seats, staring at an urn. Straight ahead, in a larger room, Rick saw a group of potbellied men whom he assumed were members of Durden Tate's sales force.

Rick stopped outside the larger state room to get in line for the guest registry. Glancing into the room where Durden was on display, Rick saw several familiar faces. There was Mindy Spencer, a face Rick had seen coming and going from more than one motel room in the company of someone else's husband. Rick had taken a couple of blurry photos that showed Mindy from behind but they weren't as good as the pictures he had from this particular husband's other trysts, so Mindy's name had never come up in the course of those divorce proceedings.

Off to the side of the room, Rick saw his first client, Lurlene Atwell. She had hired Rick to follow her husband, Tommy, whom she suspected of being inconstant in his marriage vows. Rick promptly provided some eight by tens of Tommy in several compromising positions, which led to a quick and comfortable divorce for Lurlene. Several months later, she referred Wanda Lee Henshaw Tate to Rick for the same purpose.

Despite the occasion, Lurlene was wearing an ivory Cheryl Tiegs shirtwaist dress from K-Mart and a pair of split-pea–green stiletto-heel pumps from Joan & David with a matching handbag sporting a chrome clasp the size of a rodeo belt buckle. As Rick shuffled forward in the line, he saw Lurlene sneak an airline bottle out of her purse and pour it into her coffee.

After signing the registry, Rick eased into the room where Durden lay in state. Rick found himself wondering if caskets came in husky sizes or if they'd had to use some sort of industrial-size shoehorn to get ole Durden in there. It looked like a tight fit.

Glancing up from the casket, he saw Wanda Lee across the room accepting condolences. From all appearances, the grieving widow was taking things in stride. She was smartly dressed in a black Ungaro suit, Jimmy Choo pointed-toe slingbacks, and a stunning black hat from the Nigel Rayment collection, to which she had added a tasteful black veil. When Rick got a moment alone with her he said, "Wanda Lee, I am so sorry for your loss."

"Oh, bless your heart," she said. "It was sweet of you to come." She dabbed a lacy handkerchief at the corner of a dry eye.

Rick lowered his voice and, with a look of astonishment and sorrow, said, "This is not what I expected when I suggested that meeting with Durden and your attorney."

Wanda Lee gave Rick a sweet pat on his arm. She ducked her head and lowered her voice. "Honey," she said, "if you could've guaranteed this result, I'd've paid you double." Behind the veil

Rick saw her eyes cut left and right before she continued, "Don't you know how much better this is?"

"Wanda Lee, I'm sure you're just in a state of shock right now and—"

"If I'm in shock," she interrupted, "it's only because I'm not used to having this much luck."

Rick smiled politely and was about to make his exit when he noticed Wanda Lee's eyes look past him, growing wide. She shouted, "Lurlene! No!"

This was followed immediately by Lurlene screaming, "You bastard!"

Rick turned just in time to see that split-pea-green purse coming at his face, too late to stop. The big chrome clasp caught his lip and busted it open. Rick stumbled backward into Durden's casket, his hands reaching behind for support. One landed on Durden's cold face, changing his expression.

Wanda Lee shrieked, "Lurlene! What're you doing?" She was trying to pull Lurlene away from Rick as Lurlene continued swinging the purse furiously.

Lurlene was hollering, "That vile S.O.B. took them pictures of my Tommy and showed 'em to me and made me look like a fool!"

As Durden's sales force stood off to the side snickering and making bets, Wanda Lee said, "Lurlene, what has gotten into you?" A possibility occurred to her. "Is it your hormones?" That's when she got a whiff of Lurlene's breath. Wanda Lee gasped and said, "Lurlene, you been drinkin'!"

"So what if I have?" Lurlene pointed at Rick and shouted, "That picture-takin' scumbag ruined my life. Tommy's done moved in with that Yetta Ann Bigsby and he's telling the whole wide world that he's never been happier. How do you think that makes me feel?"

"Lurlene, you brought this on yourself with your drinkin' and everything."

"No, unh-unh." She wagged her finger violently. "It ain't my fault Tommy divorced me. It's that private detective." She pointed at Rick. "He made this happen."

"Lurlene, you hired him to catch Tommy."

"Yeah, but I was drinkin' when I did that! I ain't responsible."

By now Wanda Lee had pulled Lurlene a few feet away from Rick. He took the opportunity to circle the casket and stand behind the open lid, as a shield. He wiped some blood from his lip and said, "Lurlene, calm down."

She struggled against Wanda Lee's grip. "Let go of me! I'm gonna grab him where the hair's short and make him pay for what he done to me!"

"Lurlene," Rick said. "It's not my fault your husband was sleeping with Mindy." He pointed across the room at her. There was a collective gasp as all eyes turned to Mindy Spencer, including the eyes of Mr. Herbert Spencer, her husband.

Rick wasn't proud of having done this, but he hoped it would divert Lurlene's anger and send the fight across the room. Instead, it just seemed to infuriate Lurlene further. "I don't care who that bottle-blond slut is sleeping with," she said as she broke free from Wanda Lee. She charged at Rick, swinging her purse overhead like a medieval mace. Rick ducked behind the raised lid of the casket. But Lurlene wasn't going to be denied her pound of flesh. She began to climb across the open casket, planting a knee on Durden's throat, causing him to emit a grim guttural sound.

Wanda Lee was aghast. "Lurlene! Stop it! You're ruining my funeral!"

"This shit-eatin' son of a bitch has ruined my *life*!" Lurlene was crying hysterically as she climbed farther up into the casket, her other knee pressing down on Durden's sternum. As she continued to swing her purse, you could hear the bottles rattling inside along with her collection of ninety-day AA chips.

Wanda Lee was tugging on the back of her dress, screaming, "Get off my Durden! Lurlene, think about what you're doing. Look at your bracelet, honey! WWJD!"

As Rick ducked behind the casket, he was thinking, Yeah, what *would* Jesus do?

- - - - - - - - -

RICK WENT BACK to his apartment to change shirts. He figured his reputation would be better served by not being seen in public with blood on his clothes. His lip was slightly swollen and split, but there was nothing he could do about that except hold some ice to it on the drive to the restaurant.

He was ten minutes late. Lollie was sitting at the bar, on her cell phone, when he walked in. She was wearing loose oyster-colored cotton trousers and a sleeveless conch pink linen top. The result was a sort of belle-on-the-half-shell look. "No, this would be a perfect time," she said as Rick ordered a drink and a side of ice. "Okay, fine," Lollie said. "I'll call you tomorrow." She flipped her phone shut and looked at Rick's mouth. "What happened to you?"

He took a gulp of his drink and said, "Another satisfied customer." He wrapped some ice in a napkin and held it to his lip. "But let's not dwell on it. We're here to celebrate."

A moment later, they followed the maître d' to their table, where they ordered appetizers. Rick opted for the sweet corn and poblano tamales. Lollie had the crab cakes. When the waiter left, she raised her glass in a toast. "To the quickest investigator either side of the Mississippi." He raised his glass to hers and accepted her praise with a humble nod. "So," she said, "tell me all about my granddaddy." She leaned forward on her elbows and smiled like it was Christmas. "Was he really a faith healer?"

"Wouldn't surprise me," Rick said. "He was certainly involved in other areas of show business."

"Really?" She seemed giddy at the prospect of hearing the tales. "Like what?"

"Well, there was the time he was run out of Tchula, Mississippi." Rick recounted Itta Bena Slim's story.

Lollie covered her face in mock shame. "The source of all my bad genes," she said. "What else did you find out?"

"Well, once I got his phone and address, I didn't do too much more research." Rick put Tucker Woolfolk's file on the table. "But I did find a few interesting items." He opened the file and tapped his finger on the top sheet. "The first thing was something he wrote for the *Times-Picayune* about twenty years ago."

"He was a writer?" She turned the file around so she could read it, but she kept her eyes on Rick. "What's this about?"

"It's a record review, one of a dozen or so I found with his byline. This one's for a Robert Junior Lockwood record."

The name seemed to confuse her. "You mean Robert Lockwood Junior?"

"No, it's Robert Junior Lockwood," Rick said. "Apparently his mom was involved with Robert Johnson, who . . . are you familiar with the blues?"

She fluttered a hand in the air and said, "More as a state of mind than an art form."

"Well, Robert Johnson is one of the key figures in the blues."

"Oh, wait." Lollie pointed at Rick and said, "He's the guy who sold his soul to the devil at the crossroads, right?"

"That's the one. So, anyway, Robert Johnson took young Robert Lockwood under his wing and taught him guitar and, apparently, was enough of a father figure that Lockwood started calling himself Robert Junior. Some sources say he was Robert Johnson's legal stepson, but that's unclear." Rick speared the last bite of his appetizer and gestured with it as he spoke. "And, ironically, it turns out that Robert Lockwood was born in Marvell, Arkansas."

Lollie thought about that for a moment before saying, "Ironic because that's where my grandfather was from?"

Rick shook his head. "No, sorry, I guess it's more ironic to me than you." He explained how his search for Tucker Woolfolk had led him from the F. S. Wolcott Rabbit Foot Minstrels to the W. S. Walcott Medicine Show, and finally to Levon Helm, who was also from Marvell. "Just some of the odd stuff I stumbled across while looking for your grandfather." Rick tipped his glass toward Lollie. "How're the crab cakes?"

Chewing, she nodded, then covered her mouth and said, "So was his writing any good, in the record review?"

"Not bad," Rick said. "He obviously knew a lot about the music."

"You think he was a musician?"

"Not that I could tell, but he worked with some." He flipped to another page in the file. "Seems that somewhere between selling hooch with the medicine show and reviewing blues records, he apparently produced some."

"Hooch or records?"

"Records. By some blues players I'd never heard of. Anyway, based on some of the things he says in the liner notes and some of the record reviews, it sounds like he was connected to a radio station somewhere up in the Delta a long time ago and he may have also promoted some blues acts on the old chitlin' circuit."

Lollie chuckled. "So he was either a jack-of-all-trades or he couldn't hold a job."

"Just depends on your point of view," Rick said with a smile.

"I suspect there's a lot more stuff out there but, like I said, once I got the information you were after, I didn't do much more research. But I can, if you'd like."

She dismissed it with a wave of her hand. "No, that's plenty. I can ask him about all that when I see him." She looked at her lap and fussed with her napkin. "But there is one thing . . ." She reached down to her purse and came up with an envelope just as the waiter arrived with their entrees. Lollie had the Creole-glazed yellowfin tuna. Rick had a filet wrapped with garlic-pepper bacon and a port-wine demi-glaze. After the waiter left, Lollie assumed an attorney's tone and said, "Let me ask you a question. How would you react if a twenty-year-old showed up at your front door saying he was your kid?" She eyed him like a cynic. "Would you believe him based on his word and a driver's license or a birth certificate?"

Rick was looking into her eyes, but his peripheral vision was consumed with the envelope in her hand. This was the sort of client he had dreamed about, a veritable fountain of cash payments. After a moment, he shook his head and said, "No. It's too easy to get fake IDs." He cut a piece of his steak. "I'd say my reaction would depend on what he wanted. You know? It's one thing if he shows up saying he just wanted to meet me, but it's a different ball game if he starts demanding money." He leaned forward and tipped his head toward Belzoni. "Are you going up there to demand money?"

She smiled softly at his mock accusation. "No, I have all the money I need." She wagged the envelope, then slipped it under Rick's plate. She said, "I just want to get to know him."

Rick gestured at the envelope with his fork, inadvertently marking it with a drop of beef blood. "What's this?"

"I was wondering if you could go to Belzoni with me. Tomorrow." She looked vaguely chagrined. "That's for your time."

She dabbed a bite of tuna into her hollandaise. "It's just that I don't want to, well, in case he has a funny reaction, you know? I just thought it would be better with someone else there."

The envelope had control of Rick at this point. The way he looked at it, making a few extra hundred bucks for taking a drive in the country with a pretty woman was good work. He was inclined to go. But he was curious. "You have a reason to think he'll react funny?"

"No, but I was thinking about how he might react when a stranger shows up at his door claiming to be kin, you know? Sure, he might throw his arms around me and say he can see my mama's eyes in mine, but he also might just slam the door in my face thinking I'm some kind of nut." She gestured at her purse and said, "Like you said, I can show him my license and birth certificate, but he still might not believe me. So I thought if you came along, told him who you are and that I hired you, well, I mean if he was suspicious, that might be just the thing." She held up her hands in all reasonableness and said, "If you don't want to or if you're busy, I understand." She held her hand out for the envelope.

Rick slipped the money into his coat and said, "You mind if I bring my cat?"

THERE WAS A time when no roads led to Belzoni, Mississippi. It was such an isolated village that there was no practical way for the county sheriff in Greenville to get there, so he didn't bother trying. Belzoni was a lawless backwater on the banks of the Yazoo River, famous for a string of saloons they called Greasy Row. The entire area was so lacking in civil order that it was known as the Dark Corner of Washington County.

Hoping to improve their fortunes, local landowners agitated the state legislature until they annexed parts of the surrounding counties to form a new one that they named Humphreys after some mid-nineteenth-century governor. And in time they built roads.

Crail Pitts was on one of them now, driving north on Highway 7 out of Belzoni. He'd come down Highway 49 from Sunflower, where he'd been staying, and just drove around until Cuffie LeFleur called and told him now would be a good time to go see about that thing. He hoped it wouldn't take long, didn't see any reason that it should. The plan was simple enough: Get in, find it, take it, and go. Of course there was the question of what to do with the man afterward. They hadn't really talked that out. In fact, it seemed to Crail that Cuffie had left that up to him. He figured he knew what that meant, and he wasn't afraid to do it either. He'd do anything for Cuffie.

Crail couldn't wait to see her again. They were a fire so hot you couldn't put it out with all the water in the Sunflower River. Lord knows, her family had tried, but it kept burning. All that pride—snobbery is what it really was—thinking they're so damn superior, all that cotton money made 'em think they had a right to hinder the destiny of two lovers. But now that her family's name was being threatened, something had to be done. So Crail was on his way to do it, see if that wouldn't sweeten his situation.

Crail turned onto Sweethome Road and slowed down. His radio was tuned to a rock station out of Greenwood. The Rolling Stones doing "Little Red Rooster." He pulled to the side of the road, crunching all that gravel, and lit a cigarette. There was nothing but cotton fields in every direction, the bolls starting to blossom looked like acres of popcorn under the moonlight. He took a long drag on the cigarette and hoped this old guy wasn't going to make things tough. Not that Crail couldn't handle tough, he could, he just hoped it wouldn't play out that way. But his knee was hurting again, and who needs any more trouble than they already got?

He was about to flip that cigarette out the window when he caught himself. He liked to be going fast when he did it, so he could look in his rearview and see the orange sparks on the road behind him like a tiny fireworks display. He pulled back onto the highway and gave it some gas. When he was going good, Crail flicked his butt out the window. His eyes locked on the mirror until he saw the sparkles, then he smiled just a little.

Cemetery Road was just up a piece, past those rusty grain bins on the old Hemphill plantation. After making the turn, he saw the headstones and crosses leaning every which a way, like the dead weren't done yet and were trying to push their way up out of the ground. After passing the graveyard, he could see a yellow light on somebody's porch. That was it. Had to be. Nobody else out here. A minute later he came to a gravel drive with one of those bigmouth-bass mailboxes sitting next to it. Crail figured this was the place, so he turned in. The driveway led to a small frame house with a few trees around, persimmons and oaks. He parked by an oak and got out. There were no other houses in sight, which made him feel better about what he had to do.

The mosquitoes got on him quick. He slapped at his neck and arms as he stepped onto the porch, wincing when he used his bad knee. The television in the living room cast blue shadows on the thin curtains covering the front window. The volume was way up, some kind of police drama. Crail figured the old man was hard of hearing and he was going to have to yell at him. He knocked loud, just in case, then stood there with a harmless look on his face, waiting for a response. But none came. The police drama continued, someone complaining about criminals having more rights than victims. Crail was about to knock again when he saw the front curtains pulled back just enough for somebody to peek out. He gave a friendly wave, then used the same hand to brush mosquitoes from around his ear. The fabric moved again, falling back into place. Crail heard the safety chain slide into its slot a moment before a man yelled, "Who the hell're you?"

Crail aimed a smile at the peephole, gave a good country nod, and said, "Mr. Woolfolk?"

"I know who I am," Tucker said. "I'm asking who you are!" He opened the door until the chain was tight and half his face showed, creased and wary.

Crail gestured over his shoulder with a hitchhiker's thumb and said, "I'm with a record company outta Memphis, Mr. Wool-folk. I wonder if I could talk to you for just a minute?" He slapped the side of his neck. Got one.

"Record cump'ny? The hell're you doin' callin' on me this time of night? I didn't invite nobody out here."

"No, sir." Crail shaded his eyes from the yellow light that didn't really seem to bother the mosquitoes much. "I'm real sorry about the time, but I was on my way to Greenwood and, well, I just wanted to come by and talk to you about some business. I apologize for not calling ahead, but my boss is real keen on ac-quiring the rights to some of your recordings."

"Izzat right?" Woolfolk squinted as he gave Crail the once-over through the crack in the door. "What record cump'ny'd you say you're with?"

"We're outta Memphis, Mr. Woolfolk. And I think you're gonna be interested to hear my offer. If we could talk just for a minute . . ." He nodded toward the living room, trying to invite himself in. "These skeeters are pretty hungry out here."

"You just hang on a second." Tucker didn't want to let on, but he was intrigued. He hadn't been involved with the record busi-ness for forty years and all the sudden people were calling and dropping by at all hours. Of course, he knew the blues had been undergoing something of a renaissance lately, and maybe the time had come for the public to get interested in what he'd done. And, after a moment's reflection, he figured it was about damn time. "All right, I tell you what." He closed the door enough to take the safety chain off.

That's when Crail lowered his shoulder and busted in.

7

RICK OFFERED TO pick Lollie up at her house Sunday morning, but she insisted on meeting him at the Vicksburg. He didn't make a big deal out of it since she kept handing him envelopes full of cash. When he walked out of the apartment building, she was in the parking lot, leaning against his truck and chewing intently on a cuticle. "You seem a little nervous," he said.

"Well, yeah." She shrugged. "Big day and all." She glanced down at the asphalt and said, "What if he doesn't like me?"

"Don't worry," Rick said, opening the passenger door for her. "You're pretty likable." He gave her the cat carrier, then went around and got behind the wheel. "I've got an idea," he said. "We need to make one stop on our way out of town." With Crusty in his carrier, between them on the seat, they headed up Clay Street. Rick pulled into the Shipley's and came out with a box of donuts and two coffees.

Lollie said, "You think he'll like me if I bring donuts?"

"Bring *him* donuts? Hadn't thought of that," Rick said. "But if there're any left, it couldn't hurt."

She smiled, then slipped on her sunglasses and said, "Belzoni, here we come."

It was a nice day for a drive through the country, relaxed, windows down, elbows sticking out in the wind. As they left Warren County, Rick took note of three crosses perched up on a hillock to their right. Two white crosses flanking a taller, yellow-gold cross in the middle. It was the first of what would turn out to be many such displays throughout the Delta. A few minutes later Rick said that it seemed like they were passing a church every two miles. "So far I've seen a First Christian, Church of God, Independent Methodist, and a First Baptist," he said.

"Yeah, so?"

"Well, Mississippi's not exactly what you'd a call a densely populated state," he said. "Just seems like there's a high ratio of churches to people, that's all."

"It's the Bible Belt," she said. "Besides, look around. These folks have a lot to pray for."

Rick gave a nod to concede the point.

"How 'bout you?" Lollie asked. "You go to church?"

"You mean in a building?" Rick stuck out his lower lip and shook his head. "Nah, I get my spirituality delivered." He turned on the radio, searching the AM band until he found a preacher preaching.

"You better get right!" he said. *"You better get right now!"* The flock filled the pause in his preaching with noises of consensus. The minister continued, *"You know you can't stop no rat comin' in yo' house to eat yo' cheese! That's how the devil work! And it's a dumb rat ain't got two holes! Can I have a amen!"* He got several, followed by a loosely played piano that prompted the congregation to song.

"Amen," Rick said over the hand clapping and hallelujahs. He held up his hand as if to testify and began imitating the preacher.

"Brothers and sisters, in my experience, it's a dumb rat ain't got no donuts! Can I have a chocolate glazed?" He held his hand out to Lollie. "I need the salvation of sugar and grease! Can I get some cholesterol?"

She handed him a donut and said, "You're going to hell. You know that, don't you?"

"I thought I was already there," Rick said. "But it turned out I was just working in radio."

The gospel song on the radio came to a rousing crescendo before yielding to the preacher again. He told a story about a cheating husband who drank too much and how his wife had tried in vain to reform him. *"You can't change no knuckleheaded man,"* he said. *"Only Jesus can, amen! Help me now! Can I get some help?"* He got plenty. The parable of the knuckleheaded husband seemed to resonate with the congregation.

In Yazoo City they picked up Highway 49, heading toward Louise, Midnight, and Silver City. Along the way they passed a Catholic church, a House of Prayer and Praise, the Grace Bible Church, and a congregation of Primitive Baptists. Rick said, "I never realized Mississippi was such a competitive market for those in the soul-saving business." Up ahead, a highway sign testified that they were five miles from Belzoni. Rick handed Lollie the map he'd printed out. "You're the navigator from here on."

She looked at the map for a moment. "Okay, we're looking for Sweethome Road."

Rick pulled out his cell phone. "Do you want to call and let him know you're coming?"

"No, let's just show up and see what happens."

"What if he's not there?"

"Where's he gonna be?"

"I don't know, church?"

"We can wait," she said.

"Have you thought about what you're going to say when you meet him?"

"Not really. You have some ideas?"

Rick rubbed his chin for a moment. "Well, as an icebreaker, you could ask him if he knows he lives in a town named after an eighteenth-century Italian circus performer known as the Great Belzoni."

"What?"

"It's true," Rick said. "I looked it up. One of the town's founders was enamored of the man, for reasons that remain murky." Rick was hoping to soothe his anxious client with a laugh, plus he really had looked it up and didn't want to waste perfectly good information. "His real name was Giovanni Battista Belzoni," he said in an exaggerated Italian accent. "He later became a great adventurer, traveling all over Egypt and—"

"You just passed it," Lollie said with a smile. "That was Sweethome back there."

"Mama mia!" Rick circled back and made the turn. When they came to Cemetery Road, he slowed down and looked at Lollie. "You nervous?"

"A little, I guess." She took a deep breath.

"Relax. We still have a few donuts." He drove on and, after a moment, they went around a bend. Ahead, no more than three hundred yards, the road was blocked by six or eight vehicles.

Lollie leaned forward and took her sunglasses off. "What's going on?"

"I don't know," Rick said.

As they came closer they could see that the cars belonged to the sheriff's department and the Mississippi Highway Patrol. Lollie put a hand to her mouth. "Oh my God, something terrible's happened."

It seemed like a fair bet. A moment later, Rick saw the crime-scene tape around Tucker Woolfolk's property. He knew there wouldn't be anything good beyond that. He assumed a worst-case scenario. Someone was dead, and not from natural causes. Since, as far as he knew, Tucker Woolfolk lived alone, that meant the family reunion was over before it started. He put his hand on Lollie's arm and said, "All right, listen. Don't say anything. Let me do the talking."

Up ahead a deputy was leaning against his patrol car. He reluctantly pushed himself to a standing position and waved them to a stop. He was about the size of Durden Tate and looked like he might expire in the summer heat. The deputy leaned down toward the window and, in a tone intended to both intimidate and insinuate, said, "Wha' chall doin' out here?"

"Just driving around," Rick said. He hoped the lie wasn't as obvious as it felt on its way out of his mouth. He gestured toward the house. "What's going on?"

The deputy didn't answer at first. He just stared at them, sweat slithering down his jowls. Something about his stare almost squeezed the truth out of Rick. It was as if the deputy knew he was lying and suspected he was deeply involved in whatever terrible thing had happened in that house or was at least connected to it in a way that would justify pulling him out of the car and billy-clubbing a confession out of him. For the brief moment it took these thoughts to careen through Rick's head, the deputy's stare continued working its mojo. He seemed to be leaning closer now, his plump, pink, moist cheeks just inches away. Rick's question about what was going on hung in the air, and the pressure to fill the silence kept building until finally it was too much for him to take. He had to say something. "No, like I said, we're just taking a Sunday drive in the country, you know? Got my cat and my, uh, girlfriend, and a box of donuts." He put a hand on the box. "You want one? Not that, I mean, I guess that's a stereotype, huh? Cops and donuts. Well, never mind. Anyway, we saw all the police cars and that's why I asked what was going on. Probably official police business and you can't tell us, so forget I asked and, hey, I guess we'll just be on our way."

The deputy seemed vaguely flummoxed by Rick's speech. He mumbled, "Uh-huh," just as a black SUV rolled past them with the words "County Coroner" painted on the side, finally answering the question. The deputy shook his head slightly and said, "Well, I guess that there let's the cat out of the bag." He turned and pointed back at the house. "Some old man ended up on the wrong side of a gun in there last night."

"Oh my God," Lollie said, covering her mouth with her hand.

"Sorry, ma'am." The deputy put his round face farther into Rick's window so he could see her. "Didn't mean to upset you."

Rick shook his head like a man both surprised by, and disappointed in, human nature. He said, "They catch who did it?"

"Nope," the deputy said. "Probably some crackhead or a tweaker. The place was all tore up. We already got the pawnshop staked out. But you know, we're finding more identity theft with these drug addicts nowadays. They look for Social Security and credit card numbers. But they not real sophisticated when they try to sell that stuff, so either way, somebody probably be in jail before tonight."

The Delta's drug problem was no secret. The grinding hopelessness, poverty, and lack of education for many in the region made it a breeding ground for anything that could make the despair go away, even for brief periods. Where they'd once cooked up moonshine to help take the edge off their suffering, now they were cooking up crack and methamphetamine. It was as if they were saying liquor wasn't strong enough anymore, that they needed a more powerful anesthesia to tolerate the conditions into which they'd been born and over which they felt powerless.

"Let's go," Lollie said. "I don't want to stay here."

Rick looked at the deputy and said, "Well, all right, I guess we'll be going."

As the car started to roll, the deputy grabbed Rick's arm and said, "Just a second there." Rick had a moment of panic, as if the cop suddenly knew who he was and what he was doing there, and that he'd had a phone conversation with the deceased, and that made him a suspect. But the deputy just nodded toward the seat, smiling. "I'd take a chocolate glazed if you had one."

- - - - - - - - - -

A 1971 COUP DeVille was rumbling down Highway 82. Drivers passing in the other direction could be forgiven for doing a double take, since it looked like there was no one behind the wheel of the enormous car. Upon closer inspection, however, one could make out the top of a porkpie hat and a pair of dark glasses peering out between the steering wheel and the dashboard. Blind Buddy Cotton wasn't a big man to begin with, and in his later years he'd shrunk a bit, so he kind of disappeared when he sank into the driver's seat of the massive car.

He had death's grip on the wheel and his right blinker had been flashing since Indianola. When he got to Leland, he finally honored the turn signal. He passed Neisa Ray's Diner, Gigi's Hair Port, and then H. R. Watson's Cash Store, where five old men in overalls were sitting out front on benches, passing the day like it was 1932. Buddy gave a honk, and one of the men held up a hand to wave for them all. Someone else would get the next one.

Buddy made his next turn without benefit of a signal. He drove up the dirt road and came to a dusty stop right in front of a small frame building, white paint peeling from the boards and a

lopsided cross perched above the gable. A handmade sign welcomed all to worship with the "Full Gospel Church of the Lord
Jesus Christ of the Apostolic Faith and Reverend W. J. Johnson."

Buddy shuffled up the stairs like a slow blues and went inside.
A row of pews faced a bare plywood lectern. The upright Fischer
piano off to the side had seen brighter days. Buddy took off his
hat and called out, "Reverend! You here?"

A voice came from a small side room at the far end of the
church. "Who's that?"

"It's Buddy," he said, moving toward the voice.

There was a pause before the voice replied, "Buddy?" A chair
pushed back. "Hang on." He heard the distinctive footfall of his
old friend, and a moment later Crippled Willie Jefferson was
standing in the doorway, his big hush-puppy nose in the middle
of a broad caramel face. "Wha' choo doin' here? Service ain't till
Sunday," he said. "And Lord knows, if you showed up then, you
might just have to preach my funeral."

Buddy tipped his head down and peeked over the top of his
dark glasses. "Next time you find me in this old church or any
other, it's gone be a funeral, and it's gone be mine," Buddy said,
trying to hide his smile. "How you doin'?" The two men came
together and embraced.

"Not bad for a jake-leg preacher." He stood back to look at
his friend.

Buddy waved his hat at Willie's right leg. "Lord still ain't fix
that for ya, huh?"

"My cross to bear," he said. "That and friends like you." He
urged Buddy back toward the room he'd come from. "Listen, you
hungry? I got some nicky-nacks back here."

"Naw, unh-unh," Buddy said. "Ain't hungry."

Willie led the way, his left leg doing most of the work, his
right leg swinging forward to catch up and slap onto the floor be-

fore the process started again. The room was spare, with a couple of folding chairs and a card table with a Bible open on top of it. There was a window, a fan, and a small shelf with some peanut butter Nabs and a few cans of Vienna sausages. An old guitar case leaned against the far wall. Willie gestured at the chairs and said, "Let's siddown, visit."

Buddy put his hat on the table and they sat, did some catching up. "You know Miss Annie Turner and Pine Bark Parker both passed."

"Yeah, and I hert old Junior Curtis had a stroke, not doin' too good."

Buddy gave a doctor's nod. "He always had the high blood."

" 'At's right, sho did."

"And somebody told me Toots Odom is up in some nursing home outside West Memphis, don't even know who he is anymore. It's a shame." Buddy aimed a crooked finger toward the guitar case and asked if Willie was still playing.

"Yeah, but not that stuff we used to do." He said he kept his chops up playing the gospel. "Much as folks wanna hear me preach," Willie said, making a little fun of himself, "I bet half of 'em come for the music."

"That's all right," Buddy said. "Nothin' wrong with that."

At one point Willie said, "Hey, you still play up at O.V.'s Place?"

"Naw, unh-unh," Buddy said. "He been closed awhile. Only a few jernts still open I know of . . Po Monkeys, Crawdads, uhh, that Club Centerfold, couple others. But you know the kids, they ain't listen to the music no more anyway. They taste is change, ain't like it used to be. All they wanna hear's that damn rap." He shook his head. "That ain't music."

"Things is change, all right," Willie said. "Never gone be way it was."

"And I tell you one thing what done it," Buddy said, sure as he could be. "Casinos."

Willie dipped his head. " 'At's right."

"Givin' 'way free liquor you put enough of yo' nickles in they machines. How's O.V. gone compete with that?"

"Ain't."

" 'At's right." They carried on like this for a while, but they both knew it wasn't why Buddy had come. Finally, when the well of small talk ran dry, Buddy rubbed the top of his head, front to back, real slow, then he nodded at the open Bible. "So," he said. "Wha' choo preachin' on Sunday?"

"I was leanin' toward Judgment Day," Willie said, finally getting around to what they had to talk about. "Gettin' ready for it, all that."

Buddy looked as if he thought the subject had some potential. "You gone include somethin' on forgiveness and mercy?"

"Gone be more about the guilty among us." Willie closed the book and laid his hand on top of it, as if to swear. "The time is come for all us sinners to account for what we done."

Their eyes met and something passed between them. Buddy said, "I guess you done heard, huh?"

"Yeah, old Cooter, he told me. You 'fraid of what's gone happen?"

"You ain't?"

Willie shook his head. "I put it in His hands long time ago." He pointed at Buddy and went solemn. "You should too."

"Naw, unh-unh." Buddy reached down and touched his suit-coat pocket like it was where he kept a straight razor or a pistol. He said, "The Lord helps those what helps themselves."

"That ain't right," Willie said, shaking his head again.

"They's a lot ain't right," Buddy shot back. He felt a cough coming, but he held it. "Most of what happened fifty years ago weren't right. And the hundred years before that. Way I sees so many people livin' today ain't right, but that don't stop a bit of it. Fact, right don't seem to have much to do with anything," he said. "Cancer ain't right, but I tell you what, it's what's gone kill me. I don't need no help from Clarence or anybody else, I don't care what happ'm fifty years ago. I'm on die natchal."

"You think he cares 'bout what you think? You don't 'spect he feels he's owed?"

Buddy pointed a broad finger at his friend and said, "He shouldn'ta drove off like he did." He hit the table with a fist. "Shouldn'ta stopped in the first place."

"Got nobody to blame but hisself, huh?"

"That ain't—" Buddy stood abruptly and put on his hat. "All's I'm sayin' is, I wants the few days I got comin' and I'm willin' to fight for evva day I can git."

THEY DROVE DOWN the road in silence, Lollie staring out the windshield, Rick sneaking glances to see if she was going to cry or show any symptom of grief. But she stayed focused on the road, steadfast, expression flat, eyes on the verge of calculation. Finally she said, "Do you think there's something wrong with me?" She didn't wait for a response. "I mean, shouldn't I be crying or something? Maybe getting angry or depressed?"

"I don't know," Rick said. "Not necessarily. You never met the man. You don't have any real emotional connection to him, do you?"

"He was my grandfather."

"Yeah, but only in the abstract. He's not somebody you have memories of, right?"

"But he was family."

Rick hesitated a moment. "Well, if you'll pardon me for saying it, he wasn't very good family. He never tried to see you, did he? Never sent you a Christmas card or a present, never told you a story or bought you ice cream or did anything."

"I know, but still, it seems like I ought to feel . . . something."

"Well, do you feel like crying? Are you mad? Depressed?"

"Disappointed, I guess. I wanted to get to know him."

"Sure," Rick said, touching her arm. "I understand."

Neither one of them spoke again until they stopped for gas. Rick went in and bought a few things before returning to the truck. At the gas-pump island, he looked in the trash and found half a cardboard box from a case of motor oil. He pulled a small bag of kitty litter from his sack and dumped it into the box. He took Crusty out of the carrier and set him down on the ground. Crusty didn't waste any time. Afterward, Rick put him back in his carrier and got back in the truck.

He was about to key the ignition when Lollie said, "Hang on a second." She went into the convenience store and the ATM. A minute later, she came back to the truck and handed Rick another two hundred dollars. "That's the ATM limit," she said.

"What's this for?"

"That's a retainer. I'm hiring you again."

"You want me to find out who killed your grandfather?"

"No, it's probably some crackhead, like he said. That deputy sounded pretty sure they'd catch whoever it was."

"Then what's this for?"

"I want you to find out whatever you can about my grandfather. People who knew him, who worked with him, anything. I just want to get to know him better."

— — — — — — — — —

THE STORY OF Tucker Woolfolk's murder got four column inches in the *Vicksburg Post* the next day. There was nothing about his life, just his death, which Rick felt was a shame since the man had apparently led such a colorful one. The reporter seemed to be regurgitating everything the sheriff's spokesman had given him and didn't bother to do any other research, identifying Woolfolk only by name, age, and manner of death. "Crack Claims Another Victim: Elderly Recluse Killed by Addict." It said funeral arrangements were on hold pending notification of relatives.

Rick picked up the phone to call the reporter and give some background on Woolfolk. But then he had a thought. It would be just his luck that the reporter would wonder why Rick had this information on, and this interest in, the dead man and, showing the sort of initiative he failed to do when writing the original story, might do enough research to find out that Rick had been hired by the victim's granddaughter. Then the suddenly enterprising reporter would throw himself into writing the most important piece of investigative journalism in his career, with the hope of moving up to the *Clarion-Ledger* over in Jackson, and the next thing you knew, Rick would be sucked into the police investigation, and who needs that headache? So he hung up.

He needed more information on the life and times of R. Tucker Woolfolk, and he had two choices. He could either continue doing the research himself or he could talk to someone who might already know the answers to his questions. He looked up the number for the River City Blues Museum, which he'd visited soon after moving to Vicksburg. They had a nice collection of rare records, photos, and instruments reflecting the history of the Delta blues. But its more valuable asset, for Rick's purposes, was the curator, one Smitty Chisholm.

Rick got Mr. Chisholm on the phone and told him what he knew about Tucker Woolfolk and asked if he could help. Chisholm said the name was vaguely familiar, said he'd go through his archives to see what he could find. He told Rick to come over later in the afternoon.

The call made, Rick went to the kitchen and got a TV tray, which he took into the living room and set up. He arranged the ointments, supplements, pills, and formula on the tray, along with some flat toothpicks, an eyedropper, and a couple of soft cotton towels. He passed by the kitty condo that Crusty refused to have anything to do with, unless you counted the time he peed on it. He went to the cat carrier and looked inside. "Hey," he said, reaching in for Crusty. "It's time for your midday food and medication extravaganza."

Sitting in the BarcaLounger with Crusty in his lap, Rick picked the gritty bits from his nose as he squirmed and scratched and almost got eye ointment in his ears. Crusty was even less cooperative with the pills. He'd learned how to work them up the back of his throat with his tongue and spit them out. And his spitting range was increasing. It took five minutes to get three pills to stay down, by which point Rick had scratches and bites on his hands and forearms. He made a note to trim the claws. Finally they got to the part that Crusty liked. As soon as he saw the eyedropper filled with formula, Crusty began kneading a spot in Rick's lap. Then he curled up and started to purr while slurping his lunch.

Afterward, Rick did some cleaning up. Over the past few days, Crusty had launched dozens of nostril rockets, leaving lumpy gray-green things drying on walls and floors throughout the apartment. This might have seemed grotesque to some, but Rick had seen the homes of people with children and he knew this was trivial by comparison.

After cleaning the litter box, Rick walked over to the museum. Opening the door, he triggered an electronic sensor that sounded the cry of a bottleneck guitar. Inside was a modest space with tidy exhibits. Over here was a framed photo of Blind Willie McTell wearing a jaunty cap and a three-piece suit as he sat in a chair holding his guitar. Over there was the only known copy of the original Skip James record, "Hard Time Killin' Floor Blues."

Across the room was a display case featuring a 1931 Stella guitar thought to have been owned (and later pawned) by none other than Charley Patton. The exhibit had a listening station featuring several of Patton's songs. Rick put on the headphones and pushed the button for "Down the Dirt Road Blues." Patton's guttural growl was hard to decipher until he came to the lyric about how every day where he was seemed like murder.

Rick closed his eyes and listened to the old recording that had been copied off worn-out 78s made from cheap bowling-ball vinyl. Despite the primitive sound quality, Patton's original fingering and churning rhythms emerged and reminded that the blues was, perhaps foremost, music played at dances. When the song ended, Rick hung the headphones back on their peg. He turned just as a man entered from the next room, dressed casually and wearing bifocals. He looked over his glasses and said, "You the guy who called?"

"Yeah, I'm Rick Shannon."

They shook hands. "Smitty Chisholm," he said. "I like your radio show."

"Thanks."

"I heard you playing Paul Butterfield the other night, 'Shake Your Money Maker.' I'd bet you were the only station on earth playing their version of that song."

"Probably right." They talked for a while about how Butterfield and Mike Bloomfield had introduced the blues to a younger, white audience and what a shame it was that fame had eluded both men.

"Speaking of fame," Rick said, gesturing at the case with the 1931 Stella guitar. "Why is it nobody seems to know Charley Patton's name like they do Robert Johnson's?"

Chisholm's head rocked back and forth for a moment. Then he said, "Patton didn't have the mythology like Johnson. Selling your soul to the devil's a powerful image. And if any of these guys' lives can be considered more doomed than the others, it's Robert Johnson's." He gestured at a nearby photo of Patton, his hair slicked to the side, ears like jug handles, and that bow tie. "Now Patton lived pretty fast himself, with all the cocaine, whiskey, and women, but the trick to immortality isn't livin' fast, it's dying young and, better yet, under mysterious circumstances, the way Johnson did." Smitty dipped his head, then looked up at an angle and said, "Dead at twenty-seven, poisoned by a jealous lover in a juke joint outside Three Forks, Mississippi?" He shook his head. "Hell, Charlie Patton died of garden-variety heart problems at forty-seven. How's that gonna compete? Still, Charley might've become more famous if he'd had the sense to die after getting his throat cut during that fight up in Holly Bluff."

Rick said, "Yeah, well, hindsight's twenty-twenty."

"Ain't that the truth? Well, listen, c'mon." Smitty gestured for Rick to follow and led him into his office. The place looked like a prison library after a riot. Books, pamphlets, LPs, and papers were shelved, stacked, and strewn all over. He pointed at a chair and said, "Just put all that stuff on the floor, have a seat."

Rick sat down and admired the mess for a moment before he asked what there was to know about Robert Tucker Woolfolk. Smitty winked and said, "Well, let's just say he's one of those guys who contributed his share of pigment to the state's colorful history. I knew his name was familiar, but I couldn't remember why till I started poking around in the dustier corners." He gestured at the bookshelves surrounding them. "Your Mr. Woolfolk had his fingers in all kinds of pies. Among other things, he was a partner with Henry and Shelby LeFleur in a radio station up around Clarksdale that was one of the first to play what they used to call 'race records.' And since they had the equipment, they also recorded some of the local talent and pressed their own records.

Most of 'em only got regional distribution, so they're pretty obscure. But they did have a small national hit with a record by Charlie 'The Hawk' Hawkins. A song called 'Marcus Bottom Blues.' "

Smitty held up a piece of paper with some handwritten notes. "Now the list you gave me is of some of the records they produced at that station. But there may be another one out there. Actually, not even a record, but some tapes that were never pressed for reasons that are . . . shall we say, obscure and lost in the mists of time?" He leaned forward and continued speaking in deliberately mysterious tones. "You ever heard of the Blind, Crippled, and Crazy sessions?"

"Can't say that I have," Rick said, taking notes.

"The story goes that one night, Blind Buddy Cotton, Crippled Willie Jefferson, and Crazy Earl Tate got together and played as a group for reasons no one now agrees on. They'd never played together before and never did again. The performances are said to have left witnesses speechless. Blues scholars and collectors have been trying to find the tapes for fifty years."

Rick looked up from his pad. "A sort of Holy Grail for blues enthusiasts . . ."

Chisholm raised a finger in the air and said, "Except the Grail was a real thing. The deal here is that nobody knows for sure if these guys were recorded that night, and, if they were, no one knows what happened to the tapes."

"How can no one know if it was recorded? Was this in a studio?"

"Depends on who's telling the story," Smitty said. "One version has it as an impromptu gathering at a juke joint where there wasn't any recording equipment, which makes the tapes nothing more than wishful thinking. Another version has it in a studio where the tape recorder wasn't working, but they didn't know it

Highway 61 Resurfaced

until it was too late. Another is that the tapes somehow got passed near a magnetic field and were erased. Still another is that the men were under contract to different record labels and, under threat of litigation, the tapes ended up in some lawyer's office somewhere. There're all sorts of crazy stories about how it all came about, and how and why the tapes were lost or stolen, if indeed there were any tapes. The only thing everybody seems to agree on is that, recorded or not, it was some of the most powerful blues ever played."

"What's Woolfolk's connection?"

"His name shows up consistently in the studio version of the story, probably because of the radio station. He's said to be one of the producers of the session."

Rick looked up from making a note. "Producers, plural?"

"Yeah," Smitty said. "After I made the connection between Woolfolk and the Blind, Crippled, Crazy sessions, I called Beau Tillman, who used to run a juke joint outside of Leland, knows all those old guys. He allowed as how Woolfolk had a partner at the radio station by the name of Lamar Suggs."

Rick glanced down at his notes. "I thought you said his partners were Henry and Shelby LeFleur."

"They were investors," Smitty said. "Father and son, old cotton money and the main gear in the political machine in that neck of the woods. Woolfolk and Suggs ran the thing for 'em. Suggs was the talent scout. He was on the road a lot of the time, out making field recordings of anybody he thought they could sell, you know. Running around with a one-celled Presto disc recorder. Ever seen one of those things? Weighs about three hundred damn pounds. How's that for portable? They used acetate-on-aluminum discs until aluminum got scarce during the war. Then they used these acetate-on-glass recording discs that broke real easy. No telling how much good stuff got lost on those damn things. Suggs'd show up at fish fries, juke joints, turpentine camps, wherever somebody was playing music. Woolfolk ran the radio station, sold some advertising, probably engaged in a little boot-legging and whatever else might turn him a nickel."

"Did Mr. Tillman say whether Suggs was still alive?"

"Funny you should ask," Smitty said as he handed Rick a slip of paper. "That's his address up in Yazoo City, at least it used to be. Beau thinks he's still living there, but he couldn't say for sure, hadn't talked to him in years."

"He say anything else?"

"Yeah, Beau said that whatever else might be true about Robert Tucker Woolfolk, he was not the man Diogenes was look-ing for. Same was true of Suggs. In fact, Beau said that Suggs and Woolfolk still owe him some money." He laughed and said, "Those two robbed every artist crossed their path, black or white. Had 'em sharecropping onstage and in the studio too." His head wagged back and forth as he said, "Granted, that was par for the course in those days, hell, I guess it still is. You know the old sayin', record company'll let you be as dumb as you wanna be. But anyway, it almost got 'em both killed, and more'n once."

"Makes you wonder if maybe one of those chickens has come home to roost," Rick said. "Though you'd have to ask why it took so long." He looked at his notes, then at Smitty. "You know if Buddy Cotton or any of those guys're still around?"

"No, and Beau wasn't sure either. Keep in mind we're talkin' about men who'd be anywhere from their midseventies to their early nineties, so if you're gonna go lookin' for 'em, you might wanna try the cemetery first."

9

RICK WALKED BACK to his apartment thinking about the blues. As long as he'd been in radio he'd been playing the songs of Sonny Boy Williamson, Howlin' Wolf, Willie Dixon, Robert Johnson, and others, though he rarely played the original artists. He played the British bands who were, on the whole, more enamored of the blues than their American counterparts. Rick figured he'd played Cream's version of "Crossroads" more times than Robert Johnson ever sang the song himself. He played the Stones, John Mayall, the Animals, early Fleetwood Mac, the Yardbirds, and Zeppelin. And the American blues-rockers, too, Allman Brothers, Paul Butterfield, and Johnny Winter, among others. He was a definite fan of the blues, but third generation and one race removed.

When Rick got home, he found Crusty exploring the apartment. Based on the mess in the kitchen and the goo all over his head, it was obvious Crusty had already explored the garbage. Rick picked him up and said, "You're not going to win any cat shows looking like this."

Rick went to his record collection to see if he had any

Bukka White or Big Bill Broonzy, something to listen to as he re-searched the Blind, Crippled, and Crazy business. He pulled out a couple of blues compilations and blew the dust off them. Crusty started sneezing immediately, sending snot everywhere. Rick grabbed a tissue and chased him around the apartment until the fit passed. That's when he noticed something green extruding from Crusty's nose. It was a blade of grass, and a big one, looked like St. Augustine sticking out of a nostril, like it was coming out of a dispenser. Crusty was cross-eyed trying to see it as he swiped at it with his paw.

Rick gently held Crusty's head. "You want me to ease that out or yank it?" He gave a test tug. "It's in there pretty far. Probably best to get it over with quick," he said. So he yanked it. It must have been quite a shock, because Crusty's tail puffed up like a toi-let brush. After a startled pause, he sneezed his way back to his cat carrier. Rick looked at the wet blade of grass wondering how the hell it had gotten up there.

Rick looked at Crusty and ad-libbed a blues, "He's a snot-nosed kitty, got grass stickin' outta one side. Yeah, he's a snot-nosed kitty, got grass stickin' outta one side. And when ya pull that blade of grass out, he's sho nuff gonna run off and hide . . ."

Rick put on one of the albums and sat at the computer. With Bumble Bee Slim singing "Cold Blooded Murder, No. 2," Rick started looking for information on the Blind, Crippled, and Crazy sessions. There were several references to the legend, but none revealed much more than what Smitty Chisholm had told him. It happened around 1953 and somewhere in Coahoma or Washington or possibly Sunflower County.

He found entries for all three of the musicians in various blues guides. Crippled Willie Jefferson was the elder statesman of the three, having been born in 1913 on the Rosedale Plantation in Bolivar County. His guitar style was compared to T-Bone

Walker's, with whom he is thought to have played for some time in the 1940s. Never traveling outside the deep south, Crippled Willie had a solid regional reputation as a guitar and harp player. At some point in the early to mid 1950s, however, he had become a minister and stopped playing the blues altogether, performing only gospel music and folk spirituals from that point on. Rick did the math and figured Crippled Willie would be ninety if he wasn't already on the wrong side of the dirt. He was a good candidate for the Social Security Death Master File.

Blind Buddy Cotton was born in 1920 in Hollandale, Mississippi, "halfway between Muddy Waters and B. B. King," as one source quoted him as saying. Highly regarded as a guitar player and singer, Buddy Cotton recorded a few sides for Trumpet Records in Jackson and a few more for Okeh Records when one of their mobile recording units passed through Louisiana in the 1940s. His distinctive rumbling voice was said to have been a commanding instrument that carried all the troubles of the time and place where he lived.

Crazy Earl Tate was the baby of the bunch at seventy-three. Born in 1930 in Eden, Mississippi. As a teenager, he was discovered on a street corner in Greenwood playing the repertoire of Son House on a lard can with three strings. Tate was equally adept on piano and guitar, but he was more famous for his shocking vocal delivery and wild-eyed stage presence, legendary for its demonic intensity. Asked about the origins of his stage persona, he claimed that his mama had been cursed by a conjure doctor when he was still in the womb and that the devil was trying to get out of him every time he performed. There was no need to ask how he got his nickname.

None of the guides indicated a date of death for any of the three men, but Rick knew that if Son House could disappear for twenty years before being rediscovered, it was possible these men had disappeared and died without anyone noticing. Rick returned to the Social Security Death Master File. None of the three was listed under the name Rick had, but given the requirements of the search engine, that wasn't surprising. He'd never find Son House there either, unless he knew to look under Eddie James House Jr.

He called Smitty Chisholm to ask if he knew their legal names. Smitty said he'd try to find out and get back to him. Finally, Rick searched for Lamar Suggs, but there was no listing in the death file, so maybe he was still in Yazoo City.

Using a reverse directory and the address Smitty had given him, Rick found a number in Yazoo and called. A machine picked up. An old man's voice, country as four rows of okra, got straight to the point: "Ain't here, leave a message." Rick figured it was the voice of Lamar Suggs, so he hung up and dialed another number.

"Lollie?" he said. "It's me. You free to go to Yazoo City tomorrow?"

NOT SINCE MARCUS Dupree was setting records for Neshoba County High School had there been a running back in Mississippi with all the promise of Crail Pitts. Scholarship offers poured in, a full ride anywhere he wanted to go, but he never gave a serious thought to anywhere but Ole Miss. It wasn't a Pitts family tradition or anything, but if he was going to have a shot at getting Cuffie LeFleur's family's approval, he was going to have to run for the Rebels.

He was redshirted as a freshman, but he started the season opener his sophomore year. He ran for 118 yards in the first half against a solid Texas Tech defense, leaving alumni salivating at what he might be capable of against Alabama, LSU, and Mississippi State. On his first carry of the second half, Crail was supposed to run off tackle on a trap play, but Big Jim Magee missed his block. Crail cut just as the linebacker hit his knee squarely from the side, tearing every tendon and ligament in the joint. The line judge was later quoted as saying that it sounded like someone had ripped a live chicken in half. The last thing Crail remembered was being carried off the field on a gurney with all his promise.

Now, seven years later, he was still rubbing his knee and wondering if it was going to hurt this bad for the rest of his life. He'd had six surgeries so far and the damn thing still wasn't right, probably never would be. Of course it didn't help that he'd twisted it the way he had when that old man started fighting back the other night. Sumbitch was a lot tougher than he looked. And what good had it done to put up a fight? Didn't keep him alive, that's a fact. All it really did was piss Crail off. And for what? For nothing. The guy didn't even have 'em.

So now Crail was just killing time until he got word on where to look next. He was down at Billy Mac's Sporting Goods in Indianola, looking at the new crossbows that had just come in. The guy behind the counter said, "That's got your trajectory compensator, an adjustable cheek piece, and the quad limbs with the turnable yokes."

Crail sounded impressed as he looked down the sight, saying, "That's the shit, iddn't it?" He was handing it back to the guy when his cell rang. It was Cuffie calling to tell him where to go. He got in his car and headed south. An hour later he was crossing the Yazoo River.

He drove up Broadway Street to the address Cuffie had given him. It was a turn-of-the-century Queen Anne Victorian, white with a black wrought-iron fence. It was the kind of place Cuffie LeFleur's people were used to. Crail imagined the place filled with sterling silver and porcelain and a grand piano and servants. He parked across the street and sat there for a while, watching the place. He counted five chimneys and wondered what kind of person needed five damn fireplaces in their house. You couldn't sit in front of but one at a time. Snobs, that's what kind, people who looked down on the likes of the Pitts family. Like they were in any position to act superior. Hell, if the LeFleurs were so damn pure, he wouldn't even be here.

He was beginning to think nobody was home until, finally, he saw a body pass slowly by a window. Crail couldn't tell if it was a man or a woman. Whichever it was, the person was canted forward and stopped every two steps before continuing. He hoped this was the only person inside and, further, he hoped it was the man he was looking for. Crail looked at his watch. It would be dark soon. He lit a cigarette and relaxed.

— — — — — — — — —

WHEN THE MEALS on Wheels van pulled up behind him, Crail had an idea. He got out of his car and intercepted the driver, a young woman, as she fetched a covered plate from a hot box in the back of the van. "Hey, you takin' that to Uncle Lamar?" He pointed at the house.

The young woman seemed surprised. "Lamar's your uncle? He never told me he had nephews."

"Well, technically he's my great-uncle," Crail said, reaching for the food. "I was just going in to visit. I'd be glad to take that for you if you'd like."

"Well, thanks." The young woman let him have the plate and the utensils wrapped in a napkin. "Tell him Carol said to take his calcium pills, all right?"

"I sure will. You have a nice night." He waved to Carol as she drove off, then he gimped across the street to the big white house and knocked. "Meals on Wheels," he said as he reached down to check the door. It was locked. He could see movement through the cut-glass sidelight, someone approaching slowly with a walker.

"Carol? Zat you?"

"No, sir, Carol's out sick. But she told me to remind you to take your calcium."

"That sounds like her," he said. "Always pestering." The door opened a little at a time as Lamar Suggs backed away from it with his walker. "Just set that in the livin' room on that table if you would."

Crail stepped in and bolted the door behind him. No wonder he'd been unsure if it was a man or a woman. He was in a night-shirt, stained and unsightly. His gray hair, oily and scraggly, fell past his stooped shoulders. And he was small, like a woman. Crail wasn't worried about this one putting up much of a fight.

The house was stuffy and smelled of mothballs, dust, and garbage that needed to be taken out. To Crail's surprise, there was no porcelain or silver or grand piano. In fact, there was vir-tually no furniture at all. Ancient wallpaper hung off some of the walls and you could almost hear the silverfish eating the glue. There were staggering piles of magazines and newspapers and empty produce boxes throughout the house. It looked like the sort of place where they find old women living in filth with a hundred cats.

Lamar shuffled into the living room and sat in an aluminum lawn chair at a folding table with a small television on it. Crail set the plate in front of the old man and removed the cover, reveal-ing three piles of mush, orange, green, and grayish-brown. Lamar teetered as if he might just go into it face-first. Crail unfurled the paper napkin wrapped around a set of institutional flatware. He put the fork in Lamar's gnarled hand and said, "Yeah, when they told me Carol was out, I said I wanted to be the one to bring you your supper."

Lamar scooped a forkful of the orange mush with his palsied hand and trembled it slowly toward his mouth. "Why's 'at?"

"Well, 'cause of who you are. I mean, all those records you produced back then. Yes, sir, I been wanting to meet you." He gestured around the room. "In fact, I'm kinda surprised. I figured you'd have gold records on the wall and autographed pictures of you and all them guys you worked with. Like that Blind Buddy Cotton and them. Where you keep all that stuff at? Upstairs? I'd sure like to see it."

Lamar smeared the sweet potatoes across the opening in his face and snarled, "What're you after?"

"I'm just gonna have a look around," Crail said. "You go on and eat."

"Well now, you just hang on there." Lamar reached for his walker. "You ain't gonna do any such—"

"Shut up, you old coot!" Crail kicked the walker across the room, then grabbed Lamar by his stringy hair, jerking his head back. "Tell me where that stuff's at!"

Lamar's milky eyes went wide as he stared up at Crail. "I ain't got nothin' 'cept that TV," he said.

Crail shoved Lamar's face into the plate of food, then pulled him back up. His teeth stayed behind and some blood from his nose was mixed with the creamed peas. "You don't tell me where it's at, you're gone end up like that Tucker Woolfolk." He put his mouth close to Lamar's ear and said, "And lemme tell you, that sumbitch's eyes are *set*."

There wasn't much Lamar could do, but he weren't no quitter, so he did what he could. He swung his arm down with all his strength and sunk that fork right into Crail's bad knee.

ON THE DRIVE to Yazoo City, Rick told Lollie about the Blind, Crippled, and Crazy legend and how her grandfather and Lamar Suggs had been partners in the radio station where they might have recorded the mythic session. When he finished, she asked if any of the musicians were still alive.

"Don't know yet. Figured we'd ask Mr. Suggs when we get there."

"You think the tapes exist?"

"Sure as hell hope so," Rick said. "Don't you?"

She shrugged. "I guess I like the idea that it stays a myth. It's a better story that way. Besides, it just seems like it would have to be a disappointment after all the hype. The music couldn't possibly be as good as your expectations, you know? It's like when they released that 'new' Beatles song ten years ago, remember that?"

"Yeah. 'Free As a Bird,' " Rick said. "Boy, did that stink. Still, if they exist, I'd love to hear the tapes, especially after the way Smitty Chisholm talked about them."

"Did you get a feeling one way or the other whether he thought my grandfather or Mr. Suggs actually had the tapes?"

"No, it's just one of the possibilities. If they recorded at the radio station or if Suggs recorded them at a rent party or something, you'd think one of them might have them. But you'd also think they'd have surfaced by now. So who knows? If they ran into legal problems, which was one of the stories, there's no telling what could've happened to them. Might be sitting in a lawyer's office somewhere." Rick glanced over at Lollie. "What about your grandfather's estate? Are you handling that?"

She turned and looked out the window before she said, "No. Speaking of lawyers, he had one taking care of that. I'll ask if he found any tapes or anything next time I talk to him."

About a mile later Rick said, "By the way, is there a date set for the funeral?"

"What?" She turned back from the window. She looked as though the thought had never crossed her mind.

"Yeah, I figured you'd worked that out by now," Rick said. "I wanted to make arrangements, so I could attend."

She looked back out the window. "Oh, there won't be a funeral," she said. "They found a will. Said he didn't want any service. But that's nice of you, thanks."

At the intersection of Highways 3 and 49, they turned and headed into Yazoo City. They drove past the old Bon Ton Cafe, its once inviting neon sign a victim of thirty-five years of rust and neglect, like so many things in the Delta. The place was a shabby convenience store now, with a hand-painted sign, cockeyed and sloppy and nailed to the exterior wall, that read "Beer & Butts," a perfect reflection of how so many things in this once splendid town had gone downhill with the changing economics of agriculture. Rick wondered what the late, great Willie Morris would have thought about it all.

Highway 49 turned into Broadway Street as it struggled up from the Delta to the Loess Hills above. They passed the once thriving downtown that was now a shallow canyon of empty brick buildings waiting for the second act to begin. They drove up the wide street lined with leafy trees shading homes that ranged from the modest to the grand. Halfway up the hill, Rick pulled to the curb and pointed across the street. "Here we are."

They went through the iron gate and up the front walk. As they stepped onto the porch, they noticed the door was ajar, provoking them to exchange a curious glance. Rick nudged the door and leaned toward the opening. "Mr. Suggs? Anybody home?" They waited for a response, but none came. He pushed the door open wide. "Mr. Suggs?"

The front hall was strewn with trash. They exchanged another glace before stepping inside. Lollie said, "Maybe he doesn't live here anymore."

"Shhh." Rick's head turned to listen. "I think I heard something." They walked slowly toward the living room. Glass crunched under their feet, apparently the screen from the shattered television. They saw the walker lying sideways, against the wall. Rick had the sense that something violent had happened. He held up a hand. They stopped. "Do you hear it?"

"Yeah," she said, pointing toward the next room. "In there."

Lollie was first into the room. She said, "Oh my God."

"What is it?" Rick stepped in behind her and saw the body lying on the floor with a fork sticking in its back.

10

LAMAR SUGGS WAS facedown on the floor next to a small bed, amid pieces of shattered black vinyl, yellowing newspapers, and the smashed parts of an old record player that looked as if it had been thrown against the wall. Suggs was scraping something on the floor.

Rick pushed Lollie back toward the living room and told her to call an ambulance. He went to Lamar's side and put his hand on the man's back. "Hang on, Mr. Suggs. Help's on the way." Rick pushed the trash away from around Lamar's head and looked in his hand. He was clutching a shard of a broken 78. "Mr. Suggs? Can you hear me?" He said something Rick couldn't understand. He leaned in close to listen, but Suggs could barely speak.

He seemed to say, "Bees cease siege."

"Okay," Rick said. "Just relax." Without thinking, he started to roll Lamar onto his back, but then, considering the fork, he thought better of it. Rick decided to wait for the paramedics instead. He stepped over Lamar to get a look at his face. All around his toothless mouth was what looked like dried orange mud. Both eyes were black. He'd taken a beating. It surprised Rick that someone this frail was still breathing. "Can you tell me what happened?"

Lamar tried to muster some strength and muttered, "Bees easy."

Lollie came back into the room. "They're on the way," she said. "Is he alive? Did he say who did it?"

"He's alive," Rick said. "But I don't think he knows what happened. He's mumbling about bees or being under siege or something. I can't understand what it is." He looked up at her. "Did you look around? Is anyone else here?"

"No," she said. "It's creepy. There's nothing but trash in the rest of the house. It looks like everything he owns is in this one room."

The ambulance arrived a few minutes later. Rick and Lollie stepped out while the paramedics worked. Rick said, "All right, look. The cops will be here in a minute and we're going to have to talk to them. Unless you want to be spending a lot of time with the police over the coming months, don't volunteer anything about your grandfather's death."

"Okay with me. What should we say?"

Rick suggested a plausible story and told Lollie not to say anything more than that. She agreed. They went out to the front porch and sat on the railing, waiting for the cops. Lollie seemed rather calm, almost inappropriately so. Rick was unnerved by what he'd seen and he wondered why she wasn't. Out of the corner of his eye, he saw Lollie checking her reflection in the window. She adjusted her blouse and brushed her hair back as if she was sitting there waiting for a date to arrive. This wasn't the first time something about her had given Rick pause. In fact, the catalog of examples was getting thick enough to strain credibility. Why did she always pay in cash? Why hadn't she hired him to find out who killed her grandfather? Was it a coincidence that the next guy he found for her was now being treated by paramedics? Why had she asked if Suggs had named his attacker? The more he thought about it, the more he was struck by the improbability of everything that had happened. An odd notion forced its way into his thoughts and he started shaking his head.

Lollie noticed this and asked what he was thinking about.

"The casinos," he said. "I was wondering if I could call someone and ask what the odds are that two men I wanted to talk to would end up dead or dying the day after I tracked them down." He gave her another sideways glance.

"Why're you looking at me like that?" It seemed to amuse her.

"How am I looking at you?"

"Like you think I beat up that old man," she said, gesturing toward the house. "Or killed my grandfather."

"Well, now that you say it out loud, it does sound a little funny."

She was incredulous. "That's what you were thinking?"

Rick offered an embarrassed grin and scratched his scalp. "Well . . ."

She stood up and faced him, arms folded across her chest. "You may want to keep in mind that you're not the one who wanted to talk to my grandfather or his partner. I am. And now I can't."

Rick mulled that over for a moment. Was he just being paranoid? Were there sensible answers to all his questions? "Maybe you're right," he said.

"Maybe?"

"It's just, well . . . what're the odds?"

"I get your point," she said. "But I don't know what the answer is. You're the PI. Figure it out and get back to me." She nodded toward the street. "Meanwhile, cops are here."

Three squad cars arrived at the same time. After talking to the paramedics, one of the cops came out to the porch. He asked Rick and Lollie if they were the ones who'd found the man.

"That's right," Rick said. "And we called 911 immediately."

"So he was conscious when you found him. Did he say anything?"

"Nothing that made sense," Rick said. "It was something that sounded like 'be easy' or 'bees cease seeing' or maybe one of the words was 'pieces,' because he had a piece of an old record in his hand when we found him." The cop dutifully wrote everything down.

Lollie said, "Is he going to make it?"

The cop shook his head. "They don't think so." Just then the paramedics brought the gurney out with the sheet covering Lamar's head. The cop pointed his clipboard at Rick and said, "So what were you doing here in the first place?"

"I work at a radio station." He handed the cop one of his WVBR business cards and told him that he and Lollie were doing research for a blues show they were planning to do. Figuring his story would sound more convincing if he piled on the facts, he went though the whole Blind, Crippled, and Crazy legend and explained that they were hoping to get Suggs to do an interview. When he finished, the cop seemed satisfied with the story and sent them on their way.

They got in Rick's truck and drove off. Lollie seemed to have put the whole episode behind her before they'd reached the bottom of Broadway. "So," she said. "Who else can we talk to who might know more about my grandfather and these tapes?"

Rick mentioned Beau Tillman, the juke-joint owner who'd said Woolfolk had died owing him money. And there were the three bluesmen, if any of them were still alive. Lollie said they ought to talk to Tillman next. Rick thought it was strange that she wasn't more concerned about finding who killed Suggs and her grandfather, and why. He didn't think coincidence could explain the two murders. But what could? He knew people were after the mythic Blind, Crippled, and Crazy tapes. But why would anybody kill these two old guys? And why now?

Maybe he was looking at it from the wrong angle. Maybe it wasn't about the tapes. Maybe it was about something else Woolfolk and Suggs had in common. If Beau Tillman was to be believed, they'd cheated their fair share of artists. Maybe somebody had been holding a grudge for a long time. Somebody who thought he'd been screwed and knew only one way to make things right. But then he had another, slightly farther-fetched idea. What if it was some blues fanatic avenging the suffering of the artists he revered? If that was the case, Rick wondered who might be next. Maybe others had already been killed. He hadn't considered that before.

And while these were all intriguing possibilities, Rick couldn't stop wondering about Lollie's casual attitude in the wake of these two killings. When they got back to the Vicksburg and pulled into the parking lot, where Lollie had again insisted on leaving her car, Rick said, "I'll find out what I can from Beau Tillman and see who else we can track down who knew your grandfather. I'll call you as soon as I get anything."

"I'll be waiting to hear from you," Lollie said as she got into her car.

He gave her a wave and a smile as she pulled out of the parking lot. He also gave her license plate a good look.

– – – – – – – – –

SMITTY CHISHOLM CALLED the station that night with the legal names for Blind Buddy Cotton (real name Bernard Lewis Cotton), Crippled Willie Jefferson (William Jeffrey John-

Highway 61 Resurfaced

son), and Crazy Earl Tate (Earle Lincoln Tate). Rick didn't find any of them in the master death file, so his next trick was trying to find them in real life. He doubted that any of them were involved in the murders of Woolfolk and Suggs, but he hoped they could give him ideas on anybody who might hold an old grudge against them. He also hoped one of them might know something about the whereabouts of the famous recording, though he couldn't believe he'd be the first to ask.

Approaching the last hour of his shift, Rick figured it was time to do the new segment of his show he'd been thinking about. He pulled a sound-effects CD and cued it up. Coming out of "Subterranean Homesick Blues," Rick opened his mike and said, "There's that Zimmerman character again with a song old enough to be your daddy. It's eleven o'clock and you're listening to WVBR-FM, Vicksburg, big rock by the big river. And now it's time for . . . " He played the sound effect of a lion's roar. "Oops, wrong cat." He hit the button again and got a meow. "There we go. It's time now for the Crippled Crusty Boogers Blues Hour, brought to you by the Vicksburg Animal Shelter." He pushed the button again and got a trumpeting elephant. "Got a big empty house that needs a little life added to it? The Vicksburg Animal Shelter has new and used elephants and convenient financing." Three goats started bleating. "Front yard overgrown? Tired of all that mowing? Hurry down today for a herd of hungry ruminants." An ominous rattlesnake rattle. "Looking for the perfect gift for that ex-boyfriend?" Cows began mooing. "Always wanted to make your own cheese? The Vicksburg Animal Shelter has herds of hungry Holsteins!" He paused before pushing the button again. A lone dog began to howl, then faded as Rick said, "But seriously, there are hundreds of abandoned cats and dogs and other household pets just waiting for a good home. And even if you can't adopt one of these guys, think about helping them out.

Monetary donations are always welcomed, but you can also volunteer some time or give blankets, towels, newspapers, collars, leashes, and food. The Vicksburg Animal Shelter is a nonprofit organization and they need your help. Do what you can. Crusty Boogers and I thank you."

Rick started a record that opened with a bluesy guitar lick. "And now it's time to sing the blues on WVBR. It's the Crippled Crusty Boogers Blues Hour with Johnny Winter from 1969 doing 'Black Cat Bone.' "

— — — — — — — — —

RICK WOKE UP the next morning in a mood to indulge his suspicions about Lollie Woolfolk. He went to his office, pulled her file, and made some calls. It didn't take long for things to unravel. The license-plate number he'd memorized turned out to have been stolen from a rental car. He drove over to the address on the client-information form. Rick hoped she hadn't paid much for the house, since it was somewhere in the middle of the Mississippi River. As he drove back to his office, he tried to call her but discovered her phone was no longer in service. Turned out it was a throwaway. Rick was starting to get agitated.

He called the police department in Belzoni, said he was writing a story for the *Vicksburg Post* about the murder of Tucker Woolfolk and was trying to confirm that his only living relative was a granddaughter named Lollie.

"No, there's a son, a Mr. John Woolfolk and his wife. Lollie's their daughter. I spoke with them at the funeral."

"Funeral?"

"Yeah," the man said. "Yesterday."

Rick was now officially pissed off. He didn't like being duped, it was bad for the reputation, bad for business. He'd been had. But by whom? And why? The why was the easier question to speculate about. Someone needed help finding the two men who were most likely to be in possession of the mythic tapes. Rick could only assume they were both killed so they couldn't identify their attacker. The who was the hard part. Two things were obvious about the woman claiming to be Lollie. First, she wasn't who she said she was, and second, she hadn't killed Tucker Woolfolk, because she'd been at dinner with Rick the night he was murdered. That meant she had a partner. But knowing that didn't help much. Since she'd tossed her cell phone, Rick figured he wasn't going to see the faux Lollie again, at least not anytime soon. If that was true, it seemed to mean one of two things: Either he'd spooked her when he'd betrayed his suspicions about her, or maybe her partner had found the tapes at Lamar Suggs's house.

That's when it hit him, oddly, from the blind side, as these things tend to. Lamar Suggs wasn't saying "bees easy" or "bees cease seeing." He was saying "BCC." The initials for Blind, Crippled, and Crazy. He was telling Rick what had caused all the trouble.

Rick called Smitty Chisholm at the museum and asked what the tapes might be worth.

"You mean in dollars?"

"Is there something else?"

"How about artistic and historical value?"

"Tell me about the money," Rick said.

Chisholm guessed they'd sell around ten thousand units in the U.S. and another ten in Europe. The Japanese market, he said, was much bigger, adding another thirty to forty thousand units. "Definitely a gold record, maybe platinum over time."

It was enough money to kill for, certainly, except for one problem. You'd have to show clear title to the master recordings before a major label would get within ten feet of them. And without big-league promotion and distribution, the value of the tapes was far less. Still, people were killed every day for virtually nothing, so maybe the folks after the tapes were the kind willing to settle for whatever they could get.

Rick did think of one scenario where killing Woolfolk and Suggs both made sense and avoided the chain-of-title problem. That was if the killer stood to inherit from the killed. But since the woman who'd hired Rick wasn't really Lollie Woolfolk, that didn't seem to make any sense. Unless she was a Suggs. Or maybe her partner was related to one of the men. Or maybe it was even more complicated than that. The whole thing was starting to give Rick a headache.

He went back to his office to start his search for the where-abouts of Blind Buddy Cotton, Crippled Willie Jefferson, and Crazy Earl Tate. He parked behind the Vicksburg and headed down Clay Street. When he walked into the antiques store, Pee Wee Milkwood waved from behind the counter and said, "Hey, wanna see something? Just got this." He held up an old rifle. "It's a model 1842 U.S. musket," he said, handing it over. "Made by the Harpers Ferry Armory around 1853."

Rick found Pee Wee's enthusiasm for and knowledge of the Civil War hard to resist. He wasn't a gun devotees but this was a piece of history and Pee Wee always had something interesting to share about the item in question. "How long is this thing?"

" 'Bout six feet," Pee Wee said. "The stock's made of walnut; just beautiful, isn't it?"

Rick looked down the forty-two-inch barrel. "Not easy keeping this thing steady."

"You ain't just whistling 'Dixie,' " Pee Wee said. "That's why you had to get toe-to-toe with the enemy, especially since it's not rifled. Shot came out of there like a knuckleball. That's the last smoothbore U.S. arm made in sixty-nine caliber. It was also the

Highway 61 Resurfaced

first U.S. weapon that the Harpers Ferry and Springfield Armories made with fully interchangeable parts."

"Interesting." Rick was aiming at the front door when it opened. He lowered the gun as a young woman walked in and looked around as though browsing.

"Be right with you," Pee Wee said. She gave a wave like she didn't need any help.

"Be kind of hard to do those Marine Corps rifle drills with this thing," Rick joked. He held it in front of him, both hands on the stock, and spun it slowly, like a propeller. "Especially if you mounted the bayonet." Next he tried to swing the musket around like he'd seen soldiers do in countless movies.

Pee Wee made a sudden gesture and said, "Careful."

What Rick didn't know was that the browsing woman was now only four feet behind him and that the tip of the barrel was going up her skirt. She let out a surprised yelp, then screamed, "Perv!"

Rick turned to see the pervert in question but instead saw the woman uncoiling from a martial-arts stance into a roundhouse punch. It caught him on the side of the head and he hit the floor like 170 pounds of paste wax.

While he was out, which was less than a minute, he dreamed he was on the battlefield at Vicksburg when a cannonball hit him square in the head and bounced off, like in a cartoon. When he came to, Pee Wee and the woman were hovering over him. Pee Wee said, "You okay?"

Rick blinked a couple of times and flexed his jaw. "What happened?"

The woman said, "I thought you were trying to look up my skirt."

He looked at her. She was a striking brunette, tall and athletic, but peeking up dresses wasn't his style. He sounded genuinely baffled when he said, "What?"

"It was the musket," Pee Wee said. "You were twirling it around and it, uh, goosed the lady."

"Oh." Rick put a hand to the side of his face, thinking how he preferred being beaned by a purse. "Uhhh, sorry."

She pointed at his head. "That's why I punched you."

"Looked like something out of a Charlie Chan movie," Pee Wee said.

"I think you mean Jackie Chan," Rick said.

"No, I mean Charlie Chan. You reacted about as slow as Warner Oland might've."

"Warner Oland?" Rick glared at Pee Wee as he pushed himself up on his elbows. "Help me up."

Pee Wee put his hand on Rick's chest and held him down. "No, I think you should lie still for a second, see if you can find any of your dignity down there." He smirked.

"I didn't hit you that hard," the woman said. "You went out pretty easy."

"I'm obliging that way," Rick said. "So don't let anybody tell you chivalry's dead."

Pee Wee gave Rick a pat on the arm. "Don't feel bad, she says she has a brown belt in karate."

Rick looked at him and said, "Yeah, that makes me feel much better." He extended his hand toward the woman and said, "By the way, I'm Rick Shannon."

She looked surprised. "The radio guy?"

"Yeah."

"And private investigator?"

"That's right."

She pointed up the stairs, toward his office. "I was on my way up to see you."

"What are you, like an assassin or something?"

"No, really. I was." She kept nodding her head.

Rick looked at her for a moment, then at Pee Wee, who had a what-do-you-know look on his face. Rick kept waiting for the woman to introduce herself, but she just smiled at him like she was as dazzled by the coincidence as Pee Wee. Finally, Rick said, "Well, who *are* you?"

"Oh, my name's Lollie Woolfolk."

11

"**HE STUCK A** fork in my knee! What was I s'posed to do?" Crail was propped up in the bed in room 122 at the Best Western in Greenwood, a pint of Jim Beam on the table next to him and a cigarette burning in the ashtray.

Cuffie was at the foot of the bed unbuttoning her shirt. "You were supposed to find the tapes, baby."

"I know," Crail said, like he didn't appreciate the implication that he was so dumb he didn't know that. "And I looked all over that big-ass house. I'm tellin' you, they weren't there."

"Well, they're somewhere," Cuffie said, sounding her frustration. She walked over to the table and took a drag off the cigarette.

Crail leaned forward to examine the three holes left by the fork's tines. "Damn thing stuck too," he said. "It was in the bone or between 'em, one. I had to pull like hell to get it loose. You ain't never felt nothing like it." He took a slug of the bourbon, then almost spit it out when Cuffie poked his wound. "Ow! Be careful. What're you doin'?"

"Hold still," she said as she prodded his knee. It was red

and tender and starting to swell like a melon. She said, "You'll live." Then she stood up, folded her arms, and clucked her tongue in disapproval. "You know, sometimes? I just can't believe you."

"Whaddya mean by that?"

"I expect you to be able to handle yourself better's all," Cuffie said. "You said that old man didn't weigh ninety pounds, but you couldn't keep him from stickin' you like a baked potato?"

Crail got a wounded look on his face and said, "Well now, sweetie, I don't think we need to start down that road. That old coot was a lot sneakier'n he looked. He'da stuck that fork in you too, you'd been standin' there." Crail took another hit off the bottle. "But c'mon now, that's done and we still ain't got those tapes, so we gotta figure out what we gone do."

"There's nothing to figure out," Cuffie said as she unbuttoned her jeans. "We're going to keep looking. We've just got to figure out who to talk to next."

"What about them three old jigs?"

"Crail Pitts!" She shook her head as she stepped out of her pants. "You know I don't like that kind of talk. You sound just like my papaw Henry."

"I thought you liked him."

"I do. I just don't like the way he talks sometimes." Cuffie stripped down to her La Perla bra and panties. She stood in front of the mirror looking at herself from different angles, her hand pressed against her flat stomach. "God, I hate going to these things," she said as she moved to the bathroom where her garment bag was hanging on the door.

"What is it this time, the Planters' Ball?" It was always some swanky social thing that Crail couldn't attend, lest Cuffie be seen with him and word get back to her daddy and he cut off her credit cards. Not that Crail wanted to go stand around that moldy old country club with all those assholes talking about their ski trips to Vail last Christmas. But he didn't appreciate being treated like the help, having to come in the back door, either.

"I told you, it's Great-Grandpa Shelby's ninety-fifth birthday party." She pulled a black Helmut Lang gown from the bag and held it up against herself. "Can you imagine being ninety-five years old?" She swayed in front of the mirror, as if dancing. "Must be awful."

Crail shook his head. "What's he like? I mean's he senile and drooling and wearing diapers?"

"No." Cuffie glared at him. "But he's grouchy most of the time, I'll say that. Course at his age I guess you can't really blame him. He doesn't approve of anything or anybody. Always complaining about how his offspring let him down and ruined the family name, especially after he's had a couple of drinks." Cuffie wiggled into the gown and stepped into some pumps. The three-inch heels were torturous, but Cuffie had always longed to be taller. "I think old people just don't like to see things change," she said. "They just wish everything would stay the way it used to be."

It used to be that the LeFleurs were a respected family in the Delta. But over the course of a few generations, they had come to be feared and then either despised or ridiculed, except by a few other old-line families who had suffered the same decline in reputation over the years.

The LeFleurs had a long and profitable history, and Crail Pitts wanted in on it before it was all gone. He took the remote control and turned on the television, surfing until he came across a NASCAR event. Cuffie was in the bathroom applying makeup when Crail said, "So I guess your papaw Henry's gone be at this thing?"

"What do you think?"

"You gone tell him? 'Bout our plan?"

She poked her head around the corner, her mouth wide open for effect. She said, "Are you crazy? If he knew what we were doing, he might try to stop us, and then what? Then what? Then how're you gonna win him and Grandpa Shelby over?" She ducked back into the bathroom saying, "Sometimes? I swear, I just can't believe you."

This was the line Cuffie had been feeding Crail from the beginning. Said they had to have Shelby Jr.'s and Henry's blessing before they could get married. And she knew Crail wanted that worse than anything except maybe getting his knee fixed. But, given Crail's social position, she said, their approval would be withheld unless Crail did something to impress the LeFleur patriarchs. Since the football thing hadn't worked out, Cuffie had convinced Crail that his best bet was to help her find these tapes she'd overheard Shelby Jr. and her papaw Henry arguing about one night ten years ago when they were deep in a bottle of bourbon. From what she'd gathered, the tapes had something to do with a man named Pigfoot Morgan, though they never said exactly what. What she did hear was that if the tapes ever surfaced, the whole family could suffer financially, might even face ruin.

While she didn't know how these tapes could do this, she did know that the bulk of the LeFleur fortune was still in Shelby Jr.'s estate and that everybody downstream had been waiting all their lives for him to kick the bucket and spread the wealth. Cuffie was no exception. It was one of the few family values all LeFleurs shared. Her dad, Monroe LeFleur, was a corrosive man who complained bitterly about how he knew he wasn't going to get a dime from his own father, though he never would explain why. Monroe said their only chance was for Shelby Jr. to give them a cut of the pie from the top. These were the hopes Monroe and Cuffie clung to. The hope that Shelby Jr. would die sooner rather than later, and the hope that the tapes would stay lost.

But not too long ago, Cuffie had heard something about this Pigfoot Morgan getting out of jail. She knew people had been looking for those tapes for years, but she worried that this Pigfoot guy might know something the others didn't and she feared he might start poking around. And if he got lucky, he might just find the tapes. And if he did, and if Papaw Henry was right, all the family money could disappear and where would that leave her? Cuffie loved Crail in her own way and all, but she wasn't about to marry poor.

Crail stuck a cigarette in his mouth and punched the remote until he found a fishing show. He watched as the host struggled with a striped bass. A few minutes later, Cuffie emerged from the bathroom and came to Crail's side. She looked at his knee with a tormented expression. "You want me to put something on that before I go?"

"Naw." He pulled back and rolled his pants leg over the wound. "It don't need nothin'," he said. "Just let it be." Crail didn't want to seem like he was the kind of man who needed to be nursed just because somebody'd stuck a fork in his knee. He could play it as tough as any of the LeFleur men could and this was his chance to prove it.

Cuffie stopped at the door on her way out. She said, "By the way, why'd you do that with the fork?"

Crail smirked and said, "Oh, I figured after he gave it to me, the polite thing to do was to give it back."

— — — — — — — —

LOLLIE WOOLFOLK SHRUGGED like it was nothing and said, "A girl needs a hobby, right?"

"Collecting records is a hobby," Rick said as Pee Wee and Lollie helped him to his feet. "Working toward a black belt's more like a career." He brushed himself off and suggested they go to his office to talk. As they walked up the stairs, Rick said, "Are you an instructor or something? You have your own dojo?"

"I have a classroom when I have a job," she said. "I'm a special-ed teacher in Jackson. You know, kids with learning disabilities."

Rick opened the door to his office and showed her in. "But you're unemployed?"

"Budget cuts," she said. "The arts, extracurricular activities, and kids with special needs are always the first to go." Lollie sat in the chair opposite Rick's desk. "But I understand the cotton subsidy is safe."

"Go figure," Rick said with a smile. Despite the punch in the head she'd given him, he was starting to like this Lollie, tough, pretty, and with a quick wit. He crossed to the water cooler and offered her a drink. She declined. He filled a glass, then went to his desk and rooted through the drawers. After a minute he looked at Lollie and said, "You happen to have an aspirin?"

She rooted through her purse. "Advil all right?"

"Anything."

She tossed him the plastic container and said, "Knock yourself out."

He made a face at her. "Thanks." Rick shook three tablets out of the bottle and popped them in his mouth, chasing them with the water. He sat back, rubbing his temples, and said, "So, how'd you track me down?"

"My grandfather hated telemarketers," she said. "So he got caller ID. I checked it when I was there going through his effects. I figured some of the calls would be from friends, and that would make it easier to know who to invite to the funeral." She was looking around the office at the framed newspaper articles on the wall. "So I started calling the numbers. When I got the voice mail

for Rockin' Vestigations, I got curious about why my grandfather
would be talking to a private investigator."

"Understandable."

Lollie waited a moment before she said, "So? Why was he talking to you?"

"He didn't know I was a PI. I was hired by someone to find him."

"Hired by whom?"

Rick smiled and leaned forward on the desk. "Said her name was Lollie Woolfolk."

"And you believed her?"

"Didn't have any reason not to, at least not until a couple of days ago." Rick told her the story of the faux Lollie and how she'd hired him to track down Tucker Woolfolk and Lamar Suggs. "After Suggs died I got suspicious. Did a little of the due diligence I should've done to begin with, I guess, and found out I'd been duped."

"In other words, you think you helped the killers find their victims?"

"It's not like I'm proud of it."

"Do the police know?"

"Well, I certainly haven't told them."

"Why not?"

"No point. All the info I have on the woman is bogus, and it'd be just as bogus in their hands."

"So, are you planning to try to find her yourself?"

Rick was starting to smell a new client, so he said, "Actually, I was planning to work on some paying cases I've got."

Lollie pulled a checkbook from her purse. She made one out to Rockin' Vestigations for five hundred dollars and handed it to Rick. "Well, consider this a paying case," she said.

Rick looked at the check. "This is pretty good money for an unemployed teacher."

"I married well."

He gestured at her left hand. "Lose your ring?"

She shook her head. "I divorced even better."

"Good for you."

"I want you to find whoever killed my grandfather."

Rick held the check up, waved it in the air, and said, "I'll need to see some ID."

— — — — — — — — —

BLIND BUDDY COTTON was sunk down in the seat of his Cadillac, his hat just visible over the steering wheel as he drove south toward Tchula. Everything he saw through his dark glasses reminded him of how things had changed and how they hadn't in his eighty-three years. Mile after mile of cotton, soybean, sorghum, and corn. He'd spent his share of time in those rows too, watering them with his own sweat. That's how it used to be. Used to be his people out there working. Used to be people and mules and plows and fine wooden barns, but that was all over. The old buildings listing under decay and neglect, replaced by fiber-glass and steel, soulless but sturdy. And the machines. Airplanes sprayed defoliant, and pivot systems stretched to the horizon, like giant wagon wheels with long, leaky axles. Machines plowed and planted and harvested and freed a lot of folks to head for Detroit and Chicago and a better life.

Some of the fields had been turned into big muddy ponds with aerator paddles churning oxygen into the water, trying to keep those nasty catfish breathin'. Aquaculture, they called it, and it was big business now. Buddy thought it was funny how it used to be that white folks turned their noses up and called it a trash fish, a po' nigger's fish. Said that fish would eat anything, but now it was grain-fed and treated like a gourmet meal.

Buddy shook his head and thought about how you could modernize the crops and the equipment all you wanted, but you couldn't modernize this land. It remained ancient.

As he passed through Greenwood, the old capital of cotton, Buddy thought back on harvest time and how the streets here would look like a train wreck of Tampax. You'd be ankle deep in a pillowy cloud when you stepped off the sidewalk to let a white lady pass. But that changed too, and in time Greenwood became a virtual ghost town until somebody started making a big fancy stove up there and built that factory that was a mile long and put a lot of people back to work and gave 'em some hope. And right there on the corner of Church and Howard Streets they'd fixed up the old Hotel Irving into a five-star joint. It was a thing to see.

Used to be a hotel like that wouldn't let a black man walk in the front door, let alone get a room. Now he could get a suite if he wanted. Lot of things had changed, Buddy thought. But one thing that hadn't was his own past. He was stuck with that. Still guilty of what he'd done, and hadn't. That wasn't ever going to change. He'd done his best not to think about it too much over the last fifty years, but he knew it was catching up with him.

He got to Tchula and turned on Two Mile Road, a neglected stretch of asphalt that looked as if it had been used for mortar practice. He worked his way around the potholes to the end of the road, where he pulled into the Starlighter's Lounge, a cinder-block monument to despair and malt liquor standing alone on a lot of gravel and broken glass. A pair of rusty oil drums, over-flowing with quart bottles and grease-stained paper sacks, stood like shabby guards next to a doorway framed with a string of Christmas lights in the middle of summer.

Buddy stepped inside and saw Billy Dee Williams leering at him from an old Colt 45 poster tacked to the wall between a handwritten sign warning dope smokers not to light up and a handbill for a circuit-judge candidate you could trust.

There were only two men in the joint, one on each side of the bar. The man on the stool said, "Point he was makin' was that black folk oughta be thankful 'bout bein' brought over here."

"What?" The bartender had never heard anything so foolish. "Be thankful 'bout slavery? You crazy."

The customer waved his hands wildly around his head. "Look at it! Them skinny-ass niggas over in Africa's starvin' to death evva day. That'd be us, we was still there. Instead we over here, all the food you can eat, like them casino buh-fays. You see these women we gots now? You can't get from here to Greenwood without seeing a dozen weigh two, three hundred pounds each. Now which nigga'd you rather be?"

The bartender shook his head. "That ain't right, you old fool."

The customer slapped the bar and said, "You the fool! I said that's the way I heard it, not that's how it was. They's a difference."

"They sho is," Buddy said from behind them. "Way I heard it, you could play a guitar."

Crazy Earl Tate turned around slowly, like somebody was fixin' to get it. He had a mug shot of a face. Jheri curls hung like kudzu vines on a kisser of bitterness and hate. With his red-rimmed eyes and that scowl, Earl had a look that could get him picked out of a lineup standing between two guilty parties. When he saw it was Buddy, he didn't skip a beat. Earl said, "Oh, you one to talk. Evva time I turn around I catch you stealin' another little bit of my technique."

Buddy was standing there with his hat cocked all acey-deucy and pulled low over his dark glasses like he was Nap Turner. He said, "Technique? That what you call that noise you made?" Buddy reached the bar, pointed at Earl's beer, then held up two fingers. "Sound to me like somebody pullin' on a cat's tail." He gave Earl a hearty slap on the back. Earl was a stout man, strong as oak. "But I'll say this, you look like you could still pull a plow through hard dirt."

"Ain't bad," Earl said, flexing slightly. He pointed at the bartender and said, "What I tell you? I'm the last of the good men." He smiled at Buddy and his whole face changed. The hate disappeared as dark freckles bunched around the corners of his eyes and showed there was still a light inside. Unfortunately, it dimmed when he was drunk, which was most of the time nowadays.

The bartender brought the beers and looked at Buddy, trying to make a sale. "You hongry?" He pointed up at a handmade menu on the wall, blue marker on a faded orange poster board touting fish sandwiches, tamales, pigs' feet, dill pickles, and chitterling plates.

"Gi' ya nickel for a brain sa'wich," Buddy said, nudging Earl.

Earl slapped the bar and laughed. "Yeah, me too," he said, pushing two nickels from the bit of change in front of him. "With lotta mustard."

The man looked at Buddy and Earl like they were both crazy. He said, "Ain't got no brain sandwich." Like it was the nastiest thing he'd ever heard. "How 'bout some hot links?"

"Naw, unh-unh," Buddy said, waving him off. "Ain't hungry."

The bartender shook his head and walked away. Earl was laughing and leaning against Buddy the whole time. "Ooooo, hadn't had no brain sa'wich in forty-'leven years," he said, shaking his head. "What made you think of that? I bet it was that time we was in St. Louis." He slapped the bar again. "Had to be."

"C'mon." Buddy picked up the two beers and said, "Let set over here." They were heading for a table in the corner when he stopped and nodded at the jukebox. "Anything good on that?" He felt like some music.

"Ain't got none our records," Earl said with a wink. "But

they's some all right. You got a quarter? I put some on." He punched a few buttons, then joined Buddy at the table. A second later a shuffling guitar riff, almost rockabilly, eased into the room. After a few bars, a pair of brushes slipped in with a wily rhythm, then somebody blew a harp and Jimmy Reed started singing "You Got Me Dizzy." They sat there for a while, Buddy tapping his feet, Earl's head rocking while they sipped cold beer and studied each other, not talking, just two run-down friends in a funky old juke joint. After a while, Earl said, "Ole Jimmy could sing now, but you know he stole that thing he do from me."

"What thing?" Buddy sounded skeptical, like it wasn't the first time he'd heard Earl make such a claim.

Earl held up a finger and waited for something only he could hear. Suddenly he pointed at the jukebox and said, "That thing right there. I's doing that 'fore Jimmy Reed even thought about bein' born." He nodded. "Sho was."

Buddy kinda laughed and shook his head. "How long we known each other?"

"Couple lifetimes."

"That's a truth. We seen some things too. Been places, showed 'em how to play a reel. Won a little money playin' skin."

"That's right," Earl said with a happy drunk's chuckle. "We the last of the good men."

"That's a truth too," Buddy said. "And you know, is almos' ova."

"What's that?"

"All this." Buddy gestured back and forth between them. "Peoples like us." He waved his hand around the room. "Places like this. Is just about done." He had a wistful tone in his voice. "But we did all right, considerin'."

Earl saw the faraway look in his friend's eyes and said, "What's got you goin' on?" He got a surprised look on his face. "Wha' choo doing here in the first place?" Like it had just occurred to into the Starlighter's Lounge and bought a round of beers.

Buddy said, "Ohhh, this 'n' that."

"You lyin'," Earl said. "You know you ain't evva get up outta bed 'less somebody's payin', so I know 'this 'n' that' ain't brought you here." He leaned on the table, concerned for his old friend. He said, "Buddy, you sick?"

He put his hand on his chest. "It's my lungs."

"You dyin'?"

"I'm tryin' to live," Buddy said. "That's why I come to see you, tell you 'bout Clarence."

A look of grim hope crossed Earl's face and he took a drink before he said, "He finally pass?"

Buddy shook his head.

"No?" Earl unconsciously reached for the string that hung around his neck. His fingers followed it down to a small sack of red flannel, his conjure bag. "He excape?"

"He got out," Buddy said. "Done his time. Big Walter figure he's gone come home."

Earl's concern for Buddy dried up all the sudden. The anger returned and he said, "So? What that gotta do with me?"

"Same thing it got to do with me and Willie. I'm tryin' to figure out what we gone do."

Earl sat back and threw a palm at Buddy. "I ain't gone do a goddamn thing."

"You just gone sit here'n wait for him to come for you?"

"I can takes care of myself."

"How?" He reached over and thumped Earl's conjure bag. "You gone make a hand with grave dirt and rusty nails? You think that's gone do?" Buddy shook his head. "I'm tellin' you, I gots a bad feeling." He pointed at Earl. "You gone need something mo' pow'ful'n that."

AFTER RICK LOOKED at her driver's license for a moment, Lollie said, "Satisfied?"

He nodded and slipped the check into his coat pocket before returning her license.

"Great." She sat back and put her feet on his desk. "So what's our next move?"

He leaned sideways to see around her size eights. He smiled and said, "Excuse me?"

Lollie shrugged like it was a no-brainer. "I'm unemployed," she said. "Two heads and all that, right?"

Rick made an ambiguous noise, then stuck his lower lip out and, nodding, said, "I usually work alone."

"Yeah, but if you got in a fight or something, you'd get the shit kicked out of you and my five hundred bucks would be down the drain." She held her hands out as if she'd proved her point. "I'm just protecting my investment."

Rick smiled at her jab and pointed to the monitor on his desk. "Most of the work's done on that," he said. "And I don't care how fast the processor is, believe me, I can beat up any computer you got." The truth was, Rick already knew he wanted Lollie's help. He just didn't want to let on too quick. She'd certainly be useful if something needed to be done at night when he was on the air, and maybe she'd teach him a few karate moves along the way. On top of that, she was single and attractive. He'd never had a relationship with a woman who could beat him up and he found the prospect oddly exciting. And, while he knew he shouldn't be thinking of a client in that way, well, it was too late to change. He opened the bottom drawer of his desk and pulled the case file. He said, "Okay. Here's where we are."

Lollie said she'd never heard of the Blind, Crippled, and Crazy sessions. "My grandfather didn't talk much about what he did in the old days," she said. "You think these tapes have something to do with his death?"

"I wasn't sure at first," Rick said. "For a while I thought there might be a serial killer out to kill old blues producers who had, uhhh, well, let's say, who had written some tricky contracts."

"You mean they were crooked."

"It was just a theory." He looked at Lollie. "No offense intended."

She waved it off. "None taken."

"I assumed it was something your grandfather and Lamar Suggs had in common."

"They knew each other a long time," Lollie said. "I suspect they had a lot in common besides the tapes."

"I'm sure that's true." Rick nodded. "But when I realized the last thing Suggs tried to say was 'BCC,' as in Blind, Crippled, and Crazy, I figured it had to be about the tapes."

"So they must be valuable."

"If they exist they're certainly worth something, but I suspect there'd be a lot of litigation about who owns the master tapes and who has the publishing rights, who was under contract to whom when they were made, and things like that. It's hard to imagine they'd be worth killing for, knowing all the legal headaches they come with."

"Especially considering the legal headaches that come with committing murder."

"True," Rick said. "At the end of the day, the only ones making any money'll be the lawyers."

"Maybe whoever did it doesn't know about the legal headaches."

"Or they don't care."

"Or they're lawyers."

"Ewww, talk about your worst-case scenario." Rick shivered theatrically and said, "Lawyers who kill."

"Maybe there's something else about the tapes."

"Like what?"

"Like I don't know." She shrugged. "That's why you make the big bucks."

They talked for a while, trying to figure out who the faux Lollie might be. "I'd guess she's five or ten years younger than you," Rick said. "Looked, acted, and sounded like she was from money."

Lollie gave him a funny look. "What do I look, act, and sound like?"

"More like you work for a living. This other one didn't seem like the employed type. She obviously knew you existed, so she either did some research or she knows your family."

"But if she knew how to do research, she probably wouldn't have hired you."

"Unless she also wanted me as her alibi," Rick said. "Maybe she's somebody you knew when you were a kid." He pointed at Lollie. "Did you grow up in Belzoni?"

She shook her head. "Greenwood until I was about fifteen," she said. "Then we moved to Memphis." Her mom was from

Batesville and had met her dad at Mississippi State. She was a homemaker and he sold agricultural supplies and equipment.

Rick told her to talk to her parents, see if they remembered Tucker talking about anybody from the old days. "Meanwhile, now that I've got legal names for Buddy Cotton and the others, maybe I can track one of them down." Rick looked at his watch and stood up. "I've got to get down to the station." He walked Lollie out to her car. "You driving back to Jackson tonight?"

She shook her head. "Staying here with a friend."

"Okay, meet me here in the morning and we'll go see Beau Tillman." He opened the door for her and said, "By the way, do you like cats?"

CLARENCE STOOD IN front of the mirror and smoothed the front of his new suit. Dark blue coat and pants, a crisp white shirt, bold tie, and the finest alligator shoes. He looked like a million bucks, maybe two, like one of those Wall Street hotshots he'd seen in the newspaper being perp-walked into court with his thousand-dollar-an-hour lawyer.

Later Clarence walked up Capitol Street just to see the looks people gave him. Like he was someone they ought to know and respect, like maybe he was a judge or a councilman or someone who'd been on television. People looked him in the eye and gave him a nod of respect, like they would with someone who could do them a favor if circumstances required. Clothes do make the man, he thought.

He caught a taxi in front of the Old Capitol Museum and asked to be taken to a car dealership. He didn't need a new car, probably couldn't get one. He didn't have any credit and wasn't about to explain why he hadn't been employed in fifty years. So he looked at the used cars. They looked just fine anyway.

There wasn't much haggling. Clarence gave the man five hundred in cash and drove off the lot in a 1978 Monte Carlo with a 133,000 miles on it. It had a sun-faded maroon body and a white landau roof that was blistered and peeling. The visors sagged and the steering column was loose, but other than burning a little oil, the car ran fine.

He drove back downtown, then over to Lynch Street, and turned on the road where he was supposed to. There were some guys hanging on the corner by the liquor store his friend had told him about. Lots of do-rags and posturing. Clarence pulled to the curb and rolled down the window. One of the toughs leaned on the car with a sneer and said, "Yo, wha' choo want here?"

"Lee sent me."

The tough guy was all attitude and Clarence knew there was no point in getting into it with him. The guy needed to feel bigger, fine. Clarence would just put up with his shit until he got what he came for. But he wondered what it was that had so many people acting like they were some bad-ass street gang rapper gonna bust a cap in yo' head for looking at him the wrong way. It wasn't like it used to be when you might shoot a man you caught with your woman or if he wouldn't pay his gambling debt. Now it was like sport, everybody acting like they deserved respect whether they'd earned it or not. The thing that made the least sense to Clarence was why black men were killing one another at wholesale rates when, compared to the Mississippi he'd grown up in, they lived in a world of opportunity. Well, maybe there was something he didn't know. Maybe it made sense somehow.

"Oh, so you Clarence, huh?"

Clarence gave a short nod and said, "Who're you?"

"You don't need to know my name, brutha." He said the "brutha" with contempt. "You just need to give me the two hundred dollars."

Clarence shook his head. "Lee said a hundred."

"Markets fluck-chate, nigga. It's two hundred, 'less you just after one bullet." He smiled and pulled back his shirt to show off the gun in his waistband. "So whassup?"

"Where is it?"

"That's what I keep asking. Where's the money?"

They went back and forth like this until money changed hands and Clarence followed the guy into an alley. He opened the trunk of his car and gave Clarence an old Remington .280 with the serial number burned off. "Where'd this come from?"

Tough guy said, "The fuck do you care? Dumb-ass white folks leave they huntin' shit in cabinets with glass fronts. We steal it, they make they puffed-up insurance claims. It's what we call a syma-lotic relationship. It's the circle of life, muthafucka. Hakuna Matata and all that shit." Clarence pulled back the bolt. The gun was empty. Tough guy pulled a cartridge clip from his pocket and held it out. When Clarence reached for it, the guy pulled it back and said, "I don't wanna see you slapping this in there before you leave. We don't need no wild-west show out here."

Clarence met his eyes and stared for a moment before putting the gun in the trunk. Then he got in and started the Monte Carlo.

Tough guy said, "So, what, you gonna go hunt you some deer?"

Clarence put the car in gear and said, "The fuck do you care?"

"HE'S GOT A weird-looking face," Lollie said. "Like his eyes are set too far apart."

"I know," Rick said. "And his ears are all out of proportion, but I love him anyway."

"Sure, you're his dad. I'm just saying, it's an unusual face. I didn't say it was hard to love."

Rick, Lollie, and Crusty were driving to Leland, Mississippi. Crusty was submitting to Lollie's examination and the unkind comments with as much patience as you'd expect from a cat with a sinus infection. When she let him go, he jumped onto the back of the seat and began pacing back and forth behind their heads. "What're you going to do with him when we get there?"

"He stays in the truck," Rick said. "Guard kitty. He mostly just lies on the dashboard in the sun. But it's deceptive, see? He's actually ready to spring into action and attack anyone who tries to steal the vehicle."

"Attacks with what, snot?"

"It's remarkably effective. The Pentagon's looking into potential military applications."

Lollie smiled. She liked Rick's sense of humor. She felt Crusty behind her, nuzzling her head and playing with her hair. "Aww," she said. "Look at— Ow!"

Rick looked. "What happened?"

"He bit me!" Lollie felt for blood. "He bit my head."

"Yeah, he does that every now and then."

"Thanks for the warning."

They reached Leland a little earlier than they'd expected, crossing the bridge over Deer Creek and pulling over at the park, where they all got out to stretch. After a moment, Lollie said, "Hey, did you know Jim Henson was from Mississippi?"

"The Muppet guy?"

"Yeah," Lollie said, reading from a roadside plaque. "Says he was born in Greenville but spent a lot of time down in that creek playing with his boyhood pal Kermit Scott."

Rick mused on that briefly before suggesting that Crusty might have been a good Muppet. Just as he said this, Crusty took off after a gray squirrel. He raced up an ash tree unaware that the squirrel had circled the trunk and was now taunting him from thirty feet up a neighboring pine. By the time they got Crusty down from the tree, it was time to go meet Beau Tillman.

He lived in a neighborhood that dated back to the 1950s. Low-slung redbrick homes set on a pleasant garden-club street with shady trees and competitively kept lawns. They passed a house with a "Yard of the Week" sign out in front and turned into the next driveway as they'd been instructed.

Beau Tillman greeted them at the front door. He was in his mid-sixties, with owlish eyebrows that seemed permanently arched and a round belly that kept him from buttoning the suit vest he wore. He took them into his living room, where he had a pitcher of sweet tea and a dish of cheese straws waiting on the table along with some scrapbooks and files of magazine and newspaper clippings. As he handed Lollie a glass of tea, he said, "I remember meeting your grandfather once. Seemed like a nice man. I was very sorry to hear about what happened."

"I appreciate that," she said. "We're kind of hoping you might know something that'll help us figure out who did it."

"So I gathered."

After they all sat down, Rick said, "My guess is that it has to do with the fabled tapes. Smitty said you know everybody who might know anything about it."

Beau proudly picked up one of the scrapbooks and said, "Well, I had my club for a while, and anybody in the blues who was still alive passed through at one point or another." He flipped through the scrapbook looking for something. "Of course, I was just a kid when those guys played together that night we're talking about. That was 1953." He found the photo he was looking for and showed it to his guests. It was Tillman, several decades earlier, still wearing the suit vest, but buttoned. He was standing in front of a small building with a sign out front that said "Beau Diddlies." "By the time I opened my place in 1968, that whole thing was local legend. You'd hear people who weren't even born yet swearing they'd been there that night." Beau took a handful of cheese straws and popped them in his mouth two at a time. "Anyway, after Smitty called and told me what you were after, I talked to some of the local old-timers about it, but it's getting harder to separate the truth from the fiction, older they get."

Rick set the scrapbook down on the table. "Smitty said there are a lot of renditions. Does one strike you as most likely?"

"Well," Beau said, "let me give you background on all this." He flipped through the scrapbook until he reached a page with several photos of musicians posing with their guitars. Beau indicated who was who as he spoke. "Now Buddy Cotton, Earl Tate, and Willie Jefferson had all been playin' around the Delta for years. They were startin' to establish names for themselves and getting out of the shadows of players like Elmore James and Willie Dixon and all that. Anyway, this scout for Paramount Records offered them a contract to record together. Now this was after the Depression, when Paramount had reopened, right? They'd been real big in the twenties, with prewar players like Blind Lemon Jefferson and Charlie Patton." He shifted in his seat before he said, "Now, Paramount was owned by the Wisconsin Chair Company."

"Wait a minute," Lollie said. "Paramount like the film studio?"

"No connection," Beau said. "See, the Wisconsin Chair Company was making cabinets for Edison phonograph players and figured it would make sense to produce records to sell in the stores along with the players. So they built a recording facility up in Grafton, Wisconsin, where they made the cabinets. And that's where Cotton, Tate, and Jefferson were supposed to go record. But before they went up there, they met here in Leland to play and make some money during one of the big skin balls that was going on."

Lollie leaned forward, grabbed some cheese straws, and asked what that meant.

"Skin was a card game popular with black gamblers at the time. Sometimes called Georgia skin, but anyway, Leland was famous for these things, put this town on the map."

"Why 'skin ball'?"

"Well, skin was the game; I think 'ball' refers to how the game went on for days or weeks at a time. Professional black gamblers came from all over—Texas, Georgia, Florida—to play at these things. We're talkin' about Stiff Hand Harry and Fast Dealing Pete and a buncha those guys, famous. They'd arrive, literally, with a suitcase full of money. Of course, people were shooting craps and playing Florida flip too, but they were mostly playin' the skin. There were weeks, and we're talking about in the thirties, forties, fifties, right? There were weeks when it was said there was more money on the streets than there was in the Bank of Leland. Every fourth storefront was a blind tiger and there were games going inside every one of 'em."

"Blind tiger being like a speakeasy?"

"Speakeasy, barrelhouse, bucket shop. I heard 'em called blind pigs in some places. You'd knock on the door and tell whoever was fronting the place that you wanted to pay to see the blind tiger you'd heard about. It was like a password sort of deal."

Rick said, "1953? That's what, twenty years after Prohibition was repealed?"

"Right, but Mississippi stayed legally dry until '67, when they started puttin' the local option on the ballot where towns and counties got to vote wet or dry." Beau chuckled and said, "But hell, that didn't stop anybody. It just let the local sheriff pad his annual income. The gamblers running the games had what they called a cut box, where a percentage of each pot went for the juke-joint owner who allowed the game to be in his club. The club owner meanwhile was selling hot tamales and illegal liquor to the gamblers and everybody else who'd come to dance and hear the music and whatnot. A percentage of the liquor money along with part of the cut from the gambling went to the sheriff, who allowed all the activity to go on as long as there wasn't too much trouble."

Lollie seemed amused. She said, "All that going on right here in little ole Mayberry."

Beau laughed again and said, "Oh yeah, you wouldn't know from visitin' the Muppet museum, but this little town used to be the hottest spot there was between Memphis and New Orleans." He opened the file and shuffled through it until he found an old article that he handed to Lollie. "This is from 1908. People were having so much fun here that a national magazine intent on promoting Prohibition called Leland 'the Hellhole of the Delta.'" Beau pointed to the phrase in the article and shook his head. "The place was knee-deep in whiskey, cocaine, and gamblers at the turn of the century." He winked at Lollie and said, "Course the Leland Chamber of Commerce prefers to tout it as the home of Kermit the frog, but back then . . ." Beau shook his head and let loose with a long, low whistle.

"So," Rick said, "Buddy Cotton, Willie Jefferson, and Earl Tate met here before going on to Wisconsin. Were they all playing at the same club?"

"Not at first. Let's see, Buddy Cotton started out at Ruby's Nightspot, that was one of Ruby Edward's places. She was a real smart lady, had several clubs around town. Earl Tate was either playing at the Key Hole Club or the Hole-in-the-Wall Club, depends on who's telling the story. And Crippled Willie was over at Mr. Brown's place, called the Roy Club. Anyway, around two that morning, Buddy, Willie, and Earl were supposed to meet up at a joint called the We-uns and You-uns Saloon where Pigfoot Morgan was playing."

"Wait." Rick looked up from making notes. "Pigfoot Morgan?"

"Guy from Drew, Mississippi, played a mean guitar, in E natural, according to those who heard him. You could hear the influence of Lightnin' Slim in his playing, but he had his own style. Also had the best car of the bunch, a beat-up twelve-year-old Packard he'd won in a card game. He'd agreed to drive the others to Memphis, where they were supposed to catch a train on to Wisconsin for the Paramount session."

"So the Blind, Crippled, and Crazy session was in Wisconsin?"

"Was supposed to be, but see, that's just it. More'n a few people swear they saw Lamar Suggs with his Presto disc recorder at the We-uns and You-uns Saloon that night after Buddy, Willie, and Earl got there and played with Pigfoot. Others say Suggs got there too late and missed the show. And a couple witnesses said they saw Suggs and Pigfoot arguing in the parking lot and that Earl Tate had to physically drag Morgan away."

"Okay, but then they'd have gone to Wisconsin and recorded there, right?"

"Sure, if Pigfoot hadn't been arrested later that night for killing Hamp Doogan."

"Who the hell's Hamp Doogan?"

Beau chuckled and said, "Well, Hamp was what you might call a local . . ." He paused, looking for the right word. ". . . entrepreneur." He winked at Rick. "He had a photography studio in town and he'd take his equipment out to the juke joints, especially during these skin balls, to take pictures to sell to the patrons. There were also rumors that he was the source for most of the cocaine in town." Beau pointed at some of the photos in his scrapbook, black-and-white shots of musicians and people dancing and sweating underneath the low ceiling of a steamy juke joint. "I doubt these were made that particular night, but Doogan took all these pictures. I bought these from his estate. But they kept some too, so I know there's more of his stuff out there. Stuff he bequeathed to people."

"You know why Pigfoot killed Doogan?"

"Well, again, there's lots of theories on that, but nobody seems to know for sure. The most popular theory revolves around cocaine. Pigfoot had a bad habit with the stuff, according to some of the stories, and Doogan ripped him off on a deal, and when he wouldn't make good, Pigfoot killed him. There's another story that it was over a woman, but you'd half expect that."

"Pigfoot do time?"

"Well, let's see," Beau said, treating it like a difficult question. "Black man killed a white man in Mississippi in 1953. I'm 'onna go out on a limb and say yeah, he did time. I s'pect he's either still doing it or died tryin'."

"You know his legal name?"

He shook his head. "Never heard him called anything but Pigfoot. I tried looking it up a few years ago, but the court records from that period all burned up back in the seventies." Beau looked like he had an idea. "But you know what, maybe the sheriff's arrest records are still around. I hadn't thought of that."

"You remember who the sheriff was?"

"Well, let me think on that for a minute." He shook his head. "Not sure. But I know who to call to find out. Hang on a second." He grabbed his phone and punched in a number. "Hey, Duff, it's Beau. Got a question. You know the name of the sheriff back in '53?" He paused a moment, then said, "No, it was the one before ole Tommy Dupree. Yeah, that's him, thanks." Beau hung up the phone, looked at Rick, and said, "That woulda been Sheriff Henry LeFleur."

13

CRAZY EARL TATE was a thoughtful man when he was
sober. That's why he drank. He didn't like the things he had to
think about. He fell down again and muttered, "Goddammit."
His bottle slipped out of his hand and he groped around in the
weeds to get it back before all his gin spilled. He found a few
empty beer cans and a crumpled cigarette pack before he
found the bottle. He took a slash and just sat there, head
slumped and legs making a wide V in front of him. "I jes take
my ress a minute," he said. All the insects that had fallen silent
when Earl hit the ground were slowly coming back to life, a
low hum at first, then returning to their full droning buzz.

After a moment Earl said, "Hell you gone do 'bout it?" He
said it like a threat with a knife behind it, but there was nobody
around to hear except the dead. He was just drunk and talking
to the cicadas and mad that if somebody was watching, they
might think he was sitting there feeling sorry for himself in the
weeds, which he wasn't. Wasn't like he was about to start
singing "Serves me right to suffer" or some such. Hell, he
never much cared for John Lee Hooker anyway. Stole one of

his best licks, or so Earl told everybody. "Seven-sided son of a bitch took that from me and I didn't see a white nickel for it," he'd said more than once.

Earl teetered as he sat there, but he didn't fall over. After a minute he struggled to his feet and continued stumbling through the graveyard outside Tchula. You wouldn't even call it a cemetery. There was no fence or gate to keep anybody out, and it was so overgrown Earl kept stumbling over the pitiful stone markers for the dead who didn't have the means or the family to stick them in a hole somewhere a little more respectful of their condition. This is where Earl figured he'd end up. Lost in the weeds for eternity.

Like his wife, Claudie. She'd been in a car accident, but her injuries were treatable. Earl was working when it happened. His boss didn't tell him about it until he got off. Somebody had carried her to a hospital, but nobody there would do anything for her. She lay unattended, on a gurney in the hallway, for twelve hours, bleeding inside. By the time Earl found her, she was gone. They told him there was nothing they could have done.

He didn't have money for anything fancy, so he had to bury her out here without so much as a small stone to mark her place. He'd made a wooden cross, but that was long gone. All these years later, with weeds everywhere, he couldn't tell where she was. "Claudie? I know you in here somewhere, baby," he said, missing her. "You just ress."

A little farther on, he paused to sit on the only tombstone in sight, like he was Ike Zinneman, waiting to teach Robert Johnson something new. He looked around and called out, "Where you at?" Earl squinted in the moonlight trying to find the fresh grave of that man he knew who had died suddenly of what the doctors called an emma-lism. He was going to get some dirt off the top to help make the hand he needed. Earl told Buddy he didn't want to kill Clarence, said he'd rather make a hand to cause him to run, but the only way to do that was to scoop some dirt from Clarence's own track, heel to toe, put it in a dried snail shell, plug it up with cotton, wet the edges with some whiskey, and bury it on the bank of a running creek with the mouth pointing downstream. But any old track was fifty years gone and Earl didn't know where to find the tracks Clarence was making now. Figured next time he was close enough to do that, Clarence was going to kill him.

So he was gone to find that grave and get the freshly turned dirt. He was gone take it home, mix it with some bad vinegar, beef gall, and ground sassafras. He'd shake it up good and tell it what he wanted it to do, because in conjuring everything depends on intentions, and Earl's were bad. Then he'd turn it upside down and bury it breast deep and be done with it.

And all because he didn't have no good options. Like always. Earl hated the choices God had given him his whole life. Like the choice they got that night fifty years ago that had him out here looking for that fresh grave now. Like God had it in for Earl Tate from the minute he came into this world, all ill-shaped, and maybe even before. It's why he never understood Blind Willie Johnson singing about how good God had been to him. Hard enough being born black in Texas in 1902, but why'd God have the child's stepmama throw lye in that seven-year-old face and blind him just so she could get back at his daddy? That's a funny way of looking at good, Earl thought. And people called *him* crazy.

THE OLDE RIVER Country Club was a crumbling relic with some fresh paint slapped on top to hold it together long enough for the last of those who cared. It was a dwindling diorama of days gone by, a place where past generations could hide from the present while squinting skeptically at the future through a cloud of unfiltered cigarette smoke, old-fashioneds, and the pink glow of roast-beef lamps. Even dressed up for a special celebration in honor of one of the club's founding members, it had the feel of ruins from a culture that had flourished briefly, of which a few specimens remained, but which was quickly becoming extinct.

As children growing up in the 1980s, Cuffie LeFleur and all her cousins saw the place as an exotic destination of strange smells and fading photographs of grim-faced white men. As teenagers they came to see it as a hideous vestige of the bad taste embraced by their grandparents. Whatever sense of status or exclusivity had once obtained by passing through the deteriorating gates was long gone. Now it was little more than a day-care center for the old guard, clinging institutionally to the way it used to be.

Cuffie's parents' generation had come to prefer the golf courses built by the gaming corporations, while Cuffie and her peers embraced the soulless, electric, and antiseptic candy sideshows that were the casinos themselves.

But once a year the extended family gathered in the Antebellum Room to celebrate the birthday of Shelby LeFleur Jr., the oldest living LeFleur. Cuffie had been coming to the Olde River Country Club once or twice a year her whole life. She recognized some of the help, men and women who had worked there for decades. They recognized her too, and they knew hers was the last generation that would see places and people like this. This time, this place, this circumstance. As she walked through the old building, toward the celebration, Cuffie felt as if all these people were characters in a tragedy that was near the end of the last act.

She walked into the Antebellum Room and saw all the usual

suspects. Lettie and Hannah LeFleur were huddled over drinks at the bar. As was typical, her father was on the opposite side of the room from her papaw Henry. Whatever grudge those two had been nurturing all her life was still in full bloom. More than once she'd seen Henry look at Monroe like he'd kill him if doing so didn't cross some line. The spaces in between members of her immediate family were filled with aunts and uncles and first, second, and third cousins. And there, in the back of the room, was the guest of honor, stooped in his wheelchair. Shelby LeFleur Jr. looked like a man who'd been carrying a burden for too long. Old, and troubled by something in his past, he had the look of a man who hadn't slept more than three or four hours a night for the past forty years.

Cuffie crossed to him, bent down, and said, "Happy birthday, Grandpa Shelby. You look great! I can't believe you're ninety-five. That's so amazing!"

"Y'ain't gotta yell," he said to his lap. He was slumped in his chair and rarely bothered to lift his head. "Old don't have to mean deaf."

Cuffie smiled sweetly and kissed his sagging jowl. She looked at his elephantine ears and thought it was no wonder his hearing was okay. They were like satellite dishes. It was a marvel he could hear himself think, all the sounds those things must pick up, especially with the hearing aids. She gave him a pat on the arm and said, "You having a good birthday? Can I get you anything? I'm going over to the bar." Cuffie was gone before he could answer any of the questions.

Grandpa Shelby shook his head in disgust. His own great-granddaughter. His own flesh and blood. He raised his head and looked at the lot of them. None of them cared. They were, all of them, just waiting for him to die so they could get a look at the will, in the hopes of getting another piece of the pie. He grunted and returned his gaze to his lap. Whatever happened to a proper show of respect for one's elders? His father, Shelby Sr., would've disowned this whole bunch of ungrateful loiterers, each new generation more oblivious than the one before, neither knowing nor caring where they'd come from or how they had reached such a privileged position, let alone accepting the duties and responsibilities that came with it. Those big ears could hear them ordering that single-barrel bourbon and grousing about how none of them was making enough money farming and how the subsidies weren't half what they ought to be. And have you seen my new Hummer?

They didn't care about anything important. They'd developed an astonishing sense of entitlement. They'd grown increasingly lazy, unprincipled, and covetous. And for reasons he could never fathom, they seemed intent on trading the family's heritage and values for the cheap, homogenized products everybody else was buying. He grunted again as he imagined their inevitable descent into ruin. And he figured they deserved whatever they got.

— — — — — — — — —

AS THEY DROVE out of Leland, Rick asked if Lollie knew any LeFleurs. She said it would've been hard to grow up where she did and not know a handful. "It's an old Delta family," she said. "They're all over. I think they still have a plantation somewhere. Why?"

"Smitty Chisholm said your grandfather was partner in a radio station with a couple of LeFleurs. I've got their names in my notes somewhere. If one of them was Henry, who also happened to be the sheriff at the time of Hamp Doogan's murder, seems like he'd be worth talking to, if he's still around."

Lollie reached over and took the pen from Rick's pocket. She wanted to find the legal name for Pigfoot Morgan, right?"

"Yeah, can't search the Mississippi correctional system with just a last name. I'll call Smitty and see if he knows anybody else who might know."

"Okay, and I'll check with the sheriff's department, see if they have records going that far back. And I might as well confirm that the trial transcripts were lost from Morgan's trial. Who knows, maybe they're on microfiche or something Mr. Tillman didn't know about." Lollie tapped the pen against her temple for a moment before she said, "What about Hamp Doogan? Any reason to talk to his family?"

"Nah, I don't see how they'd have come into possession of the tapes if he died the night they were made."

There was a pause before Rick and Lollie simultaneously said, "*If* they were made." They looked at each other and laughed. Her eyes lingered on his a moment longer than she intended and the only way to break it off was with a shy smile that simply compounded the moment. She made a perfunctory glance at the notepad, tapping it with the pen. "You know, it occurs to me that if these tapes don't exist, we have no idea what the murders are about."

"It's better than that," Rick said. "Even if the tapes do exist, we don't know what the murders are about."

"I guess that helps keep the job interesting."

Rick looked into her eyes and said, "Well, that's one of the things."

CRIPPLED WILLIE JEFFERSON could have made a good living playing the blues if he'd kept at it. He had the chops on guitar and harp and he wrote a good song. But after that night he played only for Jesus. Over the years he'd been invited to play at folk-blues revivals and to tour Europe and Japan. But he never accepted, never even responded, like he wanted folks to think that that man had already died.

Instead he turned to preaching and a life of atonement. Returning to his surname, Crippled Willie Jefferson became the reverend Johnson and vowed never again to play the devil's music. He gave up life on the road and all its temptations, just stayed near home, found a congregation, and tried to save them and himself at the same time.

He lived in a simple country house off old Highway 61, halfway between Leland and Stoneville. It was comfortable, with a small front room, a little kitchen in the back, and a skinny space on the side he called his bedroom. His backyard was five hundred acres of soybeans that was somebody else's problem. To the east they were growing cotton that looked good this year. To the west was a creek and a stand of trees that broke the monotony of the landscape and gave some of God's creatures a place to nest, while others used it as a place to hide.

Willie had put in a long day at the Full Gospel Church. At ninety he still mopped the floor, wrote the sermons, and helped with the choir. It was past dark when he got home, and now he was standing in the kitchen with an old two-pronged barbecue fork in his hand. He'd found it on the side of the road one time when he was walking home, figured it was still good for something even with the one prong bent the way it was. At the moment he was using it to stir the contents of the pot on the stovetop. He was simmering some collards with a strip of salt pork and a couple of chicken neckbones. Willie put in a couple dashes of hot sauce while a rattling fan set on a chair in the doorway pushed the pungent air around the room. The heat from the flame caught Willie's eyes and he stared for a moment as the fat boiled off in the water.

Even with the fan, it was hot in that little kitchen. Periodically Willie dabbed the sweat off his forehead and sipped water from a blue plastic cup that he'd set on the kitchen table next to a place setting, a pencil, and some papers that started off by saying something about being of sound mind and body. Willie had been giving things some serious thought since he'd heard about Clarence getting out of jail. He wanted to make sure the people of his congregation who were most in need would get most of his few possessions when his time came. He felt like it was the least he could do after all they'd given him.

He turned down the heat under the pot and sat at the table thinking about toothless old Miss Dobbs. He thought she could use that fan of his, so he wrote that down. His little saucepan too. Bless her heart, she didn't have much, but every Sunday when that plate went by, she put something in it. Willie wished he could do more for her.

He was thinking about who might be able to use his kitchen table and chair when the first shot came through the window. Glass scattered across Willie's hands like sparkling ice. The pot on the stove exploded, sending greens and neckbones flying. Willie didn't know whether to duck and try to put off the inevitable or stand up and get it over with. The second shot blew the plastic cup across the room and helped Willie make up his mind. He moved away from the table and made for the light switch quicker than your average ninety-year-old jake-legged preacher. His good limb was doing double time and the bad one was swinging like Benny Goodman to catch up and plop out in front of him.

He switched the light off just as the third shot shattered the window completely. The splintering glass cascaded noisily onto the floor. Then everything was quiet. The only light in the room was the blue flame on the stove. Willie stared at it, wondering if Clarence would wait for him to come outside or if he'd come in to do the killing. He decided he'd rather die inside, so he crouched in the corner and started to pray. Deep in his heart he knew that a good Christian would be praying for Clarence to see the error of his ways and praying for God to forgive him. But at the moment, Willie wasn't praying that way. Instead he was asking for some of God's mercy, a little something for hisself for a change.

14

IT WAS ELEVEN forty-five when Rick opened his mike and said, "Welcome back to the Crippled Crusty Boogers Blues Hour. It's time now for the part of the show where we spotlight a blues tune you never knew was there." Rick started Emerson, Lake and Palmer's version of Scott Joplin's "Maple Leaf Rag" and talked over it, saying, "It was somewhere in the late 1950s when Pete and John met in a London high school. Embracing an early form of American jazz, they played in a teenage Dixieland band, with Pete on banjo and John on trumpet. They later joined two other English boys named Roger and Keith to form a little rock outfit known as The Who."

Here, Rick dropped out of the Emerson, Lake and Palmer and went into the crashing guitar and synthesizer intro for "Won't Get Fooled Again."

"Somewhere in the late 1960s, ex–banjo picker Pete Townsend wrote twenty-one of the twenty-four songs for his groundbreaking rock opera, *Tommy*. Around the same time, former trumpeter John Entwistle wrote two of the remaining three songs. The opera's other tune had been written thirty years earlier by a guy from Glendora, Mississippi, of all places. He called himself the Original Sonny Boy Williamson after the *original* Original Sonny Boy Williamson was murdered in Chicago in 1948, but that's another story," Rick said as he faded out of "Won't Get Fooled Again." "So now, from the opera about that deaf, dumb, and blind kid who played from Soho down to Brighton, here's 'Eyesight to the Blind' on WVBR-FM."

The overnight guy walked into the building and waved at Rick through the studio window. Rick was getting up to file his CDs when his cell phone rang. He didn't recognize the number, but he answered anyway. It was Lollie Woolfolk. She said, "Did you make that up?"

"Oh, hey. I was thinking about you earlier."

Lollie paused, then said, "Really? That's intriguing. We'll get to that in a minute. First, answer my question."

"Did I make what up?"

"The banjo and trumpet business."

"No, that's the story."

"Fascinating. The things you know."

"So," Rick said. "You're listening?"

"Is there some other way I'd know to ask about banjos and trumpets?"

"Well, there's this one girl who calls saying she gets the radio-station signals through the fillings in her teeth."

Lollie laughed. "I bet you do meet a lot of interesting people in your job."

"Jobsssssss, plural," Rick said. "And you're a good example of the type I meet. So, what're you doing?"

"Calling in with research. I'm probably the best employee you have."

"Certainly the one who pays me the most."

"I'm also the one you claim to have been thinking about earlier," she said. "What was that about, hmmmm?"

"Oh, I got an address and a phone number for Buddy Cotton," he said. "I did a title search with the county recorders up in the Delta. Turns out Bernard Lewis Cotton owns a bit of property up in Sunflower County, just outside Ruleville."

"And that's why you were thinking about me?" She tried to make it sound as if her feelings were hurt. "It wasn't because of my winning smile or my stunning figure, or some intangible you couldn't quite put a finger on?"

"You sound disappointed."

"Men always disappoint me," she said. "I'm used to it. Though I must say I had higher expectations for you."

"I appreciate that and I'll try not to let you down again. Oh, hang on a second." Rick cued another record and started it, then came back on the phone. "So, what did you find out?"

"The sheriff's department records before '75 were lost in the same fire with the court records. But," she said with dramatic emphasis, "it was all stored on microfiche."

"That's great."

"Woulda been," she said. "Except they were stored in the same building. It's all gone."

"Damn," Rick said. "I talked to Smitty Chisholm. He didn't have any more leads on Pigfoot's real name."

"Oh, don't worry," Lollie said. "I've got an idea on that."

"You do?" He paused, waiting to hear the idea, but she didn't say anything. "What is it?"

"A surprise," she said. "Play me a song."

"What?"

"I said play me a song."

"No, I mean which one?"

"Surprise me."

"I'm off the air in seven minutes," he said. "That's not a lot of time to work with. Plus it has to be a blues."

"You're not going to disappoint me again, are you?"

"Jesus. Okay, hang on." Rick looked through his song database and found one. He cued it up, then put on his headphones. He held the phone near the mike as he said, "That about does it for the Crippled Crusty Boogers Blues Hour. We're going to wrap it up with a request from our favorite unemployed teacher. Here's Champion Jack Dupree doing 'School Days,' on WVBR-FM." He took off his headphones and let the overnight guy slip behind the board.

Rick returned to Lollie on the cell phone. They made small talk while he gathered his stuff and got ready to leave. He put Crusty into his carrier and headed for the door. "So what's your idea on Pigfoot Morgan?"

"You'll find out," she said.

With the phone in one hand and the cat carrier in the other, Rick turned and pushed backward through the door leading outside. "When?" There was no reply. "Hello?" He'd lost her signal. "Can you hear me now?"

Rick nearly dropped Crusty when she tapped him on the shoulder and said, "I can hear you better if you turn around."

"Jesus!" He turned around. "You could've given me a heart attack!"

She gave him a funny look. "Such a drama queen."

"You've been out here the whole time?"

She shook her head. "Just got here."

"Okay, so what's your idea?"

Lollie turned and headed for her car. She said, "Follow me and you'll find out."

Capri. As they walked toward the front doors, Rick said, "Do they let cats into casinos?"

"For crying out loud, we're just going to the bar," Lollie said.

It was twelve-thirty when they sat down in a corner booth. The crowd was thin for a Friday night. Rick was bent down, situating Crusty's carrier on the floor, when he saw the waitress's feet arrive. Lollie said, "I'll have a vodka martini with a twist, please."

"And what can I get for . . ." The waitress paused when Rick came up from under the table. ". . . you."

"Oh, hi," Rick said, obviously surprised. "It's . . . Veronica." After spending time with Lollie, he wondered what he'd ever seen in this aggressively unpleasant woman. He just said, "I'll have a beer."

Veronica said, "What's that?"

"I think it's barley, rice, and water cooked up with some hops."

Veronica smiled, but not in a nice way. She pointed under the table. "That."

"Oh, that's my cat," Rick said, reaching for the carrier. "More of a kitten really. He's pretty cute. Wanna see him?"

"I'm allergic to cats."

"And for some reason that doesn't surprise me," he said.

She tossed two napkins on the table and went to get the drinks, leaving a chill in the air.

Lollie wasn't sure of all the dynamics in play, but she sensed some sort of history between the two. "Friend of yours?"

"She lives in my building," Rick said. "I sort of flirted with her for a while."

"Yeah? How'd that work out?"

"Well, as you can see, she plays hard to get."

Lollie grabbed a handful of peanuts from the bowl on the table, tossing a couple in her mouth before she said, "Well, magical thinking's better than nothing."

"One does what one must," Rick said.

A moment later, Veronica returned with their drinks. She gave Rick an unpleasant look and left without saying anything else.

"She's crazy about you," Lollie said, sipping her martini. "No question."

"All right, here's a thought," Rick said. "Instead of ridiculing my skills as a Casanova, why don't you just tell me why we're here and what you know about Pigfoot's real name and maybe we'll get closer to finding out who killed your grandfather."

She looked at her watch. "I don't know anything yet. It's too early. Now relax." She waved a hand at his glass. "Drink your beer. Pretend we're on a date, maybe that'll drive Veronica so wild with jealousy that she'll have to have you."

"Okay, here's another thought," Rick said. "If you're not going to tell me why we're here, let's at least make fun of your love life instead of mine."

She held up her left hand, wiggling her bare ring finger. "You already know about me."

"I don't know much," Rick said. "Like, for instance, who divorced whom?"

Lollie hesitated before saying, "I divorced him."

"Unfaithful or violent?"

"Aren't you the cynic? Why not irreconcilable differences?"

"You're not the irreconcilable type."

She smirked. "You're right. He cheated."

"How'd you find out?"

Her expression darkened before she said, "I hired a guy like you, got a stack of ugly photographs, and only lost a couple years of my life." She shrugged. "Unlucky in love. End of story." She flashed an exaggerated smile. "But enough about me. You're a decent-looking guy. Surely you have a girlfriend other than Veronica."

"Nope, and for the life of me I can't figure out why," he said in mock confusion. "I've lived in sixteen cities in twenty years, so I've cruised lots of bars in lots of towns looking for Miss Right. I've got a steady, low-paying job at the bottom rung of a medium whose prestige has been dwindling since Burns and Allen went off the air. And the private investigation business I started with the hope of escaping radio has turned out to be a break-even affair at best."

"With a résumé like that, you'd think women would be throwing themselves at you."

"Exactly," Rick said. "But here I am, sitting in a bar at one in the morning with a woman whose only bad intention appears to be mocking my chaste existence."

"I'm sorry. I shouldn't do that." She poked a finger at the twist of lemon floating in her drink. "I just thought since I told you about me . . ." She offered him a wounded pout.

"Okay," Rick said. "There was a girl named Traci, when I was working down in McRae. And there were some others before that."

"A lot of others?"

"Let's see, if I've lived in sixteen cities during my radio career, there must be at least seventeen broken hearts out there. But that's if you only count mine once." He made a woeful face and looked at her. Their eyes connected for a moment.

Lollie held up her glass, smiled sympathetically, and said, "Well, here's to better luck all around."

Rick joined her in the toast and took a long drink from his beer. "Now, would you please tell me why we're here?"

"You know," Lollie said, "in addition to getting laid, you need to relax." She checked her watch. "Patience is a virtue."

"Getting laid's a virtue. Curiosity's a curse," Rick said. "I can't help myself. So, let me ask again, why are we—"

Lollie suddenly grabbed Rick's arm. "There he is." She was look-ing over Rick's shoulder at a man who had just come into the room.

Rick turned and saw an elderly black man walking toward the bar. He was alone and looking around as if lost or there to meet a stranger. Rick said, "That's him? That's Pigfoot Morgan? How the hell did you—" Rick stopped when he heard Lollie giggling. He turned back around and in a defeated tone said, "That's not him, is it?" He watched as the bartender directed the man toward the rest room.

"Sorry." Lollie gave a sheepish grin. "Just having fun."

Rick stared at her. "You're a regular barrel of monkeys."

She gave him a big smile, trying to be contagious with it. "Let me ask, what do you usually do on a Friday when you get off work, I mean for fun? You go home and hit your thumb with a hammer? Maybe watch some dreary Swedish movies? What?"

"As a matter of fact, yes. I go home, smoke some pot, and watch Ingmar Bergman films until the sun comes up."

Her face lit up with mischief. "You have some pot? I haven't smoked pot in years." Lollie stood up. "Let's go to your place."

"What?" He was incredulous. "Why did we come here?"

"To have a drink and kill some time." She held her hand out to pull Rick from the booth. "Which we've done, now let's go."

"You said if I followed you here, you'd tell me your idea."

"Yes, but I didn't say when. C'mon. You'll find out soon."

— — — — — — — —

THEY LEFT THEIR cars in the parking garage and walked the few blocks to Rick's apartment. It was an uphill climb from the river, but it was a nice night for a walk, not too warm and a steady breeze coming across the water. A tugboat's horn sounded to the south as it headed for Natchez.

When they got to Rick's place, Crusty went straight to the litter box. Rick put on a Delta blues anthology that opened with "Stack-a-Lee," then he made martinis and got out his cigar box. He loaded the little pipe and handed it to Lollie. She took a hit and coughed. "Heap powerful stuff," she said. "I hope you've got some Oreos in the kitchen for later."

He sat on the sofa and took a hit, then leaned back and started to sing along with Big Bill Broonzy. " 'Stack-a-Lee turned to Billy Lyons and shot him right through the head. It only took the one shot to kill Billy Lyons dead.' "

"This is such a happy song." Lollie listened for a minute. "All that over a hat?"

Rick smiled but didn't say anything. He figured he'd just stay quiet until she decided to tell him her idea about finding Pigfoot's name. Lollie didn't seem to mind. She sipped her martini and listened to the song. It was two in the morning when the cops finally caught Stack-a-Lee and put him in jail and the song ended. Lollie looked at her watch and said, "Okay. Time to make a call. You do your long distance on your cell or your land line?"

"Cell. Why?"

"This is business, so I figure it ought to be on Rockin' Vestigations' dime." His curiosity piqued, Rick handed her his cell phone. She pulled a piece of paper from her pocket and began punching in a number.

"That's a pretty long number," Rick said.

"It's a pretty long distance." She covered the mouthpiece and looked at the stereo. "Could you turn that down?" Rick did, and a moment later someone came on the line causing Lollie to say, *"Bonjour!"*

Rick turned and looked. *"Bonjour?* You better be calling New Orleans."

Lollie's French was flawless. Rick's wasn't. *"Bonjour"* was the last thing he understood until she said, "Pigfoot Morgan," which sounded funnier in a French accent than Rick would have imagined. She chattered exuberantly with whoever was at the other end. At one point she said, "Vicksburg, Mississippi," which apparently caused a great deal of excitement for someone in France. *"Oui, le lieu de naissance de Willie Dixon!"* She and the French person carried on for a few more minutes before Lollie said, *"Merci beaucoup, au revoir!"* She ended the call and handed the phone back to Rick.

"You're grinning like a smug French possum," he said. "Or are you just stoned?"

"That was Renaud Chassery," she said. "His company produces blues and folk festivals in Europe. He says Pigfoot's real name is Clarence Ezekiel Morgan."

"Ezekiel?" Rick stood there shaking his head. "Can't find a soul in the whole state of Mississippi with the answer, but a guy in Paris knows Pigfoot's middle name."

"That's why we had to wait," Lollie said, tapping her watch. "Seven-hour time difference. He just got to work, so . . ."

"You couldn't just tell me that's what we were doing?"

She gave him a friendly punch in the shoulder. "What's the fun in that? Don't you like surprises?"

Rick gestured for her to follow as he walked over to his computer and logged on to the state correctional institution site. He typed "Clarence E. Morgan" in the search field. A second later a record blipped on the screen. "I'll be damned," Rick said. "That's him. Born in 1931. Sentenced to fifty years for murder in 1953, which would put him in his early seventies if he's still alive." He scrolled down the page reading Morgan's file until he said, "Well now, you see? I do like surprises." He pointed at the screen. "Clarence Ezekiel 'Pigfoot' Morgan was released from Parchman two days before your grandfather was killed."

15

RICK AND LOLLIE stayed up for a while trying to figure out how this new piece of information fit into the overall puzzle. It didn't help that they were stoned and more than a little drunk as they attempted this, but that didn't keep them from trying. Lollie was on her third martini when she said, "I'm just saying it seems like an awfully big coincidence that a convicted murderer with connections to guys who were connected to my grandfather gets out of prison after fifty years and two days later my grandfather gets killed."

"We agree on that," Rick said as he looked out the window, toward the red lights moving on the river. "But what's his motive? The only thing that makes half a teaspoon of sense would be if your grandfather and Suggs cheated him on a record deal."

Lollie wagged a finger at him. "There you go again casting dispersions on my family."

Rick looked over his shoulder at her and said, "Aspersions."

"What?" Her bloodshot eyes were beginning to droop as she lay down on the sofa.

"One casts aspersions," Rick said as he finished his second martini. "Though I suppose one could disperse aspersions. Anyway, I didn't say for a fact that your grandfather was a crooked record producer. I'm just supposing, looking for a reason worth killing over."

"Fine. Thank you so much for restoring his good name."

"And besides, even if they did cheat the guy, it was half a century ago. I can't believe any deal they might've made would be worth killing over now. Which brings us back to motive."

"Hey!" Lollie held a finger in the air as if she suddenly had the answer. "Maybe," she said. Then she fell silent and pursed her lips in confusion.

"Maybe what?"

"I forgot what I was going to say." She sat up. "Hey, you got any cookies?"

Rick went to the kitchen. He called out, "No cookies." He came back a moment later and handed Lollie an old jar of olives. "Best I could do," he said.

"I love olives!" She opened the jar and began trying to fish one out. She tilted it this way and that and shook it and looked inside and said, "Why do they even make these jars with this tiny opening? I can't get two fingers down there and my fingers aren't that big." She held her hand up to examination. "Do you think my fingers are fat?"

"I think we're getting off point," Rick said on his way back to the kitchen. "Let's start over." He returned with a fork, which he handed to Lollie. "All along we've been assuming that the killer is after the tapes, right?" He plopped into his BarcaLounger and kicked back, putting his feet up. "Now, what would Pigfoot Morgan want with the tapes?"

Lollie held up the fork and, switching to a British accent, said, "Elementary, my dear Watson. He's been in prison for fifty years and now he's dead broke and too old to work, so he plans to sell them to fund his retirement."

Rick figured the third martini had just reached her head. "He wouldn't have the slightest idea how or where to begin selling the tapes. I mean, I don't think that's the sort of thing you learn in the prison yard or the fields of Parchman farm. Besides, why would he risk going back to jail?"

Lollie was chewing a mouthful of olives and looking at her hands. "I think I have very elegant fingers." She wiggled them in front of her face. "Look at that, slender and graceful. I could have been a piano player. Or a surgeon. Or a jeweler."

At this point she'd gone from cute to useless, so Rick continued theorizing on his own. "Maybe we're looking for the motive to the wrong killing," he said. "Maybe the connection has to do with why he killed Hamp Doogan. Didn't Tillman say witnesses saw Pigfoot and Doogan arguing outside that juke joint the night everything happened?" He thought about it for a moment. "No, it was Suggs, so that doesn't make any sense. Damn."

Lollie was curling up in the fetal position on the sofa just as he said this, tucking her elegant hands between her knees. She said, "Hmmm?"

"It'd be good to know what they were arguing about, though."

Eyes closed, she responded with a lazy "Mmmm."

Rick figured that would be something to ask Buddy Cotton when they saw him. He sat up in the chair. "What do you say we call it a night?"

There was a short pause before Lollie responded with the sort of snoring Rick imagined Keith Richards might be capable of. Rick pushed himself out of the BarcaLounger and went to his room, returning a moment later with a blanket. He covered Lollie and said, "Sweet dreams, Sherlock."

— — — — — — — —

"**BITE IT,**" **RICK** said. "Don't just lick it." He looked at Lollie. "Does that seem weird to you?"

"Yeah, he'll bite my head but not his food?" She was rooting through her purse looking for the Advil. "Listen, do me a favor," she said. "Next time you see me going for a third martini, stop me." She opened the fridge and found some orange juice. She drank straight from the carton.

Rick pointed at Crusty, hunched over his food. "He just licks the stuff around the dish until it's all in the corners and then he just stares at it until I scrape it all back into a pile in the middle of the dish for him."

"Maybe if you make it into the shape of my head."

"I don't think he'd make it in the wild."

"I wouldn't either," Lollie said, turning to head for the bathroom. "I couldn't live without a hot shower."

Rick made coffee while she steamed up the apartment. Afterward, they walked down to the casino to get Rick's truck. It was a soft summer morning, billowy clouds drifting across the Mississippi. Lollie was wearing jeans and a "Springsteen 2003 Tour" T-shirt she'd borrowed from Rick since she hadn't thought to bring a change of clothes. She admitted this was at least partly her fault, as she had failed to anticipate three martinis and the improvements they'd made in marijuana over the past ten years. Lollie had Crusty, in his case. "You know, a certain someone crept into my bed late last night and cuddled up with me."

"Fickle slut," Rick said.

"What?"

"The cat."

"Oh. Well, at least he didn't bite me again." She stuck a finger into the carrier and stroked his head. "I tell you what surprised me, though. He snores like a goddamn Harley."

Rick wagged a finger at Lollie. "Uhh, people in glass houses." He shook his head.

She stopped cold and said, "I don't snore."

"No, you're right," Rick said, stopping to look back at her. "There's probably a better word for that noise you were making, a medical term perhaps."

After her momentary huff, she started walking again. "I don't have to listen to this."

"Have you tried those adhesive strips?"

They got in the truck and headed for Shipley's Donuts. They picked up a couple of chocolate-glazed donuts and two coffees for the road before starting the drive to Ruleville.

Lollie asked if Blind Buddy Cotton knew they were coming. Rick said he hadn't called ahead, said he'd found people will tell you not to come or they'll be gone when you get there if they know a private investigator is coming to ask a bunch of questions. "If you just show up," he said, "and catch them off guard, you have a better chance of getting them to talk, at least a little."

When they got to Ruleville, which was essentially the intersection of Highways 8 and 49, they pulled into a convenience store to ask for directions. There was a guy milling around in front, apparently working on the old Ford Galaxy with the hood popped open. Lollie kept her eye on him while Rick went inside.

The guy looked worse than Merle Haggard at the end of a bender. He was shirtless and his right arm was in a filthy sling. Lollie thought it looked like somebody had tried to skin the guy, starting with the arm, but had stopped when they saw the stringy quality of the meat. It was the sort of wound most people would gob up with ointment and cover in gauze, but this was open to

Highway 61 Resurfaced

the air, all raw and nervy. He was smoking a cigarette like it would save his sorry life if he sucked on it hard enough, and his eyes had that I-stopped-taking-my-meds look: angry, agitated, and one false move from making the news.

Rick came out with a paper sack and directions. He handed Lollie a cranberry juice. "The guy said it's the first left after the Murray Gin sign."

Five minutes later they turned onto a dirt driveway. They could see the house up ahead. Getting closer, they spotted an old man sitting on the porch in the heat of the day. He was wearing a brown suit, dark glasses, and a gray felt hat. He was rocking slightly in a metal lawn chair, a guitar at his side. Rick said, "I'm gonna go out on a limb and say that's your Blind Buddy Cotton."

- - - - - - - - -

IT WASN'T EVERY day that a car turned onto Buddy's property. And on those days when it did happen, Buddy never knew what to expect. Sometimes people just got lost and needed to ask directions, other times it was a writer working on a story about the lost bluesmen of the Delta. Every now and then it was a carload of newly hatched blues fans who thought they could just show up and get him to play a song or two, as if the Mississippi Board of Tourism had installed him on that porch for their personal entertainment.

Over time Buddy had come to look forward to these unannounced visits; they gave him a chance to puff up and strut a little about his place in what used to be. It was the taste of fame he hungered for, the recognition he felt he'd been denied. But lately, every time a car pulled onto his property, Buddy tensed up, thinking the Grim Reaper might be in the driver's seat. He didn't know if Pigfoot would just pull up in broad daylight to take care of his business, but he might. So Buddy sat on his porch with his **165**

guitar, his walking stick, and his pistol in his pocket.

At first, from a distance, all he could see was a truck he didn't recognize. When it got closer, Buddy could see it was just a white couple, so he relaxed a bit. They looked like the types who might be looking to do some kind of interview, so he got his Blind Buddy persona ready to go. He let loose of the pistol and picked up the guitar just as Rick pulled to a stop in front of the house.

They got out and approached the front porch. Buddy gave a courtly nod and, aiming his glasses slightly off center from where his guests were standing, said, "All right now, who'm I talkin' to?"

"Mr. Cotton? My name's Rick Shannon. This is Lollie Woolfolk." They were standing directly in the sunlight, shading their eyes to see. Rick's shirt was already sticking to his back.

Lollie said, "Good afternoon."

Buddy touched the rim of his hat. "Aft'noon," he said, thinking that since they already knew who he was, they probably wanted to do an interview with him. He gestured for them to join him on the porch. "C'mon up here in the shade," he said.

They stepped up to the porch and shook hands. Rick pulled out his business card; it had "Rockin' Vestigations" on one side and "WVBR" on the other. He held it out to Buddy without considering his eyesight. To his surprise, Buddy took it, slipped it in his pocket, and said, "Tell me what I can do for you."

"Thanks," Lollie said. "We'd like to talk to you if you have a moment."

Buddy nodded. Just as he'd suspected. He said, "Well now, lemme guess. You wanna interview me for something you writing? About my music?" He held the guitar and lightly brushed the strings. "Well, you come to the right place. But I ain't gone tell you I played with Robert Johnson, 'cause I didn't. Most people say they did are lyin' anyway. But I did spend some times on

Highway 61 Resurfaced

Stovall's Plantation and I made plenny sounds with Muddy Waters and Elmore James and whole bunch others and—"

"No, sir," Rick said, cutting him off. "That's not why we're here. I'm a private investigator. I'm looking into a couple of murders."

Buddy's surprise was obvious. "Two murders?" The words gave him pause. He figured it had to be Crippled Willie and Crazy Earl. Damn. Pigfoot wasn't wasting any time, probably because at his age he didn't have much to waste. He would come gunning for Buddy any day now, that much was certain. And he'd be expecting it to be easy. But he was gone get a fight. Not like his friends. Earl was probably drunk and Willie probably just stood there and prayed. Easy targets.

But what about these two standing on his porch? he wondered. If they looked hard enough, they might start shining a light on things Buddy would just as soon keep in the dark. He figured the best thing was to play along, give 'em some answers that'd send 'em the wrong way, act like none of it mattered. He turned his dark glasses toward Rick and said, "What's it got to do with me?"

"Nothing directly, as far as we know," Rick said.

By this point Buddy's expression and tone changed from happy ambassador of the blues to fearful and wary prey. "Wha' choo mean by 'nothing d'rectly'?"

"Well, it's sort of a roundabout connection," Rick said, sensing the sudden tension. "I was talking to the man who runs the blues museum in Vicksburg and he told me about a recording session in the early 1950s with you and Crippled Willie Jefferson and a guy named Earl Tate."

"That's who been killed, innit?" He said it like he already knew it to be true.

"No, sir," Rick said. "It was Tucker Woolfolk and Lamar Suggs."

Buddy shook his head, his expression still grim. This news wasn't any better. It just meant Pigfoot was working off a longer list of people. He turned his face toward Lollie. "You say your name is Woolfolk?"

"Yes, sir, Tucker was my grandfather. I hired Mr. Shannon here to find out who killed him."

Buddy touched the rim of his hat again. "My condolences," he said. "When'd all this happen?"

"In the past week or so," Rick said. "A couple of days after a man named Clarence Morgan got out of Parchman. He used to go by the name of—"

"Pigfoot."

"Yes, sir. You knew him?"

"Just narrowly. We wasn't associates or anything. I considered myself about ten years elder to him. He used to work at this cotton-compress company where I—" Without warning, Buddy hunched over and launched into a deep, rasping cough. He reached to his pocket, then covered his mouth until the spasm passed and his tongue pushed the matter into the waiting handkerchief.

Lollie bent down, putting her hand on his back. "Are you all right?"

He shook his head and waved the handkerchief at Rick. "Last I heard about that Morgan, he'd gone to prison for killing a man."

"Yes, sir. That's right," Rick said. "A guy named Hamp Doogan. I was wondering if you knew anything about it?"

"Why would I?"

"Well, it goes back to that recording session. We think the murders have something to do with the tapes." Rick recounted the version of the story Beau Tillman had told, including the part about Pigfoot agreeing to drive them to Memphis.

When he finished, Buddy said, "You know, peoples been

talkin' about that for an extensive time and I ain't ever heard the whole story tolt right. See, Mr. Suggs was s'posed to come and cut some sides on account of he knew we was fiddna sign with Paramount up there in Grafton, Wisconsin, and he wanted to get some before that happened. But as I recall, he was late getting to where we was playin' on account of he had to drive down from Memphis and the roads back then weren't all that much, you know. Time he got there, we was packed up, fiddna leave, goin' right back up the road he'd just come down. But I had my own car. We didn't need Pigfoot Morgan to carry us nowhere. I don't know where that come from."

"You have any idea why Morgan killed Mr. Doogan?"

"I heard it was over some money. Usual thing." Buddy shook his head. "But I can't say for sho, weren't none of my affair. You been to the courthouse?"

Lollie said, "All the records were destroyed in a fire."

"That right?" Buddy smiled just a little and said, "Tha's a shame. Well, I guess you gone have to ax him yourself."

"I'd like to," Rick said. "But I don't know where he is. Does he have family in the area?"

"Not as I know of."

Rick asked if the Blind, Crippled, and Crazy session had ever happened.

"Oh yeah," Buddy said. "We went on up to Wisconsin and cut us some lively sides, mostly my compositions, as I recall. But they never did release them, as far as I know, at least I never heard 'em. Not sure why either. They give us our little nickels and we took the train back on down here. Ever since then, peoples just been telling stories they don't know nothin' 'bout."

16

CRAIL WAS LOATH to admit it, especially under the current circumstances, but the pain was almost unbearable. Finally he said, "Cuffie, honey, can we do this in a different position? This knee's really startin' to hurt."

Without breaking stride, she looked over her shoulder and said, "I know it is, baby." She sounded sympathetic. "But don't worry about that right now." Cuffie bit her lower lip and started rocking faster. "You can put some ice on it when we're done." She faced forward, gripped the headboard, and shortened her stroke. "Just a little more for your Cuffums. Just a little. Just . . ."

The truth of the matter was that Crail could have put the entire polar ice cap on his knee and it wouldn't have made any difference. And the reason for that went back to the summer of 1957, when Lamar Suggs paid five dollars to have his way with a hustlin' gal out behind the Midnight Special, a juke joint on the outskirts of (ironically) Rolling Fork, Mississippi. This dalliance had resulted in a state-of-the-art case of gonorrhea for which Lamar eventually sought treatment and was cured.

However, being the opportunistic bacteria that it is, the gram-negative intracellular diplococci had taken up residence and lived happily for five decades in the membranes of his rancid old mouth, whence it migrated to every spoon and fork that passed his lips.

Crail's knee flexed with each thrust, a white-hot needle plunging again and again into his nerves. For a moment he thought he might pass out. It was a testament to his masculinity that he could keep his erection throughout the torture.

"Just, just, just . . ."

He flashed back to his high school football coach screaming about how a man has to learn to play through pain. And all those years ago Crail had been happy to suffer for the team, but this was pure agony. Couldn't she just get on top?

"Just." She was pushing back harder now. "Uh." Breathing heavier. "Littlllle." One last thrust. "Morrrrre." Then a long exhale as she collapsed onto the bed. "Oh, baby."

Crail withdrew and stumbled backward, his hands reaching for the wall behind him. He caught himself and, putting his weight on his one good leg, thanked God it was over. Cuffie rolled to the bedside table and took a cigarette from Crail's pack. She lit up, took a drag, then said, "Oh, hey, you know, I been meaning to ask you. How's your mama doing?"

" 'Bout the same," Crail said as he looked down at his throbbing knee. "Hasslin' with those insurance people about those treatments she needs."

"Ohh, bless her heart."

"Yeah, they keep sayin' it's not on their list of approved procedures even though that doctor said it was what she needed. So we told 'em that and they sent more forms to fill out, you know, that old game." He took the cigarette from Cuffie and said, "But, you know, she's hangin' in there."

"That's good." Cuffie took the cigarette back and had a drag. "So I've been thinking about what we're going to do next." She blew some smoke out of the side of her mouth.

Crail limped over to the chair where he'd thrown his sweatpants. "You sure your papaw ain't got those tapes? It was his radio station, right?" He eased himself down into the chair and struggled into the pants.

"Baby." She looked at him as she took another drag on the cigarette. "Sometimes? I just don't believe you." Shaking her head, she exhaled in his direction.

"What?"

"You think we'd be bothering with all this if he had 'em?" She rolled her eyes. "Let's just concentrate on finding that Mr. Morgan."

He picked up his Jim Beam and took a slug. "Okay. But what about my leg?"

"Oh, yeah." She reached over and pulled a plastic prescription bottle from her purse. "I brought you some antibiotics." She tossed them to him and said, "Just take those. You'll be fine."

--- --- --- --- ---

EARL TATE WAS an ill-shaped baby, born with three birthmarks on his back. His mama told him it was a sign, that he'd been marked, that he was special. His foot was deformed and the woman who helped bring him out of his mama said he had a look in one eye that scared her half to death. These were the sorts of things he told people when they came around wanting to meet Crazy Earl. Some of it was true, but mostly he liked the attention, the identity, and the respect it earned him. He liked that others thought he was special that way. And the drunker he was, the more special he got.

On Saturday nights in the old days, after he'd done a few sets, wailing on his guitar or a piano if there was one in the house, he'd be all worked up on his gin and he'd fix some stranger with his Judas eye and start hollerin' about how he was a blue-gummed nigger could kill you with one bite. He'd get that crazy look about him, wobbling his jaw and swearing that even hard-shelled hoodoos gave him respect. It was a stunning performance, and it convinced more than a few that Earl was a genuine fetish man, the real thing, primitive and powerful. After a while, they came offering good money for him to lay tricks on enemies and engage in all kinds of conjuration, from making love potions to curing the sick.

The blues business being what it was, Earl studied up on the black crafts. He lived in a sharecropper's shack between the Morgan Brake Wildlife Refuge and Milestone Bayou, so it was easy to find the things he needed to make the charms and signs and cures people wanted. His little place was choked with clay jars and tin cans and odd little boxes filled with bird wings, jaws of small mammals, rattlesnake fangs, the ashes and powders of things burned on red-hot metal, dirt from the graves of the old and wicked, congealed blood from pig-eating sows, a can of rusty nails, some patches of red flannel, and all the other ingredients necessary to bring about everything from love to sorrow to death.

Since he hadn't yet heard of Pigfoot Morgan dying or going away, Earl was drunk and getting more so. He was about as special as he'd been in quite some time. So he figured his best chance to stay alive was to keep conjuring hands, each one more powerful than the last, until his enemy was gone—literally or figuratively, it didn't matter.

It was past dark and he was sitting at his rough little table with a bottle of gin and two dozen containers spread out around him like chess pieces. Problem was, when Earl got special enough, he'd forget if he was supposed to cook the snakeroot with the sand-burr and the fish eye to blind his enemy or if it was black cat hair, and a chicken-snake skin wrapped up in a tobacco sack to crip-ple him. This went a long way toward explaining why he'd ground up a dried rattlesnake head and mixed it in an old Silver Crest lard can with some pine resin, tobacco spit, and stewed coon root in an attempt to drive Pigfoot crazy.

Earl sat there, swaying side to side, trying to remember if he had to wait for a waning moon before he hung the bag from the branch of a black willow or if he could just invoke Pigfoot's name as he flung the thing into a slough. He figured the answer was in-side the bottle of gin, so he grabbed it and was throwing his head back when from out of nowhere, the goddamn lard can ex-ploded. Earl jumped backward more than a little and blinked a few times when he came to a stop. He was too drunk to realize what had happened, and, for a moment, he thought maybe he'd conjured up some bad mojo. He scratched his head wondering if he should've used some John the conquer root instead of the pine resin. But the second shot, which shattered a corked bottle of four thieves vinegar, disabused him of the notion that his recipie was the thing at fault.

When it dawned on him that Pigfoot Morgan was taking pot-shots at him from the edge of the wildlife refuge, Earl got mad. The gin and adrenaline moved him across the shack and toward the drawer with the real cure in it. He started shouting about how he was sho gone come out there and demonstrate the proper way to shoot a man. He snatched a .38 from the drawer and, standing to the side of the door, got to thinking about his next move.

At seventy-three, Earl figured he and his deformed foot weren't going to make much of a run for it out the front door, even if it was dark out and the man shooting at him was seventy-two. But what was it going to look like if he slipped out the back way? It would look like he was half a man, that's what. Damn. What kinda choice was that? Same as always, that's what. The Lord had never once put Earl on equal footing with his situations, always made it harder for him, like testing him, like he did Abraham. "Nothin' but bad luck and troubles," he mumbled. And frankly, he was tired of it.

All his life people been stealin' from him and blaming him for things he didn't deserve blame for. And now one of 'em was out there shootin' at him. Earl shook his head, disappointed in his fate, thinking that son of a bitch had his nerve shooting at him the way he was. Ain't my fault what happened. It was one of those wrong-place-at-the-wrong-time kinda situations. Sorta thing where it all would've been okay if they'd just stuck together. But driving off the way he did, leaving them to face the consequences? What'd he expect? Done brought it all on hisself. Deserved everything he got and then some. And now, gots the nerve to come shooting? Well, Earl Tate wasn't so crazy that he was fixin' to step out that door and make things any easier. The way he figured it, being half a man alive beat the other choice. So he slipped out the back and headed for the bayou.

And that's just what Pigfoot was waitin' on. Because it gave him the angle he hadn't had before. The light shined out the back door and lit up his sluggish target. He propped the rifle on a fence post and looked down the barrel. Then he took one last shot.

- - - - - - - - -

IN THE DAYS following Tucker Woolfolk's death, Lollie befriended the lead investigator on the case, a Detective Cruger. She told him no offense, but she planned to hire a private investigator to help and said they would share any information they got. Detective Cruger was fine with that, said he was glad to have extra manpower at no extra cost. Lollie said she just wanted the guilty caught and punished.

On the drive back from Ruleville, Lollie called him. Detective Cruger said he was sorry but that he didn't have anything new to tell her, said they were still pursuing the crackhead theory. Though she knew better, Lollie told him she thought he was probably on the right track. "But I wanted to let you know we're still looking into the possibility it has something to do with his days as a record producer." She had mentioned this theory to Detective Cruger before, but he hadn't lent it much credence. "I know you think it's a dead end," Lollie said. "But I told you I'd keep you informed, so I wanted you to know we just talked to Blind Buddy Cotton."

"Dee say anything useful?"

"Not really."

"Uh-huh."

"I know, you were right," Lollie said. She always told him he was right, figuring it was the best way to keep him on her side and willing to help if she asked. "But do you think you might be able to get an address on Willie Jefferson or Earl Tate? We can't find either of them."

Cruger snickered and said, "Maybe you need a better private investigator."

Lollie studied Rick's profile for a moment before she smiled and said, "No, I like the one I've got." Cruger said he'd see what he could do.

Rick wasn't listening. He was thinking about something Buddy Cotton had said. When Lollie flipped the phone shut, she noticed his expression. "You look flummoxed," she said.

"I'm trying to understand something. You remember after we told Buddy we were investigating two murders and he asked what it had to do with him? And then I mentioned Willie Jefferson and Earl Tate? Buddy immediately assumed they were the two men who'd been killed. Now why would he assume that?"

Lollie remembered. She said, "He did, didn't he? Should we go back and ask?"

Rick shook his head. "We're almost home and I'm too hungry to turn around. We can ask him next time we're up that way. But it seems odd." He glanced at Crusty, who was curled up in Lollie's lap. "Besides, booger boy there needs his medicine."

She looked at Crusty's nose. "Yeah, he needs a tissue too." A bubble formed on one of his nostrils each time he exhaled. Lollie pulled a Kleenex from her purse and wiped the trouble spot. "But you know, Buddy's assumption isn't so odd if we're right," she said. "I mean, if this is about the tapes, Earl Tate and Crippled Willie are as connected to them as Suggs or my grandfather." She looked out the window, then back at Rick. "I don't know, the more we find out, the less sense it makes."

"Welcome to my little corner of the world," Rick said. "And here's something else. Buddy's not as blind as he acts. I held out my business card and he took it. I didn't have to put it in his hand."

"You handed a business card to a blind man?"

"It was reflex, but that's not the point." He paused before he said, "I really don't have a point, other than . . . it's weird."

Lollie changed the subject to Beau Tillman's characterization of late-nineteenth-century Leland, Mississippi. "A little Sodom and Gomorrah right in the middle of the Bible Belt. You gotta love that," she said. "And what about that Hamp Doogan character? I mean, maybe I'm naive, but a coke-dealing photographer in 1950s small-town Mississippi?"

"He sounds colorful, I'll grant you," Rick said. "But he's way too dead to be answering questions. I'm more interested in talking to Henry LeFleur if he's still around. He was the sheriff when Doogan was killed, and according to Smitty Chisholm he was a partner in the radio station with Suggs and your grandfather."

"Sure, but we should at least try to find somebody in Doogan's family. Maybe one of them went to the trial or heard stories and might be able to tell us why Pigfoot killed him. Maybe there's a connection to this somehow."

As they drove along, kicking around theories and strategies on how to proceed, Rick kept stealing glances at Lollie. Her profile charmed him as she explored possible scenarios and followed the threads stemming from the clues. She beamed an enthusiastic smile whenever she thought she was onto something, gesturing excitedly as she arranged and rearranged possibilities in an attempt to explain what might have happened. Rick kept marveling at the French-speaking martial artist in the passenger seat and found himself wondering what else she was good at.

A few minutes later, they pulled into a funky little beer-and-tamale joint on the outskirts of Vicksburg. Rick ran in and grabbed an order to go, then headed back to his office.

The antiques shop closed at five on Saturdays, so they had to use the metal stairway up the back of the building. Lollie was behind Rick the whole way up the stairs and wasn't shy about admiring his back pockets. She had the urge to say something nice, something flirty, like, Don't take this the wrong way, but you've got a nice butt. Then she might add something like, For a guy your age, just to take the curse off it, but not so much that he wouldn't get her meaning. She'd noticed him sneaking glances at her for the past few days, but he seemed to be adhering to some sort of professional code about not hitting on his client, which was admirable but wasn't doing her, a woman with urges like anybody else, any damn good. Maybe it was her own fault, she thought. Maybe she needed to let him know she'd be open to a little this and that. So she resolved to say something to see if she could move things forward. She just couldn't think of the right words.

They stopped on the landing while Rick fumbled with his keys. Lollie said, "So you never really told me why you're not seeing anybody. Are you gay?" During the awkward moment that followed, she thought: Boy, that came out wrong.

Rick turned to her with a confused look. He looked down at Crusty, then back at Lollie. "No," he said. "Why do you ask?"

Embarrassed, she tried to shrug it off. "Just curious." Oh, jeez, what an idiot, she thought. Why didn't I say "just kidding" instead of "just curious"? Oh my God, now he thinks I think he's . . . She looked over the edge of the landing and thought for a moment that if they were higher, she just might jump off.

Rick wondered what made her think he was gay. Was it the cat? He was about to open the door but stopped and said, "Wait a second. Are you implying that you don't think I could get a boyfriend? I mean, if I was gay?"

"No," she said. "No. I'm sure you'd find somebody." She smiled, trying to make it all better or hoping to make it all go away, like if she showed enough charm and teeth, time itself would go backward. Then she thought maybe she should just grab him and kiss him right there on the landing and say, My point is, you've been looking at me and I've been looking at you, so let's forget our professional relationship for a moment and just have sex and get it over with. But instead she held up the grocery sack she was carrying and said, "Boy, these sure smell good. Are they pork or beef?"

"Pork," Rick said, trying to sound as heterosexual as possible. He opened the door, picked up Crusty's carrier, then followed Lollie inside. As she led the way down the hall, Rick admired the swing of her slim hips. Truth was, he'd been infatuated with Lollie ever since he'd regained consciousness after she'd punched him in the head. Still, he didn't want to make any moves based on a misconstrued signal. Given her brown belt and her willingness to use it, he thought he should be careful. Then again, aside from the gay question, he was pretty sure she was flirting with him, so when they reached the door to his office, he said, "No real reason."

Lollie was still kicking herself over the gay thing, so she wasn't sure what Rick meant. "Reason for what?"

"For why I'm not seeing anybody, who, if I was seeing, would be a girl. Woman." Then, thinking maybe he'd put too fine a point on it, he pointed at the sack and said, "We better eat those before they get cold."

"Good idea." They went in and sat on either side of his desk. Lollie pulled two large coffee cans from the grocery bag. They were packed with steaming-hot tamales. Rick folded the bag and set it on the table between them, like a place mat. Lollie thumped one of the cans with a finger and asked how he'd found the place that made them. He said a listener had turned him on to the joint after he'd said something on the air about his preference for local restaurants over franchised food places.

Lollie unfolded a corn husk, then leaned over to take in the aroma. "You know why they sell these things all over the Delta?"

"World War Two," Rick said. "The workforce joined the army, and Mexican labor came to fill the gap, brought their food."

"That's what I heard too," Lollie said, glad that they'd found something else to talk about. "So how come nobody sells burritos?" She made a sweeping gesture with her tamale hand. "Why don't you see taco stands anywhere? Why just tamales?"

"Don't know. I'm just repeating what I heard."

While they ate, Rick tried not to think about her flirtations and her hips. Instead, he talked about the databases they would search for Henry LeFleur and members of the Doogan clan.

At one point, Lollie glanced up and saw Rick licking his fingers. His lips were glistening with oil and pork broth, red from the chili powder, and she couldn't take it anymore. She said, "Oh, what the hell." She dropped her tamale, stood up, and leaned across the table. "I just have to get this out of the way." Then she kissed him. It was a long, spicy, hot-tamale kiss, their mouths warm with garlic, bay leaf, and corn. Finally she pulled back, sat down, and smacked her lips. "There. Much better. Thanks."

Rick blinked a couple of times and said, "You're welcome. At Rockin' Vestigations, we'll do whatever it takes to keep our clients happy."

She arched her eyebrows and said, "Whatever it takes?" She unwrapped the last tamale and gave a lecherous smile. "Well, maybe we should get back to work and save that for later."

17

NOW THERE WERE three things Rick knew about her: karate, French, and French kissing. Based on how good she was at these, Rick assumed Lollie was a pretty good special-ed teacher. So that was four things. He wondered how long the list was. And how long would it be until he learned more? As he wiped the last bits of grease from his fingers, Rick said, "You any good with computers?"

She wiggled in her seat and said, "Try me," like she was Mae West.

"I thought we were saving that for later."

"Down, boy," she said, pointing at the monitor. "Data-bases. How to search. Try to focus."

"You started it," he said. He showed her the basics, gave her his Web site passwords, and turned it over to her. "I've gotta feed Puff Kitty. Holler if you need help."

"Puff Kitty?"

"That's his rap name. When he gets scared, his tail puffs up like a gang member." Rick was about to go when an e-mail pinged in. It was from Smitty Chisholm. He'd talked to a professor at Ole Miss who had done research on minor figures of the Delta blues. He had a phone number and an address for Crippled Willie Jefferson, just outside Greenville. The professor also said he was trying to track one down for Earl Tate. Lollie hit the print button.

With this little bit of good news, Rick went into the reception area to medicate and feed Crusty. As he applied the ointments and pills, he could hear Lollie typing at a fever pitch. A few minutes later, he heard the printer spooling up. Then more typing, some disgruntled noises, then more typing, and so on. Rick took a minute to trim Crusty's claws. "How's it going in there?"

"So far so good," she said.

As Rick picked Crusty's nose, he heard the printer going again. A minute later she said, "All done."

"What?" He couldn't believe it. He walked back into the office with a flat toothpick in one hand and a boogery cat in the other. She waved a few sheets of paper in the air as Rick stared in disbelief. He traded Crusty for the papers and started reading. The first thing was a newspaper article with a grainy photograph, the others pages looked like part of a complaint or a deposition from a lawsuit entitled *Sunflower Retirement Village v. Good Move Transit Group,* the parent company for several large moving firms. The summary indicated that the retirement community had relocated recently and had hired one of Good Move's subsidiary companies to do the heavy lifting. When it came time to unload, the drivers said they couldn't until the residents paid for some unexpected expenses, which amounted to several thousand dollars apiece above the contracted price. Rick looked at the plaintiffs' names, but there were no LeFleurs or Doogans. He said, "Okay, they're bad guys, but what's it got to do with the price of tamales in Vicksburg?"

"Maybe nothing," she said. "Maybe something."

"Maybe you want to explain."

"Okay." Lollie put Crusty on the floor and rubbed her hands together excitedly. "First I found Hamp Doogan's death certificate on file with the state," she said. "At the bottom they list a next of kin, a woman named Ruby Finch. So I did a search and found her name in this lawsuit." She pointed at the date on the document. "And she was alive as of two months ago."

"Yeah, but in a nursing home."

"That's why I checked the master death file. She's still not there."

"Okay, score one for you." Rick turned his attention to the newspaper article and said, "Ow! Dammit." Crusty shot out of the room with his tail puffed. "He bit my ankle."

"Yeah," Lollie said. "He'll do that every now and then."

Rick returned his attention to the document. It was from a recent issue of the *Delta Democrat Times*. The accompanying photo had been taken at the Olde River Country Club. According to the story, Shelby LeFleur Jr. had just celebrated his ninety-fifth birthday with friends and family. The birthday boy was in the middle of the picture, in a wheelchair, staring at his lap. Flanking him was his son Henry and Henry's wife, Lettie, neither of whom were exactly spring chickens. Also present was grandson Monroe LeFleur and his wife, Hannah. There were a couple of litters of great-grandchildren packed around the fringes of the picture and, according to the caption, one of them was Cuffie LeFleur. But the name meant nothing to Rick, and though he might have recognized her in a clean shot, the photo was grainy and Cuffie was standing behind a tall cousin with big hair, so her face was obscured.

"Well now, we're just lousy with options," Rick said. "Who do you think we should talk to first?"

"Given everybody's age, I think we should split up and talk to everybody as fast as we can get to them. You want Ruby, Crippled Willie, or Henry LeFleur?"

"I'll take Crippled Willie," Rick said. "That way I can drop by the *Delta Democrat Times* to do some research on the LeFleur clan before we visit Henry."

"Fine. I'll take Ruby Finch."

THE WOMEN AT the Sunflower Retirement Village formed a sort of blue-rinse-and-sweatsuit mafia, armed with walkers and canes and a certain amount of surrender. Among this crowd Ruby Finch stood out like a sparkler in a dark room. She was tall and maintained an elegant finishing-school posture, as though refusing to stoop to age or arthritis. Silver hair that would have tumbled past her shoulders was pulled into a bun at the back of her head, anchored by a distinctive pair of hand-carved chopsticks.

The man at the reception desk told Lollie to look for the woman wearing the tailored linen suit. She was sitting in the sunroom, reading Walker Percy's *Love in the Ruins*. "Mrs. Finch?"

Ruby marked her place on the page with a manicured fingertip and looked up. "It's Ms."

"Oh." Not exactly the sort of thing Lollie expected to hear from a seventy-year-old at a retirement home in Sunflower County, Mississippi. "I'm sorry."

"No need for that, I'm just saying." She moved her bookmark to the page and closed the book, settling it on her lap and folding her hands over the top.

"Ms. Finch, my name's Lollie Woolfolk."

"Yes?" Her tone was guarded.

"I hate to interrupt your reading, but I was hoping we could talk for a moment."

"Were you?" As Lollie moved to sit down, Ruby said, "I haven't invited you to join me, young lady. Simply because you know my name and you've told me yours, that doesn't make us friends." She sat up even straighter than she had been. "You haven't stated your business, but I suspect I know what it is. So you needn't bother getting comfortable."

"Well, ma'am, I—"

"Don't interrupt when I'm talking, please. It's rude. Honestly. Now, Miss Woolfolk, you can just return to your office and tell them that neither I nor any of the other residents here have any intention of withdrawing from the lawsuit, and it doesn't matter how many young lawyers they send out to try to buy us off, and on Sunday, no less." She cast a withering glance Lollie's way and said, "We are going to see this through to the end."

"Ohhh," Lollie said as she took a seat.

The temerity of the move pushed Ruby's head backward. "Oh? What is that supposed to mean?"

"It means you've mistaken me for someone else, Ms. Finch." She smiled sweetly, hoping to break the barrier Ruby had thrown up. "I'm not a lawyer and I'm not here about the lawsuit. In fact, I hope you win."

"Oh." Ruby looked down at the book in her lap and gave it an embarrassed pat. "Well, in that case, I apologize. They sent a man out here last week trying to intimidate a few of the older residents and I just assumed they'd switched tactics by sending a woman this time."

"I understand," Lollie said. "But that's not why I'm here."

"So you said." She set her book on the coffee table, then looked back at Lollie. "But you still haven't stated your business. What did you want to see me about?"

"A relative of yours."

"Who?"

"Hamp Doogan."

"Oh my." Ruby's face changed completely and, in a dreamy voice, she said, "Hamp Doogan." His name seemed to transform her. Lollie had never seen anything quite like it. Ruby glanced around the room before saying, "Hamp and I weren't related, dear." She was shaking her head as she leaned toward Lollie with an almost devilish smile. "We were lovers." She put her hand to her face as if she'd said something she knew a proper lady shouldn't, though it also served to hide the smile of guilty pleasure that threatened to split her face in half. She scooted closer to Lollie. "What on earth made you think we were related?"

"You signed his death certificate as next of kin." Lollie glanced out the window as two blue-rinsed heads floated by, apparently attached to bodies in a golf cart.

"Oh, that. Hamp didn't have any family down here, so . . ." She shrugged. "They needed someone to sign the thing and the sheriff knew I knew Hamp well enough, so I signed it, much to my parents' dismay."

"Why dismay?"

"Well, Hamp had a . . . reputation." Her inflection made it a bad word. "He wasn't welcome among pra-pah society," she said, mocking the word. "He was an artist, more bohemian than they approved of. Worse, he was from Boston. And he was a charmer like you've never seen. Handsome and smooth, ohh, he was all that and more."

"The sheriff was Henry LeFleur?"

"That's right." Ruby's wistful demeanor drifted toward suspicion. "What's all this about?"

Lollie told her the whole story, including the part about Pigfoot Morgan's release from Parchman two days before her grandfather was killed. When she finished she said, "Do you know why he killed Hamp?"

"Oh, I don't know that that poor man did it at all," Ruby said. "They probably just didn't have a good suspect and he somehow ended up being their scapegoat." A sadness passed over her face and she looked away. "So many awful things happened in those days."

"Did you attend the trial?"

She waved a hand at Lollie like she was crazy. "No, my parents would never allow anything like that. I had shamed them enough by then," she said with a small laugh.

"Were you called to testify about anything?"

"Well, I was subpoenaed, of course. But, after a meeting with my father, the prosecutor just had me into his office so he could record my testimony."

"What did you say?"

"What could I say? I hadn't seen anything. I'd only heard a secondhand account of what had happened, so that's all I could tell him."

"What had you heard?"

"Well, there was this friend of Hamp's, a black gambler by the name of Shorty Parker. He was in the jail that night, arrested for stabbing a man with an ice pick, but he said it was in self-defense and I never had any reason to doubt him about that. Anyway, Shorty was in the jail when they brought those men in, those musicians? And he overheard their conversations in the next cell."

Lollie asked if Buddy, Willie, and Earl were the men who had been brought to the jail.

"Those names sound right," Ruby said. "But I can't be a hundred percent sure."

"How about Pigfoot Morgan?"

"No," she said. "I think Shorty said he had escaped."

"What did Mr. Parker tell you had happened?"

"Well, Shorty said he didn't know what had happened so much as he had an idea of what *hadn't* happened."

"Which was?"

"Well, as I said, I don't believe that Mr. Morgan killed Hamp. It was somebody else. So that's what I said in my testimony."

"Do you know if the defense brought that up at the trial?"

Ruby shook her head. "How much of a defense do you think that man got?"

Lollie understood her point so she didn't press it. "Why'd the prosecutor let you testify in his office instead of the courtroom?"

"He was a friend of the family. And my father told him I wasn't going to be available at the time of the trial."

"Why was that?"

Ruby allowed herself another small laugh before saying, "I was being sent away to avoid embarrassing my poor family any further."

"Where did you go?"

"New York City." Ruby nodded at the novel she'd been reading. "My parents were close friends with the Percy family and of course Walker had attended the College of Physicians and Surgeons at Columbia. So they sent me to New York before the trial started. I studied art and literature and looked for a husband among Walker's old crowd." Her eyes sparkled, back to her youth. "Moved into the Barbizon Hotel for Young Women, classes during the day, dancing at night. It was glorious. At one point I even did some modeling for Claire McCardell, which was a big thing. It was all wonderful, but I never did find a husband, and after a couple of years, my father got sick and I moved back to Mississippi. And let me tell you, New York may have been the center of everything, all the lights and the bustle, but the Mississippi Delta wasn't all church meetings and lazy Sunday afternoon picnics. It was a pretty lively place."

"So I gathered," Lollie said with a smile. "I've heard stories about some wild times in Leland and the joints where Mr. Doogan used to take photos."

Ruby seemed startled by Lollie's words. She paused. Then, with a certain amount of caution, she said, "Have you seen any of his work?"

"Just a few, pictures of Blind Buddy Cotton and some others at a juke joint."

Ruby looked into Lollie's eyes as if measuring something. She hesitated before she said, "You know, he took my picture." She paused a moment, as if wrestling with a decision. Then she said, "Would you like to see?"

Lollie said sure and followed Ruby down the hallway. They went to her room and Ruby closed the door behind them. She opened a closet and pointed into a dark corner and asked Lollie to pull out the big box in the back. "I haven't shown these to anyone in years," she said. "But they are such lovely memories." Lollie took a heavy banker's box from the closet and put it on the bed. Ruby lifted off the top and pulled out several old folios made of a soft brown cardboard. "Hamp Doogan Photography" was embossed in the upper-left corner. Ruby brushed her palm over the front of the top folio and said, "He took this in 1950, when I was, well, when I was younguh." This time she was mocking herself instead of the word. She handed the folio to Lollie and watched, keen to see her reaction.

Lollie opened the folio and looked. Her eyes widened and her mouth fell open.

Ruby took great pleasure in the response. She said, "Quite the dish, wasn't I?"

18

RICK DROVE DOWN Old Highway 61 until he came to the two tractors rusting in the weeds next to the listing toolshed with the faded Coca-Cola sign on it. The gravel road after that was the turnoff he was looking for. A minute later he was parked in front of a shotgun shack with knobby pine trunks holding up a tin roof over the porch. As Rick approached, the front door opened and an old man with an odd gait stepped outside, leading with his left leg. His hip turned and pitched the right leg forward in an expert motion until the foot flopped out in front of him. He wiped his hands on his overalls and said, "Can I help you?"

Rick looked up at the man who was supposed to be ninety but whose smooth caramel face was ageless. "Reverend Johnson?"

"That's right." He stood at the top of the steps like a roadblock, his hands dropped into his pockets. "Who're you?"

"I'm Rick Shannon," he said. "Sorry to bother you on a Sunday."

He shook his head. "Already done my preachin'," he said. "What can I do for you?"

"I'm a private investigator." He pulled a business card from his pocket and handed it to Willie.

Willie glanced at it and said, "All right. Wha' choo want with me?" Like it could be any number of things and he didn't want to waste anybody's time answering the wrong questions.

"I'm looking into the murder of a man named Tucker Wool-folk. I was hoping we could talk for a minute."

This seemed to change things considerably. Crippled Willie sort of bowed at the waist and said, "Yeah, you know, I heard old Mr. Tucker had got kilt." He shook his head slowly. " 'At's too bad, he was a good man." As he stood there, Willie was thinking about how things seemed to be going from bad to worse. Bad enough that Pigfoot Morgan was back and stirring things up, but worse, now there was a professional investigator looking into this mess. And didn't nobody need that.

Up until the moment Willie found himself crouched in the corner petitioning the Lord, he might've been willing to confess all he knew, which wasn't everything but was enough to get the can of worms completely open. But after coming so close to a bloody end and praying on it the way he had, the answer was re-vealed to him. Willie came to accept that it wasn't his place to mess with the Lord's plan. He wasn't so arrogant as to think he could understand it, and he didn't have to, His ways being mys-terious and all. He just had to believe that since the Almighty had brought these things to pass, it wasn't his job to undo any of it by shining light in dark places. He figured the best thing was to in-vite the man in, act accommodating, then send him on his way with the belief that he knew more than when he'd arrived.

"I be glad to help if I can." Willie took an awkward step back-ward, turning at the same time he waved at Rick to join him. "Why don't you c'mon in and we can talk, ax me whatever you think."

Rick followed Willie into the small house, wondering what had happened to the man's leg. At first he imagined something violent and romantic, like a war injury, or maybe he'd been shot during a fight at a juke joint. But it was just as likely something mundane, like an accident involving a cotton gin, or maybe it was just an old hip that needed replacing. They went to the kitchen where Willie stepped and flopped over to a cabinet and then to the sink to pour a couple of glasses of water.

Rick sat at the table and noticed the scissors and tape and the cut-up box on the counter. He looked at the window and the square of cardboard that had been put up to replace the missing glass. He imagined grandchildren, or maybe great-grandchildren coming to visit and causing trouble with their roughhousing. He said, "Kids bust that out?"

Willie swung his dead leg around and handed Rick his glass without spilling a drop. He shook his head as he sat down. "Naw, done that to myself." He pointed at the floor. "Went to clean up a mess of greens I spilt and busted the window with the mop handle. Just old and careless, I s'pose." He pushed his right leg under the table with a strong hand. "Of course this sorry old leg don't help any."

"It's none of my business," Rick said, gesturing underneath the table. "But what's wrong with it?"

Willie assumed a grave expression, leaned onto the table, and said, "Old jake got me."

Rick assumed this was yet another character from the old days and he wondered why Smitty Chisholm or Beau Tillman hadn't mentioned him. He pulled out his notebook and said, "Jake who?"

Willie slapped the table and laughed. He said, "You too young to know, I guess." He shook his head at how old he was and how much he'd seen and how so many things happened in his lifetime that younger people had never even heard of. "It was in 1930,"

Willie said. "That's when I turned seventeen and I figured that was close to being a man as I was gone get, you know? So I figure that called for a little celebration, like any man. Well, this show come through town that day, all right, with dancers and one of them string bands playing reels and what have you." He chuckled and said, "What we used to call the Ethiopian Opera. Anyway, I went down to where they was and found they was selling the jake." He held his hand as if closing around a small container. "Them little-bitty brown bottles. I can see 'em in my mind's eye." He tapped the side of his head, then pointed at Rick. "See, that's one way they got around the bone-dry laws, was calling it medicine. Sho was." Willie got a faraway look in his eyes as he thought back on things.

Rick listened to the story, so gripped by its telling that he forgot for a moment why he was there. The reverend's voice was deep and captivating and Rick figured he preached a fine sermon. As the story unfolded, Rick imagined a young Tucker Woolfolk with a fistful of cash, carnival-barking from the back of an old flatbed truck and handing bottles down to the customers, the way he'd done before being run out of Tchula back in the 1940s. But then it occurred to Rick that Woolfolk would've been too young to be selling jake to Crippled Willie in 1930.

"So I gots me a couple little bottles and stayed to watch they show," Willie said. "Now at first I was interested in the music, 'cause I was already playing some myself, and the man they had on the guitar was pretty good. I never caught his name, but he did more of a ragtime style than I was playing, but real danceable, you know." Willie took a sip of his water, then looked at the glass as he said, "But by the time I's done with that second bottle, my eyes was cut more toward this dancer what was up on the stage. Sho was." He scratched at the back of his head. "I can still see her too." He smiled. "But the Lord will forgive me for that."

Willie went on to explain that the bottles were filled with something called Jamaican Ginger Extract, a "patent medicine" they claimed was the cure for just about anything that ailed you. He said he couldn't remember why they called it jake. All he knew was that it came in a two-ounce glass bottle, it was 85 percent alcohol, and sales were brisk. "But," Willie said with a severe scowl, "they'd done cut it with something bad, you see. And it wasn't no time before they was a thousand men or more out on the streets, crippled, all across the country, and most a lot worse than me." He waved a hand in the air. "They's a buncha songs came out behind all that too. You know Ishman Bracey from down there in Byram?"

Rick remembered a display he'd seen at the blues museum. He said, "Heard the name."

"He did that song 'Jake Liquor Blues' behind that, and the Mississippi Sheiks did a 'Jake Leg Blues' too." He tapped a fingertip on the table, thinking. "Let's see, who else? Oh, the Ray Brothers did a couple jake songs, but one was instrumental, so you wouldn't know 'less he said the name. Daddy Stovepipe and Mississippi Sarah did something too. I don't recall the others right off, but they was more. Sho was. All around 1930, '31."

Rick wondered how much truth there was to this story. It might've just been a wild tale to explain his gimpy leg where the truth wasn't colorful enough. Regardless, Rick figured he could listen to this old man talk all day, no matter how much of what he said was actually true. The only problem was, he'd made arrangements to meet someone that afternooon at the *Delta Democrat Times* over in Greenville, so he guided the conversation back toward the murders, eventually asking about what had happened the night Hamp Doogan was killed.

Crippled Willie gave Rick a sideways glance and said, "Now you understand that was longer ago than you even been alive?"

They shared a smile and Rick said, "Whatever you remember. That's all I'm asking."

Willie leaned back in his chair and said, "Well now, that was a weekend of a skin ball down in Leland. All the big money come to town, and by that I'm talking 'bout Puddin' Hatchet, Baby Buddy, Hardface, Big Hand Ed, and ole fella called hisself Link. They was all there and more. Tell you truth, it was just some good times, and I admit I had some too before I found the Lord, you know. But it was just hardworking people taking some time to enjoy theyselves. Everybody had a little something jingle in they pocket and getting a drink and playing some cards with it and what have you. Now the way I remember, I'd been playin' at Ruby Edward's place. I believe Earl was over to the We-uns and You-uns Saloon and Buddy Cotton was over to the Roy Club. Anyway, around two that morning, we all ended up at Buster's Joint, just outside of town. It wasn't no plan, just how it turned out. And ole Stumpy Rivers was there picking his box. He could play good early in the night, but soon as he get too much in him, forget it. Wasn't too long after we got there, ole Stumpy took drunk bad, and I mean droopy lipped." Willie chuckled a bit before he said, "Stumpy was a fish now, and I'd say some of his ways could be contributed to his drinking. I seen him more than once just tip off the stage, still playin' till he hit the floor. Sho did." He chuckled some more before continuing, "Well, Buster finally had to get him off the stage, you know, so Buddy, Earl, and me just got on up there and made some pretty good sounds and a couple nickels too."

"Was Pigfoot Morgan there?"

Willie was beginning to wonder if Rick was ever going to stop asking questions. He screwed his face up and looked like he was thinking as hard as he could. "Now some of this is real faint to me, you know. You play all the nip joints we did, all sortsa people packed in there like sardines, it all get kinda scrambled on you, you know? But I don't recall him being there." He shook his head. "Sho don't. And if he was, he sho didn't play none with us." He frowned hard and shook his head. "Me and him I know never played together."

"What about Lamar Suggs? Was he there recording it?"

"No, sir. Not that night." Willie shook his head solemnly this time, then pointed at Rick and said, "Now that was the sort of thing he did, but he wasn't there as I recall that night out at Buster's." Rick asked about the recording session in Grafton. Willie said, "We didn't have no contract with Paramount or anybody else." When Rick mentioned the long-standing rumors about the Blind, Crippled, and Crazy sessions, Willie shot him a contentious look. "You know anybody ever heard these records?" He shook his head in answer to his own question. "I don't know where that story come from. You'd think somebody woulda heard 'em by now, don'tcha? Sho would." Willie put his hand to his mouth and feigned a yawn. " 'Scuse me," he said. "I guess I needs to try and take my rest."

Rick said he only had a couple more questions. When he asked why Willie had stopped playing, he got a vague answer about a spiritual awakening. When he pressed for details, Willie dodged it by telling a story about a wild weekend he once spent with Bukka White and Muddy Waters. Rick didn't mind the evasiveness. He was fascinated being in the presence of a guy who had played with so many of the great Delta bluesmen. When he finished his story, Willie yawned real big and apologized, said he was getting too tired to go on.

Rick apologized in turn but pressed on, asking if Willie knew why Pigfoot Morgan had killed Hamp Doogan.

"Nope. You'll have to ax him yourself. I hear he's just got out." He pushed back from the table, trying to bring things to an end.

Rick ignored it and kept going. "You didn't read about it in the paper? Hear rumors, anything?"

"Oh, I remember talk about some woman he was after bein' at the base of the thing, but I also heard talk about some money he owed behind thowin' some dice. It's always something like that though, iddn' it? Don't put much stock in rumors, like those ones about us recording together. I think people be sayin' stuff just to hear they own voices sometimes." He looked at his watch and said, "It's gettin' late now."

Rick knew he was pressing his luck, but he still had a few questions. "You have any idea where I might find Pigfoot?"

Willie rapped his knuckles once on the table and said, "Now I ain't seen the man in fitty years. Why you think I know where he's stayin'?" He waved toward the south and said, "I know he had some family over to Hollandale, but I don't know as he'd go there." He put his palms on the table to push himself up. "Now if you don't mind . . ."

"Just one last question." Rick looked at his notepad and said, "What kind of sheriff was Henry LeFleur?"

Willie stood up, glared at Rick, and said, "The white kind."

OF THE 1,700 employees at the Mississippi State Penitentiary, Crail Pitts knew about a dozen. They were guards. And tackles. And linebackers. Or at least they had been when Crail played football with them. Now they were correctional officers, criminal justice being one of the more popular majors for athletes of a certain size.

Big Jim Magee was a starting offensive tackle for Ole Miss until he got booted for violating several of the team's substance-abuse policies, primary among which was the policy about not getting caught using and selling steroids and painkillers. Big Jim opted not to disclose this on his Parchman job application, stressing instead the fact that he was six-four and weighed 275 pounds. He got the job and had been working there for eight years. So Crail figured nobody would ask what he was doing if they saw him looking in the old visitors' logs, which were otherwise not for public consumption. Big Jim had agreed to help because, as the guy who had missed the block on the Texas A&M linebacker who ended Crail's career, he felt obliged.

They were nursing bourbons in the bar at the Bayou Caddy Jubilee Casino in Greenville. Crail was wearing a pair of blue jeans with one knee cut out. Big Jim reached over and gave the swollen joint a playful poke. "Ouch! Goddammit! Stop doing that," Crail said. "It hurts like a mofo."

Big Jim chuckled. "Damn sure looks like it ought to." He did it again.

"Jesus! Would you stop?" Crail sank an elbow into Big Jim's ribs.

Big Jim laughed and said, "I can get you some OxyContins if you want."

"Oxy what?"

"Hillbilly heroin," Big Jim said. "You know, that stuff Rush likes."

"Oh yeah," Crail said. "What is 'at stuff?"

Without resorting to large words or facts, Big Jim explained, in his own way, that OxyContin was a Schedule II controlled substance containing the opioid agonist oxycodone HCL, a substance roughly as addictive as morphine. It blocked the transmission of pain messages by attaching to opioid receptors in the brain. Or, as Big Jim put it, "You take one of those, you won't mind if I hit you with a baseball bat."

That sounded good to Crail. He asked how much.

"For you? Twenty a pop. And I'm losing money at that price."

"Got any on you?"

Big Jim nodded toward the parking lot. "Out in the car."

Crail finished his drink and waved for another as he lit a cig-arette. He glanced up at the baseball game on the big screen when somebody hit a dinger. Then he turned to Big Jim and said, "What about that other thing?" Big Jim pulled a slip of paper from his shirt pocket and handed it over. Crail looked at it for a moment before he said, "This is it? One lousy visitor?"

"I think that's the one you need," Big Jim said. "All the oth-ers were from forty years ago or more, which is pretty typical. Everybody swears they're gonna come visit as long as you're in there, but that peters out pretty quick. The drive's too long or the place is too depressing or whatever. Old man didn't have a single visitor for like thirty-eight years until that guy showed up." He pointed to the slip of paper. "So, I figure that's who you wanna talk to. That's his office address down in Jackson."

"A lawyer, huh?" Crail snorted a mean laugh. "Seems a little late for . . . Ow! Fuck!"

Big Jim had poked the knee again. He sniggered, hunched over the bar, and said, "Sorry, my bad." He shook his head. "You know, I don't think I've ever seen that shade of red before."

"Jesus H.!" Crail downed his new bourbon and gingerly stood up. "Let's go get those Oxys."

As they crossed the parking lot in the warm night air, Big Jim said, "You seein' a doctor for that leg?"

"Nah." Crail shook his head. "Taking some antibiotics."

"Good idea."

Though not really. Like many people, Crail and Big Jim be-lieved one antibiotic was as good as the next. Unfortunately for Crail, such is not the case. In fact, taking the wrong antibiotic more likely kills off the "better" bacteria in one's system, clearing the way for the bad stuff to bloom and lead to far bigger troubles. In other words, while the Bactrim Cuffie had given him was ideal for treating urinary-tract infections, it had no effect on the gram-negative intracellular diplococci that is gonorrhea and which was, at this very moment, breeding like rogue Mormons in his knee.

When they reached the car, Big Jim popped open the trunk to reveal several large fishing-tackle boxes. He opened one and there, among the Hawaiian wigglers, was a cornucopia of pharmacopoeia. He counted out half a dozen OxyContins, then threw in a couple extra out of guilt. Crail looked at the handful of pills and said, "These things make you sleepy?"

Big Jim's head rocked from side to side as he said, "Ehhh, you know, a little. Depends how much you drink with 'em."

Crail nodded and said, "Huh." He wiggled a finger at the tackle boxes. "Got anything to, you know, counter that? I gotta drive to Jackson."

"Got some crank."

"Yeah." Crail nodded again. "Better give me some of that too."

19

AFTER CRIPPLED WILLIE threw him out, Rick made the short drive to Greenville and the offices of the *Delta Democrat Times*. There, with the help of a young reporter he'd contacted, Rick went through the archives and patched together a thumbnail history of a regional dynasty.

The roots of the LeFleur family tree were deep in old cotton money and, in time, the branches had reached into politics and law enforcement, making for a powerful local machine. The earliest references Rick found were to the long-dead Shelby LeFleur Sr. According to accounts in the archives, Shelby Sr. had inherited a patch of farmland from his father in 1907 and began buying up surrounding parcels until he'd built what came to be known as LeFleur Plantation, ten thousand acres of the richest soil on earth. By all accounts, black or white, Shelby Sr. was a fair employer and an honest, God-fearing man.

His son, Shelby Jr., inherited LeFleur Plantation and, employing increasingly modern farming techniques, increased per-acre yield while maintaining the good family name. He was active civically and attended church regularly, and not just for the sake of appearances. He did what he could, within the context of his time and place, to help the poor, regardless of their race.

Shelby Jr.'s son, Henry LeFleur, would eventually take control of the land but, before he did, he got elected to the newly created office of state tax collector, which turned out to be a more profitable venture, and a damn sight less work, than farming cotton. And the reason for that was none other than John Barleycorn.

Liquor remained illegal in Mississippi even after Prohibition ended in 1933. Still, most of the river counties and the Gulf Coast sold whiskey openly, at the county sheriff's pleasure. It was well known that more than a few of those sheriffs retired for life after two terms, and not because of the county's generous pension plan. Package stores on Highway 61 displayed the wares in plain sight, despite the law. The state legislature, recognizing an opportunity when it saw one, created the office of state tax collector specifically to tax the illegal hooch. In the course of his research, Rick stumbled across a *Life* magazine article from the 1950s which reported that the person holding that office—at the time a man named William Winter, who would go on to become governor—was the highest-paid public official in the United States, including the president.

After holding that job for two terms, Henry LeFleur found himself in a highly liquid position. As it happened, his sudden accumulation of cash coincided with the postwar radio boom that saw the number of commercial AM radio stations jump from nine hundred to two thousand, mostly in rural America, which previously had been underserved. So, with his father as an investment partner, Henry LeFleur obtained a license from the FCC and built a radio station. This turned out to be a savvy move on his part because it gave the LeFleurs control of the primary form of electronic media in the region, which in turn made it remarkably easy to get elected to public office.

Thus Henry LeFleur became sheriff, a position just slightly less lucrative than state tax collector. But it required far less travel and it had the added benefit of allowing him to jail or otherwise harass and intimidate anyone he felt like, including political opponents and their supporters. Henry remained in office long enough to guarantee a comfortable retirement. After leaving law enforcement, he spent time as the general manager of the radio station, where he also ran his own classical-music program, but in a few years he grew bored and sold his interest in the station to his father.

Before calling it a day, Rick tracked down archive photos of Shelby LeFleur Sr. and Jr., as well as a clean copy of the family portrait taken at Shelby Jr.'s birthday party. Then he drove home. He found Lollie waiting for him in the parking lot of the Vicksburg, leaning against her car with the box she'd pulled from Ruby's closet. Before Rick could ask about it she said, "It's a surprise."

As they headed upstairs to the apartment, Rick recounted his conversation with Crippled Willie, pointing out the inconsistencies between his version of the story and Buddy Cotton's. "I understand how they might forget the names of clubs where they were one night fifty years ago," he said as they reached the door. "But you'd think they could remember whether or not they'd gone to Wisconsin and recorded together."

"So if it's not faulty memory, what is it?"

"The good money says it's somebody hiding something." He keyed the door and opened it. Crusty Boogers was sitting just inside. And he looked pissed. His nostrils were pasted shut and each breath came with a lewd rasping sound. His expression was both indignant and accusing, like he was an opposable thumb away from calling animal welfare if somebody didn't pick his nose. And quick.

Lollie made coffee while Rick took care of Crusty, after which

Highway 61 Resurfaced

he joined her in the kitchen. He leaned against the counter wondering what was in the box she was hovering over. She asked about his research at the *Delta Democrat Times* and, as he recited the LeFleur family history, she used the new photos he had brought from the paper to follow along, matching faces to names. Shelby LeFleur Jr., as a man in his fifties, was the spitting image of his father. Henry had Shelby Jr.'s nose and mouth but, Lollie figured, the eyes must have come from the other side of the family.

Lollie tapped the photo and said, "What about this Monroe LeFleur? Where's he fit in?" Monroe didn't look much like Henry or either one of the Shelbys. Lollie figured he was more a reflection of his mother's genes and some characteristics that had skipped a generation or two.

"Monroe is Henry's son," Rick said. "From what I gathered, whatever gene had been triggering ambition in the family all those years got bred out of the line by the time he came along. Monroe's got a little family money and a big house and doesn't really have a job, unless you count the way he's selling off the plantation a few acres at a time. There was a fluff piece on him in an old issue of *Mississippi* magazine, part of a series they did on descendants of the great Delta families. He tells people he's a gentleman fah-mah and he occasionally floats a plan to build a casino on their land, but since they're not Native Americans and their land isn't on the river, the idea hardly reaches the level of pipe dream," Rick said. "Reading between the lines you get the sense that, depending on the season, Monroe spends his days hunting, fishing, drinking, gambling, cheating on his wife, and going to Ole Miss games."

"Well hotty-totty," Lollie said. "But does that get us any closer to finding who killed my grandfather, which, after all, is why I hired you."

"Seems pretty obvious that the killer is the partner of the mysterious faux Lollie. And I still think if we find out why Pigfoot

Morgan killed Hamp Doogan, we'll be able to figure out who faux Lollie and her partner are." He grabbed the coffeepot and joined Lollie at the table, topping off their cups. She was resting her arms and drumming her fingers on the top of Ruby's old box. Rick had been staring at it, waiting for an explanation. Lollie tortured him for another moment with silence and a smile, waiting for him to ask. Finally he said, "So, are you going to tell me what's in there?"

"I thought you'd never ask." She lifted the top just enough to slip her hand inside. She pulled out a folio and held it up before handing it to Rick.

"What's this?"

"A picture taken by Hamp Doogan."

Rick opened the folio and stared for a moment. "Wow." He looked at Lollie and said, "You're trying to tell me this is Ruby Finch?"

"It *was*," Lollie said. "Fifty years ago."

"She was like . . . a porn star?"

Lollie rolled her eyes. "It's not like she had a Web site. She was more like . . . a free spirit living in a repressive time and place."

Rick inspected the picture more closely. "Free spirit maybe," he said. "But I bet that ass was expensive. Was she a hooker?"

Lollie clucked her tongue disapprovingly and said, "Posing for a couple of risqué photos doesn't make you a prostitute."

"No, it puts you in the porn business," Rick said.

"Only if you sell them."

"And were these for public consumption?"

Reluctantly Lollie said, "Well, yeah, but Ruby said Doogan never sold the pictures locally, only in New Orleans and St. Louis."

"She say anything about being blackmailed? That has a tendency to lead to murder," Rick said, thinking back to what had happened in McRae.

"No, in fact, she said Doogan split the money fifty-fifty with the models. It was just an easy way to make some money during hard times."

"She was poor?"

"No, she actually came from money, but got cut off for associating with the wrong people."

"People like Hamp Doogan."

"Carpetbagger," Lollie said. "Got run out of Boston on morals charges, settled here and prospered."

"Until someone killed him."

"True, the plan wasn't without its flaws," Lollie said.

Rick opened the box and looked inside. "She just let you have all these?"

"We hit it off," Lollie said with a shrug. "She trusts me. Said I reminded her of herself when she was young."

Rick gawked at one photo after another. There were several different women. "These are wild," he said. "I mean, most nudie photos of that era were so coy you were lucky to see the side of a breast, let alone a nipple." He flipped to another one. "Oooo, nice beauty mark on this one."

Lollie looked. "Yeah, very Cindy Crawford."

Rick looked at a few more before he stopped and thumped one with his finger. "That's a late-eighties pose right there, and I'm talking *Penthouse,* not *Playboy.*"

"Such a connoisseur," Lollie said in mock admiration.

"Just something you pick up along the way."

Lollie gave a soft laugh and said, "As I was looking at these, Ruby suggested I get my boyfriend to take some pictures of me so I can prove how good I looked when I was young."

Rick glanced up from the photo and said, "You're in luck. I have a camera."

Lollie smiled. "Yeah, I was going to ask if that was a telephoto lens in your pocket."

Rick returned to the first picture. On the back he noticed something written in pencil. He traced his finger over it and said, "051251RF."

"Date and initials," Lollie said. "May 12, 1951. Ruby Finch." The box contained several dozen folios with pictures of half a dozen different women in different poses, all of whom were identified only by initials.

Rick looked at the backs of several of the photos. "Did RF give you the names for KG, LL, BW, or any of these other fine ladies?"

Lollie fanned herself with one of the folios and slipped into a southern belle accent. "No, suh. She said that wouldn't be pra-pah."

They laughed at that, then Rick said, "Reverend Johnson said one of the stories he'd heard was that Pigfoot killed Doogan over a woman. Maybe Ruby Finch or one of these others is the woman in question." He held up a photo. "I could see how a man might kill over this."

Lollie shook her head. "Ruby doesn't think Pigfoot was the killer."

"She have any evidence or alternative suspects?"

"Not that she shared. But she did offer one interesting tidbit." Lollie told Rick what Ruby had said about giving her testimony at the prosecutor's office. "The gist of what she said revolved around what she'd heard from Shorty Parker, who seemed convinced that Pigfoot wasn't the murderer."

"That's all hearsay, right?"

She shrugged. "I got my law degree from television. What do I know?"

Rick scratched the back of his neck. "She said it was recorded? Like a court reporter or on tape?"

Lollie shook her head. "I didn't think to ask. I assumed a court reporter, but I suppose it could be the other. Either way, you'd have to assume it was lost in the same fire as all the other material."

Rick nodded. "Did she say if her testimony was used at trial?"

"Nope, she was living in New York by the time of the trial, so she had no way to know. But she implied that it seemed unlikely since the prosecutor and the defense were essentially on the same side when it came to black murder defendants."

"Did you ask if she had any ideas about who might've killed your grandfather or Suggs?"

"I did, but she didn't. How about the reverend?"

"Nope, but I got the feeling he wasn't telling the whole truth and nothing but the truth."

"Which brings us back to somebody hiding something," Lollie said in frustration.

"Yeah, and for fifty years."

They sat there for a while, idly flipping through the box of photos and weighing the status of the investigation. Lollie slumped glumly in her chair as she recited the litany of dead ends and contradictions and unanswered questions they'd piled up. It was the first time Rick had seen her gloomy side. Her unflagging enthusiasm for the process and her air of invincibility was giving way to a growing sense of discouragement. She shook her head slowly, her eyes fixed on nothing. "So in other words, we don't know any more now than when we started."

"Sure we do," Rick said, trying to cheer her up. "We just don't know what it means. There's a difference."

She looked at him with the expression of a woman who wasn't about to join the optimists' club. "This isn't funny," she said. "Tucker Woolfolk was my grandfather. He was just an old man. He wasn't hurting anybody. Whatever he might've done fifty years ago . . ." Her voice trailed off and it looked like she was on the verge of tears, but she blinked them back and said, "I want to find out who killed him, so stop making jokes."

"I'm not joking," Rick said. "Look, I know it seems like we're sort of lost in the woods, but we're making progress. That's how this works. It's like doing a jigsaw puzzle where you first have to go out and find the pieces; they don't just come in a box for your convenience. After you find them, you still have to put them together."

"We don't even know what the picture is supposed to look like."

"Yeah, but finding the pieces *is* progress."

"All right, fine." Lollie folded her arms across the top of the box and laid her head down with a long sigh. "So what do we do next?"

"Well, I think Ruby Finch had the best idea." Rick stood up and said, "I'll go get my camera."

Lollie didn't even raise her head to reply. "Very funny."

"No, seriously." Rick stepped out of the kitchen for a moment and returned with his camera and his Eric Idle impersonation, determined to put a smile back on her face. "Interested in a little pho-tog-raphy, nudge, nudge, wink, wink? I can tell you're a goer!" He began to circle the kitchen table, snapping one picture after another. *Flash!* "Lovely, lovely, but we need a bit of the peachy flesh."

"Cut it out," Lollie said without much feeling.

"Off with the shirt then," he said. "Let's see those headlights, eh?" *Flash!*

"I'm serious." Though it sounded like she was smiling.

"Musn't keep those melons in the package, eh?" *Flash!*

"You're insane."

"Right! C'mon, dear, get yer ya-yas out!"

Hard as she tried, Lollie couldn't resist. He was a lunatic. She started laughing and she lifted her head just as Rick released the shutter. *Flash!* Her eyes twinkling and her smile wide. She blinked at the yellow spots in her field of vision and said, "If you don't put the camera down, I'm going to punch you in the head again."

"Ahh, the magic words." Rick put the camera on the counter and looked at her. After a moment he said, "Just trying to cheer you up. You okay?"

She shrugged. "Tired and frustrated. What time is it?" Lollie glanced at the clock on the wall. It was midnight. "Jeez," she said. "I should be getting home." But she didn't make a move to leave.

"You're welcome to stay."

Lollie looked at him, considering the offer from all the angles. He'd said it without the slightest innuendo, which scored him points. She liked him and his sense of humor and the way he kissed. And she appreciated the way he'd tried to buoy her spirits. She said, "You know—"

Rick held up a hand to cut her off, figuring the answer was no and wanting to save her the trouble of explaining. "Or, if you'd rather not . . ." He picked up the box and said, "I'll walk you down to your car."

She said, "No, I'd like to stay."

— — — — — — — — —

LOLLIE WAS ASLEEP as soon as her head hit the pillow. Rick wasn't tired, so he grabbed his cigar box, loaded his pipe, and surfed the Net. The first thing he found was a sticky cat booger on the space bar of the keyboard. After cleaning it off, Rick found a Web site run by a blues fan in Wisconsin. The site had a page featuring the history of Paramount Records. Rick sent the guy an e-mail asking if he could confirm whether or not Cotton, Jefferson, or Tate had ever recorded for the label. To Rick's surprise the guy responded ten minutes later. He said he had a complete discography of every side the label had released as well as a list of recording sessions that had never been pressed onto vinyl. Cotton, Jefferson, and Tate weren't on either list. But he said the original logs showed that the three men had been booked into the studio in 1953 and that their names had been crossed out without any explanation in the margins.

Rick thought it was unlikely that the session logs and the discography would both be wrong, though it was possible they'd recorded under false names, especially if one or more of the men were under contract to other labels at the time. But why had they been listed to record and then scratched out? And why did Blind Buddy Cotton say they had recorded there? It all came back to someone with something to hide. But who and what?

Rick surfed for a little longer before logging off. He went to the kitchen, ate the last two tamales, then brushed his teeth and headed for bed. Lollie was curled up in the fetal position, clutching her pillow. Rick remembered an expert from a talk show who said people who slept this way were shy and sensitive but were likely to exhibit a tough exterior. As he thrashed around to get comfortable, she mumbled something he couldn't understand. Then he drifted off.

20

RICK WOKE UP the next morning with Lollie's arm draped over him. She snuggled closer and said, "Sorry I fell asleep so fast last night. Was the sex hot?"

"Off the scale."

"Thanks for not waking me."

Rick smiled. "I put the 'gentle' back in 'gentleman.' " A moment later he said, "And by the way, you didn't snore."

"Told you."

"Not so smug. Last time was a different story. Maybe you only do it after three martinis."

"Maybe," she said. "We can experiment later." She threw back the covers. "Right now we've got a murder to solve."

"Two, actually."

"Three if you count Hamp Doogan."

They got up, showered, grabbed Crusty, then hit the road. On the way to Shipley's, Rick recounted what the Paramount Records expert had said in his e-mail. "Which means Reverend Johnson and Buddy Cotton are telling different stories," he said.

Lollie made a note of that and slipped it into the case file. "Though it could just as easily mean that one or both of them are senile or might just be screwing with us."

"Yeah," Rick said, "take your pick on that one. But it also means that if the three of them ever did record together, it was either at a local club or at Henry LeFleur's radio station. So if the tapes exist, maybe he's got them or knows where they are."

"Which would make him a potential target for whoever killed my grandfather."

Rick looked at her, surprised. "That's true, hadn't thought of that. You want to use him for bait? Just stake him out and wait to see if the killer shows up?"

"Nah, I suppose we ought to be neighborly and give him a heads-up on that," Lollie said. "Might buy us some goodwill with the guy."

"Goodwill? You think he won't just answer our questions?"

Lollie gazed at him as she would a child in one of her classes. "Such an innocent," she said. "Look, I don't think it's too much of a stereotype to say that lawmen of his time and place weren't always the most savory of characters, right? Power corrupting and all that. We know he took kickbacks on illegal liquor sales, so it's not unreasonable to assume he might have some other skeletons in his little sheriff's closet. And if that's true, he might not take kindly to a lot of questions that, however inadvertently, might poke into some of those areas, whatever they might be. All I'm saying is that we should talk about how we're going to approach him, don't you think?"

Rick didn't respond. Somewhere around "illegal liquor sales" his eyes had narrowed to slits as he noodled a thought.

"Hey," Lollie said. "Light's green." The car behind them honked, snapping Rick back to attention. After a moment he said, "Sometimes I'm astounded by how slow I am."

She gave him a patronizing pat on the arm. "You're not slow, Ricky, you just learn . . . *differently* from others, that's all." She pointed above his head and said, "So, what's the hundred-watt bulb you got going on?"

"A stroke of genius," Rick said.

"Let me be the judge of that."

"I'm serious," he said. "You can feel the muscles in the neck of this idea, it's so good." He dropped into his radio voice. "This Saturday night, an historical blues event." He did a drumroll on the steering wheel, causing Crusty to look up. "It's been fifty years since they played together, but now, for one night, they're back. The Blind, Crippled, and Crazy reunion concert," Rick said. "Live, on WVBR-FM."

The merit of the idea registered immediately on Lollie's face. "That *is* good," she said just as Crusty hopped into her lap. "Except, didn't you tell me Crippled Willie gave up playing the devil's music?"

"Yeah, but—"

"And we don't even know where to find Crazy Earl."

"Not yet, but—"

"And even if we got them together to play, how does any of that help us catch the killer?"

Rick's mouth curved into a sly smile. He held a finger in the air and said, "We announce that we've found the long-lost tapes and that we're going to broadcast them as part of the reunion show." He looked at Lollie, waiting for her to figure out the ending.

She pointed at him. "And the killer will come to get them. That's not bad," she said. "Of course it puts our lives in grave danger, but otherwise . . ."

Rick delivered a look of mock irritation. "See now, that's the problem with people these days, always looking for no-muss, no-fuss solutions. One minute you're complaining about not making any progress, the next you're whining about your life being in grave danger. There's just no keepin' you happy." Rick pulled into the Shipley's parking lot. "Whaddya want?"

"Chocolate glazed will keep me happy," she said. "And a large coffee."

After securing what had become their traditional breakfast, they hit the road north. Crusty was in Lollie's lap, licking sugar from her fingers, when Rick gestured at the case file. "Look in there and find Buddy's and Willie's phone numbers." He handed her his cell phone. "We need to call and invite them to do the reunion show."

Lollie called, but neither man answered. She left a message and asked them to call back. She looked at the note with Henry LeFleur's address and said, "Where the hell is Moorhead?"

Rick slipped into his best Rhett Butler accent and said, "Why, Scarlett, it's where the Southern crosses the Dog."

She looked at him, batting her eyelashes. "Oh, tell me, Rhett," she said. "Do tell me."

"Blues legend," he said plainly. "You know who W. C. Handy was?" Lollie shook her head. "Started as a musician in minstrel shows at the turn of the century. Ended up being called the father of the blues."

"I thought that was Robert Johnson."

"Different kind of father," Rick said. "Handy came first. He was at a train station up in Tutwiler, Mississippi, in 1903, and there was a man sitting there playing his guitar, using a knife to slide up and down the neck while singing about where the Southern crossed the Dog. Handy said it was the weirdest music he'd ever heard, but it stuck with him and he started incorporating the blue notes he'd heard into the songs he wrote and published. One of which he called 'Yellow Dog Blues.' "

"That's fascinating," Lollie said. "All that and you still haven't answered the question."

"I'm not surprised," Rick said. "I was just hoping I could remember that story from that plaque I read at the blues museum. What was the question? Oh, railroad lines. The Southern was an east-west line and the Yazoo and Mississippi Valley line, which was called the Dawg, ran north-south and crossed in Moorhead. That's what the guy in Tutwiler was singing about a hundred years ago." Lollie kept staring at him until he said, "It's between Greenwood and Greenville on Highway 82."

"See? How hard was that?"

TWO HOURS AND a sugar rush later, Rick, Lollie, and Crusty turned onto the twenty-acre LeFleur estate. At the end of the long driveway was a vaguely gaudy neoclassical revival that suggested the family had more money than taste. Rick parked in the shade and left Crusty sleeping on the dashboard.

A black woman of indeterminate age and disposition, wearing a crisp maid's uniform, answered the door. Rick gave her a nod and said, "Hi, we're here to—"

The woman held up a hand to interrupt. "It's right in here." She stepped back inside and picked up a large box filled with clothes that she tried to hand to Rick. "Miss LeFleur said she's sorry, but they changed her plane in Memphis to earlier or she'd've brought these."

Rick took the box and said, "I think there's a misunderstanding. We're here—"

"You ain't the Junior League people?"

"No, we're here to see Mr. LeFleur."

"Oh." She took the box back. "They supposed to come pick these up today."

"Is Mr. LeFleur here?"

"He's in the garden." The woman saw no point in letting them through the house, tracking in all that dirt, since they were just going right back outside, so she leaned out the door a bit and pointed. "Go on around that way," she said. "You'll see him."

It was a sunny, blue day and hot enough to bust open peas on the vine. And there, stooped in the middle of a large vegetable garden, was seventy-five-year-old Henry LeFleur pinching the suckers from his tomato plants. He had on a pair of brown gardening gloves, baggy trousers, a sleeveless shirt, and a baseball cap with the National Cotton Council logo on it. An old blue tick hound sat at the end of a row contentedly licking himself.

Henry and the dog noticed the two strangers at the same time. The dog didn't seem to mind, just returned to what he was doing. Henry, on the other hand, eyed them contentiously but didn't speak. After a moment he turned to the house and hollered, "Annie Mae!"

The woman in the maid's uniform materialized at the back door with aggravation in her voice. "Yassuh?"

He gestured at Rick and Lollie. "Who's this?"

"Didn't say. Come to see you." She shook her head just a bit, then turned to disappear into the shadows.

Rick waved as they approached, but Henry didn't see it. He was still looking at the back door, shaking his own head. "Twenty years," he said to himself, "and still don't know how to bring a guest through the house." He stood his hoe up on end and turned suspicious eyes on his visitors. "Who're you?" It seemed as much a threat as it did a question.

"Mr. LeFleur, my name's Rick Shannon. This is Lollie Woolfolk."

Henry tipped the hoe in her direction. "Sunflower County Woolfolk?"

"That's right," she said.

"So you're kin to Robert Tucker."

"Yes, sir. He was my grandfather."

Henry doffed his cap and gave a courteous nod. "I hear he passed on just recent. I's sorry to hear that." Lollie nodded back and thanked him. "We had some dealings long time ago," Henry said. "He was a good man, toted his own skillet."

"Yes, sir, thank you," she said. "Actually, he's one of the reasons we came to see you."

"Issat right?" He cocked his head up at the sun. They were sweating like racehorses as the humidity weighed down on them like extra gravity. Henry stepped out of the tomatoes while pointing toward the back patio. "Let's talk in the shade, why don't we?" He hollered, "Annie Mae! Bring us some tea!" The dog got to his feet and trotted toward his master. Henry gave him a rub on the head when he caught up.

"I work at WVBR-FM in Vicksburg," Rick said. "I understand you used to be in radio."

" 'At's right, owned a station for a while with my daddy. Even did my own show, playing the great symphonies. Trying to provide a little culture, you know?" Henry paused when they reached the patio. He worked the gloves off and gestured at the patio furniture. "Here, make yourself at home," he said. They sat at a large wrought-iron, glass-topped table in the shade of a pair of canvas umbrellas. Henry took off his cap and wiped his liver-spotted head with a handkerchief. "Wha' cha wanna see me about?" He leaned forward and made a funny face. "You wanna hire me as a disc jockey?" He winked at Lollie, then rubbed his dog's head as if to bring him in on the joke.

"Well, no, sir," Lollie said with a polite chuckle. "We're doing research for a radio show we're producing. And we started looking into an old rumor about a recording session my grandfather might have been involved with when he worked at your radio station."

Annie Mae came out with a pitcher and three glasses already filled with ice and sweet tea. She set them on the table and said, " 'Sat all, Mistah LeFleur?"

"Yeah, thank you, Annie Mae." Henry pushed a glass toward Lollie and said, "I think I know what you're talkin' about and I'm afraid you gone off on a wild-goose chase." He took a long drink of his tea and then put the cold glass against his leathery forehead. "You talkin' 'bout them three old jigs, uhhh . . ." He snapped his fingers once or twice, causing the dog to look up. ". . . Blind what's-his-name and them boys, right?"

Rick helped him with the other names and told him the story he'd heard from Smitty Chisholm as well as what he'd learned from the blues fan with the Paramount Records Web site. "Since they didn't record in Wisconsin," Rick said, "we figured that narrowed it down to a juke joint or your radio station, so we came to see you hoping you might be able to put us on the right track."

This brought a satisfied smile to Henry's face. "Well, I don't know 'bout that," he said. "What in particular you lookin' to find out? I mean, you ain't exactly the first folks come along lookin' to find them tapes, which, I'm here to tell you, is just old fairy tale."

"You're probably right," Rick said. "But you remember Lamar Suggs?"

"Yeah, and I heard he'd passed on too, just recent." He looked up to the sky and said, "What's that old sayin'? 'People dyin' today ain't *never* died before.' " Henry shook his head, half sad. "Gettin' on that time in my life when eva-body I know's got the dwindles."

"Actually, Mr. Suggs didn't dwindle so much as he was murdered," Rick said. "Found him with a fork stuck in his back." He gestured at Lollie. "Mr. Woolfolk was murdered too."

Henry turned on Rick, firm and irritated. "Now, son, don't you think I know that? I was a sheriff around here for a long time and I still got feelers out, so I know what goes on. They was killed by crackheads, what I heard. I was just trying to show some respect for Miss Woolfolk's feelings. Something you might wanna think about."

"Of course. I apologize," Rick said, turning to Lollie to appease Mr. LeFleur's apparent old-world sensibility. "The reason I bring up Mr. Suggs is that I went to talk to him about the tapes and happened to be the one who found him after he'd been attacked. Before he died he said something about Blind, Crippled, and Crazy that makes us think whoever killed him and Mr. Woolfolk believes the tapes are more than a fairy tale."

Henry took a deep, philosophical breath and let it out before saying, "You know, I recall a man down in Humphreys County one time, killed his mother-in-law 'cause he believed she was a large raccoon up in his attic. Of course, believing that didn't make it so." He tilted his head to one side and said, "Trust me, they ain't no tapes." He looked at Rick to see if he wanted to argue.

Lollie sensed the start of a pissing contest, so she said, "That's a real good point, Mr. LeFleur. And you're probably right, but we figure as long as we're going to do this show, it'd be nice if we could settle the issue once and for all, even if we prove they never existed. Now—"

Rick held up a hand to interrupt. He said, "The point is that it doesn't matter if the tapes are real or not, Mr. LeFleur, as long as someone believes they are. Mr. Suggs and Mr. Woolfolk are just as dead, and if whoever killed them connects the dots to you owning the radio station, they might come calling. I thought you should know that, that's all."

Henry responded with a nod and a smirk. He leaned sideways in his chair and reached into his pocket. He said, "Well, if they manage to get past ole Annie Mae, and that .22 she keeps in her apron . . ." Henry smiled as he laid a chrome .38 on the tabletop. "I'm more'n happy to see 'em."

"Oh, I doubt it'll come to that," Lollie said, adding a nervous laugh. She leaned over and scratched the dog behind the ears as she said, "The way we understand it, Cotton, Jefferson, and Tate were playing at a juke joint the same night a man named Pigfoot Morgan was arrested for killing a man."

"That's right," Henry said. "Piece of trash name of Hamp Doogan."

"What can you tell us about that night?"

21

HENRY LAUGHED AND said, "I can tell you one thing for certain, it was a long damn time ago." He laughed again and gestured at the pitcher of tea. "Help yourself to more, if you'd like." He sat back, as if to think about it for a minute, before he gave a nod to the west and said, "Now I can't say what all was going on over in Leland that night other'n they was having one of them skin balls like they did. I was north of town patrolling on old Highway 61 when I come across these three jigs standing over a man's body in the middle of the road. Now that's not good any time of day or night, so I stopped to see what was what, and sure enough, the man was dead. Shot. Several times, as I recall, like somebody's mad, real hot blooded, you know how they get."

Henry glanced at the underside of the umbrella and said, "I believe it was right about then Lamar Suggs come along, headin' to or comin' back from Memphis, one. I forget which way he was going. But he stopped to see if I needed any help, which I didn't, so he went on about his business. Now, since none of them jigs had a gun on 'em and they weren't trying to get away, I figure it weren't none of them who'd done the killin'. So I asked about the car I'd seen fleeing north. Long story short, they got around to admittin' it was Pigfoot Morgan had killed Doogan."

"They say why?"

Henry shook his head. "Just said he'd done it and run off when he seen me coming, left them just standing there, which didn't seem to please them a whole lot, as you can understand. Anyway, we got us arrest warrant out and finally caught him up near Friar's Point, trying to get across the river."

"Did he confess?"

"Didn't have to," Henry said. "Sumbitch had the murder weapon on him. That pretty much cinched his sack as far as the jury was concerned." Rick chuckled at that, and Henry didn't seem to appreciate it. He said, "What's so funny?"

"Nothing," Rick said, waving it off. "Something made me think of Blind Boy Grunt all the sudden."

"He one of them blues players?"

"Yeah," Rick lied. "One of them."

Blind Boy Grunt was actually the pseudonym Bob Dylan used when he recorded for the Broadside label in the early 1960s. One of the songs he cut under that name was "The Death of Emmett Till," a folky indictment of the all-white Mississippi jury that refused, in 1955, to convict the men who had proudly admitted to the brutal murder of a fourteen-year-old black boy who, in their estimation, had failed to show the proper respect for their cherished way of life. So Henry LeFleur's solemn claim that a jury in that same time and place had been persuaded of a black man's guilt rang somewhat hollow. When it dawned on Rick that it was entirely possible Henry LeFleur knew every last man on that panel, he said, "Of course, juries back then were fairly predictable, especially when a black man was on trial for killing a white one."

Henry squinted suspiciously. He pointed at Rick and said, "Where're you from, son?"

"Jackson."

"Wyoming?"

"Mississippi."

"Huh." Henry shook his head. "Sure don't sound like it."

Rick wasn't sure if he was talking about what Rick was saying or how he was saying it. "I guess I lost my accent, all these years in radio."

"I guess." Henry shrugged, but he'd made his point. "Anyway, what're you gettin' at, talkin' about juries?"

"Not gettin' at anything," Rick said. He was thinking about Ruby Finch's comment that Pigfoot was probably a scapegoat. "I'm just talking about the way things used to be."

"Yeah, well, thangs change," Henry said as he picked up his pistol. He admired it in a way that he hoped was intimidating before he slipped it back in his pocket. "And not always for the bettah."

They sat there for a moment without speaking. Henry's comment reminded Rick of something a Mississippi senator had said not that long ago, but he couldn't see any reason to bring that up. The dog scratched under his chin and the cubes in Lollie's glass melted and tumbled down on themselves. She was afraid that if she didn't say something to guide the conversation, it would lapse into a debate on race relations that wouldn't solve a thing. So she said, "I take it Cotton, Jefferson, and Tate were the main witnesses?"

"Woulda been, they'd shown up," Henry said, again with a slight smirk. "After we took their sworn statements, we sent 'em on. Told 'em they was witnesses and had to be available for the trial, but they skedaddled like they thought their friend wouldn't be convicted if they weren't there." He shook his head at their foolishness. "Prosecutor read their statements into the record and that satisfied the jury. They weren't out for ten minutes 'fore they come back with a guilty." Henry slapped the table and pointed a finger at Lollie. "You know, I bet that's where that story about them tapes comes from. Those three jigs weren't nowhere to be found till long after that trial was over, and I bet you that was the story one of 'em made up, said they was off making a record up in Wisconsin. After that, story just took on a life of its own."

Lollie poured some more tea and recounted her conversation with Ruby Finch. She asked Henry if he remembered whether the defense entered her testimony at the trial.

"Testimony about what she heard from some jig locked up in my jail?" Henry shook his head. "Tell you the truth, her name don't ring a bell. Anyway, I was only there on the days I had to testify. But it would appear that if it *was* read into the record, it didn't help Mr. Morgan none."

By now LeFleur had worked his way under all three layers of Rick's skin with all his "jigs" and his smug inferences about how a good, honest jury of Pigfoot Morgan's peers had found him guilty. On top of that, there was something about Henry's story that didn't quite pass the sniff test. Rick said, "So when you came across the body in the road and all that, there must've been another car there."

Henry didn't appreciate Rick's suggestion that he hadn't told the whole story, and he didn't do much to hide his irritation. He said, "If you'd been liss'nin', you'da heard me say there was a car on the horizon, heading for Memphis fast as it could go."

Rick figured he was starting to get under Henry's skin too, and he was enjoying it. "No," he said, "I mean I don't understand what Hamp Doogan was doing out in the middle of nowhere. Did his car break down? And if it did, I'm trying to imagine the series of events where these four guys stop to help, yet one of them ends up killing him."

Henry didn't like the tone of Rick's voice or his questions, but he didn't want to say anything because of how it might look. He snorted a chuckle and then, for emphasis, spoke slowly. "Like . . . I . . . said, this was a long time ago. I don't recall if there was another damn car. Maybe there was farther up the road and he was walking away from it. Maybe Hamp Doogan was in the car with them to start with and they got in an argument and that led to it. I can't remember every last little detail." He waved a hand at a fly circling his tea. " 'Sides, don't much matter, far as I can see."

"But wouldn't it have been unusual for a white man to be riding in the car with four black men?"

"Well, like . . . I . . . said, that Doogan was trash, and a Yankee to boot, involved in bringing marijuana and cocaine into the county." He sneered and shook his head. "Man willin' to do that don't care who he rides with, now does he?" He shooed the fly away again and drank his tea.

Lollie tapped her fingernails on the glass-topped table and said, "Somebody told us Doogan was a photographer."

The comment seemed to take Henry by surprise. He froze for a moment as he went to set his glass on the table, then he put it down and said, "Yeah, that's right, I'd forgot about that. Had a studio that was his front. Fact, we executed a search on it once but didn't find what we was lookin' for, and we tore that place up, I'm tellin' you. Figure he got tipped off beforehand, you know, probably somebody in the judge's office what was buyin' from him. That kinda thing happened."

Rick and Lollie exchanged a glance, surprised that Henry either didn't know about Doogan's sideline as a pornographer or that he didn't mention it.

"Now that I think on it," Henry said, "lotta folks said we might shoulda let that Morgan boy off for doing the community a service killin' ole Hamp, but the judge didn't have any wiggle room on that, so ..." He gave a shrug. "Off he went."

"And since you still got your feelers out," Rick said, "I guess you know Pigfoot Morgan got out of Parchman two days before Mr. Woolfolk was killed."

This was news to Henry LeFleur, and it showed in his eyes. Something that looked a lot like fear flashed across his face and he said, "No. I can't say as I was aware of that."

— — — — — — — — —

TURNING ONTO HIGHWAY 82, Rick adjusted his rearview mirror and said, "Ladies and gentlemen, that concludes our little journey back to the nineteen-fifties."

Lollie held up a stiff index finger and shook it. "I swear, I thought if he said 'jig' one more time, I was gonna grab his pistol and shoot him." They rode in silence for a moment before she gestured behind them with a hitchhiker's thumb and said, "You know, it's people like him that made me want to be a teacher in the first place."

"It wasn't because you just wanted your summers free?"

She shook her head. "I was in fifth grade. We were at recess, out on the playground, and this white kid named Kenny pushed this little black girl to the ground and kicked her, called her a 'no-good nigger.' Then he just walked away, like he was entitled to do that sort of thing. To this day, I've never been so mad at anything as I was at that moment. But I didn't know what to do, so I just stood there and cried. When our teacher, Mrs. Powers, heard about it, she canceled our normal classes, saying there was no point in teaching anything else until we learned one thing, that the only reason people hate that way is because they were taught that way. She got Kenny and Wanda—that was the little girl's name—Mrs. Powers had them sit next to each other and talk for an hour in front of the class. At first Kenny tried to act all tough, but Wanda was so sweet and sincere he caved after about ten minutes. Finally, he said he was sorry. Wanda forgave him, and after that, they were best buddies." Lollie smiled in admiration as she said, "In one hour, Mrs. Powers polished up what someone else had spent ten years tarnishing. That's when I knew I wanted to teach."

"That's a tall order with so many Kennys and Henry LeFleurs out there."

"I tell you what," Lollie said. "The good people in this state outnumber the bad, always have. Unfortunately, some of the bad folks ran things for too long. But things're changing."

"Moves too slow for my taste," Rick said.

"Mine too," Lollie said. "But we're working against powerful stuff. There are old things in place here, things that are strong and resist change. And I swear, every time they cut our budget I'm tempted to think they've figured out the connection between lack of education and our ability to make those changes." She looked out the window at a vast cotton field rolling by at sixty miles an hour. "But you gotta try, you know? Just keep chipping away."

"Yeah," Rick said with a nod. "Sort of like what we're doing. Feels like we're pickin' at a scab and we're starting to draw a little blood."

"You think so?"

"Did you see the look in LeFleur's eyes when I told him about Pigfoot?" Rick shook his head. "That .38 didn't seem to bring him as much comfort as it did when he thought he was dealing with crackheads."

Lollie said, "I might be scared too if somebody I'd sent to prison for fifty years had just gotten out."

Rick shook his head. "Sounds to me like Cotton, Jefferson, and Tate sent him to prison. Which would explain why *they* might be scared. But neither Buddy nor Willie seemed to care that he was out. And since both of them failed to mention their role in the trial—in fact, didn't just fail to mention it, they flat out denied knowing anything about it—you gotta wonder who all's lying and why."

"Maybe they felt bad about sending a friend to jail, didn't want to talk about it."

"I don't think so," Rick said. "They both acted like they hardly knew the guy. Besides, I can't think of any reason to deny testifying against a murderer, even if you know him. I mean, I can see why you wouldn't brag on it, but why deny it?"

"LeFleur got any reason to lie about that?"

"None that we know of," Rick said.

"And there was nothing in the *Delta Democrat Times* about the trial?"

"Three column inches about the murder, the conviction, and the sentence. Didn't mention witnesses, testimony, or evidence."

"So maybe Ruby Finch is right."

Rick thought about that for a moment. "Okay, but if Pigfoot didn't kill Doogan, who did? And why would Cotton, Jefferson, and Tate say he had?"

"Maybe they had a history we don't know about."

"You mean maybe Pigfoot did something to all three of them that made them mad enough to send him to prison for life for something he didn't do?" Rick shook his head. "You know, if just one of them had done that, I might buy it, but not all three. I mean, what could he do? Sleep with all their women? I think they'd just go shoot him for that, they wouldn't wait around for an opportunity to frame him."

"Okay, maybe they were coerced."

Rick gave that some thought. "It's starting to look that way, isn't it?" he said. "And if that's the case, then we get a whole new set of questions, like coerced by whom? And did someone just need a scapegoat and Pigfoot was in the wrong place at the wrong time or did someone specifically want to frame him? And if so, why?"

"All of which brings us back to the questions of who really killed Doogan and why and how it connects to whoever killed my grandfather."

Rick looked at her with a fractured smile and said, "Ain't this some fun?"

They kept batting ideas around as they drove back to Vicksburg. They agreed that Henry LeFleur had raised more questions than he'd answered. They didn't believe he could be involved from the arrest to the trial and not know what Doogan was doing out on Highway 61 in the middle of the night, and where his car was, especially if he could remember something as trivial as Lamar Suggs driving by. Lollie also thought it was odd that LeFleur acted so certain the tapes didn't exist. "I mean, that's like proving a negative, isn't it? The only thing he could know for sure is whether he saw it happen or not," she said. "If he didn't witness them recording together, he still doesn't know for a fact that they didn't record somewhere else. So why act so cocksure that he knows what he's talking about?"

"He did seem to protest too much, didn't he?"

She threw up her hands in frustration. "Everybody we talk to seems to be hiding something."

"Except that Ruby Finch. Bless her heart, she didn't hide a thing."

Lollie smiled and turned on the radio, tired of the endless theorizing. She scanned the dial until she came across a local call-in show from a station out of Yazoo City. The man on the phone sounded incredulous when he said, *"What'd they fire him for?"*

The host said, *"Well, he mailed a possum's head to some woman."*

"What for?" Like there might be a good reason.

"He was trying to intimidate her over some unionizing activities she was involved with over in their district."

"And they fired him for that? Well, that's just crazy," the caller said. *"Coach Parks was ten and one last season. Had most of his starting offense coming back. They was a lock for conference. Coulda gone to state."*

The host tried to explain to the distraught football fan how the mailing of a decapitated marsupial head might be considered inappropriate behavior, even in Mississippi. The fan tried a desperate First Amendment argument that the host deflected before going to a commercial break. Lollie laughed as she turned down the volume. Then she said, "What made you go into radio?"

Rick got a serious look on his face and said, "Well, I wanted to make the world a better place by using mass communication to bring about social justice and equality." After a pause, he added, "Plus you get free T-shirts and albums, and girls."

"So it was the whole Dire Straits thing," she said. "Money for nothing, chicks for free."

"You bet, except I started long before Dire Straits showed up." He thought about her question for a moment before he said, "You know, I can tell you *how* I ended up in radio, but I'm not sure I know *why*. I mean, on the one hand I've never had the disposition to thrive in what is commonly referred to as a 'regular' job. Radio's always been irregular enough to accommodate people like me. So that's one thing, but the music's what really drew me in. I've loved music since I can remember. Can't play an instrument, but I've got an ear for records. There's a cliché that deejays are just frustrated musicians. Maybe that's true. I don't know." He shrugged. "But I know, as a kid, every dime I got my hands on ended up in a jukebox or buying records. And I listened to

Highway 61 Resurfaced

radio all the time, knew the names of every band and every song and every B side." He smiled nostalgically. "At night, after I got sent to bed, I had a little crystal radio with an earpiece and I'd listen to WLS in Chicago. I thought that was the coolest thing, to hear that big-city station in my little room in Jackson. By the time I was in junior high, I was the de facto class deejay. If somebody had a party, I was the guy with the records. And there was something about that that I really liked. Still, it never occurred to me that I might be allowed to do it for a living. But I stumbled into an opportunity when I was in high school and I've been living hand to mouth ever since."

"You have a favorite song from when you were a kid?"

"Whole bunch of 'em," Rick said. 'In the Year 2525,' by Zager and Evans. 'Red Rubber Ball' by Cyrkle—"

"I love that song!"

"Bet you don't know who wrote it."

"I bet you're right."

"Paul Simon and Bruce Woodley of the Seekers."

"Really, Paul Simon?"

"Yep. But my all-time favorite from that era is 'Walk Away Renee' by The Left Banke. That was a perfect pop song." Rick pointed at the radio dial and said, "Now radio's mostly talk with a little country and lots of rap." He shook his head. "Just ain't what it used to be."

"Yeah, well, things change."

"And not always for the bettah."

BETWEEN THE OXYCONTIN and the methamphetamine, Crail got to feeling like he should just drive right through Jackson and get on down to New Orleans to try out for the Saints. But then he got to thinking about Cuffie and his mission, so he pulled off the road at Northside Drive like he was supposed to and went looking for the address Big Jim had supplied. Crail pulled into an Exxon station to gas up and get directions. When he got out of his car, he noticed a barbecue rig smoking on the corner of the service station's lot. Crail bought a rack of the baby backs, along with a six-pack, and got directions to the place that turned out to be just around the corner, on McWillie Drive.

The law offices of Jeremy Lynch, Esquire, were located in a one-story cinder-block affair that looked to have been built in the sixties. The street was lined with similar buildings that collectively gave the impression of being a failed prototype for the modern office park. It was around ten when Crail pulled into the dark, empty parking lot. He backed into a space and cased the building to the extent that he could while sitting there eating ribs and baked beans.

Twenty minutes later, he tossed the final bone out his window, finished his second beer, burped, then popped another can. All things considered, he felt pretty good. He opened the glove compartment to look for the antibiotics Cuffie had given him, but it was too dark, so he turned on the car's interior light. That's when he noticed that the skin on the back of his hand had turned somewhat yellow and scaly. Inspecting both arms, Crail noticed a couple of eruptions and some peeling and, for a moment, wondered what that was all about.

It would turn out that it was all about something called sulfamethoxazole, one of the ingredients of the Bactrim he'd been taking at twice the prescribed dosage. Sulfamethoxazole can lead to a variety of interesting side effects, including progressive disintegration of the outer layer of the skin, liver damage, and weeping eruptions around the mouth, eyes, and anus.

Rooting through the glove compartment, Crail figured that whatever had caused the skin problems would probably respond to the antibiotics if he just took enough of them. So when he found the bottle, he took two more and finished his beer.

Crail grabbed a flashlight from the backseat and took a look around the outside of the building. He didn't see anything that looked like a security system, so he just busted out a window and climbed in. Cuffie had told him to look for any kind of papers with Pigfoot Morgan's name on them. She also said to look for the tapes in case this lawyer had already found them somehow. There was nothing on the desk, so he looked in the drawers. That's where he found a glass and a fresh bottle of Crown Royal and he got to thinking about how good that would taste on top of those ribs. So he filled himself a glass and began rooting through the filing cabinets.

It didn't take him long to find several files with Clarence "Pigfoot" Morgan's name on the tabs. One contained a copy of a letter Lynch had sent to Pigfoot at Parchman. It said he had read something about Pigfoot's case and was interested in looking into the matter. But it was the contents of the other files that caught Crail's eye. Jeremy Lynch had discovered these documents among the papers of the Washington County district attorney who had prosecuted the case in 1953. These hadn't been destroyed in the courthouse fire because they had been kept in the man's private collection and, upon his death, donated to the University of Mississippi law school's special-collections library, where Lynch had tracked them down. Among the documents were what appeared to be transcripts of several lengthy interviews. At the top of this file was a handwritten note on Washington County letterhead that said, "DO NOT DISCLOSE." Crail scanned the documents for a reference to the Blind, Crippled, and Crazy tapes, but they were never mentioned. Crail wasn't sure what all the documents proved, but he figured Lynch wouldn't have saved them if they weren't important. So he fed them into the shredder next to the trash can underneath the desk.

Crail poured another drink and lit a cigarette before continuing. His persistence paid off when he slid back the panels on the credenza and found a safe. He stared at it for a minute, sipping the sweet Canadian whiskey, growing more convinced with each swig, and the time-release OxyContin, that the tapes had to be inside and wouldn't Cuffie be proud of him for finding them. If he could only figure out how to get it open.

He went back out to his car and looked in the trunk. A few small tools wrapped in a rag, a can of gas, and a tire iron. He wasn't sure how, but he figured some combination of these things would pop that puppy open, so he took them back into the office.

He poured another drink before he started trying to pry the safe open, but it was sturdier than it looked. It was going to take some time. If he could just make a small opening, he thought, enough to pour a little of the gasoline inside and let the fumes collect, he might be able to rig a fuse of some sort and blow the thing open. Hell yeah, he thought, damn good idea. He opened the paper shredder. Bingo. It was a strip cutter. It took him another hour, but he worked the tire iron into a spot and bent the door just enough. He pulled the ink cylinder from a ballpoint pen and used that to funnel some gas into the safe. It was a messy proposition, with gas spilling on his hands, but he was sure some of the fuel was getting inside. Next, using tape and his limited weaving skills, Crail braided some of the shredded documents together to make a fuse. During this process it dawned on Crail that with a certain amount of diligence, a person could actually reassemble the strips of shredded paper into their original form. He knew what Cuffie would say about that, so he determined that he had to destroy them more fully. But first he wanted to get a look inside that safe.

He fed the homemade fuse through the opening, then gave the safe a little pat on the top. He pulled a pack of matches from his pocket and struck one. Crail's hands ignited immediately. Rushing for the watercooler, he knocked over the shredder and the match flew from his grip. When it landed in the pool of gas on the floor by the safe, Cuffie's voice began to echo in his head: *Sometimes I just can't believe you.*

After extinguishing the fire on his hands, Crail yanked the curtains off a window and got on the floor to smother the flames before they spread. What he failed to notice was the lit fuse. So, a moment later, when the safe's door blew open, it knocked Crail out cold.

— — — — — — — — —

BUDDY HAD GONE over to Cleveland that afternoon to see his doctor. He did some more scans and X rays and they poked and prodded and said things had progressed as expected. Doctor didn't say how long he thought Buddy had, and Buddy didn't ask. He figured that knowing one way or the other wouldn't change it. But he allowed as how it was starting to cause some pain and so they talked about drugs he could take to help cope. Buddy said he'd wait on that, never did like drugs much. He figured a stiff drink or two would ease the pain for now. Besides, he wanted to keep his wits about him as best he could, in case Pigfoot showed up.

Buddy was sunk deep into his Coup DeVille for the short drive back to Ruleville, his eyes peeking out from under the porkpie hat that floated over the dashboard. Straight ahead, a fat, peachy moon perched on the horizon, like it was sitting smack in the middle of Highway 8 and Buddy could just drive right onto the surface and ride it to heaven. Wouldn't that be something, he thought, a fine way to leave this world and get to the next. He didn't even realize he was nodding his head, thinking about how much better that would be than what he was really facing.

Buddy was tempted to keep driving, right past his turnoff, not so he could catch the moon and ride it to his reward but because he enjoyed it so. He'd seen a fair bit of the country in his day, traveling around, playing his music, but none was more beautiful to him than where he lived. And he didn't know how many more nights he had left to appreciate such things. He thought it might be nice to let the window down and ease up a country road, take in the smells and sounds of the circumstance that was the Mississippi Delta. But the pain grabbed him again, twisted him, and when he reached his turn, he went on and took it, thinking that drink would do the trick.

Halfway up the dirt road to where he stayed, something caught Buddy's eye and he did a sort of chin-up on the steering wheel to get a better look. He wasn't sure what it was and he couldn't see it now anyway. Figured his old eyes were starting to play tricks on him, that's all.

Buddy parked the car and shuffled to the front door, everything right where it was supposed to be. He stepped inside, turning on the light and shutting the door at the same time. It was only when he turned to hang his hat on the rack that he saw the man sitting in his TV chair, holding a rifle. They stared at each other for what seemed like a long time, the only sound in the room a clock ticking. Buddy didn't recognize the face but he knew the man. He wondered if the man recognized his after all this time. Finally Buddy said, "I figured you'd get here sooner or later."

Pigfoot sat there, the Remington .280 not quite pointed at Buddy but close enough. He said, "Sorry to keep you waitin'."

There was a moment before Buddy said, "Wasn't in no hurry." He revealed neither fear nor daring as he stood there weighing his options. His heart was pounding and he could feel the blood pulsing in his teeth. He'd left his pistol and his razor in a kitchen drawer. Hospital and their damn metal detectors. There was no question, his tail was stuck in the gate. He knew he couldn't get back out the door he'd just shut, so he started measuring the distance between himself and Pigfoot. He figured: you're gonna go out, might as well go out trying.

Pigfoot could read his face. He said, "Nigger, yo' bones ain't thick enough to break on a man holding a rifle. You just gonna stand there till I say so or something happens."

Buddy knew he was right. He knew when Pigfoot cut loose with that Remington, he was done for. It was gonna hurt too, but not for long. And there wouldn't be any talking his way out of this, either. No, sir, it was too late to try and fix or patch it. Time to pay. He said, "You already find Willie and Earl?"

Pigfoot nodded without expression as he slid the bolt into place. "You can get on yo' knees and pray if you want."

Buddy shook his head. "Man ain't gotta be on his knees to pray," he said.

"Suit yourself." He raised the gun, leveling it at Buddy. "Things shoulda turned out different."

"Yeah," Buddy said. "For everybody." He set his jaw and braced himself as Pigfoot squeezed the trigger.

— — — — — — — — —

CRUSTY WAS CURLED up in Lollie's lap, snoring like one of the Marx Brothers. Lollie was at the reception desk at WVBR with papers spread out in front of her. She was scouring her notes, hoping to find a clue they had missed. On her left was a large coffee can with a couple of tamales still in it, on her right the box with Ruby's photos.

Rick was in the studio finishing his shift with Skynyrd's "Swamp Music," J. J. Cale's "Cajun Moon," and Creedence Clearwater's "Born on the Bayou." He was signing off the program log when the request line lit up. He grabbed it, saying, "VBR."

"Rick? Smitty Chisholm."

"Too late for requests," he said. "I'm on my way out of here."

"I doubt you've got any of the songs I'd request," he said. "But I gotta tell you, that one you just played with the line about the barking dog sounding like Son House singing the blues, that's what reminded me to call."

"Well, good for Mr. Skynyrd," Rick said. "You got something?"

"Yeah, remember that Ole Miss professor? He sent me an address for Crazy Earl Tate. Said it was current, just outside Tchula."

Rick took the address, then told Smitty about his conversation with Crippled Willie. He said, "When I asked about his leg, he told me this wild story about a patent medicine that was poisoned and—"

"The jake," Smitty said.

"Yeah, that's true?"

"Oh, yeah," he said. "Probably crippled a thousand men in Mississippi alone. I hadn't thought of it before, but Crippled Willie would've been about twenty when it happened." Smitty told the same basic story Willie had about the Jamaican Ginger Extract, but added some details. "These two guys in Boston had been making the stuff since the late twenties," he said. "It was mostly alcohol, like most of those cures were, so the Prohibition Bureau passed a law requiring them to contain a certain percentage of solids."

"Solids being the alleged active ingredients?"

"Exactly. To test for that, they'd burn off the alcohol to see how much was left. So the jake makers needed something to help them pass. These guys were looking for additives with high boiling points, stuff like fusel oil and butyl Carbitol. But they didn't use any of those since they were all toxic, and who wants to kill their customers, right?"

"The tobacco industry springs to mind."

"Well, yeah, but that's slow poisoning. Some of these thing's'd kill you before you could buy a second bottle. Anyway, these guys finally settled on this plasticizer with a chemical called tri-ortho-something-or-other-phosphate. It was supposed to be nontoxic, right? So these guys cut half a million bottles of the ginger extract with the stuff and shipped it all around the country," he said. "In a matter of days, somewhere between fifty and a hundred thousand men, mostly poor alcoholics, were showing up in hospitals and on the streets, some of them literally crawling. Some, like Willie, kept the use of one leg, others were permanently crippled. There're fifteen or twenty songs about it. Tommy Johnson recorded 'Alcohol and Jake Blues' up in Grafton, Wisconsin. Ray Brothers had one called the 'Jake Leg Wobble.' " Smitty chuckled a bit before he said, "The stuff also tended to cripple the middle leg too, so some of the songs have a line about how the man done got the limber leg and can't do no lovin'."

Just then the overnight jock came into the studio to take over.

Rick ended the call, then went out to the front office, where Lollie was hunched over the desk studying something. He said, "Hey, we got Earl Tate's address."

"Great." She looked up. "Where's he live?"

"Tchula."

"Bless you," she said. "Where is that?"

" 'Bout halfway between Yazoo City and Greenwood." He looked at the stuff on the desk. Handwritten notes, a few of Ruby's photos, articles from the *Delta Democrat Times*. "What're you working on?"

Lollie pursed her lips and blew out a long breath before she said, "No idea." She gathered everything and put it in the box, with Crusty on top like a paperweight, then headed for the door.

— — — — — — — — —

THEY WERE ALMOST back to the Vicksburg when Lollie said, "You don't think Crazy Earl's just going to give us the same story Buddy or Willie did?"

"Well, if he gives us the same story as one or the other, at least we'll know who's lying," Rick said. "But if we're going to do the reunion concert, we have to talk to him anyway."

She nodded for a moment before saying, "What do you think about Pigfoot?"

"I'd love to talk to him too," Rick said. "But he's made himself scarce."

"No, the fact he got out of prison just before my grandfather was killed. You think that's just a coincidence?"

"At first I thought it made him a pretty good suspect," Rick said. "Then I thought it was just a coincidence. Now? Well, you talked to both Ruby Finch and Henry LeFleur; which one do you believe?"

"My money's on Ruby," she said.

"Me too. Which makes me think faux Lollie and her partner waited for Pigfoot to get out before they started killing people."

"To make it look like he was the killer."

Rick pulled into his parking spot at the apartment building. "That's my guess."

They were standing in the lobby waiting for the elevator when Lollie said, "What about this? What if Pigfoot is faux Lollie's partner?" She tilted her head to the side as soon as she said it. "Does that make any sense?"

When they got on the elevator, Rick punched 7 and said, "Not if we're right about Ruby."

Once they were in the apartment, Rick fed and medicated Crusty. Lollie flopped on the sofa, kicked off her shoes, and said, "I think we should try the martini-and-snoring experiment."

"A capital idea." Rick put on B. B. King's *Indianola Mississippi Seeds* and poured the drinks. They made perfunctory talk about what they'd do if they actually lured faux Lollie and her murderous partner from their lair, but the way they looked at each other meant they were thinking about other things. When the opportunity finally presented itself, Rick kissed her. It was a good one too. When they came up for air, Lollie smiled and excused herself to the bathroom. A few moments later she came out and walked past Rick, casually unbuttoning her blouse. She said, "Pour us another one, then come find me." She sashayed into the bedroom twirling her shirt over her head.

Rick mixed another round, then grabbed his cigar box and went looking for Lollie. Fortunately it was a small bedroom and she was right in the middle of the mattress wearing one of Rick's T-shirts and a silly grin. They took a hit on the pipe and started fooling around. After a little of this, Rick paused. He gently brushed the hair from her eyes and looked at her. She smiled at him and said, "What?"

He gestured back and forth between them, saying, "So. What do you think? Is this something? Me and you?"

"Sure. It's something."

"But, I mean, specifically. What do you think it is?"

She pressed her hips against his. "Who can say?"

"I was hoping you could."

She put her mouth to his ear and whispered, "Do you really want to talk the life out of whatever it is?" Her tongue touched his lobe and he quivered.

Rick gave it a moment's thought before saying, "You're right. Forget I said anything." He told himself to leave well enough alone. It was sex. Why try to turn it into something more than that? If it turned into something down the road, great. If not, it was still sex, and why complain about that? He disappeared beneath the blankets and commenced investigating the southern precincts with a great deal of enthusiasm.

At first Lollie giggled, but it wasn't long before he heard her say, "Oh my God."

Rick smiled, but he didn't stop. He wanted to stay focused, knowing how critical technique is when you're performing magic.

His confidence soared when she said it again, this time more intensely. "Ohhh my God."

Rick paused long enough to say, "It gets better." He tried to prove it.

"No . . . no . . . no . . ."

"Yes," he said. "It's true, but only if I don't talk so much."

"This is unbelievable."

"Just wait."

But she couldn't. She nearly broke Rick's nose when she threw back the covers and jumped out of bed. She seemed terribly excited about something, and Rick figured it wasn't him when she said, "Do you have a magnifying glass?"

He mumbled, "Yeah, I was going to use it to find my penis."

"You can do that later." She tugged on one of his feet. "C'mon." She went to the living room with Rick following. She grabbed Ruth's box of photos and put it on the coffee table. After finding the magnifying glass, he joined her on the sofa.

"I'm sorry," she said, giving him a kiss on the cheek. "But I thought of something."

"Okay," he said. "But I want a rain check."

"You got it." She opened the box, pulled out the photo from Shelby LeFleur's birthday party, and examined it through the lens.

Rick said, "What're we looking at?"

"Not sure we're looking at anything." She pointed at the face of one of the women in the picture. "Does that look like a beauty mark to you?"

He looked closer. "Yeah. Why?"

Lollie sorted through the photos in Ruth's box until she

Cindy Crawford beauty mark. "Remember her?"

Rick nodded. "Yeah, so?"

She turned it over and pointed at the writing: "042251LL."
"April 22, 1951, LL." She pointed at the names in the caption of
the newspaper photo. "LL," she said, "Lettie LeFleur."

PIGFOOT'S EARS WERE ringing like Christmas bells. The Remington thundered like a cannon in the confines of Buddy's front room. The smell of gunpowder hung in the air as Pigfoot stared at what he'd done.

Buddy had a look about him that suggested a rich mixture of confusion and surprise. He couldn't understand why he was still on his feet when he should have been knocked backward and slumped against the wall, dead or dying. He'd expected the pain to be far worse too. His hands felt for the wound, but there was nothing. Pigfoot had missed. Or had he? Maybe he'd hit what he was aiming at. Buddy turned to see where the shot had gone and saw a hole in his porkpie. He was so surprised that all he could think to say was "You shot my hat."

Pigfoot seemed disappointed by the level of gratitude. He said, "Nigger, be thankful I let you take it off first."

Buddy looked at the hat again, then at Pigfoot. "I figured you'd come to kill me."

Pigfoot worked the bolt action, spitting out the empty cartridge and chambering a new load. "Can't think of but a few things I'd like more," he said.

Buddy was getting angry now. The pain in his back and side was awful. He needed his drink or, if he was going to die by Pigfoot's hand, he just wanted it over with. A curling vein rose on his temple as he raised his voice and said, "Well, go on then, nigger, what're you waitin' on?"

"Waitin'? You don't know nothin' 'bout that," Pigfoot said. "I waited fifty years." He raised the gun and fired again, punching another hole in the porkpie.

Buddy looked at his hat again, then back at Pigfoot and said, "I think it's dead already. Now you gone kill me or what?"

Pigfoot shook his head gravely. "You ain't no use to me dead." He worked the bolt again. The hot brass casing chimed as it hit the wood floor. The new load slid into place.

Buddy didn't understand this at all. Man's been sitting in a prison cell, waiting fifty years for this moment, and now, instead of killing him, says he's got some use for him. "What that's supposed to mean?"

"Means I'm giving you a chance to make good."

Buddy had mixed feelings about that notion. He'd spent most of his life trying to convince himself that he hadn't done anything wrong in the first place, or at least that he'd done the same as anybody would have in that situation. And he'd been able to sell that to himself as long as he wasn't looking Pigfoot in the eye. But now? Seeing the lines in that face? Those eyes with fifty years of prison in them? Buddy was torn by his rage on the one hand and his urge to confess and beg forgiveness on the other. He knew a man's true character was revealed under pressure, and this chance to make good, as Pigfoot called it, threatened to show people what kind of man he really was. And that pissed him off. If he'd been anywhere but that hospital earlier, somebody'd already be dead.

Staring down that rifle barrel, the pain worse with every breath, Buddy thought it might be better if Pigfoot just went on and put him out of his misery. Kill two birds and one old black man with the one stone. Hoping to antagonize Pigfoot enough that he'd forget about giving him that chance to make good, Buddy took a step forward, pointing at his own chest. "Go on, shoot!"

Pigfoot never changed expression as he squeezed the trigger. This time, the hat flew off the rack. "Like I said, you ain't no use to me dead."

Buddy was about to take another step when the pain snapped on him like a bear trap. He staggered sideways and lowered himself weakly onto the sofa. Pigfoot watched impassively as Buddy struggled to catch his breath and keep his eyes open. He'd seen men suffer worse, and it didn't bother him to watch this, though it didn't bring him as much pleasure as he might have expected.

When it passed, Buddy heaved a sigh and said, "Well, if you ain't got no use for me dead, you best hurry and use me."

Pigfoot tilted his head back and scratched under his neck. He'd seen it before. "Cancer?"

"It ain't a cold." Buddy pointed across the room. "You wanna drink? I know I do."

Pigfoot had already found the pistol and razor in the kitchen and he didn't think Buddy would come at him with a bottle. Besides, they needed to talk and he thought some whiskey would help lubricate the conversation. So he said, "I take some."

Buddy struggled to his feet and crossed the room. As he passed Pigfoot he said, "That's a nice-lookin' suit." He grabbed two glasses and the bottle of whiskey and came back pouring. They didn't talk much at first, just sat there and drank. The more whiskey he got in him, the sorrier Buddy felt about everything, from what happened to Pigfoot to his own imminent demise. He kept looking at this man he used to know, searching for a sign of humanity, but it looked like they'd taken that from him and left him with a face of stone. So it came as a surprise to Buddy when, a couple of drinks later, Pigfoot said, "I shouldn'tuh drove off like I did."

Buddy shook his head. "We were all scared," he said. "They knew where our families lived. My sister had those chirren and I was tryin' to protect 'em."

"You had to do what you did."

"We was stuck with some bad choices."

"I shouldn'tuh stopped in the first place. None of this woulda happened."

"They threatened Willie's chirren too." He finished his drink in a gulp. "And you know they'da done it."

"You couldn't take the chance," Pigfoot said. "Nobody gone blame you for that."

"We all felt bad. Willie went and found Jesus, Earl just about gone outta his mind, and I'd bet I worried this cancer onto myself."

"Can't change the past," Pigfoot said.

"No, you can't."

He looked at his glass and said, "So I come back, try and change the future."

"How you gone do that?"

"I got this lawyer."

— — — — — — — —

RICK LOOKED UP from comparing the two pictures. "Okay, let's say it's her. So what?"

"I hate to generalize," Lollie said. "But if a girl's willing to pose like that for a man who's not her husband, I bet she's willing to have an affair with him too. And if Henry LeFleur caught his wife with Yankee trash like Hamp Doogan, you know he'd do like any good southern gentleman and kill him. Then he'd just coerce Buddy, Willie, and Earl into framing Pigfoot."

"It's a neat package all right, but it hinges on a lot we don't know."

"Like?"

"Like does she even have the beauty mark?"

"True."

"And like, when did the LeFleurs get married? And what was Lettie's maiden name?"

"Why would that matter?"

"Because if she was L.L. before she got married, and if that's when she posed for Doogan, that would mitigate Henry's motive a bit."

"Maybe Lettie killed Hamp and Henry had to clean up the mess."

Rick seemed doubtful. "Why would Lettie kill him?"

"I don't know, to get her respect back?"

Rick gave her a skeptical look. "Is that what you'd do?"

"I'd have to kill too many people to get mine back but . . ." She shrugged. "Okay, maybe not." After a moment, Lollie said, "Maybe she posed for him before getting married and then after she got married, Hamp tried to blackmail her."

"I thought Ruby said Hamp wasn't the blackmailing sort."

"Oh, that's right. Okay, let's say Henry did it and framed Pigfoot. How does that help us identify faux Lollie and her partner?"

He shook his head. "Don't know. But I've got a hunch they're connected."

"A hunch." Lollie shrugged, then smiled and said, "Well, I've worked with less."

They went to the computer and found that Lettie's maiden

name was Biggs and that she was, in fact, Lettie LeFleur at the time the photo was taken. "So," Rick said, "now we need to find out about the beauty mark."

"Well, Miss Lettie done gone to Memphis to catch a plane," Lollie said in an exaggerated accent. "You want to go back to the LeFleurs and ask Henry or Annie Mae?"

"No thanks." Rick shook his head. "Let's go ask someone else who'd know."

Lollie looked at the caption of the newspaper photo. "She's got a son named Monroe, a daugher-in-law, and a truckful of cousins, take your pick."

Rick shook his head, pointing at the guy in the front of the picture. "Her father-in-law."

"He's ninety-five," Lollie said, pointing at the picture. "The poor guy looks like he's made out of pipe cleaners."

"It's worth a shot."

"What about Crazy Earl Tate?"

"Hell, he's only seventy-three," Rick said. "He can wait."

C R A I L   W O K E   T O the dull thud of a car door slamming shut in the distance. His eyes trembled open as he tried to remember where he was and why he was there, not to mention why he was turning yellow and losing patches of blistered skin. Without lifting his head from the carpet, he could see some tools scattered on the floor and, beyond that, a safe with its door dangling by a hinge. He could smell ash, gasoline, and singed hair. It was all familiar and distant at the same time. Oh yeah, he remembered, the lawyer's office. The Crown Royal, the files, the fire. He blinked to clear his vision and that's when he saw what appeared to be two plastic reels, the sort used on professional tape machines. A wave of euphoria swept over Crail as it dawned on him. He'd found the tapes. They'd been in the safe, just as he'd suspected. Lord, wasn't Cuffie going to be proud? He blinked again and, as things came into focus, he noticed something funny about the reels of tape. But it wasn't ha-ha funny so much as it was peculiar funny. The reels had been warped by heat and the tapes were, for lack of a better word, melted, fused together and useless.

Was this good or bad or did it matter at all? Before he could explore the question more fully, he heard keys jangling outside the door. He figured it was either the cops or the lawyer; either way it was bad news. He could hear Cuffie now, telling him he had to get up, do whatever he had to. He couldn't let her down, so, using the chair to hoist himself up, Crail tried to get to his feet. He didn't realize, for a moment, that the OxyContin had worn off. When he put weight on his bad leg, it felt like that linebacker had hit his knee again. It gave out and he crumpled into a pile on the floor behind the desk, cursing in a low voice.

A moment later, the door to the office creaked open. Jeremy Lynch stepped into the room slowly, suspicious, and said, "What the hell?"

Between the hangover and the fear, Crail's head was throbbing like a twenty-inch subwoofer. Confident in his inability to talk his way out of the situation, Crail grabbed the tire iron, rolled onto his stomach, and played dead.

A moment later, Lynch came around the desk and, seeing a body lying there, was moved to say, "Jesus!"

The room went quiet for a few seconds and Crail imagined the guy standing there wondering what the hell this body was doing in his office. He heard Lynch mumble, "Oh, man, I just bought that." This was followed by the sound of a wing tip kicking an empty Crown Royal bottle. A second later Crail felt a shoe

nudging his ribs. "Hey, you!" Crail kept playing possum even as
Lynch said, "You dead or alive?"

Crail opened his mouth to say "Dead" before he realized it was
the sort of trick question a lawyer would ask. He lay there trying to
think of something he could do that would make Cuffie proud. But
before he had any ideas, Lynch kicked him pretty good. Well, feeling
the way he did, this was the sort of shit Crail wasn't going to put up
with, so he gritted his teeth and rolled over, swinging the tire iron.

Jeremy Lynch jumped, but not fast or far enough. The tool
took a bite out of his shin and he tumbled into a cursing pile of
his own. "Sonofabitchgoddammitthathurtslikeamutherfucker!"

While the lawyer rolled around cursing, Crail pulled himself
up and leaned against the desk. It felt like his brain was swelling
to burst. He wagged the tire iron weakly and said, "Shut up or I'll
hit you again."

Lynch was still rolling from side to side, clutching his leg with
two bloody hands and blinking back tears. There were two screw-
drivers, both flathead, part of a ballpoint pen, and a pair of needle-
nose pliers on the floor near where he had landed. It didn't take
him long to figure out that he'd interrupted this guy in the middle of what appeared to be a bizarre combination of attempted
burglary and arson. Either that or the guy was just a total fuckup.

As an attorney with some experience in criminal law, Jeremy
Lynch had it on good authority that people who walked in on
this sort of crime frequently ended up dead. Since he figured this
guy was going to kill him, or try to anyway, he started thinking
about how to escape. When Crail looked up at the window with
the missing curtain, Lynch furtively picked up one of the screw-
drivers and cupped it, waiting for a chance to . . . to what? he
thought. He wasn't a violent man. What was he going to do? Stab
the guy in the neck? No, he needed something smarter than that
and certainly less messy.

Crail rubbed his free hand across his face and took a deep breath. "You got any aspirin?"

"Top drawer," Lynch said, pointing at the desk. That's when he noticed Crail's knee ballooning out of the hole in his pants. It was swollen and grotesquely discolored. And it gave him an idea. Lynch pointed at it and said, "What the hell happened to you?"

Chewing on three aspirin, Crail looked down with red-rimmed eyes and said, "Guy stabbed me with a fork."

Lynch gave him a sympathetic wince. "Ewww, man," he said. "That must've hurt like a sonofabitch."

Crail nodded. "Hit the bone."

"Ewww." He gestured at it. "Looks like it might be a little infected too."

"Yeah, but I got some antibiotics."

"Well, that's good," Lynch said. "Those things are great, a marvel of science."

While that much was true, one of the many things neither Crail nor Jeremy Lynch knew was that when bacteria enters bone tissue (as had happened when Lamar Suggs sank that fork into Crail's knee), the resulting infection is known as osteomyelitis. And given that the proper treatment for that was a six-week course of penicillinase-resistant synthetic penicillin and a third-generation cephalosporin, it was going to do Crail precious little good to keep taking the Bactrim.

Jeremy Lynch took a moment to make the sort of face he hoped would convey the impression that he was recalling a fine and pertinent point of law. Then he pointed a lawyerly finger at Crail and said, "I tell you what, you ought to sue the shit out of whoever did that to you."

The notion took Crail by surprise and, at first blush, he liked the sound of it. He said, "Really?"

"Hell yes," Lynch said, wagging his finger in a judicial fashion.

"I do it all the time." He waved a hand in the air and said, "Case like this is probably worth five, ten million dollars, especially if we can try it down in Jefferson County." He pointed at Crail. "Those are some plaintiffs' juries down there, I'm telling you."

Crail gave it some thought as he struggled to choke down the aspirin. He'd heard about how trial lawyers were making big bucks for the good people of Mississippi. He'd seen those billboards advertising their services: "Have you been injured? You may have a claim! Contact the law offices of Strut, Swagger, and Preen." Things like that. But as much as he liked the idea, he thought there might be a small hitch, so he said, "I don't think we can sue him."

"What makes you say that?" Like a parent to an insecure child.

Crail tipped his head to one side and shrugged. "Guy's dead."

Lynch waved him off as if he'd said the guy was out of town for a day. "No problem." He reached up to his desk. "Slide me a legal pad, would you?" Crail pushed one into his hand while Lynch pulled a pen from his coat. "We'll sue his estate." He clicked his pen and prepared to write. "Now, tell me, when did this happen?"

"Pretty recent."

"And how did he die?"

Crail actually looked a bit embarrassed when he said, "Uhhh, I sorta killed him."

Without batting an eye Lynch said, "But in self-defense, right?"

Crail looked down at his throbbing knee, hesitating as he said, "I guess you could *say* that."

"Of course you can! He stabbed you with a fork. That's why you came to see me."

"I dunno . . ."

"Trust me." He pointed at Crail. "You need legal help."

CRAIL AND HIS new attorney left Jackson driving north on Highway 49. After stopping for a cold six-pack, Crail swallowed three Bactrim, snorted two lines of meth, and popped another OxyContin. By the time they reached Bentonia, all of his pain had subsided.

The same, however, could not be said for his attorney, who was nursing a busted lip, a loose tooth, and an eye that was swelling shut. And his leg still hurt like hell where the tire iron had landed. Lynch thought his tibia might be broken or, at the very least, fractured. He wanted to look at it, see if it needed to be set or stitched or something. But that would have to wait, since he currently found himself curled up in the pitch-black trunk of Crail's car.

What had happened was this: Lynch honestly thought he'd sold Crail on the lawsuit idea. He said they should go down to the courthouse immediately to file the papers, figuring once they got outside he could make a run for it. Though he knew his sore leg would slow him a bit, he was confident he could outrun anybody with a knee the size and color of Crail's. Crail, for his part, played along until they got to the parking lot, where he opened his trunk, put the tools in, then turned to Jeremy with his hand extended and said, "Now gimme that screwdriver you palmed."

Lynch, whose skills at prevarication were surprisingly unpolished for an attorney, tried to back away as he said, "Screwdriver? I don't know what—" There followed a brief scuffle during which Crail, hopping around on his one good leg, somehow managed to disarm his limping lawyer and stuff him in the trunk of his car, telling him they'd file the papers later. Then Crail stunned him with a right jab, closed the lid, and hit the road.

Highway 49 took them from the flat Jackson prairies through the rolling, kudzu-covered loess hills that loomed over the southeastern edge of the Delta. Along the way Crail cranked up the stereo, listening to a classic rocker out of Jackson. Foreigner, Heart, Journey, a dull mix even by the lowered standards of today's rock radio. The two huge speakers mounted in the rear dash of the car were pounding the tedious power chords and threatening to drive Lynch either crazy or deaf. He knew he could reach up and punch holes in the speakers from where he was, but he figured that would just result in another beating, so he stuck his fingers in his ears and prayed for the signal to fade.

Fortunately, just as they crossed into Yazoo County, the music stopped. Lynch pulled his fingers from his ears and could hear beeps as Crail punched a number into his cell phone. After a moment he heard him say, "Hey, Mama, it's me. How you feelin'? Uh-huh, yeah. Well, what'd the doctor say? Ohhh. Are you sure you paid it? You call the customer-service number? Well, you just have to stay on hold till somebody answers. Yeah, I know. It takes 'em a long time." Crail listened for a moment before saying, "Oh, I'm doin' all right. My knee's a little sore, but I, uhhh, I got me a lawyer says he thinks we might be able to sue somebody about that. Make a little money finally. Yeah, me too, Mama. Wouldn't that be something?"

Crail knew better, of course. There would be no lawsuit. He was just trying to give her some hope here at the end. She'd been born poor and had worked hard her whole life, trying to give him a better chance than she'd had. The setbacks seemed to come into her life by the dozens, but she'd endured, teaching her son the value of persistence. And with that they'd managed to get the football scholarship and what seemed to be a guarantee to a better life. But then his knee blew out, ending what had been his one good chance. She didn't care what the loss meant to her, which was plenty, but she was so disappointed for him that it would break your heart. And now Crail just wanted her to believe that things were going to work out okay.

They made small talk for a minute before he said, "Well, all right, Mama. You take care. I'll come see you soon as I can. I love you too."

As soon as Crail ended the call, Lynch yelled from the trunk, "Hey, listen, I've sued a bunch of those HMOs and insurance companies, and based on what I just heard? It sounds like we got a good case. Why don't you pull over? I can make a few calls and get the ball rolling on that," he said. "I tell you what. I'll even waive my usual retainer." He paused, but there was no response. "Hey, you listening?"

Crail didn't say anything because he'd just noticed something out of the corner of his eye. It wasn't anything specific, just some combination of light and motion, coming toward his head, and fast. He jerked the steering wheel reflexively, pinballing Lynch to the trunk's wall and knocking him out. Crail managed to keep the car on the road, but just barely. He looked around wild-eyed, trying to see what had caused his reaction, but there was nothing to be seen. It turned out that hallucinations were just another of the many side effects of the sulfamethoxazole.

As they came into Yazoo City at the top of Broadway Street, Crail's cell phone rang. He recognized the number on the display. He said, "Hey, Cuffie, honey. Listen, those antibiotics you gave me don't seem to be—"

"Crail, baby, guess what! Guess what!" Her voice pitched high and fast.

He sure hoped she wasn't pregnant. He said, "I dunno, uhhhh."

She blurted, "You'll never guess! I just got off the phone with Papaw Henry." Then, in a stage whisper, "He told me he wants to talk to you about a job!"

At the moment these improbable words were coming out of her mouth, Crail was driving down Broadway past the house where he'd killed Lamar Suggs. The scene advanced in slow motion as his opiated brain disconnected. His lover's voice drifted to the background as he wondered why that old guy had put up such a fight. Why not just let him have a look around? What was that going to hurt? He didn't have to stick that fork in him the way he did. He didn't even have the damn tapes. How stupid was that? He remembered how frail the old man had looked and that made him think of his mama, down to ninety pounds last time he saw her, dying in her bed. He hoped he could get to see her before she passed.

After a long silence, Cuffie said, "Crail, honey, can you hear me?" Her voice brought him back. "A what?"

"A job!"

"Doing what?"

She let out a disappointed sigh. "Sometimes? I just can't believe you."

"I'm just asking what kind of job's all."

"It doesn't matter, sweetie. Look at it. If Daddy sees that

Papaw Henry trusts you enough to do something for him, Daddy'll have to accept you too. Don't you see?"

"But what kind of job is it?"

"Well, he wasn't real clear, said he didn't want to be, being on the phone, but get this. He said he'd had a couple of visitors come by asking questions about people and things that he'd just as soon leave unanswered, right?"

"D'ee say who it was?"

"Yes! You're not going to believe this. Said it was Lollie Woolfolk and Rick Shannon. Can you believe that?"

"How'd they get together?"

"I don't know, honey, but it doesn't matter. Papaw said some things—and it was just as much in the way he said it as the actual words, you know? But I got the feeling he needs you to do something that'll let us walk away from this other thing, if you know what I mean." She paused, waiting for a response, but there was nothing. "Are you there?"

"Yeah," Crail said, reaching for a cigarette.

"You haven't been to see that . . . that guy we talked about, have you? That lawyer?"

Crail glanced in the rearview mirror. "Well, yeah. I got him here in the car with me."

"What?"

"Now don't worry," Crail said. "I got some good news too." He couldn't wait to hear how she'd change her tune when he told her he'd found the tapes.

"What do you mean he's in the car with you? Are you out of your mind?"

Crail's jaw clenched. Sometimes? The way she underestimated him just pissed him off. He tried to maintain his composure as he said, "Well now, Cuffie, you weren't there. You don't know what all happened, so don't be talkin' like that. I got it under control.

Damn." He could hear the sound of tobacco crackling over the phone as she sucked hard on a cigarette. He could see her eyes burning. She was like that sometimes.

Finally she said, "What kinda good news?"

"I got rid of all the papers he had in his files, just like you said. That's all taken care of. And guess what I found in his safe?"

There was a pause before Cuffie answered. "No."

"Yes."

"You have 'em?"

"No I, uh, burned 'em. You said you didn't want any evidence left, right? Well, they can't ever be played now, I guarantee."

"Why didn't you tell me?"

"I just did, baby."

"You're right, I'm sorry." She took another drag on the cigarette. "Baby, I'm so proud of you. I can't wait to tell Papaw." She paused a moment before she said, "Uh, but how come you have the lawyer with you?"

"I couldn't just leave him there," Crail said without further explanation.

"Okay." Cuffie accepted the fact that she couldn't change things. At the same time, she was thrilled that the tapes were no longer a threat. She said, "Baby, you just need to keep it under control, all right?"

"Don't worry," he said. "It's cool."

Cuffie had her doubts, but she didn't have time to debate things. The toothpaste was out of the tube on this and all they could do was move forward while cleaning up behind themselves. With that in mind she said, "Look, Papaw wants you to meet him over at his deer camp near Perry Farm. You know where I'm talking about?"

"Over by Holly Bluff?"

"Yeah. He's there now, waitin' on you."

"I can be over there in fifteen minutes."

"You do that," Cuffie said. "But don't tell him about the tapes. I'll tell him when the time's right. You just get over there and see what he wants you to do."

"Okay."

"And long as you're there," Cuffie said, more darkly, "you might as well see about finding a place to leave that lawyer *behind*."

— — — — — — — —

ON THEIR WAY to visit Shelby LeFleur Jr., Rick and Lollie got stuck at a railroad crossing a few miles outside Greenville. Looking out her side of the truck, Lollie thought about how the flowering cotton was so much prettier when you weren't driving past it at sixty miles an hour.

Rick looked out his side of the truck at a shotgun shack sitting hard by the railroad tracks. There was an old black woman in a weary housecoat, sitting on her front porch in a rusty lawn chair, rocking just slightly. Rick figured she had to be eighty. He'd never seen a face so spent, like she was too tired to make an expression, unable to do anything but stare straight ahead. It looked like she'd earned the right to sit and rest, like she deserved a better chair but wasn't going to get one because what you deserve and what you get don't always turn out to be the same thing.

After a moment, Rick turned to look at Lollie, who seemed lost in a daydream as she stared out at the cotton. Was there something between them? he wondered. Something that could last, or was it just a passing thing? The sort of thing that tended to happen to two people who'd been in proximity long enough. It wasn't as if he fell for every woman who came into his office, right? He thought about raising the question, as long as they were sitting there, but then he remembered what she'd said about not wanting to talk the life out of whatever it was, and he thought that was a good idea. He just hoped he got to cash that rain check before she disappeared from his life.

She turned from looking out the window and said, "It's hard to believe something as pretty as cotton could cause so much pain."

"I believe I've said the same thing about women." Rick reached over and began tuning the radio dial. He found some ag reports on cotton-seed production and got an update on soybean acreage. Then they got a little Jesus and a little Elvis and some other oldies before they came across a distant signal, Led Zeppelin playing through the static. Lollie gave him a sour look and shook her head, prompting him to turn off the radio. "Not a big Zep fan," she said.

He nodded. "Even the blues stuff?"

"What blues stuff? I thought they were just heavy-metal rockers."

"Au contraire." Rick outlined the band's connection to the music, including the unsavory charge of plagiarism.

"No kidding?"

"Oh yeah," he said. " 'Bring It on Home' and 'Whole Lotta Love.' "

"And they just stole them?"

"Well, they settled out of court, in Willie Dixon's favor," Rick said. "What does that tell you?"

She shrugged. "I guess they either stole the songs or figured a jury would say they had."

Rick tapped his nose, then pointed at her, saying, "Arc Music was the publishing arm for Chess Records, where Dixon was under contract as a songwriter. Arc first sued over 'Bring It on Home,' which was credited to Jimmy Page and Roger Plant on

Zeppelin II. Arc claimed it was Dixon's song and got a settlement, but they didn't bother to share the proceeds with Dixon until his manager did an audit and caught them. Later, Dixon sued Zeppelin, saying that 'Whole Lotta Love' was his song 'You Need Love.' " Rick saw the train's caboose approaching, so he started the truck. He looked over at the shack, but the woman with the weary face was gone.

"I thought they revered the old blues guys," Lollie said. "Why steal from your heroes?"

The truck rumbled over the railroad tracks, prompting Crusty to peek out of his carrier. Rick said, "Probably subconscious plagiarism. Like Harrison cribbing the riffs from 'He's So Fine' to make 'My Sweet Lord.' "

"That's a more charitable explanation than I'd expect from you."

"Not my words," Rick said. "The jury's. If I had to guess, I'd say they figured they could get away with it."

Lollie pointed at the coming intersection. "Turn up there."

A few minutes later they were standing in front of a spacious colonial revival, fresh yellow paint with white trim. Rick's head tilted back as he looked up at the second floor and said, "Awful lot of house for one old man."

"By the way," Lollie said. "What's the plan here? Just introduce ourselves and ask if Lettie has a beauty mark?"

"Plan? The plan is to wing it."

A black woman opened the door. Didn't say a word. Just stood there looking at them.

Rick waited for a moment before he said, "Hi, we'd like to see Mr. LeFleur, if we could." Then he said, "Ma'am." She looked professional and somewhat reproachful. Rick figured she was more likely a nurse than the housekeeper.

The woman squinted at Rick and said, "He expectin' you?"

"No, ma'am," Rick said. "And we're sorry to just drop in like this, but we were hoping we could see him."

The woman showed no sign of stepping aside to let them in. She put her fists on her hips. "Wha' choo wanna see him about?"

Lollie smiled at Shelby's protector. She said, "We want to talk to him about a radio station he used to own. It shouldn't take long."

"Huh," the woman said with a little smile. "Take a lot longer'n you think." She glanced over her shoulder into the house, then back at Lollie. She lowered her voice. "You get that man talkin', sometimes hard to get him stopped." She nodded at her own statement. "Wanna tell you everything ever crossed his mind. You'd think at his age he'd get tired, but . . ." She shook her head and assumed a sympathetic expression. "Main thing is, he's lonely, you know? All his friends gone, none his family visits 'cept on occasions. Bless his heart, he just want somebody to listen to him while he's still here, is all."

"Happy to oblige," Rick said.

"All right, then," she said. "Who should I say's callin'?"

"Tell him it's Tucker Woolfolk's granddaughter and a friend," Lollie said.

"Well, all right." She stepped back and gestured for them to come in, then she led them to a large sitting room. "You can wait in here," she said. "I'll go check with him."

The room was filled with beautiful antiques and LeFleur family photos from the past seventy years, a documentary of the clan's couplings, offspring, and progress. Rick glanced around and said, "First one to find a mole wins?" He went to the baby grand piano, which was occupied by an army of framed snapshots.

Lollie wandered in the other direction, marveling at the scope of the gallery. On an antique drum table stood a sterling-silver frame with a picture of a proud man and his boy. "1920" was etched in the corner. Lollie figured this was Shelby LeFleur Sr., with his twelve-year-old son, standing proudly with arms extended over the high cotton they had nurtured.

On the mantel was a series of hand-tinted photos of a beautiful young woman in Victorian dress, glancing coyly at the lens. On the back of the frames, she was identified as Wynona Dunaway LeFleur, Shelby Jr.'s long departed mother. Lollie moved to a large framed photo hanging on the wall. It appeared to have been taken at a recent family reunion. She studied it for a moment before gesturing to Rick, saying, "Hey, look at this." Rick came over to see what she'd found. Lollie tapped her finger on the glass. "That's Henry," she said. "So I'm guessing that's Lettie." She pointed at the woman's cheek, saying, "And that's a beauty mark."

Rick looked at it, nodding. "It sure is," he said. "And in the same place." His eyes drifted across the photograph, surveying the other faces. After a moment, he fixed on something and leaned closer to be sure. "Well, hello there," he said.

Lollie looked but didn't see whatever Rick did. "What is it?"

He pointed at a younger woman in the picture and said, "I'll see your beauty mark and raise you one faux Lollie."

DRIVING THROUGH THE flat, virtually featureless Mississippi Delta, one would never guess that the entire region was once a primeval forest. It was only after the government built levees along the river in the late 1800s and slaves cut down the vast, steaming, wooded swamps that the land that made cotton king came to exist in its present form.

But there was still a reminder of how it used to be, and Henry LeFleur's deer camp was nestled in the midst of it. He owned a couple hundred acres between the Delta National Forest and the Panther Swamp Wildlife Refuge, one of the few remaining large tracts of mature bottomland hardwoods in the region and home to white-tailed deer, fox, gray squirrels, swamp and cottontail rabbits, raccoon, opossum, and wild turkeys. A hunter's paradise.

Crail was on his way over there now, barreling down the road, eyes twitching as he played air guitar on top of the steering wheel and sang along with some classic rock. " 'I still remember everything 'at used to be.' " He'd snorted another line of meth on his way out of Yazoo City, just to take the edge off.

" 'Lack the love, it's always easy loving you or me.' "The euphoria from the speed had Crail focused on how good things were going for him all the sudden. First of all, as far as he knew, the cops had no idea that he had killed Tucker Woolfolk or Lamar Suggs. Second, Cuffie's grandfather was prepared to offer him a job, and third, that lawyer in the trunk had finally shut up. Hell yes, he was feelin' damn lucky.

All things considered, Jeremy Lynch was pretty lucky too, though he didn't feel that way. On top of his other injuries, he had a new gash in his scalp from when Crail had dodged his first hallucination and sent Jeremy headfirst into the wall of the trunk. Since he had regained consciousness only a couple of minutes after being knocked out, the odds were good that the brain damage would be limited. He was, however, suffering from retrograde amnesia, which explained his state of confusion when he woke up in the trunk of a moving car. But again Jeremy was lucky in that he'd lost only a few hours of his life, whereas this ilk of amnesia sometimes erases memories going back years. He remembered waking up, showering, and leaving for work. After that, he was drawing blanks. But this much he knew: His head and his leg hurt like two sons of bitches and it didn't help that the driver of the car was playing .38 Special loud enough to make his ears bleed.

Jeremy wondered if there could possibly be a reasonable explanation. Maybe someone was taking him to the hospital to see about his injuries. But in the trunk? No, that didn't make any sense, even to a man suffering a transient neurologic deficit. No, unless this was a prank by some of his bar association pals, this was almost certainly some sort of criminal activity. And since Jeremy liked to think he didn't associate with the kinds of people who listened to second-tier post-Skynyrd southern-fried boogie-blues rock, things were pointing toward the unlawful.

Jeremy considered calling out for help, except the stereo was too loud to yell over with his head hurting the way it was. Besides, he figured that since they were driving down a highway, no one would hear him anyway. But then the car slowed and turned off the pavement onto gravel. He got a sick feeling in the pit of his stomach as the image of a shallow grave in the woods came to him. The .38 Special got even louder and the tires began to rumble on the washboard road and the car began to sway to and fro. The driver let loose with a Rebel yell and the car pitched violently sideways, knocking Jeremy out cold again.

Spurred by the methamphetamine, Crail imagined himself on the NASCAR circuit. He was fishtailing down the gravel road screaming and singing along with the radio. " 'I'm a man on the run, always under the gun, gonna have me some fun . . .' " Rocks were shooting out behind him like he was driving an automatic weapon. Crail hadn't had this much fun since he didn't know when. He thought about pulling over to snort another line of crank, but then he came around a corner and saw the cabin up ahead. He killed the radio, brought the car under control, and checked the mirror to make sure he didn't have any powder on his nose.

As Crail pulled up to the hand-hewn cabin, he saw Henry on the front porch talking on his cell phone, decked out in full camouflage even though the only legal game at the moment—raccoon and frog—were easily approached without such stealth technology. Crail threw the car into park just as Henry flipped his phone shut and held up a hand. "Don't get out," he said, pointing south. "Let's take a ride." He got in the car and directed Crail toward Lake George.

They'd met before, several years ago, when Crail was still enjoying the residual fame from his high school football career and that first half against Texas Tech. He was still on crutches when

Cuffie brought him to a family function with high hopes, only to have her parents give him the cold shoulder. But Crail and Henry hit it off and spent the entire evening drinking beer and talking football. "I saw that game," Henry had said, putting his arm over Crail's shoulder. "You was runnin' through that line like a four-horned billy goat. It's a damn shame about that missed block," he said. "Damn shame." They talked about getting together to do some duck hunting, but nothing ever came of it. Next time they saw each other was when they happened to end up side by side at the urinal trough in Vaught-Hemingway Stadium at an Ole Miss homecoming game a few years later.

Now, as they drove through the deer camp's cypress-tupelo brakes and bayous, Henry was thinking that the boy looked about half-past jaundiced with his yellowed eyes and skin. Of course, his sight wasn't what it used to be, so maybe it was just a trick of the light. Still, he wondered, what was causing those eruptions starting on his neck?

Crail could feel Henry's eyes on him and he was starting to wonder if the man was waiting for him to ask about the job, so he said, "Cuffie told me you wanted to talk about—"

Henry cut him off, gesturing out the window at a small oxbow lake and a stand of tupelo gum and buttonbush. "This some beautiful country, ain't it?"

"Yes, sir. Sure is." When Crail twitched at another hallucination, Henry acted like he didn't notice.

With his arm hanging out the window, Henry slapped the door and looked at Crail. "Say, you do any bow huntin'?"

"A little," he said. "Mostly just gun hunt though."

"Pretty good with a shot?"

"I don't waste too many."

This prompted a smile from Henry, who just then noticed the beers sitting in the backseat. He said, "You savin' those for later?"

"No, sir. Help yourself." He figured maybe Henry would tell him about the job after having a drink.

Henry opened two, handing one to Crail and tossing the caps out the window, and said, "You ever hunt primitive weapon?"

"I shot a few muzzle loaders," Crail said. "But those things are screwy. Hard to shoot straight."

Henry agreed, and they drove down the dirt road a ways, drinking beer and making small talk. After a minute Henry casually said, "Say, how's your mama doin'?"

Crail didn't even think to wonder how he knew to ask. He shook his head sadly and said, "Tell you the truth, she's been in some low cotton for a while."

"You don't say. I'm sorry to hear it."

"Yes, sir. Having some troubles with her health and the insurance comp'ny."

Henry already knew this, but he acted surprised, hurt, and disappointed all at once. He said, "No. Issat right?" He shook his head sympathetically and seemed to give some thought to the situation. "Well, I tell you what. Where's she at, up there at the Delta Regional Hospital?"

"She oughta be," Crail said. "But she's back at home till they get that insurance thing straightened out."

"Well, that ain't right," Henry said. "Hell, if she needs some treatment . . ." He made a sound to indicate his disgust at a system that would do a boy's mama that way. He said, "I tell you what, I'm 'onna make a coupla calls, take care of that this afternoon. I know some folks up there. You can just rest your mind on that."

With these words, tears began to well in Crail's yellow eyes. The combination of gratitude along with the elevated amounts of drugs in his system triggered a profound mood swing. His lower lip began to tremble as a wave of emotion swept over him. Then he began to weep openly.

This raw display of human feeling set Henry to squirming. He'd never been comfortable around men who showed their emotions in ways that didn't involve cussing at and hitting one another. He looked away long enough to let the boy regain his composure.

Crail was naturally embarrassed and confused about his exhibition. He seemed to have lost control of his feelings, and he wasn't sure how to get back to where he used to be, emotionally speaking. He sniffled, then wiped a tear from his cheek and said, "I'd appreciate whatever you could do, Mr. LeFleur." His voice began to quiver. "She's all the family I got."

Henry gave him a nervous glance. "Get a grip, son. It'll be okay."

"Yes, sir," Crail said, wiping his face with his sleeve. "I don't know what came over me. I guess I just love her so much." After a few moments, he managed to pull himself back together. He cleared his throat and said, "Listen, Mr. LeFleur? If there's ever anything I can do for you, all you got to do is call."

Henry gave a nod to accept the offer. He said, "Well, now, it's funny you should say that. 'Cause I got this thing needs takin' care of." He pointed at a spot up ahead. "Why don't you park up there and we'll talk about it."

"You just name it," Crail said as he brought the car to a stop.

In light of Crail's delicate emotional condition, Henry was starting to have doubts about asking the favor. He thought back on the days when he had a whole stable of folks he could turn to on something like this, people who owed him or wanted to curry favor. And every one of them experienced at the task. But now? Everybody he might've called was either dead or on the waiting list. That's the only reason he'd called Cuffie in the first place. He had nowhere else to turn. And what's family for if you can't count on 'em when your tit's in the wringer?

"All right," Henry said. "Here's the deal. Long time ago, there was somebody tried to tangle with me, threatened to ruin my family. Fortunately, I was in a position to put it to rest, you know. But, well, somebody's come around recently and they's stirring things up, jeopardizing my family again, and I ain't gone put up with it. Can't afford to." Henry reached into a pocket of his camouflage and pulled out an envelope, thick with cash. "So, this thing . . . this guy's gotta be taken care of. You think you can do it?" He held the money out to Crail.

Crail didn't hesitate. He nodded, saying, "You need me to scare him off?" He took hold of the envelope, but Henry didn't let go.

Lord, he thought, this boy is thicker'n two dogs' heads. "Okay," Henry said. "Now listen up. I'm just gone put this out on the porch for you, so follow along. I need you to make him disappear."

Crail's head tilted backward and his eyes went wide. "Scare him off real good, then?"

"Scare him to *death*," Henry said, still hanging on to the envelope.

There was a brief silence as Crail struggled with the subtext. Finally he said, "Ohhh, yeah. No problem." And Henry let go of the money.

It was somewhere around the time Henry had said "this guy's gotta be taken care of" that Jeremy Lynch had regained consciousness for the second time that day. He listened intently as the two men discussed what he assumed was his fate. When it became apparent that one of them was hiring the other to finish him off, Jeremy wormed his way toward the speakers mounted in the rear dash. He thrust a hand up through one of the speakers and waved as he shouted, "I'll double his offer!"

Henry just about went through the roof. He jerked around,

like a puppet on a string, looking for the source of the voice. All he saw was a disembodied hand coming up from the speaker hole. "What the hell is that?"

Crail gestured with his thumb. "Oh, I got a lawyer in the trunk."

26

RICK AND LOLLIE stared at the tiny man in the wheelchair as his nurse rolled him into the room. She faced him toward the sofa, where Rick and Lollie were seated. The nurse set the brake, then put her hand on Shelby's shoulder, saying, "I'll be right back."

Shelby LeFleur Jr., all ninety-five years of him, just sat there, curled up like a question mark. He looked smaller now than he had as a child in 1920, standing in that cotton field with his daddy. "Which one of you is the Woolfolk?" he asked his lap.

Lollie bent down and slightly sideways, trying to get some eye contact from underneath Shelby's stooped body. "I am, Mr. LeFleur. My name's Lollie Woolfolk."

His body rocked a little as he tried to nod. "I knew a man named Woolfolk once."

"Yes, sir," she said, leaning over farther, sort of waving at him to get his attention. "That was my grandfather, Robert Tucker. He worked at your radio station back in the fifties."

"No, I believe the man's name was Woolfolk. Don't know

any Tuckers. Worked for me at my radio station. Of course that was back in the fifties."

Rick looked at Lollie and tapped his ear, then he bent sideways and waved at the old man, shouting, "Yes, sir. By the way, my name's Rick Shannon! I work at W-V-B-R in Vicksburg."

The nurse came back carrying a small plastic case. While she was still behind Shelby, she gestured at Rick and Lollie and said, "Now, I warned you." She opened the case and helped Shelby put the hearing aids into his expansive ears. Then she gave him a pat on the arm and said, "How's that?"

"That's fine, Jessie," he said, touching her hand. "Thank you."

She reached into his pocket and removed a pendant button on a lanyard that she put around his neck. "You just push your button if you need me."

As the nurse left the room, Shelby pointed in her direction. "Jessie said you want to talk about my radio station."

"Yes, sir," Rick said. "We're curious about—"

"Well, I tell you what I can," he said. "It was a class-B licensed AM station, a thousand watts, I believe. Or maybe that was the nighttime power. It mighta been more during the day. That was a long time ago." Shelby seemed to spark a bit as he talked about the past. His stooped and withered vessel grew increasingly animated as his words floated out in a southern accent from a different era, educated and discontinued long ago. "See, you have to lower the power because, at night, changes in the atmosphere can extend the coverage of AM radio signals. So that's that. But, anyway, we were the first radio station in that part of the Delta."

Lollie started to speak, but Shelby cut her off. "Of course, we'd been listening to radio for a long time before that." The subject seemed to warm Shelby's blood and loosen his joints. He cranked his head back and continued, "I remember when I was a young man, there was this one fella we could pick up out of northwest

Louisiana. He'd come on the air saying, 'Hello, world, doggone you! This is K-W-K-H in Shreveport, Lou-ee-siana, and it's W. K. Henderson talkin' to you.'" Shelby hit the wheelchair's armrest with his waxy fist and chuckled at his imitation of the man.

Rick said, "You could pick up Shreveport here?"

"Well," Shelby said with a new snicker, "truth was, Mr. Henderson had a tendency to exceed his authorized power while at the same time expropriating frequencies that, strictly speaking, hadn't been assigned to him. That's how he reached a third of the country." Shelby pushed himself up a bit more in his chair. "You know, I tell you something interesting about him too. Somewhere in the late 1920s, W. K. Henderson started a campaign against national retail chain stores, the 'damnable thieves from Wall Street,' he called 'em. He saw how they were putting local merchants out of business, taking money out of the local economy, and he could see where it was going." Shelby gestured toward another room in the house. "I saw on the news recently that folks are protesting against some of those cheap chain stores doing the same thing."

"He was a man ahead of his time," Rick said. "Now—"

"That he was," Shelby said. "But I believe he went under during the Depression, like a lot of people, had to sell out to a new owner." He paused for a moment as something occurred to him. "But I don't suppose you came to hear me talk about that."

"No, sir," Lollie said with a smile. "We wanted to ask about your station."

"Oh, sure, I understand." He figured they wanted to hear funny stories about running a small station in a rural community. "Well, there was this one time I had to climb the transmitter tower to put in a new lightbulb, and I was up there, must've been three hundred feet up in the air, and I ain't no fan of heights, I should say that, but I was up there screwing the old one out when ole Bobby Gunnison flew by in his crop duster so close he almost knocked me off. I was hanging on by a safety belt for half an hour. My wife wouldn't let me up there after that."

They all shared a laugh over the story before Rick said, "Your son, Henry, was a partner in the station, is that right?"

Shelby thought that was an odd question since it didn't seem likely to lead to an amusing anecdote. Still, he said, "That's right, and my wife—Henry's mother—wouldn't let him climb the tower either. Had to hire somebody to do that. But to answer your question, yes. Henry had some money and he asked me to go in on it with him. Seemed like a good investment, so I bought in. At first he ran the thing and did a good job for being the son of an old dirt farmer. Even did a classical music show; he liked the German composers, as I recall. But the new wore off after a few years and he sold his interest in the station back to me. I kept it for another ten years or so before I finally sold it and went back to planting full-time. Made out all right on the deal, as I recall."

"From what I understand," Lollie said, "my grandfather and a man named Lamar Suggs worked at the station and made records of local musicians."

Shelby's body rocked as he tried to nod his head. "That's right. Had an old Presto disc recorder in the studio, least I think that's what they used. Didn't make much money though, distribution was always a problem."

Somewhere in the house a clock began to chime, prompting Rick to look at his watch. He had to get back to the station for his show, so he cut to the chase. He said, "Mr. LeFleur, this is a little off the subject, but do you remember anything about the murder of a man by the name of Hamp Doogan? This would've been back in the midfifties, when your son was sheriff."

Shelby cranked his head up and looked at Rick. It seemed to strike him all the sudden that these two hadn't come to ask innocent questions about his life in the radio business. He said, "What's this all about?"

"It's a long story," Rick said.

"Well, talk fast, son, I'm ninety-five."

Rick shrugged and said, "All right. A woman claiming to be Lollie Woolfolk hired me to find her grandfather. The day after I found him, he was murdered. The same woman then hired me to find Lamar Suggs. I tracked him down in Yazoo City, and a day later, he got killed too."

"Well, I hope nobody hired you to find me," he said. "What's that got to do with my old radio station?"

"Both of those men worked there."

"We employed a lot of people over the years," Shelby said. "I can't help it if two of them got tangled up in something fifty years later and got killed over it."

Lollie said, "Well, we think they were involved with something fifty years ago, Mr. LeFleur. We believe the woman who pretended to be me has a partner and they're after some tapes that were made at your station. They're known as the Blind, Crippled, and Crazy tapes. Does that ring a bell?"

It was hard to gauge Shelby's reaction, since they couldn't see his face, but based on body language it looked like they'd struck a functioning nerve. Shelby's friendly demeanor hardened into defiance and he said, "No. Never heard of 'em. And you oughta be ashamed coming into my house, asking questions under false pretenses."

Rick cleared his throat and, in mollifying tones, said, "Well, sir, I apologize if that's what you think, but we said we wanted to talk about your station and that's what we're doing." He explained the connection between Cotton, Jefferson, Tate, and Pigfoot Morgan, and how Pigfoot had been arrested for the murder of Hamp Doogan. "So," Rick said, "to the extent that your son, Henry, was involved in the case and was also running the radio station—"

"I remember all that," Shelby snarled. "I remember they tried that man and convicted him based on eyewitness testimony. All that was put to rest a long time ago."

"Well," Rick said. "Some things have come to light that make us wonder about that testimony. Do you want to hear about it, or should we leave?" He didn't care if Shelby threw them out, since they'd already gotten more information than they'd come for. In fact, he was sorry he'd asked the question, since he wasn't keen on telling the old man about the nefarious activities he suspected his family had engaged in.

Shelby sat there for a few moments, wrestling with his principles. On the one hand, he had to think about his family, even if they had been letting him down one generation after the next. But on the other hand, the truth was exerting a mighty pull on his conscience. Finally, begrudgingly, he said, "What new things have come to light?"

Lollie looked at Rick like she couldn't believe he would tell this old man such scandalous things about his family, especially since it was, for the most part, pure speculation. She pointed at her chest and shook her head no.

Rick shrugged and said, "Mr. LeFleur, how's your heart?"

"Strong enough for the truth."

Lollie felt sorry for the old guy and suggested that Rick reconsider. But Shelby insisted on hearing whatever it was. Rick decided to take it one disgrace at a time. After he told the story about Ruby Finch and the boxful of photographs, Shelby said, "That's why you came here? To find out if Lettie had a beauty mark on her face?" He grunted his dismissal of this bit of evidence, then said, "I don't even know what you think that proves."

"You're right," Rick said. "I don't think it proves anything by itself. And we wouldn't be here if this was just about a little adult photography."

"Well, spit it out, man. Just what are you here about?"

Rick explained his theory that the photos might suggest an affair between Doogan and Lettie, and that if Henry had learned of the affair, he might have killed Doogan, and if that was the case, it meant Pigfoot Morgan had been framed, presumably by Henry. "So," Rick said, "we're trying to connect all these dots. And one of them led us here."

"Huh." Shelby seemed unimpressed. "Even if you're right about all your what-ifs, and you got plenty, seems to me you're looking at the wrong people. Seems like you ought to be looking for this woman who came to hire you in the first place."

"Yes, sir. We've been trying to find her," Lollie said, getting to her feet. "But we didn't know where to start looking until a few minutes ago." She headed for the family photograph.

"What do you mean by that?" Shelby said.

Rick tried to catch her eye before she could say or do anything else, but Lollie was caught up in the moment. She grabbed the picture off the wall and held it in front of Shelby so he could see. She pointed and said, "It was her."

The news landed in Shelby's lap like life's final disappointment. "Cuffie?" He stared at the picture and Lollie's accusing finger hovering over it. "No," he said. "You're mistaken."

Rick was trying to figure out how to undo the damage, but it was too late. He had to go with it and see what happened. "I don't think so," Rick replied. "But I understand your reluctance to believe us."

"It must have been someone else," Shelby said, grasping at straws. "Someone who looks like her." He pushed the picture away.

"No, sir. I'm sorry," Rick said, sympathetically. "Do you know where we can find her?"

"I wouldn't tell you if I did." Shelby reached for the pendant button around his neck and pushed it. "It's time for you to leave."

"Mr. LeFleur, we're going to find her," Rick said.

"And what if you do? You can't prove a thing. I can say she was with me when these men were killed, just as easy as you can say she's the woman who hired you."

"Except you'd be lying under oath," Rick said.

"You're talking about my family!" Shelby raised a crooked finger and pointed to the door. "Now get out. I am not going to listen to another word of your nonsense."

They stood to leave just as Jessie came into the room. Rick said, "I'm sorry to be the one to tell you."

"Get out!" Shelby, hands trembling with rage, reached up and removed his hearing aids. "I don't want to hear another word of this!"

— — — — — — — —

CLARENCE MORGAN FIRST picked up a guitar when he was nine. By his tenth birthday, he could imitate any style he heard, from jazz to gospel to blues. They said he was a natural. When he was sixteen he went down to Orleans Parish in Louisiana to visit relatives. While he was there, he happened to see Lightnin' Slim playing guitar. He'd never heard anything like it. The sound of his instrument stuck in Clarence's heart like a knife. The look on the women's faces who were listening stuck with him too. That's when he knew he wanted to play guitar for a living.

For the next two weeks, he followed Slim from show to show, studying his technique, trying to learn how he got the sounds he did. When Pigfoot returned to the Delta, he kept trying to imitate Slim's sound, but the resulting style was distinctly his own. By the time he was arrested, six years later, he had found his voice and he had things to say, but he never got to share either.

That gnawed at him the whole time he was at Parchman because he figured he could've been as big as Howlin' Wolf or Magic Sam or Muddy Waters or any of 'em. He dreamed of playing on radio programs and television too. He dreamed of traveling the world, his name in lights. He could see himself up on the stage, wearing a glossy, tailor-made suit. And he could see those women too. There would be so many of 'em, he'd have some to share. Pigfoot Morgan, they'd say, was the sharpest-dressed axman you ever laid your eyes on. The only thing prettier than the man himself were the sounds he coaxed out of his guitar.

All those days in Parchman's fields pickin' cotton, all those nights locked up behind bars, and all he could do was dream of the life he never had, a glamorous life with a chauffeur and a personal assistant and his own tailor.

Pigfoot had been working on the details of his dream for fifty years. Sometimes he stayed up nights polishing it, getting everything just right. And now, as he approached seventy-three, Pigfoot was making his dream come true, or at least part of it. He knew he wasn't long for this world, so he was going to do his damnedest to live the life he imagined had been taken from him. The life of a star, a sharp-dressed man with an entourage. He straightened his tie and said, "Driver, slow yo' ass down. Road man pull us over, you gone be the first one he sees kilt."

Buddy aimed his dark glasses at the rearview mirror. "Yah, suh," he said, a bit thicker than he'd intended.

"Listen here, you can just cut cho eyes thata way," Pigfoot said, pointing forward from the backseat of Buddy's Cadillac. "And you best watch how you talk." He held up the rifle and said, "If I have to let you go, it's gone be the hard way."

Buddy tugged down on the front brim of his hat and looked over at Crippled Willie, who was in the front passenger seat looking a little nervous himself. They were both wearing their best suits, at Pigfoot's command, said his driver and personal assistant had to look respectable.

They were on Highway 12, heading for Tchula. A little past Belzoni, Pigfoot nudged Crippled Willie's shoulder with his rifle and said, "Go on, Reverend, call him again."

Willie nodded and pushed the redial button, then pressed the phone to his ear. After a few moments, he began to shake his head. He turned to the backseat and said, "They's still no answer."

"No answer, what?"

"No answer, Mr. Morgan."

Pigfoot leaned back in his seat, satisfied by Willie's performance but concerned about his lawyer. "All right," he said. "We'll try again in a little while."

Fifteen minutes later, Buddy turned the Cadillac onto Two Mile Road. He slowed down to navigate through the gaping potholes. When they reached the dead end, Buddy pulled into the rocky parking lot of the Starlighter's Lounge and, owing to a lack of depth perception, hit one of the rusty oil drums out front, knocking it over. "Damn." He looked in the mirror. "Sorry, Mr. Morgan." Try as he might, Buddy couldn't keep the sarcasm out of his voice.

"You think you halfway slick, but you ain't," Pigfoot said. "I know you tryin' to work evva last nerve I got." He shook his head. "But it's all right. You just do like you supposed to, things'll work out."

Buddy threw the car into park and slowly got out. Half of him wanted to take a chance and break on Pigfoot when the moment was right, get the gun away from him and just go a round with him to settle up, but the other half knew it wouldn't be enough. He owed Pigfoot more than he could pay, so he'd just endure these little humiliations and hope to come out close to even. He adjusted the knot in his tie and checked his reflection in the window. Then he opened the door and Pigfoot stepped out like he was the king of Holmes County. Buddy and Crippled Willie followed him to the front of the building, where Pigfoot came to a regal stop. He waited a beat, then turned to look at Buddy, who mumbled something as he stepped up to open this door too.

THE WOMAN SITTING at the bar didn't seem as amused as she had earlier in the day. Crazy Earl had been steady working on her, but he wasn't any closer now than when he'd started two hours ago. An empty gin bottle stood by the ashtray. Earl waved at the bartender and said, "Give us another drink, all right?"

"Can't do it," the bartender said from behind the newspaper he was reading.

"How come?"

"You ain't got no goddamn money."

Earl's head went back. "I know I ain't got no goddamn money," he said. "I don't need you to remind me. That ain't your job. Your job is pouring drinks."

The woman pushed back from the bar. "All right then. I think I'm gone."

Earl looked insulted and said, "Oh, it's like that, huh? You go on then." He waved a hand at the door. "You ain't no big thing. I can replace you right away."

The bartender turned the page and said, "You gonna sing the whole song or just that line?"

"John Lee Hooker stole that from me!"

The woman said she was going to see if she could find old Tommy Lester.

Earl said, "What's he got I didn't used to have?"

She said something about his wallet.

Earl laughed and said, "You'll be back. And I'll be at both doors waitin' on you."

She walked right out the front door when Buddy opened it for Pigfoot.

Pigfoot went in and paused next to Billy Dee Williams on the Colt 45 poster and gestured for the others to go ahead of him, like bodyguards clearing the way.

The place was empty except for the bartender and Crazy Earl, perched on his stool near the empty gin bottle. Hearing the footsteps he steadied himself on the rail and turned to see who was coming in. When he saw Buddy and Willie standing there in their suits, he said, "Damn. We got us two inta*national* niggers comin' up in here. And just the ones I need to talk to. C'mon over here and buy me a drink." He waved for them to join him at the bar. "Listen," he said, thinking they were approaching. "I been thinkin'. We gotta do somethin' 'bout Pigfoot." He slapped the bar and said, "That salty, shad-mouthed nigger shot up my house, tryin' to kill me. He's gone come for you too, 'less we get his black ass first." He turned and noticed that they hadn't budged, so he waved for them again. "C'mon, we'll figure it out." They just stood their ground, so Earl said, "Wha' choo waitin' on?"

Buddy and Willie stepped aside, and Pigfoot moved forward into a dim pool of light. The bartender, who didn't have a dog in this particular fight, disappeared slowly behind the bar with his paper. Pigfoot stood there with the Remington down at his side where Earl couldn't see it. Pigfoot said, "Who you calling a shad-mouthed nigga?"

The voice was both familiar and strange. Earl hung on to the bar rail as he leaned out to get a closer look at who had said that. He hadn't seen the face in fifty years, but he knew it was Pigfoot the second he saw him. "Shit!" The way he jumped, it looked like someone had hit him with a cattle prod. He snatched the gin bottle by the neck and broke it on the bar as he jumped to his feet swinging the jagged glass in front of him, cutting the air and sending a thin mist of gin across the room. He gestured for Pigfoot to bring it on, saying, "Ain't afraid of yo' black ass."

"Y'ain't, huh?" Pigfoot raised the rifle from his hip, bringing it into the light for the first time. "You 'fraid of this?"

Even somebody crazy as Earl knew a broken gin bottle wasn't much good in a gunfight. He muttered something obscene before he dropped it to the floor.

"Listen here," Pigfoot said with the authority of an armed man. "I shot up your raggedy-ass house to put some fear into that hard-shell hoodoo head of yours. If I'd wanted to kill you, you'd be dead. And it don't matter how many damn rusty nails you wrap up in that conjure sack of yours. Man ain't made no hand strong enough to keep you safe from me now."

Sensing that the danger had passed, the bartender stood up, pointed at the menu board, and said, "Any y'all hongry? Got some hot links, some tamales."

"Naw, unh-unh," Buddy said, speaking for everybody. "We ain't hungry."

Crazy Earl had bad intentions as he stared at Pigfoot and fingered the flannel sack in his pocket. Pigfoot kept the rifle on Earl while he turned to Willie. "Call him again."

Willie did as he was told and, a few moments later, said, "Still no answer." He hung up.

"Damn." Pigfoot thought on it for a second. "Somethin' wrong," he said. "We gotta go see about it." He gestured at Earl again with the rifle. "You own a suit?"

Earl squinted at him. "Say what?"

"You ain't gone be in my entourage lookin' like that."

"Wha' choo talkin' about, entourage?"

"Nigger, are you deaf *and* crazy? I axed if you owned a suit."

Earl looked at the way Pigfoot was holding the rifle before he said, "Got's old one."

"All right then, we gone get it."

"The hell you talkin' 'bout? What I need a suit for?"

"We goin' to see my lawyer."

— — — — — — — — —

IT NEVER CROSSED Crail's mind that a man could get so dirty digging such a shallow grave. But Cuffie was right, there was no point in carrying the lawyer around with him any longer, so he had to do something with him. When they got back to the cabin, Henry gave him an old U.S. Army M21, one of many weapons he'd confiscated during his tenure in law enforcement. He'd seized this sniper rifle from a bootlegger near Wayside who had refused to pay proper tribute. Henry directed Crail to a secluded spot on his camp where he might leave his attorney. "After you're done with him," Henry said, "you find those two down in Vicksburg and make it look like a lover's quarrel, you know? Somethin' like that."

Crail took the lawyer, the gun, and the money and told Henry not to worry. He'd take care of everything. Henry had his doubts, but he didn't have any better options, so he said good luck and hoped for the best. Thirty minutes and two shots later, Crail was tossing dirt on the body when Lynch's cell phone started to ring.

He threw on one last shovel of dirt and said, "Leave a message at the tone." Then he got in his car and headed for Greenville.

Two hours later Crail found himself in an awkward position. He was in the bathroom of the Bayou Caddy Jubilee Casino bent over and trying to get his head underneath the warm-air hand dryer. He'd used all the paper towels in the dispenser to wash himself and now he was trying to get the back of his neck dry. But since he could no longer flex his knee, it was tough sledding. Even with one hand against the wall and his bad leg stretched out straight, he couldn't get low enough. He finally gave up and shuffled over to a stall. Toilet paper would have to do. Once he was dried off, he went to the bar and had a double shot of Wild Turkey, then he lit a cigarette and headed outside.

Big Jim Magee was leaning against the trunk of his car in the parking lot when he saw Crail coming his way. He wasn't limping so much as he was dragging his bad leg behind him like a mad scientist's assistant. "Where you been?"

"Bathroom," Crail said. "Had to wash up." He ducked suddenly when he thought he saw the green head of a large mallard flying straight at him. He straightened up and looked at Big Jim, wild-eyed. "You see that?"

Big Jim shook his head. "See what?"

"Never mind," Crail said, looking around for more low-flying ducks. He pulled the envelope of cash from his pocket and counted some out. "You get that stuff?"

Big Jim opened his trunk and pulled a sack from one of his tackle boxes. He tossed it to Crail, who looked inside at the pills and the sparkly methamphetamine. It made him happy just to see it. He pulled one of the OxyContins from the bag and, rolling it between his thumb and index finger, said, "You know, these things come on kinda slow and last awhile, but they never really have a punch."

"Yeah," Big Jim said, rubbing his fingers together. "You gotta grind 'em up to get around that damn time-release thing. You wanna real buzz, you gotta snort it or shoot it." He looked in a different tackle box and came up with a hypodermic. "You need a rig?"

"Naw, I'll just chew 'em."

"Cool." Big Jim slammed his trunk shut and said, "So, where you headin'?"

He nodded south and said, "Vicksburg."

— — — — — — — — —

BLIND BUDDY COTTON pulled into the parking lot, crushing the pork bones Crail had left behind. Pigfoot leaned forward and pointed at a late-model BMW, the only car there. "That's his," he said.

Buddy pulled into the handicapped spot, then got out and opened the door for his new boss. Pigfoot stepped onto the asphalt like he was the head of the mob. He made the others wait as he straightened his tie and buttoned his coat. When he gave the nod, the four men in their dark suits moved toward the building in a stately procession. Crazy Earl led the way, wearing the same suit he'd worn to his wife's funeral. Crippled Willie brought up the rear, swinging his dead leg like a proud veteran from a forgotten war.

A minute later they were inside, standing at the door to Lynch's office. Buddy's head tilted back as he sniffed the air. "Smells like gasoline," he said. They looked at one another, knowing something was wrong. Pigfoot gave another nod and Buddy pushed open the door.

Pigfoot went in first, the others followed. They stood there for a moment, surveying the damage, drawers open, files strewn about. The smell of gasoline and burned paper and carpeting filled the air. After a moment, Crazy Earl said, "Damn. This a mess."

Crippled Willie kicked the empty Crown bottle and looked at the charred curtain crumpled on the floor. Absently he said, "Lord, Lord, Lord."

Buddy walked around the desk and stooped to look at the pile of half-burned documents and the two melted reels of tape on the floor by the safe.

When Pigfoot came around the desk and saw the melted reels, he felt a knot tighten in his stomach. He picked them up and stared at them. They were destroyed. He stood there trying to imagine what had happened. The tapes were his salvation. Without them, he had nothing.

Crazy Earl leaned over and peeked into the unhinged safe. He said, "You think this about you, boss?"

Pigfoot couldn't respond, rendered mute by his hopelessness.

"It's about him, all right," Buddy said, standing up. He was holding what was left of a burned file folder. The tab read: "Clarence Morgan—Trial Notes, Washington County DA." He handed it to Pigfoot.

The words sucked the remaining life from his eyes. He knew what this meant. It felt like a knife twisted in his gut. He kept staring at his name, wondering how it had come to this, how his plans had unraveled so easily. The simple flick of a match had reduced his future to ashes. He leaned against the desk as if it might help him resist the gravitational pull of despair. After a minute he said, "That was it." He shook his head slowly and pointed at the warped reels on the floor. "Man said those tapes, those files, was all we needed." Pigfoot let go and the tab fluttered to the ground.

Buddy and Willie were both wondering if these were the tapes from that night they'd recorded together, though neither

Pigfoot said, "It don't matter now, does it?"

After a moment, Crippled Willie put his hand on Pigfoot's shoulder and said maybe the lawyer had made a copy of the tape and the documents. The others agreed that this made sense and they made a show of combing through all the files and drawers, hoping to buoy his spirits, but there was nothing to be found and finally Pigfoot said what they were all thinking. "Ain't nothing here. Somebody beat me to it."

Earl said, "What're we gone do?"

Pigfoot took a deep breath and shook his head. "Earl," he said. "I don't know. That was all I had."

Crippled Willie said, "Well, now, you don't know that. Maybe the lawyer's took the copies with him wherever he's gone."

Pigfoot turned and stared at Willie. "It look to you like that lawyer left here with anything?" He looked at his shoes and shook his head. "I don't know what we gone do now."

Buddy wanted to keep his mouth shut and let the whole thing end right there, get back in the Cadillac, go back home. But his conscience wouldn't let him. It threatened to tear him in half, as he thought about what he'd done and all that Pigfoot had lost as a result. But it was more than that. It was more than the fear that had cracked in his bones when Pigfoot fired that rifle. And it was more than the trivial humiliation he felt every time he opened the door for Pigfoot and called him Mr. Morgan. They shared something stronger than all that bundled up with wire. The unrelenting assault on their dignity that had kept them in their place all their lives, that had kept them in fear and silence, was the deciding factor. They had a common enemy, and now they had a chance to strike back. Buddy reached into his pocket and pulled out Rick's card. He said, "I got an idea."

"DAMMIT!" LOLLIE HAMMERED the dashboard with her fist and said, "Why didn't you stop me?"

"You were going too fast," Rick said as he fishtailed the truck from Shelby's driveway onto the highway, spinning Crusty's carrier around on the floor. "Besides, I thought it was obvious we wouldn't want him to know we'd identified Cuffie." He shot her an incredulous look and said, "I can't believe you did that."

Lollie cinched her seat belt up a notch and said, "Yeah, well, looking back I can see how obvious it seems." She hit the dashboard again. "God, I'm an idiot!"

"I wouldn't say you're an idiot," Rick said as he pulled out his cell phone and punched in a number. "It's more like you learn ... *differently* from others." She was about to respond when Rick held up a hand. "Mike? It's Rick. Listen, I need a favor. There's a file on my desk that says 'BCC Reunion.' It's spot copy. Can you produce that, nothing fancy, just read it and get it on the air twice an hour? I'll explain when I get there. Thanks." Rick eased into the other lane and craned his neck to see around a slow-moving SUV in front of them. He ducked back just in time to avoid an oncoming combine harvester.

Lollie said, "What do you think he's going to do?"

"It's family," Rick said. "I suspect he'll warn her and do what he can to help her avoid the authorities." When he saw an opportunity, Rick punched it and shot past the SUV and toward oncoming traffic. As the engine strained to pass, Crusty poked his head out of his carrier and looked at Rick as if he was crazy.

Lollie stomped on an imaginary brake pedal and said, "Slow down!"

"No can do. If we're going to pull a rabbit out of this hat, we've got to move fast." They could hear the horn of the on-coming car as Rick pulled back into their lane with few yards to spare. He looked at Lollie, who had turned a whiter shade of pale, and said, "Call Detective Cruger."

She pulled her phone from her purse. "And say what?"

"Tell him to arrest Cuffie LeFleur."

"On what grounds?"

"Conspiracy to commit murder."

"But we can't prove it."

"Please, work with me! Make it sound like we can."

While Lollie tried to get Cruger, Rick hit redial on his cell. "Mike? Me again. Another favor." He dictated a press release announcing the discovery of the legendary Blind, Crippled, and Crazy tapes. "WVBR is going to broadcast them for the first time in conjunction with a reunion concert featuring the original artists in a couple of days," he said. "Get that to every radio and television station from Port Gibson to Memphis," he said. "And every newspaper in the state. And fax a copy over to Smitty Chisholm at the blues museum, tell him to e-mail it to everybody who gets his newsletter. I need everybody in the Delta to know about this."

Rick hung up and listened as Lollie tried to make the case to Detective Cruger. She told him about Doogan's photographs and Lettie's beauty mark and how Henry and Shelby had reacted to their questions. When she told him Rick had identified Cuffie as the woman who'd hired him, using Lollie's name, Cruger agreed that it looked like she might have something to do with the deaths of Woolfolk and Suggs. But, all things considered, he said he wasn't about to arrest Henry LeFleur's granddaughter without more than that. He told Lollie they would check Cuffie's phone records and, if warranted, try to contact her for an interview. She tried to argue with him, explaining that Shelby knew the whole story, that he was bound to tip her off, but Cruger just repeated his position and ended the call.

After Lollie recounted the conversation, Rick said, "That's the best he can do? We serve up a prime suspect in an open murder investigation and he says he *might* interview her? Hell, they ought to be kicking her door in."

"And I get the feeling they would be if she wasn't one of the nuts hanging in the LeFleur family tree."

"Son of a bitch!" He slammed the steering wheel. "She's going to get a helluva head start, thanks to him."

Lollie shook her head. "It's not his fault," she said. "I'm the one who screwed this up." She turned and looked out her window, thinking about her grandfather.

Rick looked at her. She was right, and he was tempted to say so. They'd stumbled across the answer to their question, just had it land in their laps like a Christmas present. All they had to do was get back to the computer, track her down, and they'd have her. Case closed. But Lollie had tipped their hand and he knew now that the odds of finding Cuffie and her partner were going past slim and heading toward none.

But at the same time, Rick knew he was the one who had led the killers to Lollie's grandfather in the first place, so he wasn't in much of a position to be throwing stones about who screwed what up. Instead, he started singing. "Baby, don't you worry, we gonna get them bad guys. I said, baby, don't worry, we sho nuff gone catch them bad guys. We gonna thow 'em in the jailhouse, and let 'em sit there till they dies."

SHELBY STAYED IN the sitting room for a long time, trying to decide what to do. He had two choices and he didn't like either one of 'em. He wheeled his chair over to the drum table and sat there, staring at the picture of himself in the cotton field with his father, wondering what he would have done. He remembered how his dad had impressed upon him the importance of reputation, how it took a lifetime to earn a good one while a single bad decision could ruin it forever.

Sitting there under the gaze of all the LeFleurs, Shelby realized that for the first time in nearly a century, he felt old. His body had been failing him for decades, but that wasn't it. It was this damn choice and all the implications, threatening his legacy and crushing his sense of propriety. He saw himself as an honorable man, principled and moral. Willing to do the right thing and accept the consequences.

But blood's thick, so he picked up the phone and dialed. When Henry answered, Shelby spoke in grave tones. He said, "Son, we have a problem."

This wasn't what Henry wanted to hear just now. He was already having second thoughts about sending that twitchy Crail Pitts to kill that smart-ass disc jockey and his nosy little girlfriend. If Pitts screwed up and got caught, they'd have more problems than they could say grace over. And now his feeble-minded father was on the phone with more. Henry took a deep breath and, though he really didn't want to know the answer, said, "What kinda problem?"

"Cuffie's got involved with something bad."

Henry could taste the acid coming up his throat. "What're you talkin' about? Bad how?" When Shelby told him what had happened, Henry went ballistic. "Are you crazy? The hell're you thinkin' lettin' them into your house? Talkin' to strangers."

"They said they wanted to talk about the radio station." Shelby felt older with every word that came out of his mouth, like his bones were turning to dust inside him, like his teeth could crumble at any moment. "I didn't know what they were after. And it was just a damn fluke that they saw her in the picture. We have to do something before they find her."

"Goddammit, you old fool, what you mean is, you done made a mess and now I gotta clean up behind you."

"Son, don't you ever call me a fool."

"I'll call you worse," Henry said, his voice rising. "And I won't think twice about it." He hung up without another word.

Shelby slowly lowered the phone until it rested in his lap. He was disgusted with himself and his son and everything else that crossed his mind. He looked around at the faces he'd known, the loved ones he'd buried and hoped to honor with a righteous life. And the longer he looked at them, the older he grew. And he stared at them until he felt ancient and found himself wishing he had died long ago so he wouldn't have to know what happened next.

INTERNAL DERANGEMENT IS the medical term for joint dysfunction, and Crail Pitts was in the process of taking the term to a whole new level. The intense swelling caused by the infection had finally choked off the flow of blood. His knee, once red, bloated, and feverish, had cooled and turned a soothing tone of bronze. At this rate, it would be black in less than twenty-four hours.

Crail was parked in a magnolia's shade by the border of the Vicksburg National Military Park. He was listening in fascination to the odd crackling sounds coming from his knee. The sounds were due to the accumulation of gas bubbles under the skin, caused by festering gangrene. The fascination was due to an internal derangement of a different sort, one stemming from the hallucinatory side effects of the sulfamethoxazole combined with the methamphetamine and OxyContin abuse, not to mention all the whiskey he was drinking to keep his keel even.

Looking down with waxy eyes, Crail gently poked his wound, coaxing a sweet-smelling watery discharge from one of the skin eruptions. He rubbed the liquid between his fingers before wiping it on the map of Vicksburg he had picked up at the visitors' center on his way into town.

He had marked the location of the WVBR studios on the map. He figured it would be the best place to ambush Rick and Lollie, first because he knew they had to show up there sooner or later, and second because it was on the edge of town, surrounded by woods.

It was time to get moving. Crail lit a cigarette and snorted another line of meth. He turned on the radio as he headed for the station, where he planned to scout for a place to lay in wait. The guy on the air was playing a Van Morrison song Crail thought was for pussies. Not only that, but it sounded even worse since that busted speaker was reproducing sound about as well as a worn-out shop rag. He wanted to call and request something that really rocked, like some Molly Hatchet or Whitesnake or Sabbath, but before he could decide what he wanted to hear, the deejay said, "WVBR with Van the man's version of 'Mean Ole Frisco.' Before that, the Allman Brothers with Elmore James's 'Done Somebody Wrong.' Of course if you're a blues fan," the jock said, "you already knew that. And if you're a blues fan, you're going to want to tune in Friday night when Rick Shannon presents what is without question an historical program."

The deejay played the spot Mike Rushing had produced for Rick. It opened with a scratchy recording of Sylvester Weaver's "Guitar Rag" before the voice-over started: "They were lost for fifty years. But now they've been found. The tapes from one of the most famous recording sessions in Mississippi history have been rediscovered. The legendary Delta bluesmen Blind Buddy Cotton, Crippled Willie Jefferson, and Crazy Earl Tate spent one night in a studio in 1953 and produced what some have called the truest blues ever recorded. The Blind, Crippled, and Crazy Sessions, coming to WVBR tomorrow night at nine."

— — — — — — — — —

CUFFIE WAS BROWSING at the Outlet Mall with a bounce in her step. Crail had destroyed the tapes and Papaw Henry was taking him under his wing. Things were working out just fine. She was admiring a pair of Gucci knockoffs when her cell phone rang. Her nerves tingled when she saw Crail's number. She wondered if he'd gotten rid of the lawyer. "Hey, baby," she said. "How's that *thing* going?"

Crail was still so bewildered by the revelation about the Blind,

Crippled, and Crazy tapes that all he could say was "What thing?" Then it hit him. "Oh, that lawyer? Don't worry, ain't nobody gonna find his body."

Cuffie dropped the bogus Guccis and, through gritted teeth, said, "Unny-hay? Ooo-yay eed-nay to be or-may airful-kay on the ell-say own-phay."

Crail held his phone in front of him and assumed the expression of a befuddled dog. "Baby," he said. "I think you're breaking up."

A second later she said, "Can you hear me now?"

"Oh, there you are. Anyway, listen, I got some bad news."

"What do you mean, bad news?"

"Well, I'm down here in Vicksburg doin' that *other* thing for your papaw Henry, right? So I was listenin' to that radio station when they ran this commercial sayin' they'd found the tapes of that Crazy, Blind, Crippled thing and they're gonna play 'em on the air."

"What?"

"Yeah, it don't make no sense to me either."

"You told me you got rid of 'em."

"That's what I'm sayin'. I thought I did. I mean, I got rid of something," Crail said. "But I didn't have any way to listen to 'em, so I guess it coulda been something else."

"Like what?"

"How am I supposed to know that? You just told me to—"

"Jesus," she interrupted. "All right, gimme a minute."

While she was thinking, Crail said, "Listen, I'm gonna need some mora them antibiotics."

"What?"

"For my knee. It's not red anymore. It just looks a little bruised," he said. "But it's still not a hundred percent."

"Yeah, all right, I'll see if I got anymore," she said. "Now listen. It's not all bad. You're down there anyway to do that other thing. And if they've got the tapes, at least you know where to find them, right? And since you're going over to the station anyway, you just need to take care of things *before* they play the tapes. You understand? We can't afford any more screwups."

"Well, baby, I don't think I've—"

The phone beeped at her. "Damn, I got another call. You just take care of that problem and I'll buzz you later." She clicked over. "Hello?"

"Cuffie." A man's voice, serious as a guilty verdict.

"Oh hey, Papaw Henry, I just talked to our *mutual friend,*" she said with a wink in her voice.

"Yeah? Well, I just talked to Shelby Jr."

"Oh, bless his heart. How's he doin'?"

"He's worried."

"Awww, about what?"

" 'Bout you hiring that private investigator to find Suggs and Woolfolk, just before they got killed."

Cuffie paused, wondering how on earth he knew this. "What are you talkin' about, Papaw?"

"Cuffie? Don't. This is serious," Henry said. "I know the whole thing. You two're trying to find those damn tapes."

Figuring she had to give her innocence one more shot, Cuffie said, "Tapes?"

"Goddammit, you know what I'm talkin' about. And you've put yourself and this whole family in harm's way over nothin', goddammit. Them tapes're long gone. And if that boyfriend of yours doesn't get to that smart-ass Shannon before he tells the cops who hired him to find those men, you're goin' to prison. Nothin' I can do to stop that."

"Papaw, that's impossible." This time she tried it with a roll of the eyes and a small chuckle in her voice. "I just talked—"

She almost dropped the phone. Her anonymity was the only thing standing between her and large matronly prison guards with butch haircuts and a taste for sorority girls.

Before she could say anything else, Henry continued, "Now let's face it, that Pitts boy ain't about to go bowlegged totin' his brains around and, frankly, I don't think the little he's got're nailed down real tight, he kept twitchin' when I saw him, so I have no doubt he screwed something up when he killed Suggs and Woolfolk, bound to have left some evidence an investigator's trying to connect to a name. And once he gets that name, I guarantee you they'll find a way to connect it to you. And we can't let that happen. You understand?"

"Yes, sir, but—"

"No buts," Henry said. "Now listen close. Let's hope it doesn't come to this, but if he gets caught, he's gonna point a finger at you. That's just how it works. And you're gonna deny every bit of it and agree to testify against him."

"Papaw, I—"

"Shut up, girl! That's how it'll play out if it goes bad. I've seen it enough to know. Your phone records'll show you and him talked, probably on the days he killed them. But you'll say you never knew what he was doing or why he was doing it. You were just in love and it turned out that son of a bitch was using you, trying to get at those tapes, 'cause he thought they were worth some money. You'll say he's the one got you to hire Shannon in the first place, threatened to hurt your family if you didn't. Now I know that's a hard pill to swallow, but it's either him alone or both of you. And I don't wanna see you strapped onto no gurney."

"Dammit, Papaw," she snapped. "Listen for a minute! They have the tapes. They're going to play 'em on that station in Vicksburg tomorrow night."

IN HIS SHAME, Shelby started to drink. The moment Henry hung up on him, Shelby's regrets got the better of him, so he sneaked a bottle out of the cabinet hoping to drown his guilt. He'd had three by the time Jessie found him in the sitting room, going from photograph to photograph, talking to his family, like Dick Nixon seeking counsel from the portraits of dead presidents.

"Mr. LeFleur, gimme that bottle," she said. "You know you ain't s'posed to drink."

Shelby fought the best he could, but she was half his age and she got it away from him. "I've dishonored his memory," he said, looking into his father's eyes.

"That's too bad," Jessie said. "But agonizing your liver just gone make it worse. What's got into you?"

"Shame," he said, slightly drunk. "Shame at what I've done and what I haven't." He gestured for Jessie to push his chair over to a table where he pointed at a photograph of himself and Henry standing next to the transmitter tower of their radio station. "That was the day we first broadcast," he said. "Boy was too lazy to farm, but he'd break a sweat looking for an easier way to earn a living."

Jessie knew Shelby was in his cups and in the mood to talk, so she sat on the sofa and said, "Yes, sir. That's a shame too. I know you and Missus raised him better'n that." She followed that with a solemn nod, as if she'd seen the whole thing.

Shelby cranked his head back and looked toward the mantel at the photograph of his beautiful young wife. "We tried to teach him right from wrong, didn't we? Went to church and read the Bible together." He turned to look at Jessie. "We didn't want him thinking the way some people around here were."

"Yes, sir. I know that's right."

"But he turned his back on everything. Got involved with that Citizens' Council, bunch of ignorant crackers, full of nothing but hate. And he used that radio station to get cozy with that jackass governor who named him to the damned Sovereignty Commission."

"Sometimes chirren just don't act right," Jessie said, as if talking about a six-year-old.

Shelby stabbed a finger in the air, saying, "You believe the things they did? Poorest state in the nation and they spent tax dollars investigating whether the sanctity of construction sites in Mississippi had been compromised by the presence of integrated toilets."

"Mmmm, mm." She shook her head. "It's a shame, all right."

"God forgive 'em," Shelby said. "Could've educated people, helped 'em get out of the hole we'd dug for 'em. And that wasn't near the worst of what they did, either."

"No, sir, sure wasn't."

"Now, you're too young to know about the way things were, that long ago."

"Oh, yeah," Jessie said with a coy laugh. "People always confusing me and that Alicia Keys. But I'm older'n you think."

"You haven't seen half what I've seen," Shelby said.

"That's true," Jessie said. "But my mama told me about how it used to be and I saw plenty of it on my own. Still do." Her mother had been a maid all her life, cooking and cleaning for other people and raising their children along with her own. She never made much but somehow saved enough to send Jessie to nursing school. And she was proud of that. Her own daughter, a registered nurse. Something unthinkable for her own generation. "She likes to say she's retired now," Jessie said with a smile, thinking about her mom, sitting on the front porch of the little house she owned, not much more than a shotgun shack by the railroad tracks on the outskirts of Greenville, just rocking away in a rusty old lawn chair, not thinking about regrets.

As Jessie talked about her mother, Shelby's mind began to wander. He started thinking about all the things he'd witnessed, all these people still suffering the terrible transition from a culture of slavery to a forced coexistence, all mixed with the Bible and the relentless humidity. He thought about how vestiges of the past continued exerting influence on the present, keeping people where they'd been for too long, all the half-assed reformers he'd seen come and go without reforming anything except maybe their bank accounts. But in the end, he returned to his biggest disappointment. His son. Shelby said, "You know why I invested in that radio station? It was a chance for that boy to make a positive difference. I remember telling him the day we took that picture. I said you don't just set up a transmitter and start broadcasting." Shelby's voice began to rise and he shook as he spoke. "You are granted a license and with that comes the responsibility to serve your community. And the Lord knows they needed that."

"Now don't get all worked up," Jessie said, thinking of his blood pressure. She got up and crossed the room, returning with a sphygmomanometer.

Shelby kept talking about how he thought the radio station could give folks a sense of belonging to something, give them a voice, bring people together, heal the collective wounds they'd all suffered. He shook his head grimly. "But that sorry-assed boy didn't give any of that a second thought. Just used it to further his ambitions."

Jessie rolled up Shelby's sleeve and fit the cuff around his thin arm. "Now, Mr. LeFleur, don't get yourself agitated."

"My own boy! Sorry as he could be!" Shelby made a derisive snorting sound as his head flopped back down. "I'm too old to be nice about it anymore, Jessie. I've been holding my tongue till it hurts not to say it." He hit the arm of his chair.

"Hold still," she said.

"Gave him every advantage, could've done anything, pursued any dream he had, but what'd he do?" Staring at the blanket covering his lap, the old man just shook his head.

"I know," Jessie said. "I know." She pointed at the meter. "Now look how your pressure is. You gotta calm yourself, you gone have a stroke."

"That boy brought us so much shame, I don't have words. He didn't care about folks too poor to afford a dream, let alone chase it. And now got the nerve to complain the government doesn't do enough for them while making sport of poor folks waiting for their checks."

"Mmmm, hmm. I heard that." Jessie removed the inflatable cuff and set it on the table. She rolled his sleeve down and gave him a comforting pat on the arm. Then she sat on the sofa and waited to see if he'd said his piece.

Shelby was quiet for a minute before he said, "Hell, everybody would've been better off if we'd just picked our own cotton."

"Now, don't get started again," Jessie said. "You just get upset."

Shelby waved her off. "No point in being upset," he said. "It's over and done."

"That's right," she said. "Ain't no goin' back to change the past."

He snorted and said, "You're right."

"Well, okay then. That's a good attitude. You just relax now."

Shelby looked up at her with his eyes as bright as she'd ever seen. He said, "But I *can* do something about the future."

CRAIL WAS STANDING at the altar with Big Jim at his side. They turned slightly when the organ began to play the wedding march. Cuffie floated down the aisle, like an angel, on her daddy's arm. Big Jim gave Crail a nudge and said something lewd about the honeymoon. Crail smiled and nudged him back 'cause he'd been thinking the same thing.

A beaming Monroe LeFleur handed over his daughter under the approving gaze of a church full of LeFleurs and Pittses. Crail glanced at the front row on the groom's side and saw his mama wiping a tear from her eye. The preacher said the words and asked the question and Cuffie said she did. And when Crail's time came, he said he did too. And when he said it, the squirrel to whom he had spoken scampered up the tree, bringing Crail back to the wooded area across from WVBR where he was having his most fully realized hallucination yet.

He was in a good spot for a shooter, directly across from the front of the station. He backed his car between a couple of large pines, then spent an hour stumbling through the woods in a narcotic haze gathering branches and moss and leaves that he used to camouflage his position. His nuptial fantasy had started when he'd paused to take a leak. It was a tremendous relief and it seemed to go on forever. The pleasurable sensation lulled his eyes shut and he began to breathe deeply and nearly fell asleep where he stood. When the squirrel chattered and Crail regained a sense of where he was and what he was doing there, he tucked himself back into his jeans and got back in the car, thinking about how beautiful Cuffie was in a wedding gown.

He'd been sitting there a few minutes when he tilted the rearview mirror down and stuck out his tongue. It seemed to be swollen. And the eruptions around his eyes and mouth were becoming increasingly difficult to ignore. He wondered if maybe the antibiotics had expired and lost some of their potency. He took a couple more and chased them with some whiskey. Then he picked up his phone and punched a number. After a moment he said, "Hey, Mama, it's me. I got some good news," he said. "Well, I talked to this man who's gonna take care of that insurance thing." He paused for her reaction. The thrill in her voice made him feel grand.

"Yeah," he said. "It's good as done." She asked how he'd managed this and he said, "Oh, I'm just gonna do him a favor, Mama, you know, no big deal. He said you'll get whatever you need. So it's all gonna be all right." When his mama told him how proud she was of him, it just about made him cry.

They talked for a few minutes before a vehicle pulled up to the station. "Listen, Mama, I gotta go do that favor right now. You just take care. I'll call you later."

Even though Cuffie had given a good description of Rick's truck, Crail couldn't say for sure if it was him. This was due to the fact that Crail had put so much foliage on his windshield that he could barely see out of it, so Crail turned on his wipers and leaned forward in full squint.

Up to that point, neither Rick nor Lollie had noticed the car in the woods opposite the station. And even now, as they turned to see what was rustling in the bushes, they didn't see Crail or his car, they were so well hidden. Crusty, however, who was draped on Lollie's arm, had some sort of primal response to the sudden movement of branches. His tail puffed and he leaped back into the truck and hid under the seat.

When Rick and Lollie turned to look his way, it dawned on Crail that he might be giving his position away, so he turned the wipers off. He took the scope off his rifle and used it to peer through an opening in the branches. He didn't see anything that looked like reels of tape.

Lollie tried to coax Crusty from his hiding place. "By the way," she said. "Now that we've invited the killers to come down here to look for the tapes, what sort of security do you have in mind?"

Rick pulled his gun from the glove compartment, clipped the holster to his belt, and gave it a pat. "We've got a gun and a stout-hearted cat, I'm not sure what else you wanted. We could call the cops, but I doubt they'll send anybody to watch over us based on our plan."

"You sayin' it's flimsy?"

"Yeah," Rick said. "But I've worked with less."

— — — — — — — — —

IN THE WANING light of the late summer sun, with mosquitoes sucking bad blood from his neck and arms, Crail began to imagine himself a Confederate sniper in the back swamps near New Carthage, preparing to fire on Grant's XIII Corps as they moved on the natural levee road looking for a route to advance on Vicksburg. He could hear cannons booming in the distance as the

big guns fired from their positions on the bluffs overlooking the
river. His task was vital, he told himself. If the tapes fell into the
wrong hands, the Confederacy was doomed, plus Cuffie wouldn't
see him anymore.

As he peered through the Redfield scope, Crail saw Rick and
Lollie go into the station with a peculiar-looking cat. Crail
picked up the transistor radio he'd brought and tuned it to
WVBR. He plugged in an earpiece and stuck the radio in his
pocket. Then he remounted the scope on the M21 and got out
of his car. Ten minutes later, after the other deejay left for the
night, Rick came on the air talking about the discovery of the
legendary recordings.

During his first commercial break, Rick ad-libbed a new
Blind, Crippled, and Crazy spot, stressing the historical value of
the long lost tapes. He took some calls from blues enthusiasts and
put them on the air, figuring the more time he dedicated to repeating his lie, the better chance he had of getting word to Cuffie
LeFleur and her partner.

Crail listened to the show as he made a wide circle around the
station, dragging his dead leg along behind him like a bad habit.
He was looking for a window, but there were none at the back
of the station, so he came around the side, where he saw a dim
yellow glow. He crept closer until he reached a large window
with curtains partially drawn. Peeking into the studio where
Rick was broadcasting, Crail saw CDs and albums and lots of
tapes but none that were obviously what he was looking for.

Crail's momentum was checked by a sudden wave of dyspho-
ria as his last dose of meth wore off. His eyes began to lose focus
as he stared into the studio, his face almost pressing against the
glass. His breath fogged the window each time he exhaled. The
tiny voice in his ear seemed to mesmerize him.

"Let's take a call," Rick said. "You're on the air."

"Yes, hello," a young man said. "I was wondering if you planned to discuss the music in more scholarly terms instead of merely the colloquial, and by that I mean a more technical discussion about the significance of employing flatted seventh and third notes of a scale and how these tones as a deviation from the major scale of a key constitute a structure inherited directly from the classical form while at the same time being drawn from the correlate in the mixolydian scale, built on the perfect fifth degree, which is adumbrated by the third harmonic of any tone."

Rick shook his head like a stunned cartoon character and said, "Yeah, I tell you what. Let me put you on hold until we get to that." He punched the button, then took another call. It was Smitty Chisholm.

"Hey, you're just the man I wanted to talk to," Rick said. "How're you tonight?" From the sound of his voice, one got the impression that Smitty was so excited he was about to wet his little curator pants. "So," Rick said. "Did you hear that last call?"

"Yeah," Smitty said. "And I just gotta say, that boy's not listening to the music if thinks it's all about deviations from the major scale. I mean, when I listen to the blues, I hear sweat and longing, joy and jealousy, anguish and envy and hatred and all the other human emotions and circumstances."

"There's some sex in there too, if I'm not mistaken," Rick said.

"Well, a back-door man ain't there to deliver the milk."

Rick asked Smitty to tell the different stories that had sprung up around the legendary recording session and how the tapes had gone missing in the first place. Smitty told the tales with gusto, including biographical bits about the musicians.

Rick said, "Listen, if you'd like to join our discussion, give us a call at 800-800-WVBR."

BILL FITZHUGH

The phone number gave Crail a great idea. Maybe he should call and tell them to cut the chatter and play something that really rocked. He hadn't heard any Deep Purple in a while, and boy, wouldn't that be good? Hey, how about a classic, he thought. He started to hum "Smoke on the Water."

Unaware that a Deep Purple fan was lurking outside the window, Lollie continued screening calls from the sound booth adjacent to the studio. She looked at Rick through the soundproof window between them and held up three fingers. "Let's go to line three," Rick said, pushing the button. "You're on the air."

"Yeah," a man said. "Where'd you find them tapes at?"

Crail had reached the lyric about Frank Zappa and the Mothers being at the best place around when the caller on line three snapped him back to attention. He pushed the earpiece in deeper and listened. He knew that voice. He rubbed his eyes and peeked into the studio again.

"Well, you know, that's a great question," Rick said. "A lot of people have looked for these tapes over the last fifty years and, obviously, without much luck. But we tracked them down to a private collection right here in Mississippi. But the owners asked us not to reveal their names. So I can't tell you exactly where or how we found them."

"Well, lemme ask you this," the man said. "You got 'em there at the station with you rat now?"

Rick hesitated as he and Lollie exchanged a glance. She gave a nod, acknowledging the familiar voice. Then Rick said, "You bet I have 'em, but we can't play them until tomorrow. That's the deal we made with the owners. They want us to promote it for a couple of days before airing them. You have a particular interest in the tapes?"

"Nope," the man said. "Just curious." Then he hung up.

"Well, all right," Rick said. "Thanks for calling. I know for a fact there are folks out there who are more than 'just curious' about these tapes. But I tell you what, we're going to take a break, and when we come back we'll talk more about the Blind, Crippled, and Crazy sessions. So stay with us." Rick started a Tampa Red record that opened with "You Can't Get That Stuff No More." He pulled off his headphones just as Lollie burst into the studio.

"That was Henry LeFleur," she said, pointing at the phone.

Rick nodded. "Sounded like he was calling from his car too."

"You think he's coming here?"

"It's possible," Rick said. "But I'm wondering how he knew to call and ask about the tapes in the first place. Our signal doesn't reach Moorhead, and, even if it did, he doesn't strike me as a classic-rock fan."

"He said he still has his feelers out," Lollie said. "Somebody must've called and told him." She paused, a curious look on her face. "But why would he ask if we have the tapes? He told us they don't exist." She looked a bit confounded as she said, "You think he's the one who killed my grandfather?"

"Fifty years after whatever happened?" Rick shook his head. "Seems unlikely."

"Should I call the cops?"

"And say what? That a man called the station after we gave out the number and asked people to call?" He shook his head. "We're on our own until something happens."

"Terrific," Lollie said. "I'll go paint a bull's-eye on the front door while we wait."

- - - - - - - - - -

BASED ON THEIR urgent expressions, Crail figured Rick and Lollie had recognized Henry's voice, though he wasn't sure what that bought him any more than he understood why Henry had called in the first place. Hadn't he hired Crail to do this? Why not just let him take care of it? Crazy old coot. Crail was trying to decide what to do next when he noticed a beam of headlights sweep across the trees behind him as a car turned into the station's parking lot. He stuck his head around the corner of the building and saw a 1971 Coup DeVille nearly clip Rick's truck before lurching to a stop. Who the hell was this? he wondered. Then it hit him. What if Shannon had lied about the tapes and this was someone delivering them? This could be his big chance. He twitched at the possibility.

The driver, a black man wearing a porkpie hat, stepped from the Cadillac and opened the back door. One by one, all the other doors opened until there were four old black men in suits, standing around the big car. None of them were carrying anything that looked like reels of tape. But, Crail noted, one of them was holding a rifle.

The four men climbed the concrete stairs to the landing at the front door of the station. The driver knocked and took a step back, waiting for someone to answer.

Rick was in the studio putting on his headphones, about to go back on the air, when Lollie burst in again. "There's someone at the door," she said with a slight panic in her voice. Rick decided to let Tampa Red go into his next song, then he went out to the front office with Lollie just as Buddy knocked again.

Rick triggered the intercom and said, "Who is it?"

"This is Bernard Cotton."

Rick and Lollie exchanged a glance before Rick responded, "Blind Buddy Cotton?"

"That's right. I got Pigfoot Morgan with me. Wanna talk to Mr. Shannon."

As he was saying this, the sound of another car pulling into the parking lot came over the speaker. Buddy, Willie, Earl, and Pigfoot all turned to see who it was. Crail craned his head farther around the corner of the building for a better view. They heard the transmission as the driver slipped it into park. The car sat there, idling, its headlights shining on the blues quartet.

Rick hit the intercom again and said, "Who just pulled up out there?"

"Don't know," Buddy said. "Ain't got out yet."

Pigfoot raised his free hand to shield his eyes from the lights just as Henry LeFleur got out of his car. He was still wearing his camos and he had his chrome .38 in his hand, though he kept it hidden behind the car door. The way the men were standing, Henry couldn't see the rifle in Pigfoot's hand. And he figured they couldn't see him with the lights in their faces, so he took his time before he said, "Well. Mr. Morgan. I see you done paid your debt to society."

Pigfoot knew that voice. He remembered it from when it was telling lies about him in that courtroom fifty years ago. He tightened his grip on the Remington and said, "Paid somebody's, that's a fact."

Buddy tilted his head down so the brim of his hat shaded his eyes. He stepped up behind Pigfoot and, in a low voice, said, "Sure wish you hadn't taken my pistol."

"It's right in front of you," Pigfoot said.

Henry brought his gun into plain sight, saying, "Wha' chall talkin' 'bout up there? Y'all here to make a request or you goin' inside to record somethin'?" He smirked.

Rick and Lollie were listening to the whole thing on the intercom. "That's LeFleur," Lollie said. "What do we do?"

"Not sure yet," Rick said.

Crail wasn't sure what to do either. He figured he'd have surprise on his side no matter what he did, so he could shoot the guy with the rifle if he wanted, but then what? He'd signed up to take care of Rick and Lollie but not these four men on top of that. What a bloodbath that would be. On the other hand, maybe if he stepped out and let them know they were surrounded, he could disarm the one guy and send them on their way before going inside to take care of the business he was hired to do. Before he could make a decision, Crail noticed the guy with the hat slipping a pistol from the back of the other guy's waistband. He tensed, realizing it was all about to happen. He imagined Cuffie watching him as he stepped out from behind the building with his M21 and shouted to Henry, "They got guns!" Then he started squeezing the semiautomatic's trigger, sending brass and bluesmen flying.

Crazy Earl and Crippled Willie hit the dirt, each man praying to a different power as they crawled toward the Cadillac for cover.

Henry yelled, "Son of a bitch!" as Crail's shots cut straight through his radiator and lodged in his engine block. He couldn't see through the cloud of steam spewing from the front of his car, but he fired a few shots anyway. One of them whizzed past Crail's ear. The others ripped into the station, near where Pigfoot and Buddy had been standing. Henry figured he needed a better position, so he took off for the tree line at the edge of the parking lot as fast as his old legs would carry him.

The moment Crail had opened his mouth to yell, Buddy and Pigfoot had jumped off the landing to crouch next to the concrete stairs. After Henry turned to run, Pigfoot fired a couple of rounds in his direction. Then he turned to Buddy. "You get that one," he said. "LeFleur is mine."

INSIDE, LOLLIE JUMPED when one of Henry's slugs shattered a clock on the wall behind her. She grabbed Crusty's carrier and crawled under a desk. "Can I call the cops now?"

Rick pulled his gun and said, "Yeah, now would be a good time. Just tell them not to shoot me when they get here," he said, putting his free hand on the doorknob.

She peeked out from under the desk. "Where are you going?"

"Outside," he said.

"Are you crazy?"

"What do you mean?"

"They're shooting out there!"

Rick looked at Lollie like she was the crazy one. "What did you think was going to happen? The killer was going to show up to surrender and then we'd all go out for pie?"

"But"—she pointed, her fingers in the shape of a gun—"they're shooting."

"Yeah, well, why should they have all the fun?" Rick gestured at the phone. "Nine-one-one," he said. "Then go play some more records. I can't stand dead air." He turned his attention to the door, trying to think of a clever strategy, but nothing came to mind. So he yanked it open only to find himself standing in the headlights of Henry's car. He dropped to one knee and fired a few shots until he blew the lights out. In the darkness that followed, Rick stepped onto the landing and saw Buddy pressed against the front of the building, his gun trained on him.

Rick made a friendly gesture and said, "Hey, Buddy. How's it going?"

Buddy coughed a bit and said, "Ain't dead yet."

"That's good," Rick said, looking around. "Who all we got out here?"

Buddy gestured with his hat. "Pigfoot went that way, after LeFleur." He wagged his pistol at the corner of the building. "Somebody else shooting from this way. Didn't give his name." He looked over at his car. "Willie and Earl're over there."

"Okay. You go see if you can help Pigfoot. I'll see where this other one went."

"All right with me."

After Lollie called 911, she crawled back into the studio and put on a John Lee Hooker CD. The signal shot out from the tower in all directions. That guitar riff coming out of radios all over the Delta, where the song had come from in the first place; that riff and the stomping foot that was the basis for everything from ZZ Top's "La Grange" to the Stones's "Shake Your Hips." And then that voice, putting death in the air. *Boom, boom, boom, boom.*

A rifle shot rang out near the tree line.

Bang, bang, bang, bang.

That was followed by the report of Henry's .38.

Gone shoot you right down.

　Lollie was crawling across the floor of the main office, heading for the desk, when several shots blew the knob off the back door.

Right offa yo' feet.

Lollie froze as the door creaked open. Looking up, she saw a wild-eyed man with yellow skin and open sores hopping into the room with a rifle. He aimed the M21 at her and said, "Where're those tapes?"

Boom, boom, boom, boom.

"Who the hell are you?" She stood up slowly.

"I'm the guy looking for the fucking tapes!"

Looking into his yellowed eyes, Lollie knew this was the son of a bitch they wanted. She said, "Are you the guy who killed Tucker Woolfolk?"

"Yer damn right." Crail fired a shot at her feet. "Now where're the goddamn tapes?"

A haw haw haw haw.

She saw his knee and knew it was the answer. She just needed to get closer. Lollie pointed at it with a sympathetic expression and said, "What happened to you?"

A hey hey hey hey.

Crail seemed oddly touched by her concern and lost focus for a second. "Oh," he said. "Guy stuck a fork in my knee."

"Bless your heart." Lollie inched closer, reaching out for the discolored joint as if she could heal it by the laying on of hands. Just as she came within reach, she felt the barrel of his gun touch the crown of her head. "I'm going to ask one more time," Crail said, wobbling slightly on his one good leg. "Where're the damn tapes?"

That's when Rick stepped into the doorway and said, "Drop the gun."

A haw haw haw haw.

It was a fleeting moment as Crail's eyes darted one way and Lollie moved the other. In a single fluid motion, she swept an arm up, knocking the barrel of the gun toward the ceiling while simultaneously snap-kicking Crail's bad leg. The gun fired as his knee folded like a jackknife, only backward. He keeled over sideways, cracking his head on the corner of a desk as he went down.

Heyyyyy, baby!

— — — — — — — —

A HUNDRED YARDS away, near the transmitter tower, Buddy was listening for anything that would tell him where Pigfoot was. The buzz from crickets and cicadas was loud enough to drown out the sounds of men running in the woods. But the sudden exchange of gunfire off to his left rose above the din. Buddy turned and headed in that direction. As he drew closer, he could hear desperate voices. He said, "Pigfoot, where're you at?"

He heard Pigfoot say, "You mine now."

"You don't put that gun down," Henry said, "you gone right back to Parchman to die."

"Not me," Pigfoot said. "No, sir. Now, get on yo' knees."

Buddy pushed through a bramble of shrubs into the clearing, where Pigfoot was holding the Remington on Henry LeFleur, whose arm was bleeding where Pigfoot had hit him with a lucky shot. It looked like he was going to execute him, right here and now, with a shot in the ear. Buddy eased over to him and said, "Don't do it."

Pigfoot said, "Gots to." And he squeezed the trigger.

— — — — — — — —

"SAY WHAT? I can't hear anything in this ear," Henry said, holding his hand to the bloody wounded thing.

"I said you ought to be thankful I didn't shoot the damn thing *off,*" Pigfoot said. He shook his head as he and Buddy frog-marched Henry at gunpoint back across the field, toward the station.

"Some people have hard time showing gratitude," Buddy said.

They were passing the transmitter tower when they saw a line of squad cars and ambulances snaking down Porters Chapel Road and squealing into the parking lot, their lights and sirens shrieking. By the time Pigfoot and Buddy got back to the studio with LeFleur, Rick and Lollie had explained the story to the cops. They arrested Henry as paramedics tended to his wound. They took photos of the scene and statements from Pigfoot, Willie, Earl, and the others. A moment later they brought Crail out of the studio, handcuffed to a gurney. He had regained consciousness and was babbling something about Grant's XIII Corps advancing on the levee road.

While the police processed the crime scene, Rick called Smitty Chisholm to say, "You know that reunion concert we talked about earlier? Well, turns out it's tonight." He held the phone away from his ear as Smitty shrieked. "No, I'm not kidding," Rick said. "Yeah, even Willie Jefferson. He's agreed to perform since it's a special occasion. Only one problem. We don't have any instruments."

Smitty arrived fifteen minutes later with a couple of harps and half a dozen guitars.

As they were loading Crail into one of the ambulances, a minivan came racing toward the station, honking urgently and weaving through the crowd. Henry, with hands cuffed behind him, looked out from the backseat of the squad car with a bewildered expression. He knew who it was, but for the life of him he couldn't imagine what he was doing here.

The minivan came to a stop and Jessie got out. She went around to open the side door. She pushed a button, extending a short ramp to the ground. A moment later, with all eyes turned their way, Shelby came rolling down the ramp in his wheelchair. He stopped at the bottom and cranked his head back, looking for Rick and Lollie. Spotting them near the front of the station, his head flopped back down and he steered his chair in their direction with Jessie walking alongside for guidance.

Rick and Lollie watched them approach in silence. Finally, Rick opened his mouth to say something but Shelby cut him off. "You can stop pretending you have those tapes," he said. "I know for a fact you ain't got 'em."

— — — — — — — — —

THE POLICE EVENTUALLY allowed everyone to go into the studio while they continued working the crime scene. Jessie accompanied Shelby into the sound booth while Rick and Lollie situated Buddy, Willie, Earl, and Pigfoot in the main studio. Smitty set up the microphones and helped tune the guitars. Once they were set, Rick opened his mike and said, "I'm honored to have in the studio with me four men tied to one of the great legends of the Delta blues. Blind Buddy Cotton, Crippled Willie Jefferson, Crazy Earl Tate, and Pigfoot Morgan. Over the past couple of weeks, we've talked to a lot of folks about what happened the night of the infamous recording session, and we've heard a lot of different stories. What we're going to do now is try to patch together the truth of it." Rick paused before continuing.

"Also in studio with us is Shelby LeFleur Jr., who has brought with him the answers to a lot of questions. Mr. LeFleur, we're going to turn to you first." Rick asked a few preliminary questions to set the stage. Then he moved on to meatier stuff.

"I wasn't there," Shelby said in answer to one question. He gestured at Buddy, Willie, and Earl. "I'll let these gentlemen tell you how they came to make the recording. All I can do is explain how it ended up in my possession." He took a deep breath and pushed himself up in his chair. "The tapes were made the night Hamp Doogan was murdered. Mr. Suggs and my son, Henry, figured they could get a few records on the market before these men signed a contract with Paramount. Later, in the wake of Mr. Morgan's trial, they looked into the matter and discovered that Mr. Cotton was under contract to Imperial Records, I believe it was, owned by a man name of Whitsett. They talked to him about buying Buddy's contract, but he had heard about the tapes by then and he tried to hold them up for more than they were willing to pay, so they just put the tapes on the shelf. They were more trouble than they were worth."

Shelby continued, "About six months later Mr. Suggs and Mr. Woolfolk made some recordings with a Mr. Charlie Hawkins. One of the records that came out of that session was a hit for them, though I don't recall the name of the song."

"That was 'Marcus Bottom Blues,'" Smitty said.

"Yes, I believe that's right," Shelby said. "In any event, they got busy promoting Mr. Hawkins all over the place and making more records with him and wasn't long before they just forgot about those other tapes. Some years later, Henry sold his interest in the station back to me, which included all the master recordings they owned. By the time I went to sell the station some years after that, I had found the tapes and I knew they were valuable for more than one reason." Shelby squirmed in his chair and said, "Maybe I should have destroyed them or edited them, but I didn't. I left them just as they were. I knew they could help Mr. Morgan, but I couldn't bring myself to release them because of what I thought it would mean to my family's name. It's a burden

I've carried my whole life." Here Shelby hardened a bit and said, "But when I heard about Cuffie and what she was involved in, that was the last straw. That's why I brought them."

Rick turned to Pigfoot and asked him to tell his story.

"Hard to know where to start," Pigfoot said. He seemed self-conscious and vaguely reluctant. "I wasn't there when they made the tapes." There was a sense of shame in his voice when he said, "I'd drove off and left 'em before that."

Buddy shook his head. "You did what you had to," he said. "I'd been in your place, might've done the same." He doubled up and coughed a bit.

"You told us to come on," Earl said. "And we shoulda." He gave a little nod. "It was just bad luck."

Crippled Willie leaned toward the microphone. It looked like he was going to sing another verse of the same song, but instead he said, "We all met at the Key Hole Club. Must've been 'round midnight . . ."

——————————

IT WAS A last-minute thing. As soon as Tucker Woolfolk found out about it, he got to a phone to call Lamar Suggs, in Memphis. Lamar had gone up there to record Limpin' Jim Crawford at a club off of Beale Street. It was around nine o'clock when he got Tucker's message that Cotton, Jefferson, and Tate were meeting at the Key Hole Club around midnight to play awhile, to make some money before heading for Wisconsin to record for Paramount. So Suggs packed the Presto disc recorder in his truck and started the long drive south on Highway 61.

The streets of Leland were electric that night. All up and down McGee Street between West Second and Railroad Avenue, men were sporting they fine suits and hats, and the women had dressed to kill. The whole town was pulsing like Chicago on a Saturday night. The gins were working overtime on all that cotton the fields had given up. Everybody had a little something jinglin' in they pocket. The time had come to have some fun. Reward for all that sweat.

A couple of women from the Negro Temperance League trudged silently along the sidewalk with small signs decrying the dangers of whiskey. Both were plagued by the proud yet defeated look of people who knew the game was over before it had started. Around the corner, "Hot Tamale" Charlie sold wares from his wagon while that little monkey of his, tethered on a leather leash, bobbed his head to the music coming from the joints.

The skin ball had been rolling three days and four nights. Blind Darby and Shorty Parker were the only ones had caused any trouble so far, and that was over at the Rexburg Club on the first day. They'd been shootin' craps when Shorty accused Darby of chokin' the dice. Well, Darby broke on him with that bone-handled knife he called his Casey Mae. But Shorty had him an ice pick. They both got in they licks, patted each other up pretty good, before one of Henry LeFleur's deputies carted both of 'em off to jail.

On the second day, Red-eyed Jesse—who was one of the luckiest skin players to draw a hot breath—got sent packing back to Texas after he scooped a low one in the rough and lost all he'd brought. Before he left town he told everybody he was gone back to Houston to get some more money, then he was gone come back and whup everybody's ass. And that made everybody laugh.

Just standing on the street corner you could feel the skin ball gathering momentum, like it was rolling down a steep hill. The music seemed to get louder as the worries lifted. It was like this all over town, hardworkin' folks havin' theyselves a time.

Stumpy Rivers had been playing at the Key Hole Club for a

few hours before he started to wobble. He always opened with some lively reels, old minstrel stuff that got the crowd going good. Always something you could dance to. He played in a vigorous style until he got enough drink in him. Then he slowed way down. The later it got, the sadder the songs became, until they were just plain draggy, and if he didn't fall off the stage, somebody'd carry him off. But for now, he had the place hoppin'.

You could hardly get across the Key Hole, the room was so crowded. A hoot and a holler rose from the dice game in the back corner near where Buddy was sippin' some good brown whiskey. One of the skin players hollered something about the big moose comin' down from the mountain and everybody laughed at that.

Buddy stood up when he saw Crippled Willie stepping and flopping through the door with his guitar case. Buddy waved a hand up over the guys shooting craps and called Willie over. He passed the table where the Florida flip game was going in the front. He nudged Puddin' Hatchet on the way by and said, "You not puttin' yo' cabbage on that hand, are you?"

"Naw, hell, I ain't beggin' yet." He laughed and slapped Willie on the back. "Just playin' with my stuff out the window, you know, jus' in case."

One of Henry LeFleur's deputies was back in the kitchen picking up the early cut from the games and the bar. He had a quick drink himself, then took a big can of tamales to go.

Earl and Pigfoot came in not too long after that. Earl never seemed to care much about how he looked. But Pigfoot looked fine in a new suit. While Buddy pulled his guitar from the case, he told Pigfoot he ought to sell Earl one of his old jackets, just out of charity. Earl fixed Buddy with one of his crazy hoodoo stares and said he didn't need no fancy bait to get no womens. That was for men didn't have nothin' else to offer. They all laughed at Crazy Earl. Then they made a toast to they good luck, wasn't everybody who got a record contract with Paramount. "We the last of the good men," Earl said. They drank a little more whiskey and tuned up.

There was a bright flash on the far side of the club as Hamp Doogan tried to get a dozen folks from Greenville all in the same frame. He lowered the camera, shaking his head. "Y'all cozy up or all we gonna get is ears on the sides of the picture," he said with a gesture that looked like he was playing accordion. "That's it," he said. "There we go. Hold it!" Another bright flash lit the room.

Over at the skin game, the players began to chant, "Let the deal go down now. Let the deal go down."

"Jack's the bet," said the dealer. "Who wants one for a dolla?"

Baby Buddy said he was dead on the turn, hadn't seen a card all night. The dealer told him to pull his narrow black ass up to the cryin' post and hitch onto it. Either that or get a new card. Everybody hooted at that, then resumed the chant: "Let the deal go down."

Temptation was floating thick under everybody's nose. The smell of pork and onions and tobacco and perfume mixed with marijuana and sweet whiskey breath whispering promises of untold delight. A big laugh rose from the crowd when Stumpy Rivers finally tipped over sideways, then got to his feet and stumbled off the stage.

Buddy was the first to get up and play. Things had gotten draggy toward the end of Stumpy's set, so Buddy picked up the pace with a sort of boogie-woogie thing. It only took about eight bars to turn the mood around. By twelve bars, Buddy had a grinding rhythm pushing hips in lewd circles. Whole bodies started rocking as he did some fast changes and threw in some dirty lyrics to get a couple of ladies up front laughing. Earl moved to the piano bench and chugged up a rhythm that worked pretty good with Buddy's thing. Then he hollered for Willie to bring it on up and bust the roof off. The three men played a couple of things together, trading leads on one song in particular that sounded like a fast train going on a track.

After a few reels, Buddy said he was gone step aside and get a drink. He waved for Pigfoot to come on up and take his spot. Pigfoot came on up and turned some heads with his sound, starting off with his favorite song, "It's Mighty Crazy," the first thing he'd learned from Lightnin' Slim. He smiled when he saw a couple of gamblers pick up their money, grab their dates, and start to dance.

Looking out on crowded rooms like this was the one time these men saw the faces of their fellows not dragged down by their place and circumstance. The food and the drink and the dance and the rhythm and the possibilities put the life back in their bones and, for those precious hours, it was all good.

31

LATER ON THAT NIGHT Hamp Doogan packed up his stuff, said he was heading out to Chick's Inn, out north of town. Had somebody out there wanted a little something and Hamp was the man to deliver. He figured he'd sell some more of his pictures there too. Plus he'd heard a rumor Elmore James was gone drop by and play later and that was sho' 'nuff gone draw a crowd.

He loaded his car and pulled away from the curb. But he failed to notice Henry LeFleur lurking in the alley, watching with an evil eye. A second later, Henry pulled out and started to follow. He stayed back a ways as Hamp turned on East Third and then north on Highway 61. It was only after they got out past Tyler and Yeager Streets that Henry began to close the distance. He knew where he wanted to stop him, and that was still a few miles out.

Hamp had drunk a few and wasn't paying as much attention as he ought to, though it wouldn't have mattered even if he had been. His time was coming.

A few miles later a car came speeding down the road

going the other direction. It was Lamar Suggs hell-bent for the Key Hole Club. When Henry's red lights popped on and started dancing in Hamp's mirror, he figured the speeder was heading for a ticket. But the sheriff didn't turn around. He kept following Hamp with his lights on. Hamp didn't give it a second thought. He'd never had a problem with anybody in the sheriff's department that a few frog skins couldn't resolve.

He'd started to pull to the side when Henry hit his spotlight and shined it toward a farm road off to the left, hidden by a line of trees. Hamp drove up there and turned on the gravel road. He started to pull over again, but Henry hit his siren and waved Hamp farther down the road. Hamp drove another fifty yards before he pulled over and killed his engine. As he sat there, waiting for the sheriff, he peeled fifty off his roll and folded it behind his driver's license, figuring that would be that.

Henry sauntered up and said, "Get out the car, nigger."

Hamp noticed Henry's revolver was still holstered, yet he had a pistol in his hand. He didn't know what to make of that or the "nigger" Henry had spit his way. The whole thing seemed hinky, put Hamp on edge. It wasn't part of the normal let-me-see-your-license-and-did-you-know-how-fast-you-was-going routine. Still, he'd never had any problem with LeFleur before—always figured he was too dumb to know all that was going on and was just happy to make his money—so Hamp played along with it, acting friendly all the way, though he did sense a little something tighten up in his gut. He looked around as he got out of his car. He'd never noticed before, but things don't get much darker than a dirt road in the Mississippi Delta at this time of night. Hamp held out his license with the money tucked underneath and said, "Evening, Sheriff, how're you to—"

Henry pistol-whipped him across the face, knocking him down. The money fluttered to the ground around him as Henry said, "Nigger, you think I'm blind? You think I don't know what's what?" Hamp was too stunned to answer. He spit a bloody gob and felt a half-broken tooth in the back of his mouth. He tried to push himself up to his knees, but Henry kicked him in the ribs, taking him down again. Henry pulled something from his shirt pocket and dropped it on the ground by Hamp's head. "You think I'm just some dumb-ass cracker?" It was a picture of his wife, Lettie, posing in a way Henry had never seen in person. He'd found it on a man he'd arrested the night before, a gambler down from Missouri for the skin ball. The man, who had no idea the woman was Henry's wife, said he'd bought it in St. Louis off a guy who sold such things.

Henry knew Doogan was making pictures like this, but in his wildest dreams he couldn't imagine Lettie was involved. He'd been so busy managing his rural empire (and getting a little on the side) that he didn't realize Lettie had grown bored sitting at home, all alone, night after night. Even with all his feelers out, Henry had no idea she'd started to spend time with that floozy, thrill-seeking Ruby Finch. And even if he had known the two of them were sneaking around behind his back having some fun, he never would have guessed that Lettie would try cocaine, let alone become fond of it. But she had. And when she wanted more and couldn't come up with the money without making Henry suspicious, Hamp suggested posing for the photos.

Henry kicked Hamp in the ribs again and shouted, "Where's the rest of 'em, nigger?"

Hamp figured Henry had finally put two and two together. If that was true, his goose was cooked. If Henry didn't kill him out here on this dark road, he was bound to search the car and find what was in there, and that would put him in a deep hole for a long time.

Henry bent over and yelled, "Answer me, nigger!" A cheap

cigar dropped from Henry's shirt pocket when he leaned down. He'd been passing them out for the past two months, ever since Lettie had given him his first son, Monroe. At first Henry told himself that the boy's unusual complexion was because he was a baby and they always looked funny. The truth crossed his mind once or twice, but he beat it back. He couldn't allow it even though it was staring up at him from the crib every single day. But when he saw the picture of Lettie, the obvious came to mind, and he knew what he had to do.

Henry knew the first time he'd laid eyes on Hamp Doogan that he was trying to pass. He wasn't trying to pass in society or anything, that wouldn't work here, but from the moment Hamp stepped off that train from up north, Henry said to himself, *octoroon*. Not that he cared. Hamp was just providing a service, and he always paid his tribute to the law. So for a long time, it didn't matter. Mattered now, though.

"I asked you a question, boy! Where're the others?"

Hamp could hardly breathe after that second kick. He wanted to explain, wanted to swear, there weren't any others, but he figured Henry wouldn't buy it. He'd seen the one, knew there were others, had to be. Hamp was fucked. The only good chance he had was his gun, but he'd left that in his car. Still, he had no intention of dying on his hands and knees on a gravel road in the middle of the night, so he grabbed Henry's ankles and yanked them out from under him. The gun fired into a tree as Hamp scrambled to his feet and took off running toward the highway.

Henry struggled to get up, his slick shoes slipping on the gravel as Hamp put distance between them. He was just about out to the highway when Henry righted himself and got off his first two shots, catching Hamp with both. They spun him around and tangled his feet, and he stumbled, face-first, onto Highway 61. As he lay there, struggling for breath, he could feel the life pulsing out of his body just as sure as he could hear Henry LeFleur coming his way.

— — — — — — — —

BUDDY AND THEM played until two, then it was time to pack up and hit the road. They had five hours to get to Memphis to catch their train. Roads and the law being what they were, it was going to be close. They were putting the last guitar case in the back of Pigfoot's old Packard when Lamar Suggs skidded into the parking lot kicking up a cloud of dust. "Hey now," Suggs said, leaning out his window with a six-toothed grin. "Y'all just gittin' here?"

"Eve'nin, Mr. Suggs," Buddy said. "No, sir. We fiddna leave."

He reacted like Buddy had just spit at him. "The hell you say." Lamar opened the door abruptly and got out. He wasn't anything to be afraid of physically. He was a scrawny bit of white trash, but he advanced on Buddy with a finger aimed at his face. "Listen to me, boy, I didn't drive back down here from Memphis in the middle of the night for the fun of it. We gone cut a few sides 'fore anybody goes anywhere. That's just the way it's gone be." He waved a bony hand at the club and said, "Now c'mon, get your stuff."

"Mr. Suggs, we can't," Buddy said, tipping his hat toward Pigfoot's car. "That's all they is to it." He bit his lower lip to make sure he didn't say anything else, though there was plenty waiting.

They glared at one another for a moment before getting into a heated argument. Suggs grew more abusive with each objection Buddy or Willie voiced. The whole thing was agitating Pigfoot, getting under his skin. He was full of piss and vinegar, and this just shook it up. He was young and strong and just finding himself, a man in all of his six feet. And he was damn tired of putting up with this kind of shit. Pigfoot was one of them troublesome coloreds. Talking about people's rights and all that kinda foolishness. How everybody is due respect, like they was white. With an attitude like that, it didn't take much of Lamar Suggs to pop Pigfoot's cork. He tried to tolerate, but the man finally said the wrong thing. Pigfoot took exception to it, and then he took a swing. Suggs partially dodged it but still took a shot on the side of his head.

A small crowd watched as Earl grabbed Pigfoot while Buddy and Willie tried to calm Suggs. It took all of Earl's strength to drag Pigfoot toward the car. He was ready to kill the man.

Buddy and Willie stood between the two parties and, in the process, Buddy did what he could to check Suggs for a gun. He seemed to be unarmed, but Buddy wasn't sure. He told Suggs they were sorry, but they had a train to catch. "But I heard Elmore James supposed to drop by and play out at Chick's Inn later on. You oughtta head out there if you wanna record something. Probably be worth somethin' someday."

Earl pushed Pigfoot into the driver's seat and said to the others, "Let's get out of here 'fore anything else happens." The rest of them got in the car, hoping the trouble was over. They weren't looking for it. They just wanted to get to Wisconsin.

Suggs was spitting and cussing and waving his fist. His face was pinched and red and furious. "Don't you drive off on me," he shouted as they pulled out of the lot. He bent over, grabbed a rock, and put another ding in the trunk of the old car. "Goddamn niggers!" Suggs stood in the parking lot for a while trying to decide what he was going to do and, after a minute, he turned and headed inside. He needed a drink or two after bein' disrespected like that.

— — — — — — — — — —

BUDDY, WILLIE, AND Earl took turns doing their imitation of Lamar Suggs trying to intimidate them. Pigfoot was still wound up a little bit but laughed and said, "You know I'da cleaned that cracker's plow, you hadn't pulled me off like you did."

"Oh yeah," Earl said. "I'm his guardian angel. Probably saved his sorry life." He turned and threw a phony punch at Willie, who twisted his head like a stuntman to play along. "I'm surprised that right of yours didn't kill him."

They were still laughing at that when the headlights shined on something in the road ahead. Pigfoot slowed down. He leaned forward, pointing, and said, "The hell is that?" A moment later they realized it was a man, facedown in a pool of blood. Pigfoot stopped about ten yards short of it, not sure what to do. They all sort of looked around, but it was pitch black and there was nothing to see. The man was lying in the other lane, one leg akimbo, one arm reaching for the stripe in the road like it might be the thing to save him. Pigfoot slowly eased the car up alongside the body. Nobody said a word until Buddy opened his door.

"What're you doin'?" Pigfoot said.

Buddy didn't answer. He just got out. Earl and Willie got out too.

Pigfoot looked into the darkness surrounding them and blurted, "What are you—" His mouth tensed as the fear crept in. "This ain't nothing but trouble. Get in here and let's go."

Willie looked down at the body and nodded. "That's Hamp, all right."

Pigfoot was half-past nervous. He knew they shouldn't be there, knew if they hadn't stopped, nothing bad would have come from this. But now? He said, "C'mon, let's go!"

Earl bent down and felt for a pulse. He stood up, shaking his head. "Ain't been dead too long."

HENRY LEFLEUR HAD been searching Hamp's car back on the farm road. He stopped when he saw the Packard slow down. He watched as the three Negroes got out and looked at the body and he figured this was as good a chance as he was going to get, so he walked back to his car and turned the key to start it.

Pigfoot heard the engine. His head snapped to look, but he didn't see anything. "Get yo' black asses back in the car or you be walkin' to Memphis!" He could feel all kinds of bad about to happen.

Henry put on his headlights and the red police light at the same time. He hit the siren and the gas and kicked up some gravel. He liked a dramatic entrance.

Buddy, Willie, Earl, and Pigfoot turned to see the lights coming down the farm road toward them. Pigfoot yelled over the siren for the others to get back in the car. But none of them moved. He yelled again and swore he was going to leave them standing there. The lights were getting closer and he screamed, "Goddammit, c'mon!" But they seemed frozen, like it was their part to play. And it didn't matter how loud he hollered. But Pigfoot wasn't going to stay for whatever happened next. If his friends were too dumb to leave, that was their problem. He knew there was no explanation four black men could give that would let them leave the county under these circumstances. They'd all end up swinging in the breeze, like Billie's strange fruit. Pigfoot couldn't stand the thought. The tires burned on the road and he shot out of there like a rocket.

LAMAR SUGGS HAD a couple of drinks before he decided he might as well go on out to Chick's Inn, see if Elmore James showed up, before he called it a night. He was heading up Highway 61, a few miles north of town, when he saw the red lights, the men standing in the road, and what looked to be a dead body. At first he figured there'd been a wreck. But then he saw who LeFleur had handcuffed together. He was smiling when he pulled up to the scene and said, "Hey, Sheriff, what's going on? You need any hep?"

LeFleur explained how he'd come across these three Negroes soon after they'd killed the other one lying on the road. Said there was another'n had driven off. Didn't get a look at him, though.

Lamar smiled. "I can tell you who that was," he said with understated enthusiasm. "It was that Pigfoot Morgan. You know, works over at the cotton compress with this one." He pointed at Buddy, then explained how he'd seen them all leave the Key Hole Club together, half an hour earlier. As he did this, he turned and gave a squinty smile to Buddy and the others.

They all denied any wrongdoing. But it didn't matter, and they knew it. They were in the wrong place at the wrong time. The ambulance arrived a moment later to take Hamp Doogan's body away. Henry put Buddy, Willie, and Earl into the squad car and said he was taking them back to the jail.

"Well now, Sheriff, hang on just a second," Suggs said. "I got a better idea."

— — — — — — — —

THEY TOOK BUDDY, Willie, and Earl over to the radio station and put them in the production room. Suggs told them to get the chairs from the far wall and circle them around the X marked on the floor with white tape. Then he set up a microphone in the middle before going to the control room to set the levels.

The men didn't speak until Henry walked in. Willie said, "Sheriff LeFleur, you know we ain't killed that man. You *know* it. You was watching from up that farm road the whole time."

"He was dead when we got there," Buddy said.

"This ain't no bad luck," Earl said. "This a setup."

Henry laughed. "Niggers, y'all crazy? Either you killed that man or it was that Morgan boy. Right? I caught you there with the body. You can't deny that. I looked around, didn't see nobody else. You see anybody else out on that road?" He shook his head to emphasize his point. "No, you didn't. And you know why? 'Cause there weren't nobody else. So, like I said, either you killed that man or it was that Morgan boy." Henry held a finger up, like he was offering a deal, and said, "But I tell you what, I'm gonna be fair about this. I'll let you pick if it was one of you or the other'n." He gave a big-hearted smile.

Buddy shook his head. "You know that ain't right."

There were no surprises in Henry's response to this comment. He leaned into Buddy's face and made things as clear as they needed to be. Then he looked over at Lamar, who was in the control room giving a thumbs-up, saying the levels were good and the tape was rolling.

Henry swaggered around the room, told them all how it was gonna be. Earl, Willie, and Buddy knew they had a choice in the matter, but it wasn't a good one. There were too many lives in the balance, women and children who didn't have anything to do with what had happened. It was a circumstance they had to accept. After he'd made that much clear, Henry said, "Well, anyway, why don't y'all just start makin' them sounds you do."

"We ain't got no guitars," Willie said, throwing a finger toward Memphis. "Pigfoot run off with 'em."

Henry hadn't thought of this until now. He got red in the face and yelled at Suggs, "Lamar! Where we keep the gi-tars?"

The gi-tars weren't that much to speak of and the harps were pretty tired too, but they played, and after everybody more or less tuned what they had, Buddy counted 'em down. Slowly. One . . . two . . .

One . . . two . . . three . . .

Buddy started with a lone note, low and troubled. He bent the thing just as Willie came in to make a chord of pure despair. Earl played along underneath, with a steady, cheerless rhythm. Their changes were brooding, dark. The lyrics full of doom and injustice.

They did six songs before Henry said they were done and made them sign the contracts and the statements naming Clarence "Pigfoot" Morgan as the killer of Hamp Doogan. He held them all in jail for a few days, until they caught Pigfoot, then he told them all to make themselves scarce. Said he didn't want to see any of their sorry black asses until Pigfoot's trial was long over, lest they get a subpoena, show up in the courtroom, and contradict their previous statements. That wouldn't do.

When they got out of jail, they all went their separate ways. They'd missed their train and their opportunity in Grafton, Wisconsin. They stayed away for a couple of months thinking about what they'd done. And when they finally returned, none of them was the same man that had left. Willie had turned to Jesus. Buddy had grown hard and self-loathing. Earl had turned up his crazy knob.

After getting out of jail, Earl tried a hand to fix things. Went to a slaughterhouse and bought him a beef tongue, split it from the tip down to the base. Wrote the name of the district attorney and Henry LeFleur on a piece of paper and put it in the split. Added eighteen pods of hot pepper and pinned the tongue back together before dropping it in a tin pail filled with vinegar. Kept it there until the day they were supposed to hand down the verdict on Pigfoot. Took the tongue out, doused it with kerosene, and burned it. But hoodoo's no different than regular praying. The prayers are always answered, just that sometimes the answer's no.

Pigfoot never had a chance. He was caught trying to cross the river at Friar's Point and was brought back to Greenville where, it would be fair to say, he received a swift trial. It would be less fair to say he was convicted by a jury of his peers. But convicted he was and sentenced to fifty years on Parchman Farm. He maintained his innocence for fifteen years before he gave up. Figured he was wasting his breath.

About thirty-five years later, a lawyer named Jeremy Lynch read an article in an obscure blues fanzine that a friend of his published. The article was titled, "Blind, Crippled, Crazy, and Railroaded—What Happened to Pigfoot Morgan?" It was a broad-strokes retelling of the legend of the night Buddy and the others were to leave for Wisconsin, including the pure speculation that Pigfoot had been framed for the death of Hamp Doogan. There was no proof offered, just a what-if, but it was enough to tickle a lawyer's antennae. Sensing an opportunity, Jeremy Lynch did some research that led him to the special-collections library at the University of Mississippi law school. There he found the prosecutor's original notes along with the tape recording of Ruby Finch's testimony which, together, brought Pigfoot's conviction into serious doubt. With this, Lynch knew he had a solid (and profitable) case, so he went to visit Pigfoot and offered his legal services.

32

"**WE'RE BACK ON** WVBR-FM," Rick said, coming out of a commercial break. "If you're just joining us, we're talking to Buddy Cotton, Willie Jefferson, Earl Tate, and Pigfoot Morgan about the legendary Blind, Crippled, and Crazy sessions. Also here in the studio is Shelby LeFleur Jr., who has been in possession of the lost tapes for all these years." Rick looked at his guests and said, "Unless any of you have something to add, I suppose it's time to play the tapes."

No one said a word. They all had their eyes on the reel to reel. So Rick reached over and hit play.

"Y'all sit over there," Suggs was heard saying. "'Ginst that wall. Bring 'em chairs out at the end, a little crescent shape, like 'at. Where 'at X is." You could almost see him pointing.

The words and the ambient sounds triggered memories as strong as smell for the men who were in the room that night. It was as if the magnetic tape had recorded their fear, preserving it for half a century, so they could experience it again. Hearing these voices was like a visit from the grave. Buddy, Willie, and Earl exchanged eerie glances.

On the tape, Henry made things clear. One of them was going to jail for Doogan's death, or they could put it on Pigfoot Morgan's plate. The choice was theirs.

"You know that ain't right," Buddy said.

Henry barked, "You know what, nigger? Turns out that me and the sovereign state of Mississippi are the ones 'round here gets to say what's right, not you."

"Levels're good," Suggs said. "Let's cut a side."

Henry gave half a laugh. "All right, boys," he said. "Here's the deal. First we gonna get that recording you's supposed to do for Mr. Suggs and then you gonna sign some statements against that friend of yours, I mean, if you can call him that. I'm not sure that's what I'd call somebody left me standing out there on the side of the road. But, you know, that's just me. Oh, then you gone sign some contracts." After a pause Henry casually inquired about the well-being of Willie's sister's children and Earl's wife, Claudie. He said he was glad to hear they were all doing well and said he hoped they stayed that way. Then he said, "Well, okay. I guess we're ready. Why don't y'all just start makin' them sounds you do."

There was a pause before Buddy counted 'em down. Slowly.

One . . . two . . .

One . . . two . . . three . . .

And then he struck that lone note.

And every note that followed lived up to the legend that had been growing for fifty years. Buddy's slide-guitar work was heartbreaking. Willie was blowing tragedy out of the harp and Earl's voice was possessed of all the misery and hopelessness of their circumstances. They started with a sorrowful version of "Goin' Down the Road Feelin' Bad." Earl's phrasing conjured the moan of a tortured man's soul at the end of each chorus when he sang, "Don't wanna be treated this way."

Henry browbeat and threatened the men between each song. They did "Big House Blues" and "Born for Bad Luck." The passionate playing and the intense vocals raised the hair on Rick's neck and made him think of Neil Young as he sang about the screaming and bullwhips cracking, especially when they did a version of Leroy Carr's "How Long, How Long."

Buddy, Willie, and Earl were moved too. They'd been so terrorized when they made the recordings that they hadn't really heard themselves. Between songs, the three men listened stoically to the words that had come out of Henry's mouth fifty years ago. It was the second time they'd heard him say these things and they didn't hear any new meaning or significance this time around. That's just how it was, the way they were treated, business as usual in a place that seemed a million miles away now.

But, as this was the first time Pigfoot had heard these words, he listened keenly. He'd heard about the tapes, but he didn't know they were real. He figured they were just the product of somebody's imagination and never thought if they *did* exist, that they were anything more than a few songs. But the tapes *were* real, as real as the threats Henry was making on them.

Not surprisingly, it was the stuff between the songs that was music to Pigfoot's ears. Every word out of Henry LeFleur's mouth helped lift the dark cloud that had descended on Pigfoot after he'd found the burned files and the melted reels in Jeremy Lynch's office.

As the tape neared the end, Rick noticed Pigfoot grinning like a small dog with a big bone. "Mr. Morgan," Rick said, "it looks like you might have something to add here."

"Well," Pigfoot said. "I had this lawyer name of Lynch contacted me a year or so ago. Said he'd found some evidence that would help prove I hadn't killed Hamp Doogan, like I'd been sayin' all along. Said he thought I might have a good lawsuit 'cause of all the time I was in jail. He said if I could get Buddy, Willie, and Earl to tell what went on out on Highway 61 that night, along with the evidence he'd found, he said he could put things all right for me. But the lawyer disappeared and somebody destroyed the evidence he'd found, so things were looking down." Then he smiled and said, "But I believe these tapes might be just the thing."

He was right. By the end of the tape, Henry had said everything necessary to back himself and Washington County into the corner that is a civil-rights lawsuit. Malice, coercion under color of state law, actions that were racially motivated. It was all there.

Pigfoot said he wasn't doing it for the money, at least not for personal enrichment. He just wanted to do something to show he'd been here and done something. He'd had things to say and he'd planned to say them with his words and his music, but they'd taken that possibility away from him. He couldn't change any of that, but he hoped he could help others say what they wanted and make their mark in the world.

IT WAS PAST three in the morning when Rick came out of a commercial break. "Maybe I'm asking too much," he said. "But I've been promising folks a reunion concert." He looked at the four old men and held his hands out in a plea. "Y'all feel up to it?"

They did.

Smitty opened the guitar cases. Buddy took the Gibson, a J-185, a couple years younger than his own, and a little dinged up, but it fit in his hands just right and it had a fine sound. Willie opted for a traditional steelbody with a mahogany neck and ivoroid-bound rosewood fretboard. Earl took the 1950 Martin

000-28 with the simple spruce top and rosewood sides. It had a big sound and nice action.

Their fingers weren't as fast or as strong as they used to be, but you could hear all that life they'd lived in the voices and the playing. They didn't repeat any of the songs they'd been forced to play that night fifty years ago. Instead they played some favorites and some originals. Crippled Willie started off by proving you can keep your chops up just fine playing gospel. He opened with a lively cover of Willie Lofton's "Jake Leg Blues" and then, moving from the profane to the sacred, he launched into a wrenching version of "I Know His Blood Can Make Me Whole." With each note, the men seemed to tap deeper into a reservoir of youth they had stored for this very moment.

As Rick watched Willie's old, dark-caramel hands moving against the gleaming body of that steel guitar, it dawned on him that he would be one of the last to see this thing, to witness the final rays of this remarkable sunset. This thing, and these men, were passing into history. Men who had been in the place, at the time, who were products of that dark circumstance. The last generation to create and contribute to the original body of work that could only be interpreted and imitated by future generations. People would always play the blues, the songs by the masters, but membership in this club was closed. To be a part of it, you had to be there.

After Willie's set, Earl winked at the others and said, "Now here's one I wrote that ole Leroy Ervin lifted from me." They all laughed as he launched into a raunchy version of "Blue, Black, and Evil." Buddy provided a churning, rhythmic backing while Willie blew some sinister sounds from a harp in the key of C. From there Earl led them into Tampa Red's bawdy "Let Me Play With Your Poodle."

Buddy took the next few songs, starting with his original,

"Dust on My Memories," before charging into the Muddy Waters classic "Trouble No More."

Somewhere in the middle of all this, Rick looked over at Lollie. She was leaning against the wall, eyes closed, her head bouncing with the bluesy rhythm. Rick allowed himself a bittersweet smile. He'd solved the case he'd been hired to and, with Lollie's help, they'd solved one of the great mysteries of the music world and, in the process, helped exonerate an innocent man. The story would get good play in the press and Rockin'Vestigations would have a surge in business.

On the other hand, Rick figured he wouldn't see much of Lollie anymore. Now that she knew who had killed her grandfather, she'd return to her life. She told Rick that she had applied for some teaching positions in Atlanta and Charlotte. He had some feeble hope that their relationship could turn into something lasting, but at the same time, he'd come to expect that in love, at least, his hopes would be dashed. And he was rarely disappointed. Still, it was fun while it lasted and, hell, he almost got to play with her poodle.

— — — — — — — —

THE SUN WAS peeking over the trees when they walked out of the studio, exhausted and exhilarated. To their surprise, there were cars parked in every direction as far as the eye could see, nearly a hundred of them. It turned out that blues fans from all over Mississippi, Louisiana, and Arkansas had driven through the night, toward the station, listening to the men tell their story and play their songs. Instead of stopping when the signal was clear, they just kept driving until they reached the studio. When they saw Buddy and Willie and Pigfoot and Earl, the people got out of their cars and began to applaud. A standing ovation. The blues-

men smiled and waved and waded into the crowd to sign auto-
graphs and revel in their new celebrity.

Afterward, Rick took them all to breakfast and then put
Buddy, Willie, Earl, and Pigfoot up at one of the casino hotels,
told them to stay as long as they liked.

As they drove back to the Vicksburg, Lollie said she was glad
to know her grandfather hadn't been there that night, that he
hadn't had anything to do with what had happened. She assumed
he eventually heard the tapes but knew he wouldn't have given a
second thought to anything Henry said on them. "That's just how
they talked back then." Of course, Lollie knew it was also the way
a lot of people thought—her grandfather included. "Still," she
said. "When they convicted Pigfoot, it would've been nice if he'd
stepped up and done the right thing."

"Give him a break," Rick said. "He was a man of his time and
place."

Lollie said she thought that was a cheap excuse used by too
many to indulge their prejudice. But she said she wouldn't hold
it against him. "I guess I'm just a little disappointed I don't come
from better stock."

"Not me," Rick said as he pulled into the Vicksburg's parking
lot. "I'm still hoping your lack of integrity will encourage you to
put out some."

Lollie smiled and shook her head. "I'm gonna have to give
you another rain check," she said. "I'm exhausted."

"Damn."

They got up to the apartment, collapsed on the bed, and slept
until noon.

After that, Rick and Lollie saw each other only periodically.
She had to get back to Jackson and follow up on the jobs she'd
applied for. She said living off alimony was boring her to death
and wasting her talents.

She attended Crail's trial in Greenville whenever she could, and Rick got up there when he had the time, but it wasn't as often as he would have liked. He was busy working his two jobs as well as producing the Blind, Crippled, and Crazy CD, as well as the reunion concert and a DVD, *The Pigfoot Morgan Story*.

One night, toward the end of the summer, Rick was on the air playing the Grateful Dead's version of "Smokestack Lightnin' " when the request line lit up. It was Lollie. "You want to meet me in Greenwood this weekend?"

"Sure," Rick said. "What's the occasion?"

"There's the matter of an uncashed rain check."

After a pause, Rick said, "Two, actually."

They spend an indulgent weekend at the Alluvian, that fancy hotel at the corner of Church and Howard Streets. They had dinner at Giardina's, the famed Delta establishment. They got one of the private booths, ordered martinis, and pulled the curtains. The mood was festive. They were celebrating the fact that the school in Atlanta had offered Lollie the job. Rick proposed a toast to her future. Then they toasted Ruby Finch and Beau Tillman and everybody else they could think of between fits of laughter and kissing.

They talked about that night at the radio station, the status of the trials, and the stuff Rick was producing with the bluesmen. At one point, straight out of left field, and not in keeping with their tacit policy of ignoring the elephant that had been in the booth with them the entire time, Rick said he was sorry to see their relationship end. Lollie gave him a sweet smile and said, "Yeah, but you don't want a girl who snores after just two martinis."

"No, of course not," Rick said. "A guy would have to be crazy to fall for a girl like that." He made a crazy face to emphasize the point. Then he looked deep in her eyes and in that moment something passed between them. "But I had to say it, at least once."

She reached over and put her hand on his. "I'm sorry too."

"On the other hand," Rick said. "At this point in my life, I've learned to take a small degree of satisfaction in knowing that if I keep my romantic expectations low enough, I'll usually have those expectations met."

Lollie smiled and said, "C'mon. Let's go cash some rain checks."

They went back to their room and disappeared beneath the 350-thread-count sheets. Some time later they fell into a sound sleep. If Lollie snored that night, Rick never heard it.

— — — — — — — — —

THE NEXT DAY, when they were leaving, Rick walked Lollie to her car. He said, "I got something for you."

She looked embarrassed. "I didn't get you anything."

"Don't worry about it," he said. "You gave me plenty." He handed her a gift-wrapped box.

"What is it?"

"Open it."

She pulled on the bow and opened the box. Inside was a picture frame. She turned it over and broke into a big smile. It was the picture Rick had taken of Lollie that night in his kitchen. She was laughing at the time and her arm was resting on the box of Ruby's photos. "It's great," she said. "I usually don't photograph that well." She kissed his cheek and said, "Thanks."

Rick pointed at the box. "There's another one."

Lollie dug through the Styrofoam peanuts until she found a photo of Rick with Crusty's face next to his. "Puff Kitty!"

"He wanted you to remember him," Rick said. "And I just happened to be in the picture."

"I'll remember."

He pointed at something on the glass. "He even sneezed a reminder there for you."

"How sweet." She gave Rick a kiss, got in her car, and drove
away.

Rick stopped at a store on the way home and bought another
frame. When he got back to the Vicksburg, he put his copy of
Lollie's photo in the frame and set it on a table by the window.
Crusty jumped up and rubbed it with his nose. Rick picked
Crusty up and held him face-to-face. "Well, Crustus, it's just the
two of us now." He rubbed Crusty on the head and said, "Here's
looking at you, kitty." As he turned to gaze out the window at the
confluence of the Mississippi and Yazoo Rivers, Crusty leaned toward Rick's ear. "Ow! Stop biting me."

Epilogue

Thanks to all the publicity, Rockin' Vestigations had a surge in business. Rick hired a few more operatives and put a little money in the bank.

At Crail's trial, the forensic expert testified that she was able to match the gram-negative intracellular diplococci from Crail's amputated leg to that in tissue samples retained from the necropsy of Lamar Suggs. Based on advice from his public defender, Crail rolled over on Henry to get off the hook on Jeremy Lynch's death. Then he confessed to killing Tucker Woolfolk as part of a plea deal to save the state a trial and avoid the death penalty. But he refused to testify against Cuffie. He was convicted of the murders of Tucker Woolfolk and Lamar Suggs and sentenced to life without the possibility of parole. While he was at Parchman, Big Jim Magee kept Crail supplied with all the drugs he needed. They talked about planning an escape, but nothing ever came of it.

At her trial, Cuffie cried on the stand and said Crail Pitts had used her. She said he had wanted to find the tapes and get rich and had threatened to harm her family if she didn't hire Rick Shannon to find Woolfolk and Suggs. The jury found her performance unconvincing and she was convicted on two counts of murder and sentenced to life.

The tapes, along with the testimony of Buddy, Willie, and Earl, were enough to prove that Clarence hadn't killed Hamp Doogan. But since no one had seen the crime, and Henry wouldn't confess, he couldn't be convicted for the murder. But he was tried for a laundry list of other crimes, ranging from civil-rights violations to hiring Crail to kill Rick and Lollie. He was convicted and sent to Parchman, where he died after nine months.

Pigfoot had lawyers lining up to bid on his business. They filed a string of lawsuits and won them all, clearing Clarence's name and bringing in enough money to establish a series of scholar-ships in the names of Buddy Cotton, Willie Jefferson, Earl Tate, and Clarence Morgan.

Shelby LeFleur donated the bulk of his estate to the scholar-ship funds. He died the next year knowing that the remaining LeFleurs would have to work for a living, so there was some hope yet.

Buddy died a few months later.

Rick produced the CD of the original Blind, Crippled, and Crazy sessions. Since there were only six songs on the tapes, he combined it with the recording of the reunion concert at WVBR. It went gold. The guys did a few concerts, a DVD, and a couple of TV specials and, when all was said and done, everybody got they nickels and went on home.